Dirty
DEVIL
by
Heather Long

Dirty Devil
82 Street Vandals #4
Copyright © 2022 by Heather Long
Cover: Crimson Phoenix Designs
Photography: Michelle Lancaster
Cover Model: Charlie Di Stefano
Illustrations: Victor Long

Dirty Devil/Heather Long – 1st ed.
ISBN-13 – 978-1-956264-21-0

For Stephanie
She believed in Freddie from the beginning.

Foreword

Dear Reader,

Welcome to book four of the 82nd Street Vandals series. If you have not read the first three, stop. Do not pass Go. Grab book one: Savage Vandal, and start there.

Seriously.

This is a series that really must be read in order.

Okay, back to my welcome. Dirty Devil was not originally a title I planned for the "then" 8-book series. However, when I added a ninth book, this was the title we included. The story is still being told in the order as intended, so yes this picks up following the end of *Ruthless Traitor* and the fallout of Emersyn's decision.

One of the things we've learned about Emersyn over the course of the last three books, and a trait she shares very much in common with the Vandals, is her sense of loyalty. While she has not had a core group to support her, her loyalty to the BFF she had to keep secret for years is intense.

The Vandals have earned that loyalty and affection from her, as has Milo, though their prickly relationship continues to develop despite Milo's desire to send her away.

That struggle highlighted not only how stubborn Emersyn can

be, but also just how torn she is about Milo's story. It's almost like she can't wrap her mind around what it means if the idea they are siblings *is* true. In fact, she just flat out denies it.

The more she gets to know Milo, however, the more she hopes that his story isn't true. Not because of what it will mean for her, but what it will mean to Milo. Along the way, her relationships with the other Vandals continue to develop—some with more success than others. (Yes, Doc, I'm looking at you.)

What happens next is a journey that pulled me in and wouldn't let me go. I would like to reiterate here, this is definitely a dark romance. The trials she faces, both internally and externally, push her. It all comes down to choices, though, hers, the Vandals, and the world around them.

The question is, can they all survive those choices? And if they do, who will they be on the other side?

And now, as always, the housekeeping notes:

For those of you who have never read a reverse harem before, first let me thank you for picking this up and giving it a shot. Second, a reverse harem means the heroine will not make a choice in this book or any other between the guys in her life. It may take her a while to reach that conclusion, but it's the journey that drives it. There are many ways to frame this kind of relationship, currently reverse harem fits it very well.

Also, this is the fourth book in a series. While there may be no specific happy endings at the end of each of these books, there will be one to the whole series, that I promise you. Some of these books will have cliffhangers, largely due to the size of the story, but the happy ending has to be earned as part of the journey.

xoxo

Heather

Chapter One

LIAM

I checked my watch for the fourth time in the last thirty minutes. Not only was Sharpe late, he was conspicuously late. When he said he was coming to Braxton Harbor for the meeting and arranged for it to be the Titian—the same hotel Hellspawn had stayed at during her show—it had set off alarm bells. From unreachable and leaving me to his staff, to arranging an in person meeting? Yeah, nothing sketchy as fuck about that.

It was why I wanted Hellspawn secure at the apartment. I'd rather she'd been at the clubhouse, but the guys had other issues that made it a less than optimal choice. Not pacing took effort, I'd gone the suit and tie route, playing up my O'Connell connection. Still, when we hit the forty-five-minute mark, I gave up any pretense and headed out.

The bike wasn't parked in their lot. In fact, I'd stashed it half a block away for a reason. Everything about Sharpe set off internal warnings. I'd mentioned him, in passing, to Adam and all Reed had to say was stay as far away from him as possible. The guy was bad news.

Emersyn hadn't tried to reach out to him at all as far as I knew. In fact, she'd done quite the opposite that day she'd gotten away. He'd been right there and she'd gone in the opposite direction. Between the telephone tag and his slow response times, I'd already decided to just play him for information and that was it.

But why call for a meeting at all? Much less one he didn't plan to show—I plucked my phone from my pocket and hit the number for Hellspawn's phone. It hadn't even begun to ring when I caught the movement from the corner of my eye.

Too many years of back-alley fights and knives in the dark looking to take me out had honed my senses. Someone rushing at me, even in broad daylight, got my attention. My phone went flying as I caught the extended wrist and deflected the blade. Twisting the guy, I slammed him into his partner. My chest still ached from the three bullets that hit my Kevlar center mass, but I'd fought worse battles in far more damaged condition.

On any other day, maybe these guys would be an even match, but I wasn't in the mood for this. I needed my phone and I needed to hear Hellspawn was fine. One guy I dropped with a broken arm, and the second I split open every knuckle on my left hand with the upper cut to his jaw.

What the fuck did he have in that thing? Titanium? Still, a swift kick to the head of the guy cradling his broken arm knocked him out, too. I didn't have time for this shit, but I still removed their weapons, both had Glocks, fully-loaded and I field stripped the weapons down to parts, dropped them in different trash cans and tossed parts into the bushes on my way to grab my phone.

The fucking screen had shattered. But it worked. Still, the phone rang and rang and rang, then went to an automated voice mail.

"Pick up the fucking phone, Hellspawn." She could be doing anything. Running on the treadmill. Dancing around in her underwear. Fucking one of the assholes on my sofa again. But she still didn't answer the phone. At the bike, I stuck the key in and got it started as I tried to pull up the cameras.

They responded but I couldn't make out shit. The hair on the back of my neck stood on end and my blood ran cold. If I hauled ass, I was twenty minutes from my place.

That was twenty minutes too far. Just as I started the engine, my phone rang.

"Hellspawn," I said as I answered it. "Why the fuck—"

"It's not her," Freddie interrupted me. "I don't know where you are or what you did, but she's leaving."

"What?"

His voice held a frantic note. "She called me. There's no car here and just the stupid fucking rats we can't leave to run around in here..." His words came out jumbled. "The guys are gone and she's going home. That's what she said."

Home.

"Not to us, to the other place, the one I know she doesn't want to go to. What the hell did you do?"

"I'll take care of it."

"Liam..."

I ground my teeth together. "I'll take care of it. Stay where you are." Then I debated what I needed him to do. Freddie needed a task or he would derail and we couldn't afford that right now.

He couldn't.

Especially if they had him on rat duty, that must mean they were circling in on whoever was leaking the shipping schedules. "Call Rome."

"What?"

"Call Rome." It would be better coming from me, but Rome could keep it to himself. "Tell him what you told me and then tell him I'm on my way to get her."

"Okay—you're *going* to get her, right?"

Hell yes, I was going to get her.

"But you don't even know where..."

"I know where."

There were only two airports locally that could handle private planes and if Sharpe was here, he'd pulled me out to get her. I didn't know what the fuck was going on, but I was going to find out.

"Freddie, just do it," I snapped. "Call Rome, tell him exactly what you told me. I'll call you as soon as I know something."

I shoved the phone in my pocket then pulled the helmet on. Two airports.

The one closest to my place was also closer to this hotel.

It was a gamble, but I went with my gut.

I hit the highway doing 100 and I pushed the bike harder. The engine was a scream as we angled our way between traffic. I closed on every single dark car. No doubt he would have sent a goon to get her, or maybe he picked her up himself.

She didn't want to see him.

I couldn't reconcile the disparate desire with the phone call to Freddie. Why Freddie? To let us know, but warn the one person least likely to stop her? She needed to learn when Freddie cared, Freddie didn't stop.

None of us did. Still, it wasn't until I closed the gap on the sixth car that I saw her. Even through my visor and the tinted windows of the car, I could make out the wide eyes and the taut expression on her face.

No uncle.

But the driver was a mule of a man. He swung the car at me twice trying to dislodge me, then he cut off at an exit.

Swearing, I took the very next one, but he'd bought himself time. The race to the airport had my heart hammering. The one thing I didn't own was a private jet. So, I had no access to this part of the airport.

The car took her straight to a plane, but I was already off the bike and yelling for her. "Don't get on that fucking plane, Hellspawn!" The engines on it were already primed and running.

Security cut me off. One guy ate my helmet and I pulled a night stick from another. For a split second, I swore she heard me. She glanced back.

No way in hell did she want to get on that plane. A taser caught me in the back. The shock jolted my system, and had me staggering. I struck out blindly. Fists. Feet. Nightstick. Them. Everything became a weapon, but it was just me and the big dude who'd been driving her when I got clear and the plane was taxiing down the runway.

I focused on the behemoth.

I only needed him alive.

Not in one piece.

The clean-up crew would be less than happy with me when I called them in. There was a lot of scrubbing that would need to be done. I'd already taken care of security at the airport. Private airfields had private owners. They also tended to not care for FAA rules or sharing their issues with local authorities.

Greasing those wheels cost a hundred grand. Easy money. The security guards cost a little more, but they understood the offer clearly. The owner would deal with them, or he'd deal with me. None of them wanted to deal with me. The behemoth hung from a hook in the old meat packing factory. This was one of those acquisitions I'd been "after" for the Royals for a while.

It also put this body squarely in the center of 19 Diamonds territory and gave me plausible deniability. I didn't give one good goddamn about deniability, but my cleaners did. Whatever. As it was, I'd already put in calls to find out where Sharpe's plane was going.

Of course, they hadn't filed a fucking flight plan. The family had a dozen properties around the world in their name that didn't count what they had in their corporate assets. I needed to go back to the apartment and check my cameras. My fucking phone was useless, but I had this guy right here and right now.

And he was going to answer my questions.

As soon as his dumb ass woke up. Blood dripped steadily from his nose. I'd enjoyed the savage beating I'd given him.

Maybe a little too much.

I wasn't going to cry over spilt blood.

The slam of a door rang through the warehouse, echoing off the old metal fridges and abandoned equipment. I sent a security team through periodically to clear out any detritus or squatters.

Hand on my gun strapped behind my back, I faced the open door to the fridge I was using for this interrogation. I'd only told two people where I would be.

"I come in peace," Freddie announced, scuffing his shoes against the dirty cement floors. "Mostly. Also—why the hell are we doing this in an old crack den?"

Relaxing my grip on the gun, I started forward and narrowly dodged the fist flying at my face as Jasper cut around the corner. I caught the next swing, and then delivered my own sharp jab before I shoved him away.

Barely stumbling a half-step, Jasper pivoted and faced me. Fists already clenched, he was already lunging at me.

"Guys!" Freddie called, before releasing a shrill whistle. The noise actually hurt with how it rebounded off the metal. "This is not about your dicks or your dickishness."

The sober note was so un-Freddie-like, I almost glanced at him but I didn't dare take my attention off Jasper. Not when the hate in his eyes had taken on a whole new dimension. His anger I could take, even the blame after I'd followed the plan and walked away from the Vandals.

This though?

No, this was him in a killing rage.

"I tried to get to her," I told him. "I wasn't fast enough."

That was on me.

"But I'm not giving up and I will fucking find her and bring her back, if it's the last thing I do."

She did *not* want to go back to her family.

Eyes narrowing, Jasper glared at me. The ice in his slate gray eyes was so jagged they threatened to leave me bleeding. "What if she doesn't want to come back?" He bit off every word like he fired bullets.

In a way, he was.

Because beneath all that anger was fear and pain.

I couldn't fix it, not yet.

But he wasn't alone. "Then she can fucking tell me she doesn't want to come back *here*. If she doesn't, fine, we'll go there to be with her if that's what she needs."

We. Not just me.

Tension still straining at his muscles and in the flex of his jaw, Jasper straightened slowly. "What did you do?"

"I didn't do anything, but make sure she knew how to defend herself. The only way they got in, was she let them in. The only way she left was if she went willingly."

"Then she wants to be gone." The rawness in his voice was brutal. If Milo could fucking see this, he'd shut up about thinking anyone was using her as a whore. Fuck me, if he ever said anything like that again, I was gonna break his jaw until he remembered the manners we'd all been taught.

"No," I said in the same breath as Freddie.

"She didn't want to," Freddie said, coming closer and still sounding so damn serious. That snagged Jasper's attention. That pulled his focus away from me. "It was in her voice. She lied to me. She was so damn sad, but she didn't want to go. They did *something*."

Jasper's expression tightened then he glanced at the man hanging from the hook. "This the guy?"

"The driver," I answered, relaxing a fraction now that Jasper's temper seemed to have been defused. Or at least had a new target. "He took her from my building straight to the airport."

"Could be a nobody," Freddie suggested, coming to stand between us.

"If he hadn't been armed for bear, I'd agree." I kept my tone mild, then motioned to his weapons, which lay across a table on the far side of the room. A pair of Glocks. Two six-inch plus long knives. A flip blade. A taser. Three sets of zip tie cuffs. His phone. The bullet proof vest.

I'd stripped him down to his pants. Even emptied his shoes.

"The car's in the larger freezer on the other side." It had a roll open door and I'd had one of my people stash it in there. If they had any kind of tracking system, the high-density lead and heavy metals in the old fridge would block it. At least until I could strip it down.

Then again, if this fucker had friends who wanted to give me something to vent on, I'd be happy to rip them up too.

"Kel and Vaughn are on the way," Jasper said as he stripped off his own jacket, then his shirt. Why get everything bloody if you didn't have to. "We were finishing a job or we'd have been back faster."

The last came out in an almost apologetic tone as he glanced at Freddie. Finally, I studied the kid. Well, not really a kid anymore, but still younger than the rest of us. His eyes were shadowed and his expression bleak, but also determined.

"What did she say?" I asked him. "*Exactly.*"

He exhaled, but stared at the man hanging from the hook as Jasper moved around the empty fridge. He was either examining what I had to work with, or cooling himself down so he could get answers, instead of just beating the guy to death.

We needed the former, but the latter might help slake some of the rage pounding through my veins. Everything was off about this situation. Her expression when she'd seen me at the airport. Even from that far away, I'd seen the sadness.

But I'd also seen fear a moment before she squared her shoulders and the emotion vanished. Buried.

Just. Like. Milo.

She'd been hiding so fucking much from us and it had been right there in front of me.

"She said she had to go home. It was time. When I told her one of us would come get her, she said no, not to the clubhouse. To my real home." His tone was dead neutral as he recited the conversation. No emotion at all. "I told her she didn't want to do that. I know she didn't. Then she said her mother was sick and her father had a heart attack."

Both of those could be fact-checked. I reached for my phone but the shattered screen was no fucking help.

"I told her not to do it. I told her to stay there, and we'd talk and make a plan." He compressed his lips. "She said, "Freddie. Stop. Thank you for wanting to do it, for making me laugh and for being you. But I have to do this. I need you to tell everyone this was my choice." If he'd just slammed a blade into my chest it would have hurt less. "I said, 'I don't want you to go.' She apologized then when I said I'd head straight there, she hung up—but only after she said, 'Thank you for caring. I'll call when I can."

When.

I.

Can.

"She didn't want to go. I don't care that she said it was her choice." Freddie finally pinned me with a look. "She didn't want her family to find her."

No.

She hadn't.

There had been far too many opportunities and instead of pressing this, we'd all just—held on and pretended it didn't matter cause she was with us, where she belonged.

"You got this here?" I said abruptly, looking at Jasper. "Get whatever you can out of him. All the details. I'm going to the apartment. I need to know what happened there."

"I'll take care of him," Jasper said, cracking his knuckles. "You tell me what you find."

"Done."

Hatchet buried.

For now.

He nodded, then looked at Freddie. "Go get some buckets of water. We're waking this fucker up."

I left them to it. My bike was also in the warehouse. There were cracks and scratches from where I'd dropped it, but I ignored those. They were unimportant.

Getting to my apartment now and looking at the surveillance

was important. It was the only thing that mattered. That and finding *where* her family was taking her.

Find her.

Then get her back.

That was the plan.

Chapter Two

JASPER

Freddie returned with two full buckets and he wasn't even staggering with them. For the first time in, I didn't know how long, he didn't stagger or crack wise. He just carried the buckets in and set them down. He'd ditched his jacket, probably in the office, and he'd rolled up the sleeves on his shirt. Before I could say a word, he lifted one of the buckets and sent the contents flying into the face of our guest.

The man sputtered and coughed as the water roused him. Half of his face was already bruised as fuck. I envied Liam the hits he'd already gotten in, but he'd done too efficient a job if the guy was unconscious. Every minute we had to wait for the guy to wake the fuck up put us behind finding where she'd gone.

My gut pitched like I was a ship on a storm-tossed sea. Emersyn wasn't gone. Not for good. We'd find her. We'd get her back. It was what we did. The guy shook his head and spit, then began to test the chains shackling him to the ceiling. I moved over and turned the crank to draw the chains up higher. I wanted him on his toes—off balance.

The minute the wheel began to pop and turn, drawing the chains tighter, our guest snapped his eyes open the rest of the way. Well, the one that wasn't swollen shut anyway. I stretched my head from side to side as I rolled up my sleeves. "You should go," I told Freddie. In general, he preferred to be away from the violence and the blood. It wasn't that he couldn't fight…

"I'm good right here." Freddie folded his arms and glared at the guy in chains. Face to face with him, he had the height but definitely not the weight. He was far too lean, and the guy tried to lunge at him.

Dumbass.

The chains yanked him backwards and Freddie didn't flinch.

"You sure?" I checked with him. I had every intention of making this bloodier.

"I'm sure. He took Boo-Boo."

"That he did, little brother." I clapped Freddie on the shoulder and turned to our guest. The guy opened his mouth but I didn't need him to talk yet, so I slammed my fist into his solar plexus. It knocked all the wind out of him and he made a gagging noise. I walked in a circle around him as he fought to catch his breath.

As soon as he stopped panting, I jabbed him in the kidneys. We repeated this a few times. Always soften the target up. I didn't ask him anything. Not yet. No, when I asked, I wanted him ready to answer me. I couldn't think about Emersyn. I had to put thoughts of her away in a locked box, where she would be away from this. The violence I wanted to rain down on this guy right now had less to do with him and everything to do with the fact that I didn't know where she was.

If finding her meant working with Liam and working this guy over? Then count me the fuck in. On my fourth round of driving my fist into his kidney, the man coughed up blood and let out another gagging groan.

"I was just *hired* to take her to the damn airport," the man spat out.

Didn't ask. I hit him from the side, a series of blows before I circled him again. He began to flinch when I would move toward him. That was what I wanted.

Fear.

Freddie stood like a sentinel, arms locked and his expression almost unreadable. Almost. But he was so laser focused on our guest that I doubted anything would get past him. The intensity threw me, but I didn't have time to focus on that. The clock was ticking, we needed info now. I walked away from our guest and over to the corner. If we'd been at the clubhouse, I would know what tools were at my disposal. As it was, I didn't know this place, but Liam and I had clearly been on the same wavelength. He had some heavy rubber balls and a dozen or so of those inside a cloth sack worked almost as well as real fruit, like oranges.

I paced back over to the guy. "I told you—I was just hi—" He choked as I swung the bag and struck him with all balls across the lower half of his abdomen and his crotch. A vein popped out on his forehead and I didn't let him catch his breath. These balls hurt, a lot. If applied correctly they would do a lot of soft-tissue damage on the inside but not leave a lot of marks on the outside.

Circling him, I kept the strikes up until he did gag and throw up some bile. That was better. There was blood in his mouth too. These kinds of injuries could hurt for weeks, lucky for him, if he answered my questions he'd win an all-expenses paid tour of our body disposal.

No pain. No gain.

Gagging and coughing, our guest leaned over and sagged hard against the chains. He wasn't trying to stay on his feet anymore, and the pain and stress on his shoulders trying to support his weight added to his discomfort. Bag in hand I stared at him and the man lifted his head.

"I'm Tony."

"I don't care," I said flatly.

"I was paid," he wheezed. "To do a job. The girl. He's had me watching her for a while."

Freddie's shoulders stiffened.

"He wanted me to keep track of her, log her movements, especially who she spent time with." He spat.

"How long?" Freddie asked.

"A few weeks." The guy couldn't hold my gaze even with that answer and he flinched as I hefted the bag.

"Months," the guy admitted on an agonized gasp. "I'm a freelancer out of California. I'm only here because he paid the fee and I had a job to do."

"Where was the plane going?" I flexed my hand around the bag as I checked the weight like I wanted to swing it again.

"New York? California? Man, I'm telling you, I don't know. Rich fucker paid me ten thousand to watch her."

"He paid ten grand just to keep an eye on her?"

"A week," Tony said, trying to stand again but he kept twitching as though every muscle hurt. "Ten grand a week. Document any sightings of her. Get pictures of anyone she was spending time with. Put names to the faces, report in daily."

"Who was *he*?" Freddie asked, squinting like he had to really strain to concentrate on him.

"You won't like my answer." Tony shot me a worried look.

"You don't know who you were working for?" I didn't have to pretend to be skeptical.

"He was paying me ten thousand dollars a week," he complained. "For that much he could have called himself George McFly or Mr. X, I'd have believed him. I didn't *care* about his name."

"Did he say *why* you were watching her?"

"No."

"Where did you send the pictures?" He'd mentioned taking pictures.

"To a cloud account, a burner email address from one of those YesMail accounts. So it could be anybody, anywhere." It had to be her family though. Freddie said she mentioned going back. The same family she never wanted us to contact.

The kernel of that thought reared its head and I frowned. Granted, it had been months since she first woke up with us, but even then—*don't contact my family. I'll pay my own ransom. I have money.*

What the hell else had I missed?

"No, I told you. I'll tell you a hundred times. I don't know anything…he paid me, I sent him pictures. Everything is on my phone. I'll give you the fucking password—" The man cut off with a gurgle as blood spurted from his neck. I hadn't even seen Freddie move and he'd sliced his throat.

"Fuck me—Freddie!" Not even slowing down, Freddie wiped the blood off his blade and looked at me with the deadest eyes I'd seen in a long time. The door to the room slammed open and Milo filled the whole frame. He cut his gaze from me to the body and then back.

"What the fuck?" Milo demanded cutting his gaze back and forth. There was blood on my face. Spray had caught me. The warmth of it seemed to burn into my skin. Freddie paced out of the room and I met Milo's gaze.

"Asshole told me everything he knew," I said. "We didn't need him." Freddie didn't need to deal with this, or Milo, at the moment.

"So, you just slit his throat?" Milo frowned. "It's messy and makes clean up harder."

"Who cares?" I snapped. "He's dead. We need to find Swan." It was also Liam's warehouse. Once I cleaned up my prints, he could deal with the clean-up.

Milo frowned and snapped his gaze toward me. "What about Emersyn?"

Fuck.

"And why the Hell were we all needed here?"

That was a damn good question. I'd had my phone on silent since we started the questioning, but when I dragged it out I found the message from Rome. Kellan and Vaughn filled the doorway one after another.

"Please tell me we're not all here on a body disposal," Vaughn drawled before he scrubbed a hand over his face. "We've been up for thirty-six hours…"

"Ignore the body for now. He was a driver, local muscle hired to pick up Swan from Liam's place and return her to her family."

Milo gave a barely perceptible jerk like he'd been shot and the heat of his glare threatened to scorch my skin. Only, Kellan and Vaughn beat him to the punch. Literally—"What about Dove?" Vaughn demanded and he did a sweep before he grabbed his phone from his back pocket. Kellan glared at me though and it wasn't hard to read the assumption in his eyes.

"What happened?" Two words, both fired out like he squeezed the trigger with deliberate focus.

I briefed them with exactly what I knew, from Freddie's urgent phone call to finding Liam here.

"Where is Liam now?" Milo asked.

"His place," I said and I kept any editorial comments to myself. We needed answers and right now Liam seemed to be acting in our interests—his, mine, and Milo's. I'd use anybody and anything to get her back. "He wanted to know what happened there precisely, and he was also going to see if he could track down—"

"She went home," Milo turned the three words over, repeating them more to himself than to us. He glanced at the body. "No struggle? This guy just drove her to the airport."

"Freddie said she didn't want to go."

"How does he know?"

Kellan glared at Milo for a minute. "Why would he lie?"

"I didn't say he lied, I asked how he knew." The emptiness in Milo's tone should have been a warning. As it was, I frowned at his tone, but I also didn't want to debate this issue. I just wanted to find her.

"She called him." That part still stung. She called Freddie. Though to be fair, I was fucking glad she'd called *someone,* even if it hadn't been me. We could talk about what she should do, or would do, *if* something like this happened again. I went over everything I knew, repeating Freddie's words verbatim.

Yet when I headed for the door, Milo didn't move. His scowl deepened and then he yanked his gaze off the dead guy and met my stare. "If she chose to go home, then we leave her alone."

"What..." Kellan began, then Vaughn said "...the..." before they both said, "*fuck.*"

"You heard me," Milo stated. "If she wanted to go home. We leave her alone." Then he swept us all up in a look. That's an order.

Not waiting for us to argue or debate the issue, he strode out of the room and left us with the corpse. Well, he stormed out more than strode. There was so much anger vibrating over the surface of his skin, I had a feeling he *couldn't* fake calm any better than that and even then, he sucked at it.

"We're not leaving her alone, right?" Vaughn asked and I yanked my stare from the door to look at him and Kellan both.

"Milo's thinking she left him," Kellan said quietly, "but you don't think she did?"

"Not willingly," I stated. "No matter what she said to Freddie. She didn't want us contacting them for ransom and she didn't want us contacting them at all."

Kellan's eyes narrowed.

"Put that together with some of her other reactions," I said and spread my hands. "She didn't want to go back there. Think about it, she said she left then she came back. She came back to us."

That fucking meant something.

It had to, especially in the shit show we'd been dealing with. "And if she wants to be there—then she can fucking tell me to my face."

Then I'd walk away.

Maybe.

Right, that was the lie we wanted to go with today, that was the lie I was going with. I didn't think I could ever let her go. Not now.

Not ever.

"Then we fucking find her," Kellan said more like he was swearing a blood oath. "Did you leave us anyone to bleed?"

Chapter Three

DOC

"There we go," I said as I laid the gauze over the three neat stitches closing up Keisha's knee. "All done. You'll have to come back in a few days and let me check on them." After I set the bandage in place and sealed it, I reached over to the dish on the shelf with the suckers in it. I pulled out the cherry ones she preferred and held it out to her. "Think you can stay off the skateboard for a couple of days, to let that heal?"

Keisha wrinkled her nose when I wouldn't let the sucker go without an answer. At eight, the world didn't interest her enough unless she was going full speed, and that was either on her bike, or the new skateboard she'd brought to the clinic a week before so we could fix it. A new set of wheels and a better set of screws and she was good to go. Course, she also had two skinned elbows, one skinned knee, and some gravel scrapes on her thighs.

Not even her "owies" slowed her down. The three stitches I'd just put on the inside of her right knee was more to help encourage it to close faster than because she needed it. I'd also added a bit of skin glue to be on the safe side.

"Fine, two days," she agreed, and I let her have the sucker. "But only two. I want to work on riding it right so I can do tricks."

"I get that," I told her before hoisting her up and then setting her on her feet. "But if you keep getting scrapes, you're gonna leave more skin on the ground than on your body and Momma over there might beat up old Doc with that skateboard."

A fresh burst of laughter left Keisha as any trace of pain or complaint vanished. "Momma says hitting people is bad."

"She's a smart lady," I told Keisha before I tugged one of her braids affectionately. I nodded to her mother. Rina—born Marina— was not a lady to be trifled with. She was about five years younger than me and had two kids. Keisha and her older brother. Like a lot of the kids I'd gone to school with, she'd popped out a baby at eighteen. Her boyfriend was doing a dime upstate and she focused on their kids.

"Momma also told her that if she couldn't learn some patience, she would never master any tricks."

I chuckled. "See? Smart lady."

The woman rolled her eyes and slapped my arm. "What do we owe you?"

"How about some oranges the next time you go to the Farmer's Market? I never get down there and I could use some fresh squeezed juice." Rina had insurance and I'd bill them first. I didn't need her copay. I'd rather she used the money to feed her kids, especially this close to graduating college for her, and a serious uptick in salary.

"You got it, Doc." At least she didn't argue with me anymore. I walked them out front and then let them out of the clinic. They were my last patients of the day. I studied the street as Rina and Keisha made their way up the block. It was after five, traffic had thickened and some of the local shops along the way had already shuttered their doors and pulled down their gates.

The bodega on the corner never closed. There was a diner a couple of streets over that would be open until eleven. But after five, this part just emptied out, save for the locals. Most of whom knew where my apartment was if they ran into issues.

A car parked a block away caught my attention as I turned back inside. Too many years of keeping one eye on my six kept me from staring. I bolted the door like I would normally and engaged the security system that rolled a gate down in front of the front windows and door. The back was left open, but the door was also three inches thicker and reinforced.

I headed upstairs after shutting off all the lights in the front and found a perch not far from the windows overlooking the street. With no lights on, there was no way to see inside. That, and the glare treatment I'd put on the windows, also kept the view obstructed.

The car parked on the street was still there, along with two guys in it. I may not recognize them, but I definitely recognized a type. There was nothing friendly about those faces or their stony expressions.

My phone started buzzing in my back pocket even as I reached for it. I'd put it on silent while I was with patients. The screen showed me Freddie's name and I frowned. Freddie didn't call me. In fact, Freddie avoided me unless—

"What's wrong?" I asked even as I put the phone to my ear.

"Boo-Boo is in trouble."

My heart sank. Goddammit, what had those boys done now? After our last encounter, I was pretty sure I would be the absolute last person she wanted to see. I needed her to want nothing to do with me. It would be better for everyone.

But it didn't change my feelings. "Where is she?" I headed for the stairs, but a pounding at the back had me diverting that way.

"We don't know," Freddie said. "That's me knocking."

I paused mid-reach for the door, but silenced the little voice that asked if Freddie was really here for Emersyn, or was he here because he needed a fix? Medical grade norco was acceptable when he couldn't score something on the street. Mostly, he wanted to blunt his mind and turn everything off. I had the stuff for it, but it was all locked up.

Hanging up, I freed the locks to open the door for Freddie. He ducked in immediately. There was a car in the back of the lot, but not one I knew. It was parked right next to my truck, so Freddie probably just "borrowed" a ride. "Do I need to worry about that vehicle?"

"It's legal," Freddie told me, pacing back and forth like a lion in its cage and needing a way out. Considering the car watching from out front, I turned on the security camera over the back door and the second one up on the roof.

After taking almost two dozen human trafficking victims in over the last few weeks, additional security measures seemed prudent. Fortunately, the last of those patients had already been moved into the system. A system I was going to end up explaining to Milo and the others sooner rather than later, but for now…

"Where is Emersyn?" I asked, tracking Freddie with my gaze and heading toward my office. The video feeds were all accessible from my laptop. It took me a couple of minutes to pull up the front camera, but what do you know, the Camry was still parked in the shadow of an alley.

"I told you," Freddie said, even as he flipped through his phone like something on the screen or in his messages would reveal everything. "We don't know."

Straightening, I kept one eye on the car in the alley, along with its two passengers, then focused on Freddie. This level of agitation usually marked him crashing or needing a hit. But there was no flop sweat.

"I know you think I'm here to score," Freddie said, meeting my gaze without a flinch. "I'm not, but I get it. I'm here because I need to know why Boo-Boo called me and not you."

While I could probably answer that, I didn't volunteer the data. "Start at the beginning. What happened to Emersyn?" Because if he didn't tell me soon, I might slam Freddie into the wall to get him to focus, and that wouldn't be good for either of us.

"She went home." His eyes and his tone were the same level of dead. No inflection. No teasing. No—nothing. Just devastated emptiness. "She said it was her idea." And the agitation was back. He worried at the corner of one of his fingers, like he had a hangnail. "But it wasn't. It couldn't be. She didn't want to go back."

Freddie resumed his pacing.

"She called me. Why did she call me, Doc? You're the one she trusts." He pivoted then stared at me. "Or did she call you?"

No. I checked my phone anyway, but there had been no calls from her. No calls or messages, not since the shooting at the club. Not since I got her off and then told her she shouldn't want me, and that I wasn't going to let myself want her. The fact I could still hear the way her breathing changed and craved another view of her eyes as she let go—right. I was a fucking liar.

"She hasn't called me. But that doesn't mean she didn't go home." After all, she'd had a chance to leave before and she'd decided against it. I dropped my phone on the desk and then sat before scrubbing my hands over my face.

"It has to mean something. I know she didn't want to go back. She didn't talk about them, you know. Her family? She never talks about them. Not in interviews. Not to us. Not even when she got high or was talking to me through the door." The frenetic energy rolling off him was giving me a headache. "So why go back to them? Why now? Milo was doing better, you know? Not giving her orders. She could come back to the clubhouse, only she decided not to."

He made a face and I glanced down at the backs of my hands. For all that they were calloused and one was tatted, there wasn't enough ink to cover up the crimes of my past, or the blood I'd spilled on the way to making myself respectable. Now?

Now I was good with doing what I could for who I could, and hopefully not hurting anyone else along the way.

"But no, she goes back to Liam's. Fine, Liam's is safe. He's good. He'll look after her. Rome goes over and sees her. She texts me all the time and we talk, sometimes for hours."

How the Hell did I not know that part? "Hours?"

"Yeah, hours. She knows it's rough for me, so we talk and sometimes we read to each other. It's cool, okay?" He fumbled with his phone and then shoved it in his pocket before he raked a hand through his hair. His knife came out next, the blade slicing out with a snick, then closed again as he kept pacing. "But today, she calls because she has to go and it's important that I tell *everyone* it was her decision. Totally means it wasn't."

I frowned. "Not saying you're wrong, but how do you get from her telling you it's her decision and you deciding it means the opposite?"

"Are you not listening to me?" Freddie gaped at me, his eyes wild and a muscle in his cheek jerking. "She doesn't talk about her family. She talks about us. She talks about dancers. Hell, she talks about that shitstain dance partner the guys ripped apart. But she doesn't talk about her family. Why don't you talk about something, Doc?"

"Because I don't want to think about it, or I don't want to deal with whatever their memory brings up." I had a lot of shit in my past I wished would stay there. "So, you think because she never talked about them…"

"I don't just think. I know. Liam knows. Jasper knows. Milo will figure it out if he can get his head out of his ass. We questioned the driver who took her to the airport. He didn't know much, just that he was hired. But this wasn't just some driver, this was real muscle."

Snagging my phone, I sent a message to Jasper and then another to Liam. There was a damn good chance Hawk would just ignore me. Liam tended to be a little more open-minded.

Was she really gone? Or was this Freddie? Because if she really went home… fuck that was gonna kill Milo, on top of everything else. The fact I hated the idea of her being gone was not something I wanted to address at the moment.

No. She was gonna be back at the clubhouse or at Liam's. One of the boys would climb back in her bed and she'd be safe with them. My phone vibrated with an incoming call. Liam's name appeared on the screen. I answered it before it even finished ringing.

"Doc, I don't have time to chat. Watch your ass. Someone has been following all of us and documenting our every move."

I cut a look at the monitors. "Really? I might have a couple of candidates right now."

"Where?" Jasper asking the question surprised me, more because he was already on the phone with Liam than that he was engaging me. My stomach pitted. Her absence. That was what drew them together.

"Outside the clinic," I said and at those words, Freddie prowled over to the monitors and stared at them. I kicked the door closed before he could head out of it, with his knife in hand. "You," I told him. "Stay. I'll deal with this. You back me up if I get into trouble."

"Who?" Liam demanded.

"Freddie's here," I said and Jasper swore.

"Rome isn't that far from you," Liam said. "Wait for him. He was already heading back that way."

"And Doc—" Jasper said. "I'm on my way, try to keep one of them breathing."

"Only one?" For whatever reason that amused me. "The doubt hurts, Hawk. It really hurts." I hung up and then reached for the keys over the top of the door. It was hidden under a loose bit of the molding. Freddie glared at me as I led the way out of my office.

"I can help."

"I don't doubt it. But you're also on edge." I glanced at him. "If she's really in trouble…she's going to need you to hold it together."

That wasn't fair to Emersyn or to Freddie, but she inspired Freddie. Fuck, she inspired all of them. She even made me want to be better. "So, stay in here, keep an eye on the cameras. If they move, call me once, hang up then call again."

I eyed him and Freddie finally nodded. "Doc…"

"Freddie, I don't care what it takes, we'll make sure she's all right. Believe that if you believe nothing else."

"Do you promise?"

Fuck my life. I stared at him. "Freddie…"

"Promise me, Doc. You promise me and I'll believe it."

"I promise."

Relief swam over Freddie's expression. "Thank you."

"Stay in here."

I left him in the office and went into the supply closet. Behind the extra towels, and linens, locked in a hidden box, were my weapons. A shotgun. A pair of handguns. A combat knife. I kept them all locked up and safe. No sense in letting anyone else get hurt, even by accident. I left the shotgun, but I took the handguns and the knife.

I had a feeling I was going to need all of it.

Chapter Four

KELLAN

Vaughn practically vibrated in the seat next to me. If it were Jasper or Freddie, the wild, chaotic energy would make sense. Hell, even Liam at the moment. He and Jasper had that on the edge quality in common. Vaughn, though? He was the calm guy, laid back, and easy going. For all his intimidating size, he was more of a puppy than a junkyard dog.

Then again, this was Sparrow.

He punched my dashboard.

The vinyl and leather console gave a little shudder. The molded plastic wouldn't take that kind of abuse for long. I flicked my gaze back to the road. We were five minutes out from Doc's clinic. The fact Doc had company watching him in the aftermath of Sparrow leaving, Liam's little court of secrets were tumbling down around him, and Jasper *finally* on the same side as Liam again, should be a cause for alarm.

At the moment, though, all I wanted was the chance to break a few bones. Possibly starting with fingers and working my way from the small bones to the bigger ones. Vaughn slammed his fist into the dashboard again and I shook my head.

"How the fuck are you not losing it?" Vaughn asked me.

I had no idea.

Well, that wasn't true. I had a few ideas. I'd grown up around a volatile crew. While we'd all had our own problems, pasts, and pains—we had been a unit. The more reckless and angry they became, the calmer I always seemed to become. Maybe it was a counterbalance to the madness. Maybe it was the fact that I needed all my wits about me to protect them.

Or maybe I was ice cold until I had what I needed, and then I could unleash.

Vaughn didn't seem to care that I wasn't answering. I took the next corner smoothly, not quite riding up on two wheels. We were pushing our luck today, wild reckless chances we would normally avoid, being performed without a second thought. If the cops tried to pull us over…

Burn that bridge when we got to it.

"Three minutes out," I told him. Liam's phone call had been clear. There were guys watching Doc's. He didn't know who they were or if they were related, but if they were at all involved, we needed answers.

No. Shit.

I kept that response to myself.

For a split second, the message to meet at the warehouse and the why flashed across my mind's eye. We'd been in the middle of trying to shred the veil concealing the group hijacking our trucks and shipments. Cutting our losses had been the smart move, but we'd also put two bullets into the head of the only potential information source in our custody.

Later, we'd deal with them later. We found some of them once. We'd find them again. Sparrow went home. Sparrow went back to her family.

That just didn't make sense.

"I don't want you to go," she said in a voice drenched in tears, pain, and fear. The sound shredded my guts. From her first waking moment, Emersyn had been a fighter. She'd had spirit and fire. A tempest ready to be unleashed on us all. She was also clever and she studied us even as we were trying to learn about her.

In so many ways, she was just like Milo. The resemblance was far more than skin deep. The sound of her ragged screams would haunt me. I'd half-thought someone had gotten in, gotten past me, and I'd shoved the door in, ready to kill whoever had their hands on her.

The problem was, she'd been captured in her dreams and tormented by a nightmare. A place none of us could follow or defeat. It just pissed me off but when she asked me to stay, I made my choice without hesitation.

"Then I'll stay."

Her lower lip trembled and her eyes were visibly swollen, even in the low light spilling over from my room.

"Please don't tell the others?"

"That you had a bad dream?" Not something any of us would judge her for. We had our own nightmares. "They won't care, except to make sure you're all right. Hell, if they'd heard your screams, they'd have ripped down the damn doors themselves."

"But I don't want them to know. I need to trust you again. I need to know you won't tell them my secret."

The fact she needed to learn to trust me again, that stung. But she wasn't wrong. I'd seen the attraction, even as I'd tried to put the kibosh on it and then... well time, truth, and circumstance had done the rest. "I'll keep your secrets, Sparrow. I won't betray your trust again. I promise." I silenced any of her potential objections when she opened her mouth with a single finger. "But believe me—we all want to protect you, and we're all very familiar with nightmares."

"I dreamt that you guys took me back. You didn't tell me where we were going or why. You put me in the car, and Jasper dragged me out of it when we got there." Every single word was a lash with a spiky whip. "Got rid of me because I wouldn't trust you."

"You know we would never do that." I'd cut off my fucking arm before I hurt her but why the hell would she know that? "Of course you don't, or you wouldn't have had that dream."

Even as I shifted her on my lap, my dick took notice of warm, delectable Emersyn curled up against me. She wasn't quite as undernourished as she'd been back during the show and the bruises were gone. If anything, she seemed healthier, happier maybe. She had been since she came back after she got away. Still, my dick could fuck off right now. This wasn't about sex, no matter how beautiful she was. The tears still drenching her lashes put paid to that.

"Are you okay with me sitting here?" Yeah, great now my dick

had her noticing it. I'd never been led around by my dick before and I wasn't about to start letting it make decisions now.

"I'm fine, ignore my dick. Dicks do that. Right now, I want you to know and to try and believe me when I say nothing—and I mean nothing—you could do or say would make us force you to go anywhere you don't want to go. In fact, I'll kill the first person who tries, whether they're my brother or not."

If she believed me about nothing else, she needed to believe this. Because I would. I loved them. I'd die for them. But I'd kill them before I let them force her to do anything else she didn't want, especially with how fucking scared she was right now.

"Why did you take me?"

"Because leaving you there seemed like a far worse idea. I can't say we thought it all the way through." We definitely didn't think this through, taking her and keeping her had been all Jasper. Maybe I was the ass who'd wanted to get her back, but that was before I knew about this. Before I knew she was afraid. "You know what, fuck it. Jasper has had plenty of time to clear this up with you. When we found out you were going to be in town, we just wanted to be close. To see you. Make sure you were all right. But you weren't all right. You were far from all right, although you are very talented at hiding it. Maybe better than I realized, and that's a discussion for another day, hopefully when you believe me about being able to trust me."

My mind jerked back to the present as I took the last corner toward the clinic. I could make this drive in my sleep. Vaughn's vibrating presence next to me went predator still. Just because he was an easygoing guy, didn't mean shit when it came to protecting what was ours. Doc stood near the corner, leaning against a lamp post like he had nowhere else to be. As we passed him, he nodded to another car.

Yeah, I saw it and the guys inside it saw us. Their wheels cut to the left like they were going to pull out. No, I didn't think so. I cut across traffic and ignored the blaring of horns. One upside, this time of day, the traffic around here was minimal. Mostly locals, who knew a fight when it was coming, and they went away.

Vaughn was out of the car before I'd even stopped it. He caught the gun the driver pointed at him and yanked the man forward. One hand on the back of his neck, he slammed the driver into the steering wheel once, twice, and on the third time let him sag into unconsciousness before he pointed the gun at the passenger.

A passenger who already had his hands up, because Doc had a gun on him. Doc.

I had to do a double take. As it was, I popped the trunk and slid out. "Put the driver in the trunk. The passenger can ride in the back with you, Doc—" Since I had a feeling he was coming. He just nodded. Vaughn didn't wait for Doc's answer, he just dragged the guy out of the driver's seat, emptied his pockets and then dumped him in the trunk. He came back with a pair of zip ties and went to the passenger and lashed his wrists before he patted him down and removed everything—phone, wallet, cigarettes.

I studied the guy. Couldn't say he was familiar. Mid-thirties, I'd guess. Though he could be older, or his hairline had started retreating earlier. Sweat decorated his face and his collar had stained dark with it. One hand on the back of his neck, Vaughn dragged him over to shove him in my backseat. I glanced at Doc.

"Freddie's in the clinic." He tossed keys to Vaughn who caught them.

"I'll get him," Vaughn said, then nodded to the car. "Bringing that too."

Right. We didn't leave anything behind.

"Catch you back at the clubhouse," I said. Liam might have his little hideaway, but I'd rather work in familiar territory. We could also break down that car and strip it faster there, out of sight.

I slid back behind the wheel as Doc dropped into the backseat next to our prisoner.

"Look," the guy said, and Doc clamped a hand down on him in brutal enough fashion that the guy let out a grunt.

"Shut up," Doc informed him and it wasn't Doc talking. That was Mickey J. That was the guy who taught us how to be runners. "You talk when we tell you and not before."

The guy swallowed and I met Mickey's gaze in the rearview mirror for a split second. The granite hardness present was also familiar. I'd joked at one point that maybe Milo wasn't the only one coming home when we picked him up, but now—now I was certain of it.

I backed up and pulled out while Vaughn crossed to the clinic. Not even five minutes from arrival to departure. I split my attention between the road and our tail. Vaughn would take a different route back.

My phone rang and I answered it one handed rather than use the car speakers. Not when we had company.

"We have company."

"Good," Liam said. "They say anything yet?"

"Nope," I replied. "You coming to the party?"

"Not yet," Liam grunted. "Rome's with me. We'll be there soon."

I had a dozen questions I wanted to ask, none I could verbalize with an audience. Even if that audience wasn't likely to survive the night. No sense in borrowing trouble. "Don't be late. I've got a few things for you."

Silence greeted me then something crashed on the other side of the phone. Shattered. "I know," was all Liam said when quiet returned. "Talk soon." Then he hung up.

The drive back to the clubhouse was silent. There were rats on point, including a pair "playing" basketball in the alley. They were already moving as the doors rolled up. In my car, I didn't need anyone to let me in.

Milo and Jasper were waiting.

That was fast.

Unless…

"Who is he?" Milo asked as he opened the back door and focused his attention on the man Doc had.

"We haven't asked him yet," Doc replied, but if Milo's temper bothered him, he didn't let it show. He pushed his way out of the car and then dragged the passenger with him. "JD," he called to one of the rats. Fucking JD man, and Sean was right there with him along with Miguel, Richie, and a punk who went by Houser. I had no idea what his real name was.

JD looked at Doc as Doc shoved the guy at him. "Put him in the fridge."

Instead of moving though, JD hesitated. I climbed out of the car to deal with him when Milo cut a look in JD's direction. Not one word did he need to say. The rat *moved*. Yeah, pissing on anything Milo wanted done wasn't a good idea, and the rats might be idiots at times, but even they had figured this out over the last few weeks.

Hauling the guy away, JD jabbed him when the guy started pleading. Yeah, better to not let him talk until we were ready, by then he'd probably be pissing his pants and his words.

As soon as the guy was out of earshot, Milo swung back to us. "What the fuck?"

"He and his buddy in the trunk were watching the clinic. I don't know what the hell is going on…"

"Emersyn went home and everyone is acting like it's the end of the world." The abrupt change in his demeanor wasn't lost on me. Or on Jasper, who glared but said nothing. "We have bigger fish to fry, and if she wants to be home then that's what we do." No matter how much it hurt him to say it.

Yeah, well, maybe it was time for some hard facts. "She had zero interest in going back."

My words landed like a grenade after the pin had been pulled and everyone froze, waiting for it to detonate. I had all of their attention.

"Freddie…" Milo began, and I cut him off with a slice of my hand.

"Not just Freddie. Though I believe him when he says he knows she didn't want to go. Because *I* know she didn't want to go back. She was terrified of them. She didn't want us ransoming her and she didn't want us to force her to go back to them."

"How can you know that for sure?" Milo asked, and I ached for the way he ruthlessly seemed to be suppressing any sense of hope.

Before I could answer, Doc said, "Because the day I took her back to her hotel and she was going to go inside, she retreated and damn near ran the other way because her uncle was coming outside."

What?

Jasper snarled. "What?"

"Save it," Milo stopped Jasper's lunge with a hand on his chest and focused on Doc. "You're sure it was her uncle?"

"He's the slimy bastard always on television, talking about how he'll bring their princess home. I know who he is. She was scared. She was scared in the alleyway when Liam grabbed her."

Jasper's eyes about fucking bulged and I pinched the bridge of my nose.

"I'm with Kellan on this. She didn't want to go back to that family."

That family. Not *her* family.

"No," I said firmly. "Because *we* are her family and with everything else going on, even as pissed at us as she was for the lies—

she was forgiving us.”

Milo’s expression went from neutral to thunderous. “Get Liam here,” he said over his shoulder to Jasper then glanced at me. “And get the fucker out of the trunk. If they’re involved, we need to know, but I don’t want to waste any more time on this than necessary.”

“Then we get her back,” Jasper said and it wasn’t a question.

While he didn’t answer right away, Milo nodded. “No one is locking her up anywhere she doesn’t want to be.”

Thank fuck.

Pivoting on my heel, I went to the trunk. These guys were in for a rough few hours. They better fucking cooperate.

Chapter Five

VAUGHN

The pair hanging from the chains had been stripped down to their briefs by the time Freddie and I arrived. We'd taken the car to a chop shop on the other side of town. It wouldn't even show up as scrap somewhere. Antonio was second only to Kellan in my opinion, but I didn't want it found in Vandals' territory.

Freddie hadn't wanted to follow me, but he'd done it. The whole way back he'd had his cell phone in his hand, and he kept calling Dove. The phone barely qualified in the smart category, though she would have been able to access Wi-Fi and apps with it. I'd paid for the service on it and put all our numbers in.

She could have called any of us.

She'd called Freddie.

The sting of that settled in to fester, not that I resented Freddie for earning her trust. I just wished…

I shoved that thought aside. What I wished was to have her right in front of me so I could *know* whatever she had decided had been because she wanted it. Yet Freddie kept trying to call her, even when she didn't answer. He sent messages. Though, according to him, none of them seemed to have been read.

He refused to give up and I wasn't going to tell him to.

Not by a long shot.

The warehouse was swarming with rats when we pulled in. JD and Sean had two trucks pulled in and they were going through the cargo. Under normal circumstances, one of us should be over there supervising. This wasn't normal circumstances. I knew where they would be questioning the pair, so that was where we went.

I still had their ID and phones. Though I had turned both phones off. I didn't want them tracked. Jasper wasn't actually the one running the interrogation. Nor was Kel.

Milo, however, was working one of the guys over with a steady kind of rhythm that had left the target sweating and bleeding. If he wasn't pissing blood before this was over, I'd be surprised.

"Freddie," Jasper said as soon as we walked in. "Don't."

I cut a glance to my right. Instead of his phone, he had his knife in his hand. "Do they know where Boo-Boo is?"

Doc moved to stand between Freddie and the targets. "We're working on it. Put it away." The command in his voice was steady. With Jasper and Doc focused on Freddie, I circled them and moved to where Kellan stood.

"Anything?"

He gave a shake of his head. "You have their phones?"

I handed them over before I pulled out the wallets. I eyed the guy and then the interior of the wallet as I flipped through the first one. "They're running spare. Identification—Nate Marcus. Sounds fake." The man's retreating hairline and faint layer of fat over his muscle made him seem a soft target, but he had meat hooks for hands, and even as Milo worked him over, he fought against his groans or revealing his pain.

His companion was unconscious, dangling from his arms. At least one of his shoulders was dislocated. I passed Marcus' wallet to Kellan then flipped open the second guy's. Jordan Levi.

Nate Marcus and Jordan Levi.

They just didn't sound real. I studied the license and it took me a minute, but I probably wouldn't have noticed it without being on the look for something. It was a fake. A *damn* good one, but a fake.

They had cash, about five hundred between them. A couple of credit cards, also in their names. A pair of blank electronic keys for a hotel room. The car itself had been pretty bare of anything we could use, except for the trash in the back. Neither man had been particular in their habits where that was concerned.

Milo walked away from "Marcus." He jerked his head toward the door and as one, all of us moved out to the office, with Jasper and Doc herding Freddie ahead of them. The last time I'd seen Freddie this agitated, he'd been strung out and desperate for a fix. He'd probably have sold his testicles if someone had offered him a hit.

No matter how far down the dark he plunged, Jasper would go in after him. So would the rest of us. That was what made us Vandals. In the office, with the door to the fridge sealed, Milo swept his gaze over us.

"These guys don't know shit." He walked over to grab a bottle of water off the desk, ignoring the blood on his hands and chest as he took a long drink. After, he said, "Where the fuck is Liam?"

"On his way," Kellan said steadily, like he'd just spoken to him. He was flipping through the wallets. "We have their phones. I can go get them cracked."

Milo nodded once, but then he focused on Freddie. "Why are you so convinced she didn't want to go back?"

Not flinching under the weight of that heavy stare, Freddie lifted his chin. "Because I heard it in her voice. She's a really good performer. Maybe the best. But she doesn't want to go back to those people. Her home *is* here."

The words landed like pebbles plinking into still water. Every single ripple shifted the mood in the room. Jasper's expression was pure fury. Kellan's had turned to stone. Doc's had gone almost flat fucking unreadable. Freddie's palpable agitation scraped against my already irritated nerves.

Why the hell had Dove not just called all of us? Or waited?

Because she knew we'd stop her. The soft voice in the back of my mind splashed icy reality onto the scorching heat of my anger. *She didn't* want *us to stop her.*

Milo asked something else, but I wasn't listening to him anymore. I was thinking back to the show. Sorting every single interaction I had with her, before she came to the clubhouse, and every single one after.

In the alley behind the theatre, there had been fear in her eyes when I caught up to them and relief when I got between them. I should have just snapped the guy's neck then and there. Jasper wanted his pound of flesh for Dove. I respected that, but she would have been safer. Maybe she wouldn't have gotten another concussion.

We wouldn't have had to take her.

Then what…? She would have left with the show while we dealt with the body? Even if she reported us to the cops, she wouldn't have known who we were and…and we wouldn't have had her here. Wouldn't have gotten to know her. Wouldn't have been able to look after her while she healed.

While I should have moved faster and dealt with the son of a bitch right there and right then, Dove *needed* to come back here with us. She *needed* the time. Freddie was right, she was a hell of a performer though. Even after seeing how badly battered and bruised she was, it was almost impossible to reconcile her injuries with the performances she'd done. The liquid flow of her movements were in complete opposition to the damage she'd taken.

That said…there was no escaping her trauma. I'd seen it more than once. At Liam's, here at the clubhouse, even in the bathroom when I'd asked her direct questions. She would evade those answers, even if she couldn't evade the clenched fist of fear that would take her captive.

Eric abused her. *Hurt* her. Raped her. We *knew* that. The cocksucker admitted it before we finished cutting his dick off and shoving it down his throat. The vicious amount of pleasure I took from how we took him apart couldn't replace the gut wrenching worry about how much she had suffered *before* and how talented she had been at hiding it.

Masking our real feelings, burying our pain, and pushing through the fear—that was something we'd all mastered early. Some of the guys were far better at it than I was, but how much had Dove endured to be so skilled? It was my third or fourth pass through the guy's wallet when I found the second seam that opened. Inside was a slip of paper with a list of names.

Our names.

Doc's was circled, but the rest of us were on here. Flipping the page over, I checked the back, but there was nothing there. Names only.

So, they were watching *us*.

"I think they know more than they're saying," I said abruptly, interrupting whatever conversation had begun to crackle between Doc,

Jasper, and Milo. When I held up the paper, Doc's eyes narrowed.

"That doesn't tie them to Little Bit," he said, almost grudging as he took the slip. "Just that they have a list of all of us."

"Liam's name is on there. He's not a Vandal. Nor are you. At least—you haven't been for a long time." I wasn't going to mince words. "Liam made his choices. You made yours. The only thing that binds all those names together is Dove."

"And our past," Milo corrected. "Don't mistake Liam's work for betrayal. Mickey had a right to make his choices, just like all of us do. That never changed who either was to the rest of us."

Jasper scoffed, even as Milo cut him a dark look. "Don't," Jasper retorted, shocking the shit out of me, and even Kellan straightened. "You made plans and cut the rest of us out of them. So no, you don't get to tell me what we can and can't believe. Liam walked the fuck away, cutting ties with us almost immediately. Now you want to say it was something *you* arranged and couldn't be bothered to trust the rest of us with?"

I scrubbed a hand over my face, even as Milo sighed.

"We don't have time for this," Freddie interrupted before the fight could even begin to escalate. "It's been *hours* since she called. *Hours*. We still don't know where she is."

"Liam followed her to the Narrows," Jasper said. "She boarded a private plane and it took off. So far, none of our contacts can even tell us the plane's registration or destination. We're all assuming it was a Sharpe family plane, we know they have two of them."

"I know someone who might be able to help," Doc said.

"And you're just telling us now?" The sharp reprimand in Kellan's voice was hard to miss. "Why haven't you called them already?"

If Kellan's tone bothered Doc, it didn't show. "Because until now, no one mentioned she'd gotten on a private plane." The last was said with a glance at Jasper, who at least had the grace to grimace.

"Can we please stop pissing on each other?" Freddie demanded. He was still dancing his knife around in his hand, the sharp blade seeming to narrowly miss his fingertips over and over. "This isn't about *us*, it's about Boo-Boo!"

A headache pounded behind my eye. "Then call their house," I said. "We know where they live." We'd always known that. We had a list of *all* the Sharpe homes. Dove tended to stay with her uncle when she wasn't touring because her parents traveled so much and he seemed more settled.

Milo met my gaze and raised his brows. "You just want us to pick up the phone and call them?"

"Yes." I tossed the wallet onto the desk and dug out my own phone. "I can fucking do it if you want. If she went home, and she's not answering the phone I gave her, then it makes sense we should be able to get a call or at least a message to her there."

Jasper's scowl deepened. "The last thing she wanted was us contacting her family."

"That was for ransom," I pointed out, but Jasper still shook his head. Phone in hand, I debated it. We needed to know. If they took her and she didn't want to be there, then we'd burn it down to get her back.

But if she wanted to be there…

Did I want to know if she really wanted to leave us?

"Call her," Freddie said abruptly. "I'll bet you *money* they won't put her on the phone."

Doc rubbed his jaw, then he shared a look with Milo. "Your call, kid."

"No," Kellan said and the ferociousness in that single syllable startled me, and seemingly everyone else present. "It's not just his fucking call. Sparrow belongs to all of us."

I liked the sound of it.

Jasper quirked a brow.

"Milo wanted her gone. He doesn't get to make the call." For Kellan to take that stand meant a lot and I nodded.

"Agreed. Love you brother," I said to Milo when his dark gaze collided with my own. "Believe me when I say that, I mean it. But Dove is ours. We took her. We protected her. We *care* and you wanted her to go back to that world. I didn't." It was the first time I'd admitted it aloud, but the truth was right there. I wanted Dove *here*. I wanted to be able to wake up to her, make love to her, play with her…

I wanted it all, and when she'd asked me for that tattoo, there was nothing in anything she said or did, that told me she wanted any different.

"We need the number for their place—" A fist hitting the door interrupted and Freddie, being the closest, jerked it open and had JD against the wall with a knife to his throat before any of us were moving.

"What the fuck do you want?" Freddie asked.

"Easy," Jasper said, having already closed the distance and he had a hand on Freddie's shoulder. A little trickle of blood appeared on JD's throat where the knife touched him. I shifted to grip Freddie's other shoulder. Right now, we didn't need more bodies to dispose of, even if JD was a pain in the ass—he was still one of the rats.

"Answer the question," Milo said in a dead neutral tone. The grit of each syllable was colorless and forced. "What do you want?"

JD's eyes cut to where Milo stood. "There's something you need to see."

"What?"

"News report…in the clubhouse."

"What the fuck were you doing in the clubhouse?" Kellan asked. "You guys were warned."

"Yes," JD said and the man looked like he wanted to squirm, but Freddie's white-knuckled grip on him kept him still. "Went to grab a drink, television was on. News report."

News.

"What news?" It was my turn to ask, and JD's whites were showing when he cut a frantic look at me.

"The princess is home."

"She doesn't like that name," Jasper growled. Something JD should fucking remember. Rome had laid his ass out the last time he called her that.

"I know," JD raised his hands. More blood trickled down his neck. "I didn't call her that. The dude on the news did. She was getting off some plane with him and reporters were everywhere—"

Reporters.

Dude.

Plane.

I let go of Freddie and stalked out of the office. In no time, I was in the clubhouse and staring at the television. There was a picture of her on the screen as a news reporter talked about the return of the Sharpe heiress and that the family was asking for their privacy to be respected. No details on where she'd been or who had held her were forthcoming. Then it cut to live footage as she walked next to her uncle. He had a hand on her arm and their security made them a way to the car.

Nothing in her demeanor said anything about not wanting to be there. If anything, she was unreadable, but I looked for something—anything to tell me what the fuck was going on.

"After months of speculation following her disappearance, the Sharpe heiress has returned home. The family has not answered any questions on her whereabouts or what transpired, but sources tell me that the FBI and law enforcement will be interviewing her in the coming days. For now, we wish the Sharpe family good fortune and we're glad to see them reunited once again."

The last image was her uncle wrapping an arm around her as she turned her face from the cameras and he spoke. She looked so small next to him.

Something shattered behind me and I didn't bother to look. But when I glanced to my right, Kellan stood there. "You believe that?"

"I don't know," he said. "I know what I want the truth to be, but I don't know if that's what it is."

Fuck.

"Then we call—" I started, but Milo cut me off.

"Leave her alone."

"Milo," Doc began, but Milo didn't even give him a chance to finish before he cut him off.

"I'm serious," he growled. "Leave her be. She made her choice. Live with it."

Then he spun on his heel and stalked out.

Fuck.

Fuck.

Fuck.

"I'm not leaving it alone," Freddie swore and goddammit—neither was I.

Chapter Six

ROME

The apartment had been hauntingly quiet when I arrived. I'd never believed in ghosts or other supernatural phenomena. They made for curious and entertaining television or movies. They weren't real. But Starling's ghost was everywhere in Liam's apartment. The floor near the equipment where she stretched. On the treadmill where she ran sometimes. On the kitchen counter where we had kissed. On the sofa where I'd held her.

The silence inside the apartment swelled. I walked back to my room and stopped at the door. The scent of her filled the air. Closing my eyes, I took a deep breath. It was there, the scent of the soap and the shampoo. There was coconut from the lotion she used. The faint undertones of sweat. Trapped in the doorway, I studied the room but couldn't bring myself to walk in. It was my room, but it had become hers. Retreating, I went back to the front. Flipping open the panel in the dining room, I keyed in the code and waited for the cameras to come up on the small screens.

While I rarely used Liam's system, I understood it. He'd explained it to me so I could access it whenever I wanted. I'd never wanted before. Entering the time code for earlier in the day, I searched for when Liam left.

There.

The lack of sound minimized distractions, but I wanted to hear her if she said *anything.* Impossible, but she moved to sit in the living room and turned on the television. Her attention seemed split between what was in her hand and what was on the screen. Maybe her phone? She watched the news. A moment later, she twisted to look toward the kitchen. I turned to scan it.

The phone.

Back to the camera. She didn't get up and answer it. She turned the television off. Then she looked at the door. Facing it, I studied it. Nothing obvious hinted why she stared at it. Had someone knocked? Had they rung the bell? She didn't answer the phone. She *shouldn't* answer the door. The waiting scraped against me like an uncomfortable sweater.

Still, I didn't move. She walked over to the door, but her hands didn't go to the knob. She was checking the view hole.

Hitting pause, I walked to the door and checked through it. The hall in front of the door, the door at the end of the hall and the elevator were visible. But only an angle of the doors, not the interior. Still, nothing moved.

I returned to the monitor and hit play. I tried not to focus too much on every step she took, how her expression shifted or her respiration. When she opened the door, I tensed. But no one was there and she just picked up a package from in front of the door.

She carried it to the table and opened it. The camera angle wasn't sharp enough for me to see. I pressed as close to the screen as I could. She went through the pages and whatever she found—it upset her. When she put it all back away, I only got a glimpse of the front of one—it looked like a photograph. I backed up the recording twice and played it again.

I still couldn't see what she was looking at. The next few minutes had her vanishing back to my room and then she came out with a bag. One final look around and then she just—left.

Liam put no cameras in my room. He had them in his, but not mine.

We would change that.

There was a note on Liam's door. I hadn't even looked at it

earlier, but there was a note stuck to it. I peeled it off and read the words written by a trembling hand. There were little fine tremors in the ink.

Liam,

Thank you for everything. It's time for me to go home.

H.

There was a watermark around the h. The note was another clue.

H.

Hellspawn.

Liam called her Hellspawn.

In my bedroom, I swept the room with a look. Starting in the closet, I searched. Her clothes—all the new things were here. The dirty clothes in the hamper, same thing. All new clothes. Opening the drawers, I checked for the items that came with her from her dressing room.

They were gone.

Nothing of ours had gone with her. My shirt that she'd been wearing was there at the end of the bed. Vaughn's was in the drawer. Pivoting, I faced the bed. The bear was still there.

She'd left him.

Something uncomfortable gnawed inside my chest and I rubbed a hand against my sternum as I looked at the room. Tried to see it as she would. She'd had her phone. Did she take it with her? I pulled out mine and found her name in my contacts.

Starling.

One press and then I hit the speaker on the phone.

It went straight to voicemail. It didn't even ring.

The message wasn't her voice either, just the standard message. Vaughn had gotten her the basic plan. One more try. Straight to voicemail. I considered leaving a message, but when I got to the end it said the voicemail box was full.

Putting my phone away, I stared at the room again. I wanted to know what she'd done in here, but there were no cameras. So, I started at one side of the room and opened, looked under, moved, and searched everything. At the bed, I paused from looking under it to study the bed itself. Under the bed was too easy, if I had to secure something I'd use the slats of the box spring. This bed had no rips or cuts in the box spring for her to get inside it.

Gripping the mattress, I lifted the whole thing up. At the edge, there was a chance of finding something when the bed was stripped or remade. Hiding it in the middle made it far less easy to find because who would hide something that far—there was a small envelope there. Manila. Smaller than the one she'd had at the table.

I snagged it and pulled it out. It had weight.

Inside?

New identification, credit cards, cash, and everything she could need to be someone else. The work on the cards was good. The electronic stamp and foil were present. The hologram too. I checked them for any other identifying marks.

Forgers could be specific, but these were clean. The cash was too. The serial numbers were sequential. It was nearly ten thousand.

Why would she leave this behind?

How long has she had it?

Why hadn't she used them?

Because she didn't want to leave us.

A single thought crystalized and I set the new IDs and cards aside with the note and continued to pull the room apart. If she had one hiding spot. She'd have another. I went back to the dresser and slid my hands inside to search above, below. I even pulled the drawers all the way out to look under.

It wasn't until I got to the bottom one that something jammed the drawer and wouldn't let me pull it all the way out. Snaking my hand under the small space between the floor and the dresser bottom, I found the phone tucked away and pulled it out.

It was hers and it was off.

I added that to my stack and then went back to my search. When Liam walked in, I'd just found the envelope with the pictures. She'd slid them into a cleaning bag in the back of the closet. It held a suit Liam had made for me that I never wore.

Good place for hiding something.

"Rome."

I met my mirror's gaze as I came out of the closet with the envelope in my hands. Then he looked away, anger had turned his jaw taut. He studied the room. The wreck that I'd left in my wake. Right now, the contents of the room mattered less than what I'd found. I took the envelope with its photos, and everything else, out to the table. When I dumped the pictures out, I stared at them.

Starling.

Us.

Liam.

Milo.

Doc.

Dozens of photos. All of us. Freddie. Jasper. Kel.

All with targets on them.

"He threatened her." Liam's words penetrated the red haze burning through me and I looked at my other half. He held up a photo of the two of them, his expression cold, remote, and murderous.

"He threatened *us*."

That snapped his attention to me. Fury burned in the tundra behind his eyes. Before he could say anything though, his phone rang and he answered it. He turned away, distracted as he answered whoever it was.

He.

No one who sent these was a friend.

This "he" was an enemy.

I picked up her note to Liam. The tremors disrupting the ink, the water stain. Starling hadn't wanted to go.

Setting the note down, I went through the pictures again. No clues on any of them. No writing. Had she known automatically who sent them? I replayed her actions on the video.

Within minutes of receiving the pictures, she was back in my room and then she was leaving. She'd known. Her family was the enemy.

It was the only way it made sense.

She knew who it was.

Turning on her phone, I waited for the screen to power up. It requested a password or pin to unlock it.

I entered her birthday.

No.

What other numbers would have any meaning?

I tried spelling dove out with numbers. It was Vaughn who gave her the phone.

It didn't work.

I tried Vandal.

No.

Frustration rifled over my skin and I gripped one of the chairs and flung it. Something crashed in the living room, but I didn't look at it. My attention was on the phone.

"I gotta go." Liam's voice re-entered my sphere. "You found her phone."

I nodded. He didn't need an answer. I had the phone in my hand. Would Vaughn have passcoded it before he gave it to her?

Milo's birthday had been the default we used for most things before we personalized them.

No.

I closed my eyes. I couldn't throw the phone. It was another tether to Starling. Until we found her and brought her home. What would *she* use as a number? Most used something valuable. Liam's was the day the O'Connells adopted him. A date that had significance for him. Vaughn's was the day his mother died. Freddie used the date of his suicide attempt. A reminder, he'd told me once.

The day of her first show. The first time Emersyn Sharpe performed. I entered the date and the phone unlocked. The mail app was empty. The messages were all to and from us. Nothing stood out. I didn't read her messages to my brothers.

Liam stood right at my shoulder, his focus on the screen. "Wait. Scroll back."

There were only two screens of apps. She didn't have very many. Not even games.

"This isn't right."

I looked at Liam. "What isn't?"

He held out his hand and I fought the initial resistance to hold onto the phone. If he could find something that could help, then I needed to relinquish it to him. He swiped back and forth between the two screens. Then he opened the apps store and checked recent purchases.

"I knew she had another one on here." He held it up to show me. I didn't know the app. Not waiting for me, he reinstalled it. When he opened it, he messed around for a few minutes. I opened and closed my hands, flexing my fists. The aggravation rippling over my skin made me want to move, but if I moved I couldn't see what he was doing.

He swore.

"What?"

"She has fading on. It went to its default settings." At my silence, he said, "This is a messaging app. Like our texts, only when you send a message, once it has been read, it wipes itself. When I reinstalled it, I was hoping the histories would come up—that happens sometimes, but she's wiped those. So, the app is here and so is her login, but there are no contacts, no message histories. Goddammit. Why didn't she call one of *us*?"

"Because she wanted to protect us. You should have been here when those came."

Liam scowled. "I know that. I told her to not answer the damn door." When he started to throw the phone I covered it in his hand and yanked it away.

The phone vibrated in my palm and we both stared down at it.

A name popped up on the screen.

"Fuck me," Liam swore.

I stared at the name Lainey.

I didn't know who that was. But from Liam's fierce expression— it seemed he might.

"Who is she?"

Chapter Seven

FREDDIE

A week. A whole week. After the one brief sighting of her on the news, Emersyn all but vanished from the public view. The family had withdrawn behind an army of lawyers and corporate double talk. In fact, the only ones still talking about her were the tabloid shows that kept speculating about everything from a legal investigation to a medical one. Worse, some had begun to suggest she had a drug problem.

Boo-Boo. A *drug* problem.

Assholes.

The one hard line had been 'the family would like their privacy during this difficult time.' "My mother is sick. My father had a heart attack." Both seemed reasonable. The news touched on them, but only in passing. So, were they really in danger? Or had she lied to me?

No. The tremor in the words. That hadn't been a lie.

I knew fear when I heard it.

Every minute that passed without something more seemed to draw blood. The jittery feeling racing over my flesh increased every single day that dawned without news. We'd all tried calling the house.

If they bothered to answer, we never got past the butler. Doc had taken a different tack. He'd called as her *doctor*. When he was told to just send a bill, he'd actually thrown his phone against the wall. The device shattered into chunky bits. After, he'd just walked out and we hadn't seen him in three days.

Liam and Rome had been curiously silent on the whole damn thing. Or maybe they were just talking to each other. I didn't know. All I knew was I couldn't sleep. Food held little appeal. I couldn't shake the quiver in her voice when she said she had to go. The almost mournful sigh. I'd told her nothing good came after a sigh like that.

I'd been right.

I was still right, only now they weren't listening. Jasper and Vaughn had been working overtime to sort out who was sabotaging our shipments, or hijacking them, and using our transportation for flesh peddling. Not even the Bay Ridge Royals, which we knew for damn sure peddled in flesh, had been so bold.

The 19 Diamonds had been keeping their heads down. Juan Ricardo probably heard Milo was back, pissed himself, and fled. We'd catch him sooner or later.

I flipped my blade in my hand as I stared down the street. The guys were cleaning house. Body disposal was a pain in the ass, but they were doing the hard part here, then separating it all out after. Drums would go on different ships, to different ports, and by the time they got there, what was left wouldn't even be recognizable as human.

We'd gotten pretty good at this part.

Still, the guys we'd taken apart had given us nothing. They didn't know who hired them. All of our tails had also vanished, almost overnight. The men watching Doc had been the only ones caught, but the guys watching Liam's had never come back. We knew very little and Milo—goddammit, Milo pissed me off. He wanted us to leave it alone.

Not a fucking chance.

"Freddie," Rome said and I twisted. Where the fuck had he come from? I scanned the street and then looked back at him. "I have an idea."

"Will it get Boo-Boo back?"

"Maybe."

"I'm in." Because *anything* was better than this.

He nodded. "We need to leave as soon as they're done."

Right. We couldn't leave them unprotected. "What do you need me to bring?"

"Just you, right now." Rome paused, the silence lasting almost too long. "Don't stab anyone."

"Now? Or later?"

"Both." With another nod, he walked away as silently as he'd approached.

"No promises," I said when he was a few feet away. I wanted to stab a lot of people. Starting with whoever convinced Boo-Boo to leave us.

When I found *that* person—all bets were off.

"Woah," I said, holding up both hands as I glanced from one twin to the other. "You've had this information for how fucking long and haven't said a word?"

"Milo doesn't want to hear it yet." Rome shrugged. "Jasper and Vaughn will not react well."

Liam gave his brother a look that said he didn't think Rome was acting well. Fuck them both.

"A week. You've done *what* with it?"

"I've been using connections to reach out to the family," Liam said. "One of the reasons Milo likes me in this world…"

"Yeah, yeah, cause you travel in the same snooty circles, only she didn't."

The bastard had the grace to at least grimace. "No. But I know people who know her."

"*I* know people who know her." Agitation invaded my system like a hive of bees had been kicked over. The stinging sensation kept me moving. "*We* know her. What good are these *people* of yours?"

"Not much," Liam admitted, his expression shuttering.

"Not much? Or nothing?" I rubbed at my chest, then the back of my neck. I wasn't quite to the point where I was going to start yanking on my hair. But I needed a fix bad—either information or—no, no or. I had to keep my fucking head on, because these guys were all chasing their own damn tails.

"Not much." Rome held out a phone to me.

"That's Boo-Boo's."

"We know." Liam cut his brother a look, but I ignored them both as I unlocked the screen. The passcode was off of it. "That's the 'not much' part."

"No incoming calls that aren't us." I panned through the apps they had open, trying and failing to stand still so I just went back to pacing. They said nothing, but did that whacked out thing where they barely looked at each other and then read the other's mind. It was both cool and creepy.

Also, a real bitch when we played cards—or any game really.

Ignoring them, I went to the ChatApp and popped it open. There was a message there.

Lainey

Call me. I saw the news.

"Who's Lainey?"

"We don't know," Liam said. "The name—it could be anybody."

"Or it could be a friend of hers." Maybe one from before. "Have you reached out to her?"

Rome glared at his brother and Liam sighed. "No," he answered before Rome could. "She was hiding this. I restored the app and the message came through. We turned off her security protocols, so it didn't just erase it."

Each word came out as though he had to chew glass to get them past his teeth. Rome's expression shifted. "I said we should message her back."

"It's a bad idea," Liam said. "We *don't* know who she is, and we have no way to check her out beforehand. It's a name."

"And a number." I clicked on the information banner next to her name.

"Yeah, it's another dead end," Liam said with a grimace. "I ran it. It's attached to a burner account for a shell that's part of a subsidiary of an LLC that was just picked up by a corporation. There's no way to track that back to that person just as there is no way to track Hellspawn's phone back to her."

"Except Vaughn just got her phone from one of our stash." Most of which we had because Liam set them up through some network of companies and other crap. I didn't pay attention to that part because I didn't *care*. "So, Boo-Boo added this number from memory."

"What…?"

"She had to add this number from memory, she didn't have *her* phone. Kel or Jasper still had it." I turned the phone over in my hand like it would offer me some insight. "She left *this* one. What about the other phone?"

Rome shook his head. "It's not here."

"So, she took the phone she had from before, but not this one. Why? Why leave one and take the other?"

"This one has our contact info in it." Liam said.

"She could have added it to her other phone before she left." I sliccd a hand through the air, my thoughts buzzing almost as much as my skin. "She was in touch with this person." For how long? And she told none of us? Then again, why would she tell us this? It was a tie to her old life.

Or was it?

Unlocking the phone, I went back to the message. The other person had to know it had been read but they'd sent nothing else. They saw the news, which meant they knew Boo-Boo had gone home. My thoughts were like a hurricane, the volume too loud for me to catch more than snippets. But she hadn't sent any other messages.

Had she already seen her? Did she know she didn't have this phone?

Well, she might have guessed.

Fingers flying, I typed in a message and hit send just as Liam snarled, "Don't."

But it was too late, the message was already on the screen.

"Goddammit, Freddie." He scowled but Rome moved to stand at my shoulder and read the message.

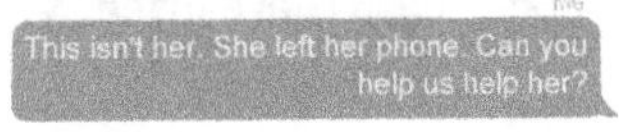

"She could throw her phone away now," Rome said.

"She could," I agreed. "Absolutely. But if she's the kind of friend you memorize their number, then you keep all your contact secret and use programs that erase the messages? Then she's the kind of friend you can trust—at least for Boo-Boo."

Rome nodded, but he didn't lift his gaze from the screen once. We stood there, like a bunch of boobs, staring at the phone like it held every answer. An hour passed before Liam moved to the kitchen and started cooking. A second hour and we were at the table, the phone plugged into a charging cord and the screen left on so we could see the message. It would also show that "Emersyn" was online.

I didn't care.

This was the first tangible fucking connection I'd had in days. The closest I'd been able to get to her. Even the news hadn't reported on her, not one word. They replayed the story of her getting off the plane over and over again. Apparently, that was what had happened to Liam's television. Rome smashed it when the news hadn't given them an updated report.

Liam just hadn't replaced it.

It was dark when a flash on the screen jerked me out of a half-doze. Rome sat forward as I did, and Liam jerked.

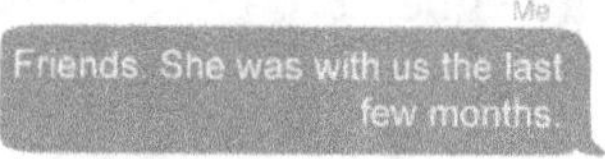

We all stared at the message. There was a green dot next to her name at the top. She was online. I flicked a look at the twins.

"Answer," Liam said. "This is your plan."

Right. My *plan*. I didn't have a plan. I had a hope and prayer. Neither of which had ever done shit for me, but maybe they would for Boo-Boo.

Not much else I could offer than that. Had Boo-Boo told her about us? Anything? Fuck. Were we about to dead-end?

That was—sad.

The screen bounced, but it wasn't the connection. It was my hands. The shakes came and went. I didn't have time for this right now. Probably should have eaten more. But food made me gag on the best days.

I stared at the words for the longest time and then shrugged. Fuck it. I wasn't a smooth talker or a charmer.

The phone connection ended. The green light vanished. Rome stood up and picked up his chair and then flung it across the room. It hit a wall and then fell to the floor. Liam scrubbed a hand over his face.

"Well, so much for that idea." He'd just stood when another phone rang. This time, his expression changed from exhaustion to one of resignation, or maybe it was irritation. "I have to take this."

He stalked out of the room, pulling a phone out of his pocket. I put Boo-Boo's phone back in front of me and stared at it.

This Lainey person would come back.

She had to.

She was Boo-Boo's friend. Real friends didn't let you fall alone. They jumped in after you. Sometimes, waded into the shit to drag you out. Those were the numbers you memorized.

"I have to go," Liam said abruptly as he stormed back through the door.

"Where?" I asked but the door had already closed behind him

I frowned at it.

"He hasn't found Starling," Rome said. "He would have told us that."

Great, so where the fuck else did he have to go?

Rome eventually crashed out on the sofa, and I sat next to the glass looking out over the city, with Boo-Boo's phone still in my hand. I didn't care how long I had to wait. If she messaged back, I was going to be right the fuck here when it came in.

The first fingers of dawn touched the sky when the phone vibrated and I snapped my eyes open. I hadn't meant to fall asleep.

I stared at the message and something punched through my

chest as I exhaled. The next three lines were an address and a phone number. Then a time to meet.

Holy shit. That was…

Shoving up from the floor, I went to Rome and kicked the sofa. He snapped his eyes open. "We gotta go," I told him. "It's gonna take forever to get there, but she said she'd help."

I showed him the phone. His whole demeanor changed as he studied the message. She hadn't waited for our answer. She was already offline. "It could be a trap," Rome said.

"Risk I'm willing to take. You?"

He pushed off the sofa. "I'm driving."

Chapter Eight

EMERSYN

One Week Earlier

"Welcome home, Princess."

My skin crawled at the affection slithering through his voice. I looked away from him and toward the window. The plane hadn't even waited for me to be seated all the way before they headed for a runway. While planes didn't move all that swiftly on the ground, this one seemed to accelerate. I didn't dare look back to where Liam had been.

I'd already given my uncle enough ammunition. As it was, he said nothing. When we reached the actual runway, the pilot came on to warn the staff to prepare for take-off. Moments later, we accelerated down the runway, racing to take off. As the nose of the plane lifted, my stomach dropped and my heart sank. Both were being left behind. No matter how hard I fixed my gaze on the window, I couldn't stop the heat burning behind my eyes.

I had to forget. I had to bury it all. The old Emersyn knew exactly how to do this, the well-worn emotional calluses were still there. Only the new Emersyn clung to regrets, something neither of us could afford. Swallowing, I tried to equalize my ears but the sudden pop just brought the noise of the engines into sharper relief. Not that I needed it to be aware of my uncle's contemplative stare.

Eventually, the plane leveled off and he said nothing as the staff joined us. Instead, one of the attendants refilled his drink and then asked me if I wanted anything. Before I could respond with a no, my uncle said, "Bring us both champagne, it's time we toasted our reunion."

Oh, I hated him so much.

The little thought snuck out of a back corner, growling and snarling even as I shoved it back. Nothing. I felt *nothing* for him. The guys couldn't afford my hatred. The whole point of me coming back was to keep them safe. I should have known I couldn't stay, even if I had begun to…

"Here you go," the attendant said as she set a flute glass on the table next to me. The golden liquid cheerfully bubbled like we were enjoying a private joke. I barely glanced at the glass before I nodded to her.

Granted, they worked for my uncle so none of them could be trusted as even potential allies. That didn't mean I couldn't be polite.

"Leave us." At his words, the women withdrew and closed the door between our cabin and the area where they worked. The slide lock and click plunged us into silence. "Pick up your glass, Princess."

"No, thank you." For a moment, pride at my even tone flooded me. There wasn't even a hint of a tremor.

Not responding, he reached across the gulf separating us and picked up my glass. It was only then I recognized he'd risen from his seat and moved around to the one next to me.

Fuck.

"Your glass." It wasn't a request, but I rested a hand over my abdomen and the tattoo that was still scabbing there. The ink I'd asked Vaughn for and that he'd drawn on me. A first. Our first.

Head up. Wings out.

I turned my head and met my uncle's stare. "No, thank you."

His eyes were cool, calculated, and dark. His stern expression seemed unforgiving as he took a seat next to me, both flute glasses in his hands. "Princess…"

"Don't. You wanted me back. I'm here. But let's not pretend that I'm here for any other reason than you blackmailed me into it." I refused to look away, even when his lips compressed and his eyes went chillier, if that was even possible. They were like twin sheets of black ice, treacherous, and unyielding.

With a heavy sigh, he set the glasses down. No matter how

braced I was, I couldn't stop the flinch when he reached out his hand to run over my hair. The gentle touch was a lie. It was always a lie. "You've been gone too long, Princess. I don't know what they did to you but…" He fisted my hair and yanked so I had to look at him. The pull against my scalp burned, but I gritted my teeth. "We will fix it. I never stopped looking for you. You know that, right?"

I didn't answer.

He tightened his hand and pulled my hair a little harder. "Right?"

"I'm aware."

"Good." All at once, he loosened his hold. "When we learned you were missing, I brought in extra security for the family. I even talked to that Benedict girl."

Don't. React. Don't react. Don't react.

"Who?"

He snorted, then picked up the flute of champagne and put it into my hand. Even as he closed my fingers around it, he pressed my hand so severely, I had a feeling the glass might shatter. While he held my hand firmly on the glass, he reached for his own. "Don't worry, Princess. We'll fix everything." The promise left dread curling in my stomach. Even more when he tapped his glass to mine and lifted his for a drink even as he pressed upwards.

I didn't want it, but unless I wanted to wear it—I drank it down in one long gulp. Approval radiated off of him as he finally released my hand. "Another," he said and it wasn't a question. Instead, he just refilled my glass and his own.

The champagne was dry as hell and the alcohol hit like a punch. Maybe that was why he wanted me to drink it, so I'd just relax. Sure. Why not? I downed the second glass without any encouragement and he finally released my hand and settled back in his chair. The fact he clamped a hand on my leg sent my skin crawling in a desperate attempt to escape the contact, but by the third glass of champagne, I didn't give a fuck anymore.

He didn't ask anything else of me, nor did he insist that I eat when the attendants brought out food. "Your chaperone has been dealt with," he told me rather conversationally at one point, but I didn't care. If that meant he paid off Marta, or killed her, it was all the same to me. "You will also not be returning to that troupe in the future. In fact, I believe you should take the next couple of years and reassess your goals and choices."

Sure. Why not? I was almost nineteen. Probably time to put away childish things. He kept talking, making plans, and I kept drinking. I finished the bottle before we landed. Instead of leaving the plane immediately though, Uncle Bradley made us wait until the new security team arrived. They came to the doors of the jet itself in order to escort us off.

The reason why was clear from the moment we descended the steps. Press was everywhere. Press. Flashing cameras. Shouted questions. My uncle drew me close and I dropped my head and looked away from all of them. One, I didn't want to be photographed. Two, I didn't want to answer their questions. Three, if I opened my mouth, I might start screaming and never stop.

All the way to the car, he kept an arm around me and the security pushed the people back. I caught the flash of a badge, but my uncle all but shoved me inside before he turned to deal with the man. The interior of the limo smelled of air freshener and faintly of cleaner and tobacco. It wasn't until Uncle Bradley climbed in that the cloying notes of his cologne were there.

I shifted on the seat but before I could move away, he clamped a hand on my knee again. His fingers bit into my skin, the pain increasing with every second until I settled back. Only then did he ease up.

"I'll introduce you to your new security detail tomorrow," Uncle Bradley said, and it took a few minutes for his words to register. That and the fact he mentioned going to his home. "Your parents are preoccupied, though your return will be good for both of them to hear."

"What security detail?" I wasn't some celebutante who needed one.

"If you think I will allow anyone to take you away again," Uncle Bradley told me in a voice devoid of emotion. "You're gravely mistaken. Those who took you will be dealt with…you're far too precious to me to be allowed to be harmed or ransomed back."

Ransomed.

"No one ransomed me."

"Weren't you?" He gave me an enigmatic look. "How else did you think I found you, Princess?"

Bullshit. Even if my thoughts were running a little slower than normal. "If I'd been ransomed, you wouldn't have had to threaten me to get me back."

"I'd never threaten you," he said before leaning in and kissing my cheek. I flinched away before he could touch my mouth. His tone hardened. "But I will undo the damage that's been done to you. You were never afraid of me before."

I stared at him, aghast. "I'm not *afraid* of you now."

"No?" Challenge dripped off that single word.

"No." Oddly, it was true. Maybe I was drunk. Or maybe I'd actually hit my limit. "I'm not afraid of you."

When he lifted his hand to my face, I jerked away. "Really? Then why do you keep flinching?"

"Because you disgust me."

The words slipped free. No matter how hard I tried to squeeze myself back into the mold of the old Emersyn, it just didn't fit me anymore. He telegraphed the move. I saw it coming and watched it as his hand came back and then struck. The hot slap against my face burned. The force drove the soft skin inside my cheek against my teeth, and I tasted blood.

The coppery flavor flooded my mouth, sobering me alongside the pain flashing fire against my skin. I didn't even have to reach up to cup a hand over it. I met his gaze, unblinking. "You still disgust me." Flecks of blood sprayed as I spoke and a drop hit his cheek. The next blow slammed me against the glass of the window and the world darkened for a bit.

I should stay awake, but I didn't want to be conscious. Not here. Not ever again. As it was, I roused again as we passed through the black gates marking the drive up to his huge home. Uncle Bradley didn't wait for the driver, he just pushed open the door and stepped out before reaching back inside. He caught my arm and dragged me across the seat.

Limp, I didn't fight him, nor did I help. Once he had me out of the car, I glanced around. There was no staff on the steps. The driver was still in the car and another vehicle was coming up the drive. Security?

I didn't recognize it, or the man behind the wheel. The last thing I wanted was to go in that house though. I came back. That was enough. "Let's go," Uncle Bradley said, tugging me into motion and I "stumbled." He wasn't prepared for me to drop like a dead weight. It pulled him off balance and he had to let me go or risk falling himself.

How many times I'd practiced the next move had my muscles responding automatically, I slammed my forehead against his crotch. As gross as it was, the impact would hit harder than my fist and it kept my hands free to wrap his knee and yank, even as I hit.

An agonized sound escaped him as he crashed to the ground and I was on my feet and running. Get away. That was what Liam had been teaching for fuck knew how long. Stun, wound, incapacitate if I could, then run like hell. I raced away from him, from his horrible house with its horrible rooms and even more horrible memories. I didn't head for the drive or the black gates.

Instead, I cut across the manicured lawn toward the trees that edged the property. There was a private reserve on the other side of the fence and state lands past there. All of it heavily wooded. I'd gotten lost out there once when I was little. I'd nearly frozen before Uncle Bradley and his search party had managed to find me.

Sometimes, I wished I had frozen. At least then it would have been me just going to sleep. Shouts came from behind me, but I ignored them. My lungs burned. All the alcohol I'd drunk didn't make this flight any easier. The tattoo on my stomach pulled and twinged with every step I took, a reminder to keep going.

All I had to do was get away. I'd figure out what to do next after that. I had their numbers. But Uncle Bradley was far away from them. Far away from Braxton Harbor. I had time. I could warn them.

Leaves crunched under my feet as I raced beneath and around the trees. Just a few more yards to freedom. The fence was absolutely not an obstacle, even with its black metal jutting spikes at the top to discourage people from climbing over.

When I was much younger, I could slip between the bars. Now, I'd just fly over them. My heart thundered in my ears as a raised voice behind me bellowed. I ignored it. Uncle Bradley. His security. It didn't matter who it was.

They couldn't help me.

I had to get away.

Finally, the fence was right there and I leapt as soon as I was on top of it. A grip on the bars and my momentum would push me up and then I'd twist over. Only instead of that, there was a loud pop and shocking burn that ran up both my arms before I flew backwards and hit the ground.

All the air whooshed out of me. Pain from the impact. Pain in my hands. Pain all through my system as I jerked and twitched.

Then a strange man filled my vision. "Silly girl, the fence is electrified." There wasn't an ounce of pity in his voice as he dragged me upward. I offered almost no resistance, I couldn't even get my brain to cooperate, much less my fingers. He threw me over his shoulder and marched back toward the house.

Everything hurt, everything swayed and when we got there, he set me down and I faced my uncle. His face was contorted in fury, an anger he made no attempt to contain. He was yelling at me, but I barely heard anything as I swayed. Fuck, I just hurt.

"Well?" he demanded. "Say something."

I opened my mouth and promptly vomited all over him. His cursing was the last thing I heard before I passed out.

Chapter Nine

EMERSYN

The next couple of days passed in a blur. When I woke up, I was in my old room and the door had been locked. There were even bars on my window. How—quaint. At least I was still dressed and there was no familiar pain anywhere else. Or there wasn't, until I tried to push myself up.

My hands hurt like hell. When I stared at my palms, I couldn't believe the red stripes across them. He'd electrified the fence. Since when? Granted, I couldn't remember the last time I'd climbed it, but I had when I was little.

Every muscle in my body protested as I dragged myself out of bed. I wanted a shower and to brush my teeth. I had a vague memory that they brought me food at some point, but I'd refused it. I didn't even want the drinks they brought. Twice, I'd dragged myself out of the bed to get water in the bathroom. Sleep and pain held me captive. Or was it drugs? The confusion was real.

Scanning the room, I found no phone or television. For the first time in years, I really looked at the pink lace bedecked curtains and the fuzzy rug, even the overstuffed fuzzy chair done in a softer shade of pink. There were stuffed animals all along the window seat. All as neat and as prim as they'd been the day they'd been delivered.

None of them were as loved or as worn as the scarred teddy bear with its stitched arms and flattened fur. I walked to the window and stared out through the bars. My room faced the south side of the property, away from the road, away from anything. The woods stood out there, taunting me. The black—electrified—fence mocked me. If I planned to climb it again, I'd need something rubber to grip it with.

Or maybe I could go up a tree and over. There were some pretty close. The fall might hurt, but I could survive it. My skin itched and crawled. I needed to check my tattoo as well. I hadn't been taking good care of it. Vaughn—

I slammed the door on his name and closed my eyes. Don't think about them. Don't let them in. Not right now. Not when I'd already gambled and lost the first round. My fingers hurt as I began to flex my hands. Burned or not, I needed the muscles to work. There were hints of blisters along the edge of them. One had broken open and wept.

Great.

They needed to be washed. So did my abdomen. The last thing I needed was an infection. That meant I also needed a change of clothes. Unsurprisingly, my duffel was nowhere to be seen. I had a feeling I'd never see it again. It was my room and when I pulled open a drawer on the dresser, I wasn't surprised to find it filled with clothes.

Lacy panties.

I slammed that drawer shut.

Just not wearing anything he bought for me there. I searched as carefully as I could with my hands protesting, until I found an old t-shirt all the way in the back of the closet and a pair of leggings I'd probably forgotten. There was a rip in the knee. I was kind of surprised they'd survived back here. But there was also a cami that I could wear under the t-shirt. It wouldn't be a bra, but it would help.

Layers were good.

I dragged a chair from the dressing table into the bathroom with me. Once there, I locked the door—look at that, it still worked. Then I wedged the chair under the door handle. It wouldn't keep them out if they really wanted in. Jasper could probably kick the door in without—

The hurt in my chest expanded like a balloon and threatened to pop. I didn't have much time. If they were watching me, they'd know I'd gone into the bathroom. I scanned the room around me. Fuck it.

Let them look.

I stripped out of my clothes and winced more than once at the pull of skin across my abdomen and from the fresh bruises on my back. The fall had been bad, but it was the landing that really sucked. My clothes stank of sweat. A fact I was oddly grateful for. As filthy as I was, no one had stripped me. I got the water going before I checked my abdomen in the mirror. It had gotten a lot scabbier during my sleep. Fuck. I needed to keep it cleaner than I had. The wrap over the tattoo seemed attached.

When trying to peel it off slowly didn't work, I waited to climb into the shower. The water stung like a bitch on my hands but I needed to clean the tattoo. I got the plastic wrap off with some of the scab. Grimacing, I went for the soap and washed my hands carefully before cleaning the tattoo. Some of the scab flaked away but not all of it.

Wash, don't scrub.

Then rinse carefully. As soon as I got that done, I hurried through the rest of it. I didn't care how much my bruises or hands complained. Washing my hair helped, so did the rest. After, I brushed my teeth while wrapped in a towel and dripping. Then I sat down on the top of the toilet to catch my breath.

The sound of a door closing told me someone was either out there or had just been out there. I blotted myself dry, but didn't waste time on it before I pulled clothes on. I didn't have any moisturizer here, I didn't think, but I waited to search for it after I had clothes on. Nothing in the bathroom proved useful. Some hair products. A bag of expired cosmetics that I just dropped into the trash. More toilet paper, extras for general toiletries and that was it. There wasn't even a hair dryer in here. I guessed they didn't want to leave me with any weapons.

Hair still dripping, I pulled a comb through it and then left it. Standing near the door, I strained to hear anything. No sounds of movement didn't mean my room was empty. My uncle's new security team had been quite liberal in their entering and exiting my room.

So far, I hadn't seen *him* since I threw up all over him before I passed out. In a way, it was almost funny.

Almost.

But not really.

I'd embarrassed him.

I'd defied him.

I'd tried to run away.

Sooner or later, he would be back to exact his punishment.

My pulse raced but I couldn't stay in the bathroom forever.

I mean, I supposed I could, but I doubted they'd let me remain hidden away. Ignoring the mess of my hands, I pulled the chair away from the door and then unlocked it. A part of me was braced for the door to slam open.

Cold dread curdled in my stomach. This was a thousand times worse than when I'd woken at the clubhouse. Even then, I'd been safer than I'd ever been here. Just wish I'd understood that sooner. Regrets clinging like the droplets of water soaking through my shirt, I opened the door. I didn't pull the chair out though. If I needed a shower, I needed everything I could between me and the rest of the world.

My company stood in the middle of the bedroom, arms folded, and expression blank. Security.

Relief turned my muscles lax, but I didn't dare drop my guard. The guy might not be my uncle, but that didn't mean he was my friend. After all, he'd peeled me off the ground and carted me back.

"Miss Sharpe," he said in the most impersonal of tones.

"Mr. Whoever-The-Fuck-You-Are."

His lips thinned as if he tried to smile and failed miserably. "You can call me, Mr. Cole."

"What. The. Fuck. Ever." I lifted my chin. "Why are you here?"

"You need to eat."

I shrugged. "I'm not hungry."

The man's smile actually grew more terrifying. "I didn't ask if you were hungry. My orders are to make sure you eat." He nodded to the table where a tray of food sat. "I do hope you choose not to cooperate."

Something in the way he said those last few words sent apprehension up my spine. "Do you get off on abusing teenagers, Mr. Shithole?"

His eyes narrowed. The guy was big. Big like Milo had been big. Big like Liam. But I could almost hear Liam in the back of my head. *You're safer if you get away from him. Guys have a longer reach, you take a risk on getting in close. So, you have to be fast. Look for a weakness Everybody has one.*

"Spoiled rotten little princesses who think they can do whatever they want without consequences?" He smirked. "I eat little bitches like you for breakfast."

"Gross." I didn't shudder at the word princesses. I refused to shudder at any of it. Instead, I walked over to the tray and lifted the lid.

Grilled cheese and tomato soup.

My stomach revolted at the sight of it. I loathed tomato soup. It was disgusting.

It was also one of Uncle Bradley's favorites. He particularly liked it in a bisque. Swallowing bile in the back of my throat, I picked up one half of the sandwich, since it had been cut into two triangles. Facing my unwanted guest, I took a bite of the sandwich. It was like chewing sandpaper and went down just as easily.

"There. I ate."

"All of it," he said. "Every bite and drop. Or I'll pour it down your throat." He smiled again and nothing friendly lived in that look. "Like I said, feel free to resist. No one is here who cares about what a pouting brat screams."

A pouting brat?

"Fuck. You." But I took another bite. He laughed at me, but I didn't care. I needed the food, even if I didn't want to eat it. I even choked down the soup. Though I took my time, standing there, chewing each bite at least a hundred times before I swallowed it. I swore he began to twitch. I managed to stretch the meal out for almost an hour. Only when I was done, did I pick up the glass of water, walk in the bathroom and dump it out before I refilled it with water from the tap.

He snorted, but made no move to come near me. The food sat like a hard lump in my stomach. After draining the glass, I set it back down on the tray. And waved a hand at him. "You may take it and leave now."

The dismissive tone struck a nerve because he clenched a fist and took a step toward me. Lifting my chin, I waited. What was he going to do? Hit me? My uncle didn't want me bruised up unless he gave me the bruises. A part of me almost wished this guy would hurt me. Hurt me enough they had to take me to a doctor.

But instead of following through with his non-verbal threat, Mr. Shithole Cole picked up the tray and stalked toward the door. He didn't have to unlock it to open it. Once he was outside, the bolts slid into place.

Locked in again.

They sounded like sliding bolts. What did it matter? I'd never gotten around to learning how to pick a lock. And I didn't think you could pick one of those anyway. Walking over to the bed, I sat down amidst all the pink frills and lace. I hated this room.

I hated this house.

The locks slid open again and the door shoved inward. I glared at Mr. Shithole-Cole as he walked back in. "The doctor is here to see you."

"I don't care."

The last thing I wanted was one of my uncle's doctors.

"I was hoping you'd resist." He stalked across the room toward me and I snatched the lamp off the night table and smashed it against him just as he got to me. He let out a roar of sound, but I was already up and over the bed and out the door. I hauled it closed and threw the locks, then turned and slammed into another man.

Goddammit.

Rock-solid, he glared down at me as he caught me by the arms to keep me from falling. Only he slammed me back against the door and it lit up the bruises on my back. Well, so much for the helpful part. "He said you'd resist," the man said as he kept me still while he unlocked the door. It yanked inward as soon as the last lock was free. If not for his grip, I would have fallen.

Hand clamped against my nape, Mr. Cole sneered down at me. There was just a trickle of blood trickling from a cut along his hairline.

"You can't," the other man told him as Cole started to drag me backwards.

"You heard what he said, if she resisted, we were allowed to punish her."

"Yeah, and if he finds out you fucked her, he'll have me cut your dick off." The new guy was a thousand times scarier than Mr. Cole. He offered the threat conversationally. "Now, stop playing with her and bring her downstairs. The doctor needs to examine her and he wants a full report."

Cole flexed his fingers against my neck. The minute my not-so-nice-savior turned his back though, Cole bent his head to whisper, "He won't always be around princess and trust me, you're going to pay for that, and I'll take it out of your ass myself."

If he wanted to play that way.

I screamed.

The sound that ripped out of me came all the way from my toes.

The guy ahead of us wheeled around and Cole almost dropped me at the sound. I fell to my knees and *sobbed*.

"What the fuck did you do?"

"I didn't do anything to the little bitch." The implied yet hung in the air.

"Oh, for fuck's sake." The new guy caught my biceps in a bruising grip and hauled me off the floor. "Stop crying." He snarled the words as he brought his face down to mine and we were practically nose to nose. "Or I will let him give you something to cry about."

My throat tightened at the threat. "I thought you said you'd cut his dick off."

"I will," he told me, then grinned. "But you'd still have a reason to cry, wouldn't you?"

The earlier dread came back a thousand-fold.

"Now," he said. "Come with me and behave or I'll let Brandon fuck you until you bleed. Then I'll bleed him."

"Asshole," Cole snarled.

"Shut it."

To my shock, Cole did.

I believed him. So did Cole.

Guess I was going to see the doctor.

"Do you have a name?" I asked him as we descended the stairs.

"Yes," he said. "Pray you never learn it."

I swallowed around the lump in my throat. The "doctor" in the drawing room wasn't the one I half-wished it could be. I didn't know him, but the minute I saw him—all I wanted to do was flee. But I couldn't. Surrounded on all sides and locked in a house of horrors.

The only one missing was the master of them.

Chapter Ten

EMERSYN

Doctor Schuitevoerder's icy presence didn't ease one ounce of my apprehension. In fact, the lingering look he pinned on me through his glasses just added to my discomfort. Nothing about his bedside manner seemed even close to supportive, much less sympathetic.

"One of you may stay," the doctor said abruptly as he rose. "The others get out."

It shouldn't have surprised me, but tall, dark, dangerous, and promising to be deadly was the one who stayed. He didn't even have to say anything. The others just left. Including Cole, who blew me a kiss before he left. Repulsive douchebag.

"Strip," the doctor said once we were alone. Well, alone except for the guard now standing in front of the double doors, arms folded.

"No." I folded my arms. Granted, I wasn't wearing much, but Doctor skater-vorder wasn't getting any of it off. "Who are you?"

The doctor focused on me and removed his glasses instead of squinting over them. "You do not recognize me, Miss Sharpe?"

"Nope." Though everything about him made my skin crawl.

Apparently, that was a prerequisite for being in this house. "And since I'm eighteen, I get to decide, so—the answer to me getting naked is not only no, it's hell no."

Tapping one of the earpieces to his glasses against his lower lip, he studied me. "You have injuries and they need to be inspected. You also received something of a shock a couple of days ago."

"And someone threatened to rape me fifteen minutes ago. I'm still not getting naked."

He glanced at our chaperone—guard dog—whatever the hell Mr. You Don't Want To Know What My Name wanted to call himself. I didn't. I could make him out in my periphery. I still refused to acknowledge him as in charge. What little control I still managed to claw to myself, I would not surrender.

Honestly, I couldn't believe my uncle *wasn't* here and that I hadn't seen him since I vomited all over him. Not that I had any desire to see him. But he'd never had me so thoroughly caged before. Not like this.

I'd never escaped him for so long before either.

"Let's start with your hands and then we'll talk," the doctor said with a sigh, when it appeared that the guard dog wasn't going to do him any favors.

"What kind of doctor are you?" Honestly, I didn't want to get anywhere near him. Doctors couldn't be trusted. I'd made the mistake of trusting two of them.

One was dead.

The other just didn't want me.

"A busy one," he said. "Now let me see your hands." After tucking his glasses back into place, he closed the distance between us. The fact we were in a formal sitting room just added to the overall weirdness. The room had windows that looked over the garden in the back just like my room did, but they were all shuttered and closed.

The scant few seconds he spent getting close to me, I was debating striking out. But there was nowhere to go. Even if I knocked him on his ass, the bulldog was right there. So, when the doctor grasped my wrist. I let him pull my right hand to him and he studied the burns. It was only then that I realized he wore gloves.

Well, that was something, though he'd been messing with his glasses and reading something on his phone, so clearly he wasn't all in on the sanitary conditions. With a hum, he motioned for my left hand.

"Are you in much pain?"

Yes, but for some reason, I really didn't want to tell him anything. Trusting my instincts, I shrugged. "I'll live."

"Clearly." Apparently, he wasn't impressed by me. Well, that made two of us. "The report indicated you took a fall and landed on your back."

"It's fine." I'd gotten worse bruises in training.

"I'll be the judge of that. Turn and let me see." The very last thing I wanted to give this man was my back or access to my skin.

"Just do it," the bulldog said. "The sooner you cooperate, the sooner this is over."

I hated to admit it, but he had a point. Turning away from both of them, I reached for the hem of my shirt, but the doctor had already shoved it upward and caught the cami beneath it and pushed it higher. The pressure on my back wasn't remotely comfortable. I tried to curl my hands into fists, but my palms added their protests to my back.

"Deep contusions. Definitely looks like you landed on something. The color is good. I don't see anything here to—"

He shifted and almost immediately, I knew he'd spotted my tattoo. I yanked my shirt down and moved away from him.

"What is that?"

"None of your business. It definitely had nothing to do with my fall."

"Miss Sharpe, belligerence isn't helping your case."

"What case would that be?"

"Your assessment," the doctor said, his frown brought out the wrinkles in his face. The salt and pepper hair did his pale features no favors. Without his glasses, the bags beneath his eyes were clearly visible. Honestly, he looked a bit like a zombie. There was a thought I wished I could unthink. "Your uncle is very concerned about you. Your whole family really. Especially after your ordeal. The fact you tried to hurt yourself so soon after coming home has just emphasized those concerns."

"What the hell are you talking about?"

"You've been through a trauma," he said. "Your uncle has had to take precautions to make sure you don't try to harm yourself further."

Harm. Myself.

"It's understandable. But… we need to address these concerns immediately." He had his phone again. "The best way to do that would be for you to talk to me…”

"Talk to you."

"Yes," he said with a smile that never reached his eyes. "I'm here to help you."

"I'd sooner gargle with household bleach." Every instinct I had said to get the hell away from him. "So, if you're done with your exam. I'll just go back to my room."

I made it halfway to the door before the doctor sighed.

"Your uncle was afraid you wouldn't be ready to talk."

"What do you know, he got something right."

The bulldog didn't move and I paused a couple of feet away. All the bravado in the world didn't seem to hold a candle to the arctic chill surrounding him.

"Miss Sharpe—may I call you Emersyn?"

"No," I told him. "You could call yourself a cab if that would get you out of here faster."

"Miss Sharpe, lashing out at me verbally is understandable."

I cut a look at him. "What kind of doctor *are* you?"

"I'm a psychiatrist."

Of course he was. "And the first thing you wanted was to see me naked? What does Freud have to say about that doctor?"

The faintest of sounds came from the bulldog and I shot him a glance, but there was absolutely no change in his expression. He just stared back at me blandly.

I hated him.

I hated the doctor.

I hated this house.

"I'm going back to my room. The last thing I need is a psychiatrist."

"This will be much easier for you if you cooperate."

"You know, that's not the first time I've heard that," I said. "It didn't make anything easier for me." Ever. "But I'm done cooperating with the people who want to assault me or hurt me. I don't care what my uncle asked you to do. I refuse treatment."

His expression tightened. "I don't think you have much choice in this."

"Since when…"

"If you'll sit down and talk to me, maybe we can work on this here. I can prescribe you some medications to help you sleep and soothe your agitation."

My agitation.

Agitation?

"I'm not agitated by anything other than this conversation. Since I'm not allowed to leave, maybe you could go so that I can go back to my room."

"Why do you think you're not allowed to leave?" The fact he could ask that question with a straight face made me laugh.

"Oh, I don't know. Bars on my windows. Threats if I didn't come home. A guard dog to follow me around and threaten me if I don't behave." I glanced at Mr. No Name. "What was it? If I didn't behave you'd let your friend rape me until I bled then you'd bleed him?"

Silence greeted the statement and the doctor exhaled. "That's very dark."

"Oh, you think?" Was this guy for real? "You know what? I'm done. You want to sit here?" I walked over to a chair and sat down. "I'll sit."

Then I folded my arms, crossed one leg over the other and tuned him out. Him. The guard dog. This house. The place. Every part of it smelled like my uncle. A hint of tobacco. His favorite bourbon. The cologne he preferred. All of it was cloying and sticking to me. But bit by bit, I shut it out. All of it.

The doctor kept talking and I ignored him.

It took what felt like hours for him to get the point, but he finally admitted defeat. "Very well, I can't force you to talk."

No, he couldn't.

"You can go—"

I didn't need to hear anything else, I was up and heading for the door. The guard dog unlocked it without waiting for me to even ask.

"I'll see you tomorrow," the doctor called.

Not if I saw him first.

Not making a break for the front hallway or door was the hardest thing I'd ever done. The fact the guard dog wasn't gripping my arm or manhandling me said he was waiting for me to make a break for it. I went straight up the stairs.

Mr. Shit Hole was waiting at the top, and I managed to brush past him without any contact, but he caught me before I made it all the way past.

"You weren't told to go to your room yet." He jerked me to him and I slammed my knee right into his crotch. I half-twisted away to avoid the retaliatory blow, but it never landed. His grip on me ended abruptly and I staggered a few steps. Glancing back, I found Mr. No Name had Mr. Shit Hole pinned against the wall, hand around his throat and his arm wrenched in such a way that it had to hurt like hell.

Good.

"Go," Mr. No Name said to me. "Now."

"I'm guessing you mean my room."

"Smart girl."

Definitely *not* a compliment. I walked toward the door, but I kept glancing toward them. Whatever he had to say, he wasn't saying it loud enough for me to hear. But there was loathing Shit Hole Cole's eyes.

Right back at you.

Once in my room though, I shut the door and leaned against it. Everything began to shake and it wasn't just from terror or anger. Laughter threaded up through me, a hysterical little giggle of sound. I was locked up in the madhouse and the inmates had the damn keys. The bars on the window were the last straw.

I was never getting out of this house if my uncle had his way. I tried to get my breathing under control but the laughter made that almost impossible. The locks clicked into place and I pushed away from the door as the tumblers rolled and slotted home.

Exhaustion hit me all at once, but I didn't want to get into the bed. I walked over to the window seat and slid onto it. At least here, I could look outside and…

My uncle sat at a table in the garden, only he was in a wheelchair. His left leg was up and there was a brace around his knee. The doctor stood a few feet away talking to him. They seemed intensely focused on each other, then as one they glanced up toward my window. I should have ducked out of sight, but I refused.

Instead, I stared at my uncle, aware that he wanted me to see this. Whatever he was telling the doctor—the psychiatrist—he wanted me to know.

Self-harm.

Uncle Bradley motioned to his knee as he looked back at the doctor, his expression one of deep concern. There was no greater actor than my uncle. He knew exactly how to put on a show. I sank down on the window seat and stared at my room rather than the garden. The light changed in the room as the day wore on.

When the locks on the door turned, I didn't even glance at it. Probably more food I didn't want to eat. Better that than my uncle—only it was worse. It was Shit Hole Cole and he carried the tray into the room, glaring fire at me.

"You're going to fight me," he said as he set the tray down and picked up a pair of pills from the tray. Then the glass of water. "Aren't you?"

I just stared at him. There were marks on his throat from where Mr. No Name strangled him earlier. The door was still open. Probably a lure to get me to run for it again. No, I wouldn't give him the satisfaction. I could fake swallow the pills and then spit them out later.

A split-second after I held out my hand, I recognized my mistake. He splashed the water everywhere as he broke the glass and the first jagged cut sliced into my arm. The pain was nothing against the shock. He yelled and I tried to get away from him as he deepened the cut and my blood raced down my arm.

"You son of a…" I tried to claw at him with my free hand to get away and he slashed the glass across my already burned palm and he shouted again.

There was a rush into the room. The blood was racing faster and I was getting lightheaded.

How fucking deep had he cut me?

Even as my vision tunneled, I tried to fight. Then my uncle said, "Stay with us, Princess. I can't lose you again."

Fuck that.

I'd rather go.

Chapter Eleven

LIAM

The king had been up my ass for days. It was like as soon as Emersyn vanished onto that plane, he'd known I had time on my hands. Or maybe he didn't care if I had time or not. Probably the latter. At least I wasn't alone in my pain. Adam had been summoned right alongside me, and seemed to be in the same mood I was. Ezra wasn't present, but I didn't worry about him. Of the two of them, Adam was probably the most lethal.

For the third time since we'd met each other in the car park and walked in, he checked his watch. As much as I wanted to be elsewhere, tracking down Emersyn or at least *why* she had left and who the hell *Lainey* was, I knew where the Sharpes lived. I knew where *all* of their properties were. At least all of those on the public records, and two I'd found that weren't.

One was actually in her name, but I somehow doubted she bought a chalet in Switzerland. Probably the parents were just hiding assets in her name. It wouldn't be the first time a wealthier parent did that. My own had done something similar and I'd tucked nest eggs away in Rome's name.

If anything happened to me… well, I'd taken care of things for him. I didn't want him to worry about his next meal or anything else. Still…

Her uncle had put the bounty out on her. He was the reason the goddamn bounty hunters had been all over the city. The asshole may have been trying to find her, but he put her in harm's way. It told me he was probably also behind the photos sent to her. So, he'd used *us* as leverage.

Dislike filled me. Her uncle needed to learn *now* that he did not get to use us against her. While I *understood* the idea she'd left to *protect* us, I might spank her ass red for not telling us first. Freddie counted, but not enough. She'd called the one person she thought *wouldn't* try to stop her.

Still, in the days since we'd made the discovery, Rome and I had been split on how to handle it. The fact we were so divided didn't sit well with me. The only reason he hadn't gone after her yet was because we weren't sure which of their properties she was at. If we risked an incursion, there was a chance they'd close ranks around her.

Admit it. A nasty little voice inside of me whispered. *You don't want to get there and find out she did want to leave us, and she doesn't want to come back.*

I closed down that line of thought and leaned back against the wall. The fact we were meeting in the empty offices of Pocket Arc Financial said this was all business. We'd been summoned to offices only twice in my recollection.

"Goddammit." Adam kicked a small trash can across the room and it chipped the drywall when it impacted. I spared him a look. While I sympathized with the agitation, he knew better. In fact, he was the one who told me to never reveal a weakness.

Ever.

When he glanced at me, I just raised my brows.

"Fuck off, O'Connell, what did you do?"

"Can't fuck off and answer at the same time," I told him with a wry smile and a half-shrug. The more restless he seemed, the calmer I became. Not revealing our cards was a part of the job. For Adam to be showing his hand this early, suggested there was more going on than I knew.

Yet.

With a dark glare, he took a step toward me. His hands curled into fists. A muscle in his cheek jumped and I swore I could almost hear the grinding of his teeth. Honestly, I wished he'd just go for it. Come at me.

I needed the fight.

I'd been avoiding the pits all week, while we tried to puzzle out what the hell was going on.

"Why are we here?" Adam asked, not moving beyond his single step.

I shrugged. "No clue. I got the call, same as you. Or at least I assume you got a call."

Why else would he be in Braxton Harbor? He and Ezra both avoided the town. I preferred it that way, personally. This was my territory and I'd marked it as such. The other Royals had their own enterprises and assignments, none of which came through Braxton. I'd made damn sure of it.

He blew out a breath, then stalked away toward the window overlooking the city. With the exception of being ridiculously empty, the whole floor was set up just like any regular corporate office. Yes, you needed a keycard to get to this level. And no, no one else worked here, there were computers, desks, plants, a lobby waiting room, and even a fish tank.

The fish tank was fucking weird, cause the fish were all alive and clearly thriving so *someone* else came through here, but never when I was present. Not that I spent a lot of time in this corporate office. It was a front. A place to funnel money, to serve as a corporate distraction for activities we didn't want anyone looking too closely at, and to host meetings like the one we didn't appear to be having.

"Five fucking minutes more," Adam snarled without looking at me. "Then I'm leaving."

When the king called, you didn't ignore him and you didn't blow off his orders. Adam was the one who told me that all those years ago. The one chance to turn him down was when you were offered a place, after that? Well, it was your life. If that was how you wanted to waste it.

I'd never turned down a job. Never missed a call. I'd given them my blood, sweat, and time. The one time he'd demanded I throw a fight, I'd done that as well. I still had scars from that fight. It was the only time he'd ever asked it of me, and he'd never done it again.

Still… all this time later, as far as I'd come and I was no closer than when I'd been in school. Maybe it was time to cut our losses with this project. I knew the layout of the operation. I knew the names and the places. I had a lot of information. I could do a lot of damage.

My phone vibrated with the arrival of a text. Adam's must have too, because he pulled it out of his pocket.

Two words on the screen.

Conference Room.

Adam strode ahead of me and through the doors into the main offices. I trailed him, more interested by the second at his level of agitation. Something was going on with him and he needed backup. Maybe I should send a message to Ezra.

The door to the conference room slammed back with a crash. Those doors were weighted.

"Man," I said, keeping my voice down. From the moment we arrived there was a high percentage chance we were under surveillance. This loss of "cool" was *not* like Adam at all. "Dial it back."

He didn't glance in my direction much less say anything. As soon as I cleared the door to the conference room with its oblong table, six chairs and an eighty-inch plus screen on the wall, the screen flashed on, then went blue for a moment, before resolving into the shape of a man.

No distinguishable features were visible. In fact, despite the screen's incredible clarity and high definition, the man was one unrelieved shadow.

"Gentlemen," the king said. I'd know that voice anywhere. "Thank you for joining me today."

Not that he'd given us a choice. Adam mirrored my stance on the opposite side of the table. We both stood, arms folded, staring at the screen. "Your Majesty," I said when Adam made no move to say a word and inclined my head. The fact I had to chew over those words in every single interaction did not make them more palatable. "What can we do for you today?"

If I'd thought the question would distract him from the fact Adam glared at the screen, I was mistaken. Instead of answering my question, the man leaned back in his seat and rested a hand against his jaw as though thinking.

"Is there a problem, Reed?"

"You've had me in Braxton Harbor for three days."

Three days? I didn't look at him.

"And?" the king replied. "You go where I want you, when I want you there."

A flash of movement I barely caught from the corner of my eye was the only indication that Adam had curled his fingers into a fist. "Of course," he said. "Your Majesty."

Glass probably tasted better than those words. No amount of even attempting a bow would soften the bitterness in his tone. "You seem to be having a problem, Reed."

"No," Adam said, the word stilted. "I am simply not used to forced idleness."

"Forced idleness?" The figure on the screen chuckled, but the sound was not remotely humorous or entertained. "Don't waste my time, Reed." Any pretense of amusement vanished. "You and your little friend think you can work a separate game and that I won't find out about it?"

The curl of unease and apprehension from earlier redoubled. Adam stiffened at his tone. What the fuck had those guys done?

"What, precisely, is it you think we've done?" If anything, the belligerence in his tone doubled. I'd give Adam this, he had balls. But then, I'd known that from the beginning. Ezra was the more personable of the two, but Adam would get his hands dirty if he deemed it necessary.

"I'd have care with your tone," the king warned him.

"Then you might consider starting to take care with your own." Adam was as far from cowed as one could be. "You didn't recruit me for my manners, but for my name, my connections, and my money."

"And because of this, you think you have leverage? Special privileges?"

"I don't think I have shit, I just know I'm not going to keep kissing your ass while you hide in the shadows and we do all the dirty work. You wanted me here. I'm here. You want me polite and respectful? You start demonstrating the same."

"Or what?"

"Or I walk."

"Mr. Reed, you are aware of the rules. You were aware when you agreed to them."

"I'm also aware that you need *me* a hell of a lot more than I *need* you."

The gauntlet had been thrown down. Whatever the king had

done to earn Adam's ire, I didn't want to imagine. He'd once tried to leverage Rome's safety in an attempt to hold his life over me. It had taken a few bloody encounters for him to get the message. My loyalty wouldn't be bought that way.

Nor would I tolerate a single threat made against my brother. Whatever leverage he had over Adam—or was that it? Had he lost his leverage over him? That would make Adam very much a wildcard.

And a wildcard could be put to my advantage.

Maybe.

"You're quiet, O'Connell."

"This conversation has nothing to do with me." Impersonal and polite. "I was merely waiting to find out why you wanted me here."

Adam didn't even spare me a look. Then again, if he'd wanted me to back his play, he should have said something earlier. But I wouldn't have looked to him for assistance either. That wasn't the relationship we had. The fact Ezra had warned me not that long ago had been an aberration, not the norm. None of the Royals were tight. Gang or not, they feasted on each other's failures, not successes.

"Interesting. You have no comment on the situation?"

Right. "Do you want me to comment on it?"

The shadowy figure shifted, leaning back in his chair. As it was the closest I'd ever come to seeing the "man" himself, I tracked every visible twitch. Not that he gave many clues. "You didn't achieve the rank of Bishop by being so careful, now did you?"

I snorted. "I'm not a bishop." I was only a knight.

"Ah, but that is where you are wrong, O'Connell."

It was the first I was hearing of it, but I didn't leap to the bait.

"In fact, that is exactly why you are here."

Adam shifted his weight and even as aware of him as I was, I didn't dare look away from the screen. Alarm bells went off in my head. This situation was about to go from bad to worse.

"Is that so?" I kept the inquiry careful. Guarded.

"Yes, to move up, the knight must take bishop you see, and Mr. Reed has decided he no longer needs us."

Fuck. My. Life.

"And you know the rules," he said, steepling his hands together. For a split second, they were out of the shadow and I could make out a ring on his right hand. Not much definition, but it was a heavy ring. "Execute, Mr. Reed, Mr. O'Connell, and take his place as Bishop."

I didn't say a word when I checked out where they were going to be. The next show was clear across the country. But I could make the drive in a couple of days. I'd get there the same day they did. Gas money and a few hundred dollars socked away for a rainy day. Her birthday was coming up. Well, the birthday she celebrated anyway. And I wanted to see *her*. I was also being selfish as fuck.

For the first time in a long time, I didn't care. I just—needed the break. A break from everything. I needed to see her and have a breather. Leaving a note for the guys, I told them I'd be back in a few days. It was better to slip away unseen or someone would take it upon themselves to follow me. Or just climb in the car.

Once on the highway, I exhaled a long breath. The agitation in my blood cooled. The tension in my spine unknotted. Music cranked, the cool wind blowing through the windows, and my foot on the accelerator as I left Braxton Harbor in the rearview mirror. I didn't run away. Didn't think I was now. Just—this damn urge to see her. I trusted my instincts. When I ignored my gut, bad shit happened.

With every mile I put on the car, I relaxed more. This was the right call. The guys would be fine for a few days. They could handle it. If they didn't—well, I'd deal with it when I got back. The drive took just under two days, a little over thirty-seven hours, including a four hour nap I took in the car at a rest stop.

I made it to Orlando in time to see her walking into the hotel. It was pure luck that I guessed the right one. Well, luck and the fact I knew their troupe had used that hotel before. She looked dead on her feet. The bitch walking with her looked like a bitch. I didn't know who the cunt was—wait—yes, I did. The chaperone. Okay, maybe a chaperone should look like someone smashed her face with a brick to create that expression.

Still…not a fan.

I followed them inside, made a show of checking the wall with all its pamphlets of local attractions while they checked in. Ivy looked so damn tired, but then it was still early and they'd been traveling.

"Since the venue is tied up with the riggers," she said while they waited on the hotel desk clerk to sort out their rooms—multiple. So, Ivy had her own room. How—lonely. Then again, maybe she wanted privacy. Having grown up with the guys all sharing the same room most of the time, I craved personal space, but it could also be too damn quiet. "I'll just do stretches and use the gym here."

The chaperone nodded. "Do not go down to the gym without me."

Ivy rolled her eyes.

I bit back a smile. I swore she gave the woman a look that just radiated "bite me." Kind of bratty, but I appreciated it. Rules were there to chafe, but also to protect. Or so Ms Stephanie often reminded us. The rules were also there to be bent carefully with just the right amount of pressure.

Pre-law had given me a lot of insight on that one.

As soon as they had their rooms and keycards, I made a note of which floor and let them disappear into the elevators, before I asked the clerk about whether they had a room available. Unfortunately, my plans had been blown at the last minute and the girl behind the desk blushed when I smiled at her.

I got a room on the same floor with Ivy and the clerk's phone number. Maybe I'd make this a vacation of my own. She said she'd be off the clock at three. Good to know. She also worked nights sometimes. Even better. The credit card I used wasn't the best idea, since it was for emergencies only. But I'd make do for now.

Instead of going straight up to a room, I went out to move my car and grab a bag. The hotel nightly fee included parking—thank fuck. Even with Sarah Jane's discount, it was still pricey. On my way back through the lobby, I winked at her on my way past. Her smile grew and mine might have made an appearance as I stepped into the elevator.

Getting laid hadn't been the original plan, but what the hell. It was still *really* early. I was just stepping off the elevator when the battle axe said, "Stay in the room, order room service, and catch up on your assignments from the tutor. You have my number." Then she was bustling up the hall.

"Whatever," Ivy called after her and the door slammed. I sidestepped the woman as she got to the elevator. She was on the phone before the doors opened.

Our gazes met briefly as she said, "Yes, three days—it's about time I had a break from the brat." Her look practically screamed fuck off as she jabbed the elevator button and the doors closed behind her.

What. A. Bitch.

She was just *leaving* Ivy here? *Alone*?

Irritated as fuck, I made my way to my room, which was just up the hall from hers. I glanced at her door, probably staring a little too long. We weren't directly across from each other, more caddy cornered. But when I checked through the viewfinder, I could see her door.

Well, the desire to be *here* fueling my blood made sense. The cunt and I were going to have words. Closing my eyes, I took a deep breath. Violence needed to serve a purpose. Carelessness was one thing. The woman was a chaperone, not a caretaker. She probably saw nothing wrong with leaving Ivy secured in a hotel room.

She was almost twelve by her standards, with Emersyn's birthday the following week. Even if she didn't look much older than eight. I was here. Here I would fucking stay, the guard dog at the goddamn door.

Every time the elevator dinged, I got up to check the door. The first was room service. Ivy opened the door, but she didn't let the delivery person in. Just asked them to leave the tray and she'd get it in a minute, like she needed to get dressed. At least the sound carried from the hall easily enough. The minute the elevator dinged that the guy was gone, she pulled the door open and wedged it with her foot.

Dressed in a t-shirt and shorts ,and apparently having showered since her hair was wet, she looked even younger. She picked up the tray and grinned. Really grinned. The door closed before it occurred to me, I should have taken a picture.

Fuck, I was creeping on my own sister. Shaking my head, I returned to the bed and dropped on it. I was a light sleeper. The doors opened and closed in the hall. The sounds of families passing by, running kids, murmuring parents, even the occasional crying baby. All of this registered, but none of it was Ivy, or a door close to mine.

The sudden fierce knock on a door had me upright and across the room before I'd even processed I was moving. A young girl stood outside Ivy's room. What the fuck? The door opened and Ivy stared out, her mouth fell open in shock.

"Lainey!" I hadn't heard that squeal in *years*. It catapulted me back as Ivy threw the door open. The girls gripped each other in a tight hug, all but dancing before Ivy dragged "Lainey" into the room. "What are you doing here?"

Whatever the answer was, the door closing cut it off. Fuck me.

Adrenaline flooded my system. After emptying my bladder, I splashed water on my face and brushed my teeth. Every hotel room came with its own coffee maker, so I brewed a cup. It tasted like ass, but caffeine was caffeine and I'd had way worse.

I'd barely downed two swallows when the door across the hall opened again. The girls were coming out. Ivy had put her hair up in a ponytail and wore sneakers. She also had a purse strung crosswise across her body. Where the hell were they going?

"I still can't believe you're here!" Ivy's excitement punctured my anger so deftly, I damn near forgot why I'd been annoyed.

"I'm so fucking grounded," the other girl said with a laugh. "Worth it."

Then arm and arm they headed for the elevators.

Son of a bitch.

I stuffed my feet into shoes. I was still in jeans and a clean t-shirt. It would have to do. I snagged a baseball cap out of my duffle and shoved it on my head. Wallet in my back pocket, I downed the rest of the scalding coffee in one swallow and headed for the stairs. I made it to the lobby in time to see them spill out of the elevator in a mini-crowd of people. It didn't take them long to separate over to the concierge desk.

The two girls, both possessing an unnatural poise, kept breaking up into giggles that had me grinning. Tickets to the parks purchased, they followed the concierge's directions to head out the doors. Why did the guy just sell them tickets? Then again, I hadn't heard exactly what they said to him.

I crossed to him and handed him the credit card. Fuck the cost. "One ticket to the parks."

"Hopper?"

"Whatever."

The guy opened his mouth to ask me another question and I just fixed him with a look. This wasn't a social call. "Of course, one moment." It took two, agonizingly long minutes. "Here you go, the hotel offers a shuttle to the—"

I didn't wait for him to finish that part. I'd already caught the bus idea. Relief swarmed me when I got outside and found the girls waiting with a group of others for the bus. It was easy enough to drift into the crowd. I surged on behind them, sunglasses keeping my eyes hidden. They sat together, still giggling, and as much as I wanted the seat right behind them, I took one a couple more rows back.

At the park entrance, the thronging crowds worried me but they also provided camouflage. I was just another kid on his way to the park. I didn't have a bag, but I also didn't set off the metal detectors. I'd left my knife back in the room. And I hadn't brought a gun. To see Ivy? I didn't think I'd need one.

For the next few hours, I soaked up both the park and the girls' reactions to it. There was no artifice. They laughed. They played. They bought each other t-shirts. Ate ice cream. Rode the rides. I did actually manage to land in the same conveyance with them more than once. They never noticed me. They didn't pay attention to anyone. I even managed to get a picture or two when they found a couple of villains, including the wicked looking chick from Alice in Wonderland.

They made no move to leave as the park segued into evening. There was a huge Halloween party and you needed a special ticket. Turned out, I'd gotten one from the dick at the hotel. Go me. They trick or treated around the park, laughing and playing madly. When the parade came through, they were right at the edge of the curb. The darker it got, the closer I drifted.

By the time the fireworks lit up the sky, I'd forgotten about the driving need to be here and just enjoyed their pleasure at it all. Then it was closing time and we were all leaving the parks. The lines to get back on the buses were long. It didn't look weird at all to be standing with them and about a thousand other people.

I didn't let anyone jostle them and this time, I parked my ass right behind them on the bus. Maybe I was being selfish, but I'd already figured out this was a birthday present from Lainey to Ivy. I hadn't realized she had such a good friend. Stupid, right? Of course, she had friends. But she'd been constantly traveling the last three, going on four, years. I wondered if she had anything "normal" in her life.

They planned together in laughing giggles everything they were going to do back at the hotel. More food, then a movie, and a sleepover. No adults. Just them. Perfection.

Good, once they were tucked into their room, maybe I'd give Miss Sarah Jane a call and —

"Oh, you've got to be *kidding* me." The snarl in Lainey's voice snapped me out of my plans and I narrowed my eyes at the two men standing between the girls and the hotel door. They weren't small, but they were pissed. Ivy was already cutting in front of Lainey like she was going to take them on.

Fuck that—

"Ignore him," Lainey ordered.

"Who is he?" Damn good question, Ivy.

One of the pair glared at Ivy briefly, before transferring that look to Lainey. Personally, I was about to pluck his fucking eyes from his head. "Do you have any idea how long it took me to find you?"

"Not long enough," Lainey told him. "And this is my mother's lover's son, or as I like to refer to him, the human version of period cramps."

The guy behind him burst out laughing and Mr. Period Cramps glowered. My lips twitched, because that was a damn good nickname. In fact, little Miss Magpie there just started forward like she was going to plow through.

"If you wanted to come see your friend," Crampy said finally. "You should have just said something."

"Adam… I don't have to tell you anything. ….let me be clear, you're like a cloud. A big, dark, ugly storm cloud and when you go away, it's a beautiful day. So, buh bye." Lainey's voice kept dropping like she was fighting for the poise they'd abandoned all day.

Awareness of the pair kept my muscles coiled. I was gonna draw attention just standing here staring, but I sure as fuck wasn't leaving them behind. The girls almost reached his laughing friend when Adam whatever the fuck said, "We came all this way and we're not leaving until your ass is in the car with us and on the way back to school."

"Sorry, my ass doesn't detach—unlike your personality. Maybe you should put a bag over it or something." With that, she stormed past them, Ivy in tow. The pair shadowed them all the way to the elevator and I was right behind them.

"Six in the morning," he ordered. "Meet us down here and don't try to sneak off somewhere."

"Six?" Lainey snorted. "Too bad your brains don't match your looks. I'll be down by ten." She waited until the elevator doors almost closed and for a split second her gaze locked on mine and then she added, "Maybe."

As one, the pair pivoted to face me.

"What the hell do you think you're looking at?" the laughing man asked.

"Good question, been trying to figure out why two jackasses are harassing little girls. Only pervs do that."

"What the fuck did you just say?" Adam the period cramp demanded.

"I said," I told him as I stepped right up to him. "Only pervs harass little girls."

"Dude, you're asking to die," his friend warned, but I ignored the laughing idiot and kept my gaze on the guy right in front of me. Anger rolled off him like a storm.

"Go send them a cake," Adam ordered. "Tell them they don't eat enough. You—outside."

I chuckled. "Oh, what's the matter big boy? Did I wound your pride?"

"Adam—"

"Fuck off, and do what I said." Then Adam went back to glaring at me.

It'd been a while, but this was a nice place—with cameras—so I just stepped to the side and motioned for him to take the lead. No way was I giving either of these assholes my back. Adam McDouche tried to shoulder check me and missed. His friend groaned, but he cut away from both of us toward the hotel desk. I followed Adam right out the doors.

He didn't slow until we were on the far side of the building and half in the shadows. I expected the next move and avoided the hard drive of his right fist. His left came up damn near as fast and I took a glancing blow from that. The dick had moves.

So did I.

A hard uppercut slammed his teeth together. I took the next blow on the shoulder and the kidney shot that followed it, but he took an elbow to the face for his trouble. Blood sprayed the pavement and the scent of copper filled the air. More familiar than mother's milk at this point. His fierce expression showed zero signs of giving up.

Our next clash was just bare boned bashing. Fuck, I took one shot to the eye that was gonna sting like a bitch, but the clap I delivered to his ear sent him staggering. The swift flow of feet was my warning that his buddy had arrived and I barely moved my head in time to avoid the fist he would have caught me with. As it was, it slammed him into his friend.

And I laughed.

They went down like some bad physical comedy.

When they got up. They were pissed.

"Come on pretty boys," I told them. "Let's see if you can take me two on one."

The laughing idiot charged me like a freight train. I took the blows, blocking a couple and then had to fend off Adam as well. It was like fighting the twins, only without the coordination. When I head butted his friend, I saw stars for a split second, then Adam caught me in the jaw and I stumbled backwards, falling over a goddamn curb.

I rolled, managed to not hit my head or leave myself to get curb stomped when there was suddenly a little girl between me and them.

"What are you doing?" Lainey shrieked.

Fuck.

I backed off, panting and shot a look around for Ivy. But only Lainey.

"Get your ass back in the hotel," Adam growled at her, but like me, he kept his distance. Even the idiot had slowed down. We were all bleeding and bruised. I hurt, but they were going to be hurting worse, even if I could barely see out of my right eye.

"No."

Arms folded, Lainey glared up at him.

"Excuse me?" He growled at her and took a step forward and I went to meet him. At my motion, he froze. For one long second, we just glared at each other. If he took another move in her direction, I'd kill him.

His expression promised much the same.

"You heard me," Lainey yelled at him. "Have you lost your mind? Fighting out here? Why are you guys beating this guy up? Do you want to get arrested? Cause if you want that, I'll call the cops. Right. Now."

The laughing idiot started laughing—again. "Fuck me, Lainey don't be such a little bitch."

Adam swung around, only this time, his fist slammed into his friend and knocked the asshole down. He didn't say a word to him, just looked at me then at Lainey.

"Fine. Get back in the hotel," he said.

"Not without you two. I apparently can't trust you and I came down to thank you for Emersyn's cake. I was going to actually ask if you wanted to join us but you're not going up there all bloody and gross."

A half-laugh escaped me.

That snagged me the angry bird's attention and she glared at me. "I don't know who you are or where you came from. But now is the time you go—*while* I have them distracted." She paused. "Oh my god, what did you do to his pretty face?"

Adam snarled when she would have taken a step toward me, halting her in place. Smart man didn't touch her though. "Lainey. On the count of three, if you aren't moving in the direction of that hotel, I'm throwing your ass in our car and going home. One…"

She made a face. "Jerk." Then shot me an apologetic look. "Sorry, I never get to see my best friend." Then she turned.

"Two."

"You really are period cramps," she snapped.

The asshole looked right at her, pulled out some bills from his wallet and tossed it at me. They fluttered into the wind and scattered around us. "For your trouble," he said, then looked at Lainey. "Now. Go."

She went and he grabbed his friend, hauled him to his feet, and said, "Don't ever let me see you again, Mister."

I chuckled. "Or what?"

He stared at me.

"And keep your money, dick. I'm not for sale."

With that, I walked away from them, awareness of them keeping me on alert. I made it back into a side door of the lobby, avoiding the main portion. Last thing I needed was cops coming after me. I made it back to my room, pausing only long enough to hear Lainey's laughter in there along with Ivy's, before I let myself in the room.

Fuck, my bruises had bruises. I stopped dead when I found Sarah Jane lying on my bed.

"Oh my god, are you all right?" She sat up, concern all over her face.

"Getting better," I told her and threw the security lock on the door.

Chapter Twelve

ROME

Freddie was quiet after finally having fallen asleep. The drive had taken us almost a day and a half with no stops except for gas and to pee. The music was off. Time wasn't the issue unless we missed her. She'd set a place and a time to meet. We were there.

The phone, we'd kept on the charger. She'd sent no more messages. The only question was whether she would show up. Freddie had checked the phone repeatedly, as though it would alter in the scant few seconds he would put it down. Rather than park in the lot of the little apartment complex, I'd picked a spot that overlooked it.

We needed to see what was coming for us. All we had was a name on the phone. The name didn't mean much, except she was important to Emersyn.

"It could be a trap," Freddie said in a muffled voice, before he began to unfold in the passenger seat. He popped his fingers as he stretched, then rolled his head from side to side until the vertebrae cracked there too.

"Maybe."

"You already thought about that?" He let out a noisy yawn

before he grabbed the half-drunk soda from the cup holder. The lid popping off released a hiss of fizz.

I nodded, but kept my gaze pinned to the area below. I'd expected something bigger, more prestigious. This apartment complex was neither. It wasn't low-rent, but it wasn't wealthy either. The choice seemed questionable at best.

"Did you think she might just be shining us on?"

I shrugged.

"Yeah, me too." He pushed open the car door. "I'm gonna take a leak. Be right back."

I'd nod but he hadn't waited for my response. The door closed behind him and I kept a firm gaze below. Five minutes later, when Freddie sauntered across the parking lot raking a hand through his hair. He shot me a grin and a thumbs up before he tucked his sunglasses on and moved to lean against a light pole.

Bait.

Leaning back in the seat, I waited.

Almost forty-five minutes later, a car pulled into the lot from the street. It was the first movement that didn't involve someone leaving their apartment and getting into a parked car before they drove away. The way Freddie leaned, he could be asleep, but I doubted it.

I tracked the low-slung black sports car. It was far too expensive for this neighborhood. A dark-haired woman was behind the wheel, barely visible behind the tinted glass. For a moment, my heart jerked.

Starling.

But no—the facial shape was wrong. If I hadn't already decided on that, I would have when she pulled into a spot just three down from where Freddie stood. The blunt cut of her hair wasn't hidden by the sunglasses. It was too short. She could have cut it, I supposed. Starling wouldn't be hesitating inside the car.

The frozen tableau seemed to hold all of us captive for far too long. I reached for the keys just as Freddie pushed away from the lamp pole. The girl inside the car seemed to come to the same decision.

The girl.

Lainey opened the door and stepped out into the sunshine. The blunt cut seemed sharper, when combined with her dark blue leather jacket, over unrelieved black jeans, ending in a pair of calf length leather boots in the same rich blue. Wealth shimmered over her like a second skin. Too far away to hear anything, I shoved my way out of the car and descended the hill.

She was alone.

That was why she'd lingered in the vehicle. Either to prove something to us or to herself.

"You're friends of Emersyn?" Her voice held a hint of an accent.

"We are," I answered before Freddie did. He still seemed puzzled by her for some reason. "You came."

"I told you I would," she said, shooting me a frowning look. "I wasn't aware there would be two of you."

"You didn't ask."

"True." She shifted her weight, then folded her arms. "Can you prove you have Emersyn's best interests at heart?"

"No." My answer seemed to galvanize Freddie from whatever lost place he'd gone.

"Rome, yes we fucking can." He narrowed the gap between us. I hadn't gone to stand too close, because while Lainey was taller than Starling, she didn't seem to have her muscle tone and she was shorter than us.

Lainey lifted a manicured hand to her sunglasses. They were a ruby red color with a hint of gold glitter on them. "How?"

She asked the one question I had, and Freddie dug his phone out of his pocket, then played a message I'd never heard before.

It was Emersyn.

The sound of her voice was startlingly clear. The ache in my chest at hearing it gouged out where my ribs should be. The hollowing effect hurt. She was talking—no, she was *reading*. Lainey took a step toward Freddie, her gaze fixed on the phone. The distraction gave me time to catch my breath and I had to look away from both of them.

Instead, I scanned the area. The echo of laughter underscoring her words as she described the scene she was reading, poured stinging soap onto the deep wounds. It seemed forever since I'd heard her voice. She'd never left me messages. Not like that.

When she came back, I'd ask for some.

"She's never mentioned you," Lainey said finally when the message ended and I could breathe again.

"She never told us about you," Freddie answered in an empty tone. "She didn't tell us a lot, but she called me and said she had to go home. That her mother was sick and her father had a heart attack."

"What?"

The sharpness in that syllable pulled my head around.

"Her father might have had a heart attack, but they aren't advertising it. Then again, they wouldn't." Impatience crept into her voice. "And her mother isn't sick, she's just…"

"She's just what?" Freddie demanded. He'd shoved his phone away, but he hovered closer like he could get her answers faster.

"It doesn't matter, she's not *sick*."

"It might."

Lainey glanced at me. "What?"

"It might matter. You can't know for certain it doesn't."

Her lips compressed into a thin line. "Yes, I can. The woman had a 'nervous' breakdown from the stress of Emersyn 'going missing.'" The stress she put on some of the words suggested she didn't believe them. "In all likelihood, she's floating on a cloud of vodka and valium."

Freddie frowned. "Emersyn doesn't know that."

"Did she say *why* she was coming home?" She tucked her sunglasses to the top of her head. "Why she'd go back when she was out? I didn't think she wanted to go back at all."

"You sent her the fake IDs."

"That's not important."

It might be.

"You keep doing that," Freddie accused. "You sent her the IDs, she trusted you—but she didn't call you before she went back?"

"No," Lainey snapped. "She didn't. I would have told her not to do it."

I believed her. "Who would threaten her to force her to come home?"

"Her uncle." She didn't even hesitate with that answer. "I've tried to see her all week, that's why I answered your message."

"You haven't been able to see her?"

"No." She frowned, the struggle playing out on her face was obvious even to me. But Freddie got a little closer. The nearness bothered her because she took a couple of steps away. "She doesn't want me contacting her through their houses and she doesn't appear to have *her* phone. I can't leave a message in case…"

"In case someone else hears it." Freddie pivoted and stared at me. "We have to go and get her."

I wasn't arguing.

"Wait—you're going to get her?" Lainey glanced from one of

us to the other.

"Yes." It wasn't a matter of if.

"Count me in."

"No."

"What?" Lainey charged toward me. "I'm her friend. I came here to help and I know things that can be useful."

"Like what?"

She opened her mouth, then snapped it closed again. Freddie glanced at me over her head, his eyes held a question. I didn't know what the question was though, because the woman radiated impatience.

"No, if I tell you, you'll just leave me here."

"I'll just leave you here if you don't tell me." She wasn't the important one. "We know where their houses are…"

"So you go after them one place at a time? The Sharpes own over half a dozen residences, easy, and have access to more than a dozen more."

"Then tell us where you think they are."

"I don't *know*." The stress she put on the last word said she was telling the truth.

"Then where have you been trying to reach her?" Freddie demanded. "If you don't know where she is, you have to have a way of getting in touch with her."

"I do," Lainey admitted. "But it's been completely quiet since the conversation we had last week." She shook her head. "This is my fault."

"How?"

"Because we added to the rewards—my grandfather did and… and a friend of ours did. I promised her it was only because we wanted to get any news before they did, so I could warn her, but…"

"But?" Freddie demanded.

"But it didn't work if she chose to go back to them." She paced away and Freddie shot me a look. I shook my head.

"If you can't help, then we need to go." We'd already spent all these hours, only to find out she didn't know any more than we did.

Maybe.

"I didn't say I couldn't help." Chin lifting, she gave me a long look. "I said I wanted to help."

"No."

"Fine," Freddie said. "Don't listen to him. Help us. Tell us where he would take her. Tell us why she didn't want to go back in the first place. Tell us why she would listen to him if he threatened us."

"He threatened you?"

"Yes," Freddie answered without a second glance at me. "He sent photographs of all of us—with crosshairs on them. It was definitely a threat."

"She went back to protect you," she said more to herself than to us. "She never wants me around him. He definitely didn't want us to be friends, but then…ugh." The sound she released bordered on painful.

Yeah, I was done. "I'm going." The last was a warning to Freddie and I pivoted on my heel. Seeing Lainey was supposed to help. But if she wouldn't part with her secrets, we would have to find Emersyn a different way.

"Wait!"

I paused, but I didn't turn around. The door to the car slammed and then the trunk opened. Glancing back, I frowned as she pulled a bag out and dropped a couple of things into the trunk before closing it.

"I'm coming."

Freddie stared at her. "Why did you get rid of your phone?"

"Because she isn't the only one who knows how to avoid being caught if she doesn't want to be. Now, I probably have another half hour before we really need to get out of here. *If* I'm lucky. So can we go?"

Taking her was a bad idea. She was Starling's friend. I couldn't let anything happen to her. "I don't want to be responsible for your safety."

She pulled out a taser from her pocket and pressed the button on the side. It crackled and sparked. "I'm more than capable of taking care of myself." After putting it back in her pocket, she headed to the hill I'd walked down while carrying her bag. "Is that your car?"

Not waiting for us, she lugged the suitcase all the way to the car then reached for the backdoor handle.

I'd locked it, so it didn't move.

Setting the bag down, she turned and looked at us.

"If she wants to help," Freddie said. "We let her help."

"But is she going to help?"

"I'll tell you what I can on the way to wherever you're going," Lainey called down to us.

"But why would she trust us?" That bothered me. "She doesn't know us."

"No," Freddie said. "But she knows Boo-Boo. Didn't you see the look on her face when I played the message?"

I shrugged.

"Do you trust me?"

Frowning at Freddie's question, I glanced at him. "Yes."

"Then trust me right now. She's trusting us because Boo-Boo does. I don't know what her beef is or why, and right now I don't care. I just want to find Boo-Boo."

"Milo and Liam won't like this." Not that their dislike of a choice had ever stopped me before.

"I don't care," Freddie said.

Agreed.

I climbed the hill with Freddie. He grabbed her suitcase when I unlocked the car, and stowed it in the back of the SUV we'd taken. She climbed into the back seat without waiting for either of us and then settled in.

"Faster would be better," she told me as I got behind the wheel and I glanced at her in the rearview mirror.

"You're not afraid."

"For me?" She shook her head. "More for the two of you and because I want to go and help. I've spent months doing nothing because they kept blocking me. No more."

As soon as Freddie was in the passenger seat, I got the car started and pulled out. We didn't look back at her car or the apartments. Aware of her concern, I kept an eye on the cars around us in case we picked up a tail.

"Okay," Freddie said, twisting in his seat. "Tell us what you know."

"It might be better to wait until we get to wherever."

"No," he said. "It won't, because it's a long drive back and I need to know we're going the right way."

I hadn't thought of it that way but Freddie was right. "Cooperate," I told her. "Or I'll leave you on the side of the road. We don't have time for games. *She* doesn't."

She was quiet long enough I thought she didn't believe me, so I changed lanes in order to pull over onto the shoulder.

"Fine," Lainey snapped. "I'll tell you."

Cages Surrounded by Thorns

LAINEY

Gala season meant a circus of events, parties, and conversation with peers, allies, clients, potential allies, potential clients, and, unfortunately, enemies. I'd exercised a little familial goodwill and reached out to some of Grandfather's contacts on the various committees. With so many events, invitations went out as many as three to six months before. The RSVPs were requested a month prior to the event.

All I had to do then, was find out which ones the Sharpes had accepted during the period Emersyn's show was closed. A month. She'd protested in her last letter that it was the longest she'd been shuttered between shows. But one had ended and the next wouldn't even begin their first round of rehearsals for four weeks.

That meant she was within arm's reach, only the first two weeks of events—she'd been at none of them. The Sharpes had accepted a handful, but the three I'd made it to had all been her parents. She never came to these with them. Adam had already figured out what I was up to and had begun trailing me like an angry shadow, constantly looming out of the darkness when I least wanted him there.

I'd tried to talk Ezra into escorting me, but he'd been in a mood and had pretty much told me to fuck off. Tally was also utterly preoccupied with her latest conquest. He was definitely *her* conquest too. An older man, by all reports, and she'd been lusting after him for months, stalking him like he was her prey and she was the big game hunter.

The very satisfied messages she'd been sending me about his place in the Poconos were downright sickeningly sweet. I didn't see the appeal, but Tally was happy and that was what was important. Tonight, however, I'd pulled off because Grandfather was in the city and I'd tagged along with him.

I just needed to see Emersyn. I needed to quell the flutters of worry about her absolute *silence* the past couple of weeks. Yes, it was harder for us to stay in touch when she was home. Her family held *her* aloof, even when they were everywhere. Their wealth and connections made them top tier on most guest lists.

But Emersyn's distance had given her an air of mystery. Everyone wanted to know her and no one got close to her. She'd joked once that she should be a social pariah. After all, she was a *performer*. Pretty common.

What she didn't see was that she was a *star* and a *headliner*. The air of celebrity just added to her mystique. Gossips wasted their time trying to squeeze blood from a stone, but they found nothing. Because the Sharpes wanted them to find nothing.

I wanted to protect her, too. The first time they sent her to Pinetree because she'd "exhausted" herself had worried me. The second time, though, had terrified me. Now, all I could think, was they'd done it again. Two weeks of absolute silence from her suggested as much. The first time, Adam had helped me find out where she was, but after that, he refused to let me be involved.

He was such an asshole.

It didn't help that the very next time I'd seen her after that, she'd been so—distant and scattered. She hadn't remembered Ezra. Hadn't remembered a few things. Not at first. Then it came back. Me?

She remembered me and I was grateful for that, but Ezra had been aggravated when I'd introduced her to him again.

Later, she'd laughed it off.

But I didn't think it was funny.

"Leave it alone," Adam snapped at me. "Can you just leave it alone?"

"She's my best friend. Do you even understand what that means? Oh wait, I forgot, your best friend is Ezra. You wouldn't care if he fell off the face of the earth."

"Hey!" Ezra said. "He'd care. Who else is he gonna get drunk with?"

I shoved the memory aside. Assholes. Both of them.

Still… there. Oh thank fuck, there she was. I'd been hovering at the top of the stairs trying to not be noticed and yet have a good view of the new arrivals. Grandfather had gone inside to the bar, where he would probably spend the rest of the evening with his friends. I would place solid money that they'd be deep into a poker game.

If I could steal Emersyn away, I'd totally do it.

She was with her uncle, so I held back, waiting for her to find me. It would be easier to make our "meeting" look like an accident. After all, we were in public. We had to be able to exchange a few words.

In the meantime, she looked absolutely *stunning* in the deep forest green dress and jewels. Emersyn was gorgeous and while her manners seemed flawless, her eyes were… lost. My heart hurt. I wanted to march down there and rip her away from her uncle. But that would be a scene and we weren't supposed to make scenes. Too many years of training, not to mention years of keeping our friendship out of the public eye, kept me in place.

Then she caught sight of me and the fake, plastic smile she wore turned real. Relief flooded me. No matter what had happened, she remembered me. That was a good first step. Still, I waited as she and her uncle worked the other guests and the hosts on the steps. As soon as they were within fifteen feet of me, I saw my chance.

He had dropped his grip on her and focused on something a pair of financiers were saying and I hurried down the steps to hold out my hand to her. Her clasp was fierce and her expression faltered.

"You look amazing," I told her. "It's been ages."

After all, we had our parts to play and I would play mine to excellence. Nothing I did would be allowed to hurt her.

"I know," she said in a breathier voice than she normally had. It was steeped in exhaustion and relief. "Was it last June?" For the briefest moment, confusion clouded her eyes and my heart sank.

No. It had been just the past Christmas. We'd stolen away for a day of shopping. I'd managed to slip away while Adam and Ezra were out of the country. It had been the best day.

"Last April," I said, laughing even if entertained was the last thing I was. "At the show in Paris." I'd tagged along with Grandfather and Mother for some meetings. Though Grandfather barely spoke to Mother the whole trip. "You were fantastic, and I was so surprised to see your name."

Her uncle cut a glance at us, so I played it up.

Shaking her head, Emersyn looked a little bemused. "I barely got out of the rehearsal rooms. I never did get any sightseeing in."

"You went to Paris and didn't actually *see* Paris?" I shook my head and made the appropriate face. "Unacceptable. I insist, girls' trip at some point."

"That sounds wonderful."

It would never happen. Not unless we both changed our names and just vanished. How tempting was that? Adam moved into my line of sight and I sighed. Why the hell was he here now? But he glanced from me to Emersyn and back. Instead of just interrupting, he shot me a questioning look.

Did he remember what I'd said about her not remembering Ezra? I shook my head a little. I didn't know if she'd recognize him. Not when she'd forgotten our last visit.

With more effort than I cared to admit, I focused my energy into my smile. "Good. Let's make it happen..."

"Elaine." Goddammit Adam. Did you *ever* listen? "Aren't you going to introduce me to your friend?"

"I didn't plan on it," I said. "Go away."

He laughed, but it was a chilly warning. One I recognized as he transferred his attention to Emersyn again and held out his hand. "Adam Reed, and you are..."

"She is utterly unimpressed," I told him and she didn't remember him. Was he *blind?* The last thing we needed to do was call attention to it in front of her uncle. The man was king of the douchebags. I slid my arm through Emersyn's. "And we're going inside."

"Adam." Her uncle's greeting killed my plan to sweep her away. Damn Adam for interrupting. "Good to see you."

Adam's expression froze into a steel mask. He didn't even nod in greeting to her uncle. Well, clearly the dislike went both ways.

"How is your father?"

"He's well, sir. I'm sure he'll be terribly upset to have missed you."

"Not to worry," Bradley Sharpe responded. "The shares I just secured will see me seated on the board. I'll catch up with him at the board meeting next week. Enjoy your evening. Princess."

There was no mistaking the order he'd just given. Emersyn let go of my arm with a small smile.

"You didn't introduce me," Adam said, his grin cold and predatory.

"You're right." Oily and smooth, the man didn't miss a beat. "I didn't." With that, he slid an arm around Emersyn and pulled her away. His knuckles whitened where he gripped her. Goddammit. Maybe I could…

But I didn't even make it two steps before Adam caught my arm and pulled me back to him. "If you follow them, I'll pick you up and haul your ass out of here like a child."

"What is wrong with you?" I demanded. "Did someone drop you on your head? I know it's not your mother. She loves you so much, she can't see you for the cold-hearted bastard you are."

"I'm not the bastard in this equation," he reminded me, his eyes chipped ice. "Stay the fuck away from Emersyn while she's here."

"No."

"Lainey, I'm warning you…"

"No, you don't get to decide my friends. I've told you this a thousand times and I thought you liked her."

"She's fine. It's her family I don't trust." He cut a look over my head and I stomped my foot on his. It was as subtle as I could make it, but I made sure to put all of my weight into it. His lips thinned when he looked back down at me. "You will be the death of me someday."

"We can only hope."

Chapter Thirteen

EMERSYN

Throbbing in my wrists penetrated the dark fog smothering me. Throbbing and whispering. The whispering was the worst. The whispers punctuated by soft kisses to my brow. The smell came next and brought reality crashing into my awareness. No matter how much I didn't want to open my eyes, I refused to hide in the blackness. The inky velvet didn't make my situation more palatable.

His room.

His bed.

Him.

All three things registered in the same breath as he lifted his head to look down at me. The concern in his eyes filled me with revulsion. Worse, he stroked my cheek. "Princess, you have no idea how worried about you I've been."

If my mouth wasn't so dry, I'd spit in his face. His *guard* slit my wrists. Wrists. I lifted one hand and the vision of white bandages wrapping it up swam across my vision. He caught my arm in a firm grip.

"Don't worry about that now," Uncle Bradley urged me. "I

should have come up to see you sooner." Then he feathered more kisses against my cheek. "But I'm here now."

I wanted to vomit.

I wanted to scream.

I wanted to just disappear.

None of those things happened. Awareness held me in its icy grip and I endured every touch as he moved against me. I was there and not there. It was like it happened to someone else and at the same time, every push and press of his flesh into mine left a vividly nauseating imprint.

I found a crack in the ceiling to focus on while he grunted and shifted. The sound threatened to drag me back into my body, but I didn't want to be there right now. I'd survived this before. I'd survive it again. I just had to endure.

Thankfully, it didn't last long. He was shaking as he clutched me to him. The wet tears against my throat almost made me laugh.

"I can't lose you," he said, over and over again. Like he truly cared. That was the sickest lie of all. Then he started all over again, more frenzied and angry. When his hands locked around my throat, I finally dragged my gaze to his eyes. The manic light in them promised me a swift end. That, too, was a lie.

But that beautiful lie I wanted and I didn't fight for a breath. Didn't try to squeeze in even a drop. When my vision darkened at the edges, I fell backward, letting it swallow me whole. The haze of darkness and pain twisted me into knots. No matter when I woke, he was there. My skin crawled from his touch.

Twice more, he offered to end me with his hands on my throat. And twice more, he reneged on the gift that would have been. When the endless night finally met the dawn, I could have wept. Whether for the fact I'd survived it or for what I'd endured, I had no idea. He had trouble getting out of bed.

There was some small satisfaction in me as he limped—badly— to the bathroom. If only I'd done more damage.

Next time, a vicious little voice inside my head whispered. We'll do worse next time.

If we survived that long. If I…

The doctor was there. Crap. When had he gotten there?

"I kept her with me all night so I could look after her," my uncle was saying. Dressed now, he played the part of a concerned family member. "If not for the nurses who checked on her, we might have lost her last night."

Nurse?

Shithole Cole was a nurse?

A laugh escaped me. It was a broken little sound, sharp and scraping. Both men shot me a look as I laughed. Now that the floodgates had opened, the laughter turned to mad giggles. It also brought the aches in my body into sharp relief. My throat burned, the sound aggravating the rawness inside.

The doctor's pitying look vied with my uncle's faux concern for which one was more hysterical. As it was, they were both hypocrites. There had to be bruises around my throat, but did the doctor ask about them? No.

No, he wouldn't. Why would he? My uncle paid him to see what my uncle wanted him to see. The only people who had ever seen the truth, the negligible handful of people who knew the real story, had all died or disappeared. No one was ever on my side. No one dared.

Not even the one person I knew would take my side in a heartbeat. I'd never told her because I never wanted her in his crosshairs. He disliked her enough as it was.

"We have room at the facility," the doctor said as my laughter evaporated. The idea of my uncle hurting Lainey filled me with rage and sadness. The competing emotions choked me more effectively than his hands. "From what you're telling me, the combination of her hysteria and hostility are probably directly related to her incarceration with her kidnappers."

Kidnappers.

My kidnappers were amazing people. So much better than my so-called family.

"After that ordeal, I can imagine she will need some time to normalize. With the right treatment and proper rest, I don't see why we can't help her regain a sense of normalcy."

"I would be most grateful," Uncle Bradley said. "You know cost is no object."

"Of course, if you'll give me a moment, I'm going to call for some orderlies to arrange transport."

"We want to keep this discreet, Doctor." Bradley's voice held a note of warning. "Both for her sake and the family's."

"Of course," the doctor assured him. "We've never had a breach at Pinetree."

Pinetree… that name?

"We will admit her under a pseudonym. That will also help to shield her and the family."

"Good."

Then the doctor was gone and it was just Bradley and me. The laughter had died as had any trace of humor, real or imagined. He limped over to the bed and with a show of exaggerated care, took a seat.

"Stockholm Syndrome," he advised me in a low voice, "is a real condition. I know you may not understand what is going on or why this is affecting you so badly, but I know. So does the doctor. He agrees with me that you need some longer-term treatment in a facility where you can't hurt yourself. It would kill your mother to lose you, and your father would never recover."

I just stared at him. But before I could tell him to go to hell, he reached out a hand to stroke the hair away from my face.

"Princess, you are too valuable to all of us to risk. If that means I have to take steps to eliminate those boys once and for all, I will do it." The promise, though offered in this tone of mock rationality and kindness, sucked up all the oxygen in the room. "They should never have taken you. Their first mistake was putting their hands on you."

In a move I didn't anticipate, he dragged the covers down so he could stare at me. I hated the feeling of any part of him on me, whether it was hands or his gaze.

"They put their mark on you." He pressed a hand against my abdomen. "We can have this removed, eventually. Don't worry."

"No," I said, in a hoarse croaking sound. The fact I managed to push out the pained syllable made me proud.

"You don't know what you're saying," he told me with a kind of assuredness that made me insane. "That's what the syndrome does, it makes you dependent on these criminals. But they aren't your family. They do not love you the way we do—the way I do."

But they were my family, I wanted to yell that fact at him. I wanted to cut at him with the knowledge that I had Milo, but I stuffed that reaction down. He was already threatening them. If I revealed Milo's connection, my uncle might do much worse.

"I need you to get better," he continued. "I need you to listen to the doctor and fight their influence. I need you to come back to me."

He skated his hand up to my throat and when he gripped it, he forced my gaze back to him. "One way or another, you're going to do that, Emersyn. You're mine. You've always been mine. I will not let them take you from me. I'll burn them and everything they hold dear to the ground first."

Real fear crystalized within me.

"Do you understand?"

His dark eyes bored into mine and I swore he could tear through layers of skin, tissue, bone, and muscle to get all the way down to my soul.

"Tell me you understand."

"I understand," I managed to squeeze out past the grip of his hand.

"Thank you, Princess." His smile was equal parts possessive and relieved. "Having you back means the world to me. I hate to send you away, but it's the best thing for you. You believe me, don't you?"

The answer he wanted was my agreement. My acquiescence. I couldn't give him either. I just stared at him, trying to empty out the anger licking up my insides like a slow-burning, relentless fire that would consume us all. If it were only me…

Fight. Fight and get away. That was what Liam had wanted me to learn. He'd pressed that over and over and over again.

Learn everything you can. That had been Kellan's promise.

Come back to me. That had been Jasper's request.

Tell him… Freddie's plea whispered up inside me. Tell him whatever he needs to hear.

Survive.

I could do this.

"I believe you," I said, finally. The words didn't taste like ash on my tongue, they didn't cut or slice my throat with their lie as they left me. No, I did believe him. My uncle was a sick, disturbed, and altogether dangerous individual. He meant every single word he said.

"I love you so much." Even that horrible combination of syllables. He meant it. He just had no concept of how much his *love* hurt me.

Or maybe he did, and just didn't care.

Bending down, he pressed a kiss to my forehead and lingered there like he needed my touch. The leaden weight of my muscles and my inability to push away or even struggle suggested he'd done more than just deposit me in his bed and use me.

They'd drugged me.

I hated him... "…so much."

"Yes, Princess," he whispered again, his breath hot against my skin. "I do love you."

Whatever else he might have added went unsaid at the firm knock on the door. "My orderlies will be here shortly," the doctor said through the door. "We should get her dressed and ready to go."

"I'll take care of it." The command in his voice ordered the doctor to stay outside. Then Uncle Bradley looked at me. "I'll get you all dressed, Princess. Won't that be nice?"

I had no idea how I managed to not throw up. The next several minutes passed in unbearable and agonizing slowness as if time itself worked against me. He brought a washcloth and soap. He cleaned me up, every touch lingering far too long. His eyes were thoughtful and assessing. I didn't want to imagine what he saw or why.

Escaping my mind and body for this proved impossible, each time I'd try to drift off, he'd bite me or pinch me. It was like he needed to mark me. Those marks hurt. They invaded the languor of the drug-fueled haze with their throbbing presence.

I wasn't even allowed to escape him in my own mind. By the time he helped me sit up and slid the t-shirt over my head, all I wanted to do was curl up into a ball and die. But the pain in my brutalized wrists denied me the ability to pass out.

Finally, he finished and after a too-long press of his lips to mine, he went to the door to let them in. His awkward movement and clear pain with each step he took made me smile. I wanted him to hurt. I wanted him to hurt *bad*.

"Have you scheduled a surgery for that knee?" the doctor asked, as two burly men I didn't recognize converged on the bed. They lifted me out and strapped me to a gurney. They even used velcro to secure my bound wrists. Like I could get away even without the tie-downs.

"Tomorrow," Uncle Bradley told him. "They expect I'll need three weeks for recovery. That will be sufficient time for the corrective treatment?"

"Of course," the doctor assured him. "We will work as quickly as we can, but we want to be thorough."

"Yes," Bradley said. "We do. I want *my* princess back."

"And you shall have her."

I almost managed to lift my middle finger in their direction, but a sharp sting in my arm pulled my attention. One of the orderlies pressed the plunger on a syringe. It was really, really full.

What was th—oh. I disconnected from my body as a gauzy haze flowed over the world. The throbbing went away. So did the anxiety. The pain. The loss. It all vanished under the floating fog. As they maneuvered me out of the room, it was almost like flying. I swore I glided down the stairs. The paintings all turned to look at me, some of them even doubled or tripled into multiple duplicates as we passed them.

Shithole Cole was there.

So was tall, dark, and terrifying. He moved alongside the orderlies. I'd forgotten they were there until he spoke to them. But his words barely registered before they vanished again. Had they stuffed my ears full of cotton too?

How rude.

A flash of Lainey appeared out of the corner of my eye and I jerked on the gurney. No, she couldn't be here. I didn't want her here. Even as I struggled, I swore I saw Milo reaching for me. Worse— Rome and Freddie were shoving through the people to get to me. Hands pressed me back and something cold was on my arm. It cut through the adrenaline and the fear.

Carved them away until I was moorless. This time when I fell, nothing pulled me back.

Everything is Broken

FREDDIE

"You know you can talk to me," Ms. Stephanie said. She had a way of offering an ear that didn't sound like we were wasting her time or someone was holding a gun to her head. She was good people. All the guys said so.

It was why I couldn't talk to her.

She didn't need to know about what happened. Not when she was the kind of lady who believed good things were still possible for rejects like us. Maybe it was selfish, but I needed her to keep believing and if I talked to her—that belief would die.

With a sigh, she left her desk and moved over to where I sat on the floor. I'd been bouncing a ball, sending it over to the opposite wall and catching it. I needed something to do with my hands. Ever since… well ever since, I always had a knife on me, but I kept it away when Ms. Stephanie came to see us.

Saying nothing, she slipped off her shoes and then slid down the wall like an expert. Ladies in suits shouldn't do that so easily.

Crossing one ankle over the other, she caught my ball on the rebound and then sent it back toward the wall. I caught it this time and gave it a little more pep in the throw.

We sat there catching and throwing the ball back and forth. Ms. Stephanie had game, she put a spin on the ball and managed two ricochets. When I made a sound, she chuckled.

"You're good, Freddie, but I've been doing this a long time." She bumped my shoulder. "Age and wisdom will always overcome youth and skill."

"Rude," was my only comment.

Her grin promised she didn't take any offense. "How is school going?"

"It sucks."

"Have you thought about the extracurriculars we discussed?"

I shrugged. "Not really."

She bounced the ball. "Why not?"

"I don't want to spend any more time at the school than I have to."

"Are you having trouble there?"

Not anymore. "Nope." Vaughn and Rome had both been swinging by on a regular basis, as had Jasper. I didn't want to admit that I needed them to walk me to and from school. Milo hadn't even asked. He'd just started the first morning I went back to school, and the guys took turns every other day.

"Freddie," she said, catching the ball. "I need you to give me something. I know pain when I see it. Let me help you."

She'd been one of the first faces I'd seen when I'd been "entered" into the system. The first real face of kindness that came back. Again and again. I never wanted to see pity in her eyes.

"I'm getting better," I told her. "I like coming back here after school. Kellan's been using his shop classes to get a job down at the mechanic's on Bay and 101st. Sometimes I go there. Vaughn's been spending more time at the tattoo shop. He's getting really good at that work."

Her eyes narrowed. "He's too young to be doing tattoos on others."

"He knows that," I said and hoped my face was a mask of innocence. I'd been getting better at lying. But only about stuff I didn't care about.

"Uh huh," she said, but her lips twitched. "Do I need to step in?"

"No," I said and this time I really did mean it. "It's fine."

Another careful look at me then she bounced the ball again. "So, you're helping Kellan at the mechanic's and working with Vaughn at the tattoo shop—"

"Not working," I said holding up two fingers in a Boy Scout salute. At least I hope it was that. It had been a while since we watched that movie and I'd rather stay at school extra hours, then actually join the troop that tried to recruit me one year.

I didn't do strangers.

Not anymore.

"Right, *hanging out* with Vaughn," she corrected herself in that soft voice and I grinned. The best thing about Ms. Stephanie, besides the fact that she genuinely seemed to care, was how she smelled. She always reminded me of a flower garden or a spring day. Just clean and nice and nothing that made my eyes water.

I grinned. "Exactly."

"What about Milo, Jasper, Rome?"

"Rome doesn't always want company, but he never complains if I tagalong and I try not to mess with his art."

"Okay."

"Milo and Jasper just give me jobs to do." I tried to make it sound like a chore, but the fact they trusted me at all was a big deal. They were also teaching me how to fight. Probably not something Ms. Stephanie would approve of. "Milo has been helping to tutor me on my math homework too."

"Still having issues with the numbers?"

I shrugged. "Not so much. He's just more patient than my teachers."

"Good." When I caught the ball and didn't toss it again, she said, "Would you consider music lessons if I arranged a private tutor?"

I tried not to flinch. I really did. "Ms. Stephanie…"

"You can take the lessons at my apartment," she continued as if I hadn't interrupted. "We can do it on Sundays. You boys are always welcome to come over for supper on Sundays." And we had a few times. There, beneath it all, was the crux of the offer. She would be there. The guys would be there.

I wouldn't have to be alone with anyone I didn't know.

"I'll think about it." It was the best I could do, especially since I was sweating at the idea alone.

"Can't ask for more," she said, then nodded to the ball. "We still playing?"

One glance at the ball and then back up at her. "You know you don't have to play with me, right?"

"You know I'm here because I want to be, right?"

I couldn't help it. I smiled.

She answered it with a grin of her own. "Now, let's go, best two out of three and then we'll get some ice cream."

Okay, I could do that.

Chapter Fourteen

KELLAN

The last of the trucks were in, emptied, and accounted for. We'd lost five total. Five out of fifty. That was a lot of trucks when you considered how long it had taken Jasper to build this operation. He took every single loss personally. Not only were they gone, their GPS transponders were gone, their drivers, their cargo—everything.

Vaughn leaned back against the wall with a weary sigh. We were all tired. No one was sleeping. Not me. Not Jasper. Not Vaughn. And definitely *not* Milo. Dark shadows underscored his eyes and he hadn't shaved in three days. Since coming back from prison, he'd taken particular care of his appearance. Always clean-shaven, hair neat, clothes clean, and it didn't matter how dirty our work got—he'd refused to be unkempt in any way.

Frankly, it reminded me of when he'd been in college and on course for law school. Only then, he'd been aiming a lot higher than we were right now. But I got it, it was all about Ivy. He'd gradually begun to accept that Ivy was Emersyn and that he didn't know her. They were both trying. It had been rewarding to watch and it had made being patient worth it.

Now?

Now, I struggled to not slug them when he and Jasper snarled at each other, or when Milo tried to tell us to let it go where she was concerned. None of us would. Now that we had the trucks shored up, Liam better have something for us. He and Rome had been "working" on a lead all week, or so Liam had said.

Rome hadn't answered any of us. Then Freddie vanished two days ago—fuck was it three now? I ran a hand over my face. I needed a shower, a shave, some coffee and—Sparrow. I just needed to see her and know she was all right. The brief glimpse we'd gotten on the news wasn't near enough. We spent years looking out for her where we could from a distance.

I couldn't go back to that. I didn't want to. I *liked* having her—

"Kel," Milo said with some force that suggested he'd said my name more than once. When I glanced at him, he frowned. "You good?"

"No," I said, not bothering to avoid the elephant in the room. I was fucking tired of ignoring it. "I'm not. But we had a job to do. We're done for now, right?"

He let out an aggravated sigh. "Don't—"

"What? Don't call you on your crap?" I met him stare for stare. Vaughn lifted his chin and Jasper lit a cigarette, but he straightened and stared at Milo with an impassive expression.

"We're going to do this now?"

"I don't see why not," I replied. "You're never going to want to do it and you know what. Fine, count yourself out. The three of us can take it from here. We know where everyone else stands."

Doc was in his corner, but he wasn't any happier about all of this than the rest of us were. He might hide it well, but I'd seen his face after he watched the news report. As determined as Doc seemed to be to support Milo, Emersyn's absence troubled him.

Fine. Whatever.

We would—

The cranking sound of the roll up doors sounded from the other end of the warehouse. We all turned. No one was due back and I slid a hand to the gun tucked into its holster at my back. But the car pulling in was one of Liam's SUVs. I knew all of his plates.

It wasn't Liam behind the wheel. I didn't think so, at least. The twins were identical, sure, but Liam and Rome rarely dressed alike.

Rome also had a way of driving that was precise, if abrupt. As soon as the vehicle would clear the underside of the still rising door, he was inside and parked. The door was already rolling down behind him.

"What the fuck?" Milo growled in an undertone. We were all heading toward the car as Freddie climbed out of the passenger seat, rolling his head from side to side and muttering. It was Rome that held my attention, because he went to the back door of the vehicle and opened it. A dark-haired woman—fuck my life, for a split second my pulse skipped, the slam of my heart almost painful—stepped out and *glared* at Rome.

Not Sparrow.

Too tall.

Lean though, but without her compact muscles.

From a distance and for like half a second, she'd been back. She'd come home. Stuffing that torn and bloodied part of my soul away, I squared my shoulders.

"You live here?" the woman demanded in a cultured tone. She enunciated every syllable, clean and deliberate. Sparrow had similar diction. The similarities were there, but she wasn't Sparrow.

"Rome?" I asked a lot, saying his name. I was aware of that. But Rome didn't usually need me to recite monologues. If anything, he preferred short and direct.

"She's a friend of Starling's," Rome explained.

"Why the fuck is she here?" Milo's question came out more a snarl of ground words, as if he had clenched his jaw in a fruitless effort to hold them back.

"Because I want to be," she snapped before Rome could say anything. "These idiots didn't tell me we were a two-day drive from where we needed to be. I could have gotten us here a lot faster, not to mention we're going to need to move faster if this is going to work at all."

Despite her claim of two days in the car, she seemed perfectly put together, save for a slight wrinkle to her shirt. She pivoted away from Rome and Freddie, who shockingly didn't say a word, just leaned against the hood of the SUV, waiting. For what?

Sparrow's friend glanced at me, then Jasper, Vaughn, and finally settled on Milo. I swore she measured, assessed, judged, and moved on. But Milo earned her *stare*. "*You're* her brother?"

Silence greeted that scandalized note and I wasn't the only one who focused on Freddie and Rome. Jasper exhaled a thin stream of smoke and said, "Freddie, what the fuck did you two do?"

"We're working on getting Boo-Boo back. She has information. She's kind of bitchy if you interrupt her, so just let her talk."

"Freddie," Milo snapped. "We don't kidnap women."

"No, we just kidnap Boo-Boo."

I didn't laugh. No matter how fucking funny the comment was.

"We didn't kidnap her."

"They didn't *kidnap* me." The woman's comment stormed right over the top of Rome's dry response.

Before that particular round of debate could begin, a door slammed and Liam was there, striding across the warehouse. The lethality in his movements and the barely suppressed rage in his expression had me tensing and shifting my balance without a second thought. Freddie moved behind Rome and closer to the girl, like he was gonna shield her, and Milo cut between all of them to meet Liam almost halfway.

The tension in the room crackled, because Liam wasn't looking at us, he was staring at his brother *and* the girl. "What the hell did you do, Rome? Why would you bring Elaine Benedict *here* of all places?"

Milo stiffened. If I hadn't been looking at him, I'd probably have missed it. His back rippled with tension and he straightened.

"Great, is there anyone else coming who is going to be shocked and awed by my presence that we'll need to stop to explain it all?" Elaine demanded. "If so, would it be possible to use the restroom now? I'd rather discuss *Emersyn's* problems instead of this, but we don't have all day."

"She can help," Rome said after Elaine finished. "Come on, I'll show you to the bathroom."

"Wait," Liam said before they even went two steps. "Having *her* here is dangerous."

"Why?" Jasper said and I ran a hand over my face. A headache was already building behind my eyes.

"Fuck this," I stated. "Rome - take her to the bathroom. Everyone else, shut up and let Freddie explain. All of you be quick. We'll do this inside—" There weren't any rats around inside right now, but if having Benedict here was going to be a problem, better to nip it in the bud. "Vaughn, call Doc and get him over here. Then we won't have to have them explain everything twice."

The door closed behind Rome and Elaine before I was even done speaking, but it was Milo who twisted to glare at me. He and Liam pinned the same damn fury in my direction. Not that I gave a fuck. Not right now.

"Be pissed at me later," I told them both. "Snarling like mad dogs isn't getting us anywhere. If she can help, she can help. But until we hear it, we won't know anything. As for the rest? I seriously don't give a fuck whether you want to be involved in finding your sister or not, Milo. I love you man, but this shit is old."

With that, I left them to follow or not, and headed inside. Freddie jogged to catch up to me and muttered, "When did you become such a badass?"

"About five minutes after everyone stopped using their brains," I retorted.

He almost snickered. Almost. It was the first Freddie-like sound out of him in days. "So, years ago?"

Fair.

I chuckled.

That helped some. Not a lot. But some.

Fifteen minutes later and with a beer in hand, I waited as Elaine Benedict glared at all of us, though Milo seemed to get her stare more than anyone else. We'd waited for Doc. Liam fumed. A layer of fresh bruises had begun to appear along his jaw. But that wasn't that unusual. Nor was the purplish bruises and broken skin along his knuckles.

Freddie had made sandwiches. A whole stack of them, and he passed them to Rome and Elaine when they came back. She eyed the sandwiches then Freddie before she'd taken a bite from one. I couldn't quite pin down what it was about her. The clothes and the mannerisms screamed money, wealth, and privilege. But the attitude? The attitude was all *fight me* and control. She hadn't said a word about the living room, the cheap furniture or the concrete walls.

She looked more out of place here than Emersyn ever had, but not in a bad way. I couldn't put my finger on it and I stopped trying to figure it out. The moment Doc walked in, Liam pinned her with a look and said, "Talk."

"Charming, I'd know you two were brothers without the looks."

Vaughn chuckled, even Jasper shook his head. The humor, no matter how needed, was far too fleeting. I didn't want to be entertained. I wanted information.

Thankfully, Elaine didn't waste anymore time. "Everyone here is trustworthy?" Of all people, she directed that question to Freddie.

"Yes," he said without equivocation.

"Good, because I'm going to need all of you to help." She rose from her seat and moved to stand in front of the dark television. It shifted the power in the room, which I assumed was her intention. It also left her standing alone and directly opposite Milo. "Emersyn's in trouble."

"And you know this—"

She cut off Milo with a slice of her hand. "Pretty boy, this will go a lot faster if you let me talk and save the questions until after the presentation."

My eyebrows weren't the only ones who shot up. Holy shit. She didn't miss a beat either.

"So, a little more this," she continued, holding her thumb and fingers together like a closed mouth. "Instead of this." She mimed yapping with her hand. After a beat, she nodded. "Good. Emersyn contacted me a few days ago because of a reward that was put out by my family and friends of ours. I knew she was okay, but my grandfather offered the reward at my request. We were hoping someone would try to collect from us before the Sharpes, and that would let me know if anyone had found her before they could sell her out."

Some of her confidence wavered, but all she did was fold her arms. "I promised her I would help in any way. I would also warn her if we heard anything. That was our last conversation. Then I heard she'd been *found* and was coming home."

A shudder raced through her.

"That was the last thing she wanted."

"Told you," Freddie said, though his tone was far from smug.

"You sound certain," Milo said.

"That's because I am, I've known Emersyn since we were five. Granted—we haven't always been in the same places, and we had a hard time keeping in touch sometimes, but we never gave up on each other and I'm *not* giving up on her now. As much as I hated not knowing exactly where she was, I was happy knowing she was *safe.*"

The emphasis she gave to that last word slayed what reservations that might have still lingered over our choices in taking her.

"She never told me why you took her and I don't care right now, I'm just glad you did. Her going back was never the plan."

"The false IDs," Liam said. "You got them for her."

"Yes, a new identity, cash, anything she needed to not be Emersyn Sharpe anymore, and disappear."

I frowned. The ferociousness in her eyes glinted with no small amount of danger. She was the real deal. She'd fight for Emersyn. Fight for her the way we would fight for each other.

Freddie and Rome were right to bring her here. "Where is she now?" I asked. "Where is she that you're so damn worried about?"

As desperate as I was to see her, I wanted the answer to be something like a beach in Mexico or the Caribbean or anywhere. I wanted this to be overkill. I wanted our concerns to be unfounded.

"If he's done what I think he has and if the rumors are true, he's sent her back to Pinetree."

"What the hell is Pinetree?" It was the first time Doc had said a word since he arrived.

"It's a psychiatric facility," Liam answered, a muscle ticking in his jaw. "A very exclusive one."

"You've heard of it?" The question seemed rhetorical because she didn't wait for his response. "All I know is that if she's there, we need to get her out. I have the money and the connections, but I have no way to get in and I don't think I could anyway—the last two times he sent her to that place—she was different when she came out."

"Different how?" Milo took two steps toward her. "There was never anything about her being in a facility."

"Of course not, it wouldn't reflect well on the family. But I knew. Some of us knew, because we saw what happened after. The only reason they sent her there was to control her—to take away who she is, and I couldn't stop it before. I *can* do something now."

"That's where we come in," Vaughn said, like Doc, he'd said almost nothing. But real fury had replaced the agony in his voice. If they were caging her, we would damn well shatter those bars.

"Exactly. I just—I just don't know how to make it happen and I need help to get her out."

"We'd need to know if she was there for sure," Doc said. "HIPPA would prevent them from admitting it, but medical requests…"

Medical requests?

Milo cut a look at him.

Right. No one wanted to admit this. No one wanted to say she was in trouble, even if it was what we'd *all* been saying.

"Tell them," Rome said and that got all of our attention. But he wasn't talking to Elaine. He was looking at Liam. "It's time. Tell them."

"He's right," Freddie said. "Tell them and then we figure out how to get me committed. It's not like anyone needs to tell me how to be crazy. They've been wanting to lock me up for years."

We Saw the Sea

MILO

Nikki said yes to joining me for the weekend. The guys had given me some shit about it, but I flipped them off. Nikki was the kind of girl who deserved nice things. She was sharp, from the neighborhood, and going places. While she hadn't been in the system, her dad died when she was a kid, leaving her mother to raise Nikki and all four of her brothers on her own.

She used to say she grew up quickly because her mama needed help, but now, the boys were mostly grown and so was she. The loyalty she had with her siblings mirrored the tightness I had with the Vandals.

That was the only bone of contention between us. Gang life was not something she wanted any part of. This was a goodbye trip. I'd accepted that from the moment she agreed. The wind blowing in off the water carried so many fleeting promises. None of them were going to come true.

I'd stripped down to swim trunks and leaned against the deck railing as I stared at the waves. The place cost a pretty penny to rent for the weekend, but it also offered us privacy and a strip of sand to call our own. Nikki was a lady and I wanted to treat her like a lady.

More, I wanted her to keep being my lady but…

"This is a nice place," she said from behind me as she trailed her fingers up my spine. I closed my eyes at the warmth in that touch. The ease of it. We'd known each other for a few years. The dance between us began sometime around the end of high school and before college.

The guys knew her. They looked out for her when I traveled. I'd taken care of some issues her brothers were having when an upstart gang filtered into the area. They thought they were being quiet, but I wasn't letting a bunch of punks paint our streets with blood.

When her brother Keith had gotten winged in a confrontation, I grabbed Jasper, Vaughn, and Kellan. We cleaned out their block and a few blocks around them. Keeping Nikki and her family safe was important.

She hadn't quite seen it the same way.

I kept my hands on the railing until she leaned into me, and then I slid an arm around her. Relief surfaced but I didn't grasp onto it. Nikki's decision was her own and I didn't think she enjoyed it any more than I did.

"Milo," she said in a sigh. "What am I going to do with you?"

The words 'keep me' refused to leave my tongue. They might as well have been superglued. Glancing down into her deep brown eyes, I turned so I could trace her features with my free hand. Her skin was both warm and silky soft. She really was one of the most beautiful women I'd ever seen, inside and out. That I got to touch her—it was a gift.

The sadness etched into her expression and worse, deeper into her eyes, left my heart heavy.

"It's okay, Nikki," I promised her. It wasn't, but I would make it okay. For her. She needed the distance, I'd give it to her. I wouldn't pull anyone into this life who didn't want to be here. Frankly, I didn't want her involved in any of it anyway. I just… Well, that didn't matter anymore. "I understand."

A wet sound escaped her and her eyes went damp in the time it took her to look down and then back up again. She pressed her hands against my bare chest. "I wish I did," she admitted. "I wish I understood why this scares the hell out of me and at the same time, I wish I was the girl who could do this."

"You don't have to be anyone except yourself." I was right there with her. I wished she was the woman who could handle it. Even if I would do everything in my power to never let it touch her. I had a plan. One we'd talked about a few times late into the night, with her wrapped in my arms. "I will never ask you to be anything more than that."

Her chin dipped again and she let out a watery laugh. "Why are you so damn perfect?"

Sliding a finger beneath her chin, I nudged her face up to look at me. "We both know that's not true."

"But it is—you're kind, you're sweet and thoughtful. At the same time, you're protective and strong. And you're so damn smart. You're going places, I know you are. I just—just how you're getting there."

"I can't change who I am." Not when who I was would give me the strength to become the person with the power and the influence I needed to be. Not when I was determined to get back to Ivy and meet her in her world. I would take my brothers with me.

I wanted to take Nikki.

"And I don't want to ask that of you—any more than you want to ask me to."

"Well, that's where you're wrong," I said evenly. "I am asking. You're saying no."

She parted her lips, then closed them again. "I guess I am," she whispered finally. The tears in her eyes escaped one at a time. Each one poured salt into the wound, so I gathered her close and pressed her against me.

"We have the weekend," I told her. "It's not goodbye."

I'd never cut her out of my life.

"If you need us, you'll know where we are." That was a promise I intended to keep. The guys all liked her. Even Rome, and he didn't like too many.

"Damn you," she whispered, her fingers curling into fists that she beat against me, but it wasn't like it hurt. "I hate that I—"

Tilting her head back, I kissed her, silencing the recriminations. The last six months had been round after round of the same conversation. We carried guns. We actively would, and had, taken out competition and those that would do more harm.

It didn't matter that we had a moral code. It mattered that we wouldn't shy away from the violence she didn't want in her life. Her mouth opened beneath mine and I plundered the sweetness. It wasn't long before her fists loosened and she wrapped her arms around my neck.

Against her lips, I said, "I know, Nikki. I know all of it. This weekend is for us to say goodbye."

It had been from the moment I asked her and she said yes.

We would just have to make the most of it.

Her groan answered something inside of me and I picked her up. It was four steps to get us back inside and I had her sprawled on the bed in moments. Gazing up at her, I found her watching me with teary eyes.

"I love you," she whispered. "You know that, right?"

I did. But it wasn't enough. Not for her. "I love you, too." Loved her enough to let her go. "But for the next two days, ma'am, you're mine and all I want to hear is you screaming my name."

In saying goodbye, I planned to leave my mark. I couldn't keep her, but I'd never forget her.

And I didn't want her to forget me.

Chapter Fifteen

DOC

"You want to be committed?" I stared at Freddie. I'd heard him clear as day. I still couldn't quite believe it. "At some exclusive treatment facility we know nothing about?"

"Liam's got the money," Freddie said with a shrug. "Elaine here—"

"Lainey," she corrected him. I had no idea who this new girl was, or how she knew so much, but Milo hadn't said a word since she shut him down. The fact she *had* shut him down so damn effectively was a conversation for another day.

"Lainey," Freddie repeated with a hint of a smirk and a thumbs up. "She knows where it is."

Arms folded, Liam dipped his chin. "We'd have to change your name, work out a fairly quick ID swap. Make you my brother for real."

Rome snorted, but Freddie grinned. A real grin. The first actual smile I'd seen on him with any animation in days. Hands over his heart, he said, "See, I knew you liked me best. Look, it'll work, we need to get in to find her. It's that, or go in there guns blazing, and I don't want Boo-Boo getting hurt, 'cause if they're locking her up like that, what else are they doing to her?"

That one question hit Milo like a fist to the head.

"She never wanted to go back," Kellan said slowly. "She didn't want us contacting them."

"And she said, repeatedly, we had no idea what we were talking about," Jasper added.

Every single sentence drew blood, but Milo didn't move. I glanced at the newcomer. The woman hadn't said anything else, no, she was watching all of us. Correction, she was watching Milo.

"What do you know about her family?" It had to be asked. I'd pushed Emersyn away because I thought it would be better for her. For Milo. For the rest of them. The hurt in her eyes though after, and the way she avoided me, raked across my soul in great big bloody gouges. Regret for that choice crawled through me, a thief coming back to chortle over its victory.

"Enough," Lainey responded. I thought she'd offer more, but that was it. Arms folded, she shifted her attention back to Milo. "Is he really her brother?"

"You could just ask me," Milo said in a low growl.

"I could pretty boy, but I wanted confirmation from someone else. Because the fact you are her brother means you were following us a few years ago and I'm not sure if that's creepy or endearing."

He'd followed—I wasn't the only one who snapped a look at Milo. A muscle ticked in his jaw. "I followed you both because you were running around a huge amusement park *alone*."

"And remarkably, we were just fine." She made a face at him.

"Until trouble found you when you got back to the hotel."

She laughed. "That was Adam and Ezra. Ignore them. I do."

Liam's whole demeanor shifted. There was no mistaking the look he and Milo shared, but we didn't have time for this.

"Tell me more about Pinetree. It's going to take more than just a recommendation to get Freddie in there." Maybe I could use my credentials to get in. But I wasn't licensed in every single state, so that might be a crap shoot.

Why the fuck would her family stick her in a place like that? The image of her hurrying away from the hotel like Hell itself was at her heels replayed through my mind. How many signs had we missed? The abuse. The trauma. We all put it down to Eric.

I had.

What if that was just a layer of it?

Irritation scraped over every nerve. I flexed my hands, the urge to break down a door or a neck flooded me. Freddie had been so damn worried. Now I was.

"Pinetree Psychiatric is a private facility located on eighty acres in upstate New York. It's not quite as far as Buffalo, but it's in the same area. It's designed to be a quiet, isolated retreat where privacy is key. No one gets in that isn't a patient or one of the staff."

The details she offered were precise.

"How many times did you try to get in?"

"Only twice," she admitted. "The first time, I let them escort me off. But the second time, I climbed the wall and tried to sneak in." She gave a little shrug. "I didn't do it as well as Em would have, but I was able to see that, while it looks like a resort on the outside, the interior is very different. I recognized some of the people there. All of them are from wealthy, influential families. The security is ridiculous and after my little excursion, I'm afraid I made it worse."

Her grimace was almost sweet, but she was a kid and maybe she had encountered resistance, but how much and why?

"Look, whatever they are and whatever they're doing, when she comes out of there—she's different. She's forgotten things. Sometimes she gets it back."

"But not always?" Milo's voice was sharp and the anger might be leashed, but it was there. He wasn't one to shout. He never had been. Quiet and deadly, his voice softening until you had to strain to hear it.

Lainey shook her head. "I don't think so, but I haven't ever been able to really ask her about it because…"

Vaughn gripped the back of the sofa. "Because she doesn't remember going to that place, does she?"

"No—and she would have told me if she had." The absolute certainty and quiet conviction convinced me. The sound of a fist crashing into a wall behind me merited a glance. Drywall flaked away from a fresh hole left by Jasper's fist. Kellan white knuckled a grip on a chair. Vaughn glared into space, a muscle in his jaw ticking.

Liam stared at the ceiling, his whole body rock still, but it was a lie. The tension coiling around him was like a viper, ready to strike. Rome was the only one who hadn't said a word. Even Freddie seemed calmer.

Then that made sense. As awful as the news was, they were a step closer to getting her back. "I need to make some calls," I told them. "Don't move until I get back."

No matter how much money Liam and the girl Lainey threw at this, I needed to know more about the facility and the doctors there. I needed to know what they'd likely done to Little Bit.

I needed to know who I was going to have to kill if they were doing what it sounded like they were doing. Liam caught me before I got to the truck. "Where are you going?"

Shaking off his grip, I gave the kid an even look. Something was tearing him up and there were more bruises in his eyes than on his face. "To take care of something and to get some information. Sort out Freddie's ID. If that place has that much security, they're going to be looking for trouble."

"They're going to be looking for *us*," Liam said abruptly. "The men investigating all of us—the pictures."

"Pictures?"

I almost wished I hadn't asked. The brief explanation left a thousand questions, not to mention a fire-fueled rage that wanted out. "The fucker blackmailed her?"

Liam nodded once. The hell in his eyes. He blamed himself. Fine. I could blame him too. Or the others. Mostly—I just blamed myself. Little Bit would have called me if I hadn't pushed her away. If I hadn't—

"Go figure out Freddie," I ordered. "And keep an eye on him. This is going to be harder on him than he thinks."

"Wait...you want him to go through with that plan?" Kellan asked from a couple of steps away. "Doc, that's a terrible idea."

"In a terrible situation, sometimes it's the worst idea that gets you out. Square things away here. Getting him in might be tough— getting them out will be tougher." And they'd need a plan.

A dozen plans turned over in my head as I got in my truck and left the warehouse. I didn't go far. Just three blocks, before I turned off the street and parked on the far side of the apartment buildings. One whole wall featured more of Rome's art. It was colors muted by shadows. As though the people in the shadows couldn't leave the dark, even for the beauty that waited for them.

Fucking poet.

Flipping open the glovebox, I pulled out a phone that I kept there. It was better to not carry this one all the time. But I couldn't bring myself to leave it somewhere I wasn't. The guys rarely called me. All of once in the last three years, and it was for an emergency bullet extraction.

I'd taken care of it. Cleaned it out, stitched him up and gave him antibiotics. They were gone within hours of arrival. Coming and going like ghosts. The only reason I saw them was, I was one of the few they trusted.

Because I'd been one of them.

Phone in hand, I called the number I had memorized and then waited for the options to leave a message. It was an anonymous voicemail. Accessible from anywhere they were. Though, there was a damn good chance they would be too busy to answer immediately. I had to trust the system.

"Situation red. Status important. I need to break a bow. Information required." I added the date and time to the message and then hung up. Leaning back in the seat, I stared out over the port. Shipping containers stacked high. Large slips. Cranes. The whole area was a warren of equipment, storage, and transportation.

Like any warren, it held its secrets in a tight grip.

The phone rang five minutes later. "Hey Doc," Alphabet's voice was both familiar and welcome, even if he sounded more than a little smug. "Long time, no see."

"Yeah well, we've all been busy."

"True—but you only call when you want something." The remark struck true.

"And you only call when you need me to save one of your lives."

"Touché, man, touché." The humor in his voice dried up. "What's wrong?"

"Pinetree Psychiatric. It's located in upstate New York. Do you know it?"

"Not personally," the man said. "Need information on it?"

"I need everything, doctors, patients, location, schematics—everything."

"Give me twelve hours," he said. A crash came from somewhere behind him and he sighed, and the next words were muffled as if he was talking away from the phone. "Gracey, feel free to take his head off, but do it somewhere else. I'm working in here."

Another crash exploded against the wall and he laughed.

Lunatic.

"Should I ask?"

"No." Laughter turned to deadly quiet. "No, you shouldn't."

Understood. "Twelve hours."

"Hang on to the phone." Then he cut the call and it was just me, the phone, and the truck. Twelve hours to do a little digging of my own. I wasn't going back to the warehouse without answers and a plan. They were all on edge, but they'd wait.

The next number I called on my regular phone. My sister answered on the second ring, she sounded a little breathless. "Mickey, hey—it's almost dinnertime, you on the way?"

Fuck. Family dinner was tonight. "No, Steph, sorry. Something came up."

"Fine, I'll just put all the extra tortellini and breadsticks into Tupperware and take it to work with me tomorrow."

"You are a cruel sister."

"Uh huh." She puffed out a breath. "What's wrong, Mickey?"

"Nothing." The lie flowed right off my tongue, but it didn't sit right with me. So, before she could call me on the crap, I just said, "Nothing you can help me with. I gotta do this. A friend needs me."

"You're always a good friend."

Thinking back to the betrayal in Little Bit's eyes in that bathroom, after feeling her come all over my fingers, I didn't think so. I'd turned out to be a pretty lousy fucking friend. "Yeah, well, I screwed up and someone else might be paying for that."

"You'll fix it." Absolute confidence.

"Steph, you always say that."

"And I'm always right. You made mistakes, Mickey. But you paid for them. You fixed it. You became a better person." The crispness of her words pulled a reluctant smile from me.

"You've always seen the best in me."

"No, I've always seen *you*. The good. The bad. The indifferent. You made mistakes. You made—big mistakes. Some of them forgivable. But you also took ownership and you've done what you could. Unfortunately, not every mistake can be fixed or even undone. The past is done, Mickey. We can mourn it, curse it, and even regret it. But we can't change it. The only thing we can do is make amends, plan to be better, and repair the future."

The words were exactly what I needed to hear. At the same

time— "What if a decision I made drove someone else to make an even worse decision?"

"We all make choices. You can't take responsibility for theirs, only your own."

"But if I…"

"Michael James, you cannot, and are not, capable of making another person's decisions for them and if you think they made them purely for you, then I would suggest you slap yourself upside that arrogant head of yours."

Ouch.

But she had a point… Little Bit was hardly a pushover.

"Love you, Sis."

"I love you, too. Look after my boys and don't do anything stupid."

We didn't linger on the phone after that, which was good, because I didn't have to tell her too late. I'd already done a lot of stupid things. Head back against the seat, I waited. Back here was as good a place as any.

My phone buzzed a few times.

Messages from Jasper.

Liam.

Milo.

One from Freddie.

I didn't answer any of them. I couldn't.

Not until I had answers.

It was nearing midnight when Alphabet called back.

"You're not going to like this," he began without preamble before he recited the information he'd uncovered.

He was right.

I didn't like it.

At all.

Trying to Grab Smoke

FREDDIE

The heated blanket didn't seem to do much about the cold in the air, but Jasper had talked a nurse into giving him another one. It was stupid that he had tucked me in. Hadn't I just been sweating my ass off? When I tried to push the blanket down and reach for the IV on my arm, Jasper caught my wrist.

"It itches," I protested. My tongue was heavy and thick. Everything inside of me alternated between freezing and burning. The itching was inside my skin too, I needed to get it out. I needed… "A hit, just one."

I wasn't above begging.

"No," Jasper told me firmly and he didn't relax his grip on my arm. "You've already had too much."

My next argument died as the door opened and Ms. Stephanie let herself in. The door. The room. Hospital room. Sweat dripped into my eyes. The thoughts were like whispers of smoke from the fire burning inside of me. Instead of anger or reproach, she gave me the kindest look.

One I really didn't deserve.

I stopped fighting Jasper and laid back down. The shivers were coming. The nausea was already there. Closing my eyes helped, but not much. "Jasper, go on, I can stay with him."

"Probably not a good idea." He sounded almost apologetic. "He's already tried to rabbit four times. They want him in restraints."

I grimaced. But Jasper's tone promised that wasn't going to happen.

Ms. Stephanie let out another long sigh. The whisper of her hand against my brow was so cool, I almost echoed her exhale. It took me a minute, but I sucked it up and opened my eyes. Even braced for disappointment, I wasn't ready to see the compassion in her eyes.

"Hey," she said and I tried to smile. It wasn't really physically possible at the moment. I wasn't even sure when I got to the hospital. "I'm not going to ask how you're feeling. You don't look good."

That seemed reasonable.

"I'm also not going to chastise you for doing this to yourself, though I think we all need to admit you need more help than what you've been getting."

I couldn't look at Jasper. If he was as disappointed as Ms. Stephanie, I was pretty sure it would kill me. All I ever did was let them down…

"But," she continued, her voice crisp if gentle. "You don't like strangers and you don't like lock-in treatment programs, so I think we're going to have to compromise."

Now I did look at Jasper. Did he know what Ms. Stephanie was talking about?

"Listen to her, I think she's right. What we're doing isn't working." While he shook his head, his words seemed at odds with that action.

"I'm sorry." The words tasted like ass. Hell, my whole mouth did. I wanted to throw up. I lurched upwards because the burn in my stomach followed my desire. Jasper caught me and had a bowl in front of me. He kept me upright while I puked up my guts.

Neither of them retreated, no matter how nasty. When it was done, he took the bowl away and Ms. Stephanie washed my face before she let me suck on some ice chips. "We're going to get you through this," she told me. "We're going to get you past this overdose and you're going to get clean. Then, we're going to go to the meetings together."

I swallowed the bitter bile in the back of my throat.

"Or?" Because that sounded like it had a hammer to make me do what she wanted me to do.

"Or we'll keep trying until we beat this," she told me. "We're not giving up on you."

I couldn't figure out why.

"Which means you cut this shit out," Jasper said, folding his arms as he stared at me. Despite the gruff tone, he wore a frown of concern. "I don't want to find you like that again."

Fuck.

I banged my head against the pillow. "I just needed it to stop for a little while."

Neither of them asked me what I needed to stop. Ms. Stephanie knew and Jasper never pushed. Sometimes—sometimes I thought he did know. But he never brought it up.

"Well, we're gonna find other ways," he told me. "And if it gets like this again, you call us first."

Nausea swarmed through me again. Some days, I really didn't know why they pushed so hard. I wasn't worth it. Maybe if Jasper really knew the truth, he'd get it. None of them would want me around…

"Whatever the fuck you're thinking kid, knock it the hell off." Jasper all but collapsed into the chair next to the bed. "Sorry, Ms. Stephanie."

"I think we can let the language go," she said, almost too lightly. "I'll give you both a pass tonight."

"You shouldn't," I mumbled.

"I think I'll do whatever the *fuck* I like," Ms. Stephanie informed me in a tone so tart, I had to blink. "What? You didn't think I knew how to use cursing as judiciously as you?"

I opened my mouth, but honestly, I had no idea what to say.

"Well then, now that I have your attention…" She wore the most serene expression, but it didn't reach her eyes. "Let's discuss what's going to happen for the next three days."

Licking my dry lips, I frowned. It was spring break. "I don't have school." The dry expression she wore promised that wasn't what she meant. "Okay." My voice came out a croak. I winced and she fed me another spoonful of ice chips. After I got those down and she gave me another, I managed, "Why three days?"

"You'll be here in the hospital for at least the next forty-eight hours. I'd like seventy-two. They've got you on a dose of methadone to get you clean, but if you leave too soon or you decide to go and do a few hits, you could overdose again."

Oh.

One glance at Jasper said he was scowling.

"What happens after three days?"

"We get through the next three days, and we'll talk about the three after that. Then the three after that. Can you hold on for three days?"

I had no idea.

"We'll do it one day at a time, but one of us is going to be here with you…"

Jasper had work and so did she. "Just suck it up, Freddie," Jasper told me as he leaned back in the chair and put his booted feet on the end of my bed, like he had every intention of sleeping in that chair. "In three days, Vaughn and Kel will take over."

Ms. Stephanie nodded. "Then Jasper and I will be back. Rome will fill in when we need him."

But not Milo or Liam?

"Milo and Liam are for the three days you decide you're going to run again," Jasper said, but he hadn't opened his eyes. "Just be ready, Liam's got money on when you're gonna bolt."

Ms. Stephanie huffed a sound so impatient, I almost laughed. "Really?"

With a shrug, Jasper said, "We gotta entertain ourselves. But Freddie's not gonna run."

Wait. "I'm not?"

"Nope," he said, then slitted his eyes open to look at me.

"You bet on me not to run." It wasn't a question and Jasper just smiled, closing his eyes again. I licked my lips. He believed in me enough to put money on me.

"You boys." Ms. Stephanie couldn't manage to keep her amusement out of her disapproval.

"Want to add some side action?" I asked and she gave me the most scandalized look, I had to laugh. It was laugh or cry, and I didn't want to cry anymore.

I didn't even think I had it in me to cry. Not after… No, I wasn't thinking of what happened before. The guys had come for me. They knew that. They hadn't rejected me then. Maybe they wouldn't if I ever told them what happened. But I didn't want to talk about that part.

"Maybe," Jasper said. "Whatcha got?"

"Oh, fine, if we're doing side action," Ms. Stephanie said, pulling something out of her purse and it took me a minute to realize it was knitting and needles. "Count me in."

"Ms. Stephanie," Jasper said in a slow teasing voice. "Have we finally corrupted you?"

When she bounced a ball of yarn off his head, I started laughing. I couldn't stop either. I laughed until I cried and neither one of them left me. They didn't go when the next wave of shakes hit either.

But they did make me a bet.

Chapter Sixteen

FREDDIE

"**O**kay, sign here and here," Liam said as he slapped the papers in front of me. It was almost entertaining. "That will make it legal and transfer power of attorney to me for the time being."

"Yeah, because being adopted at twenty-one is what we all dreamed of." I kept it light because I'd rather get this shit over and done with and get moving. But Doc insisted we needed a paper trail. Fortunately, I had an easily accessible history of substance abuse and a troubled psyche. Even my school records said so. We didn't have to manufacture shit.

"Cleary?" I double-checked the name. "Not O'Connell?"

Rome glanced at us from where he'd been leaning against the wall. Everyone was in the sitting room, including our guest, who refused to be removed from the discussion no matter how much Milo huffed and he puffed. Man was gonna have a damn heart attack if he kept it up. As it was, she hadn't taken her gaze off Liam since he'd arrived.

He'd barely glanced at her when he'd walked in and flipped

open folders with a dozen different legal forms. Some were dated today, others for years past.

"The O'Connells only adopted one son," Liam said without a look at his twin. "Though they were more than willing to adopt my siblings. The rumors about having other brothers are strong enough, we can just lean into it. Your medical history will help out there, too."

"Cause I'm a fuckup."

Jasper glared at me and I shrugged.

"Just saying," I told him as I signed the first sheet and followed it to the next tab. Whatever it took to just get us moving. We'd been away from Boo-Boo for days. *Days*. If what Lainey told us was true, and she seemed pretty damn confident it was, then Boo-Boo needed us to move our asses.

Exactly as I'd been telling them all along.

"I'm the kind you keep hidden so that it doesn't affect your reputation."

"Right," Liam said with a snort. "The point is, that world knows I have at least one brother. Very few actually know he's a twin. Enough think I have others." He made a sweeping motion to the rest of them. I half-expected Jasper to comment, but he just took a long pull from his beer. "Okay, Doc, you need to go over these." Liam dropped another packet of paper in front of Doc.

"I'm not even going to ask where you got these." Doc had the folder open and I leaned over to look. Medical records. But...those weren't mine.

I glanced at Liam and raised my brows. His bland look told me to just shut up. I shrugged. Cause really, whatever.

"Okay," Doc said. "This means I'm recommending you to a treatment of at least thirty days but no more than ninety." Scratching his jaw, he cut a glance at me. "That means you could be stuck in this place for thirty days before we can even move legally to get you out."

"Yeah, if they can keep me," I said with a shrug. "My plan is simple. Get in. Get Boo-Boo. Get out. It's easier if I'm all the way in."

"You're gonna have to watch it," Doc told me. "You won't be armed. They can medicate you—not a fan of that considering your history, but I'll make sure I note it."

No one said anything.

"You also need to remember…"

"Doc," I said before he could push on. "Nobody has to tell me how to act like a whackjob who needs to be committed. I got this."

"Freddie," Kellan said and that surprised me. I actually thought that comment would rankle Jasper, but he'd just shaken his head. "No one likes leaving you in there with no one to watch your back."

"Cause I'm a fuckup?" I could take the heat.

"Pretty sure if you were that bad of a fuckup," Lainey said and that yanked all of our attention, "none of these guys would be okay with it. But let's continue to debate your worthiness, we've got all the time in the world."

I grinned. "I like her. She's my kind of people."

Milo stared at the ceiling. Jasper snorted. Kellan frowned then looked at Lainey. The remoteness in his expression shut me up. "You're here as a guest," he informed her. "You brought us information. We appreciate it. This is about *our* family, so if you'd be so kind as to sit down and shut the fuck up, the rest of us would appreciate it."

"Kel," Milo snapped, but Kellan didn't even look at him. His icy gaze was fixed on Lainey. The firecracker with the balls of steel just raised her hands.

"I'm worried about *my* friend."

"So are we," Vaughn informed her. "Freddie is also our brother. Tell me again why we can't just go in, shoot these people, and take her out?"

The last wasn't directed at Lainey but at Liam and Doc. To be honest, I was okay with that plan too. However, Vaughn wasn't usually the guy advocating blunt force. That was Jasper.

He was still silent as hell though. That was—weird.

"Would you like me to start at the top?" Doc asked.

"How about, because the minute we go in there guns blazing we bring in law enforcement, their security, and more. The heat that comes down on us would be one thing," Milo said, his expression stone. "The other is Ivy—fuck my life—Emersyn could be hurt."

"Not risking Boo-Boo. Besides, I look harmless. That's all they're going to see. My pretty face, my shitty history, and my weak character. I'm not a threat." I knew my strengths.

Jasper said something under his breath and stood. Then he was gone, stalking out of the room.

Scrubbing a hand over his face, Kellan asked, "What happens if they do to him what we're worried about them doing to Emersyn?"

"I'll deal with it." Not much they could do that would hurt me.

"Look, if you have a better plan, spit it out. If you don't, can we finish this paperwork? We still have to get to this joint and that's a long fucking trip. Not to mention—Doc, don't you gotta have a medical license in New York to do this?"

Liam set another folder on the table. "That's covered."

"Where the hell are you getting all of this?" Vaughn gaped.

"Does it matter?" Lainey asked. "I can get papers if we need them. I have friends who can do excellent work. But the longer we debate this, the longer she's there."

Instead of snapping at her, Kellan just scowled. "Fine. Let's do this. How close are we sticking to this?"

"You can't," Liam said and that just started another round of objections. Rome silenced them all with a whistle. It cut right through the noise.

"No more arguments. Freddie can do this. Liam or I will be there. Everyone else needs to be here." Rome offered no more explanations. Vaughn just slammed his fist to the side table and stood up, before he stalked out to follow Jasper to wherever.

Good times. I raked a hand through my hair. Now would be a great time to get high, except—I needed to be sober. Or did I? Would it be better if I was high going in?

Doc stared down at the papers, then he started signing them.

No, getting high could cause other problems and I didn't want to fuck this up. Boo-Boo needed me. She needed me to be sober. I could be sober. Besides, they were gonna probably hook me up to some shit to flush my system anyway. Easier to not be puking everywhere if I wasn't fucked up when I got there.

"I can help," Lainey offered into the disquiet of the room.

"No," Milo said before anyone else could say anything. "You need to go home."

Yeah. That was gonna end well.

"I'll go where I damn well please and I'm not going anywhere until I know she's all right."

They glared at each other. "You'll go or I'll dump you in a trunk and drive you back myself."

"Yeah, that's the way to do it, Milo," I said as I stood up and stretched. I should probably go pack a bag. They'd let me bring a bag to Garnet Bay for the whole two weeks I'd been stuck there. This was thirty days. What the hell should I take? "I mean, take her home and she can take off and do whatever she wants."

Oh, books would be good.

Lainey and Milo both glared at me. I blew the ball-cracker a kiss. I kind of liked her. She needed to stay safe. Especially since she and Boo-Boo were friends.

"She can stay in Emersyn's room—" Kellan began but Milo cut him off.

"I'll take care of her."

And on that note, count me out. "I'm getting my shit. Tell me when you're ready to leave." I said that more to Liam than anyone else, but he was staring at Lainey and Milo with a troubled frown.

Yeah, nope.

In my room, I stared around at the mess. I should probably clean up more. But that wasn't my problem today. In fact, today all I really needed was some clean underwear, a couple of t-shirts, some jeans and her books. She'd been reading to me, but she hated reading the sex scenes. It was kind of funny.

Though she never complained when I read them. Course—they were hilarious cause dude, I needed the stamina these guys had. The sheer number of girls I could bang with that kind of stamina.

Not that I wanted to bang any.

Liar.

The little whisper of a voice in the back of my head sounded a lot like Jasper, so I just flipped it off and got my shit together. I probably couldn't take my knife. That would suck. But I didn't want to take anything I might not be able to get back out with, so if I had to leave it. I left it.

Everything had to be nondescript too.

Once I had everything in the bag, a job that took all of five minutes, I sat down and waited. I wanted Boo-Boo back. Just back. She didn't have to talk or hang out or read. I just wanted her back where she was safe.

The nightmare Ball-Cracker described though, was the kind of thing I never wanted to think about. Without a knife, I'd only have my hands. I needed to keep it together long enough to not kill them before I got her out.

After? All bets were off.

My mood soured the longer I waited. If those assholes were out there still arguing—

At the first knock on my door, I bounced to my feet with my bag in hand. Yes, let's get the fuck out of here.

Only it wasn't Liam at the door. It was Jasper. His expression was fierce, but not angry. "If I told you don't go, would you listen?"

The question knocked me on my ass. "You don't want me to go get Boo-Boo? Who the fuck are you and what did you do with Jas?"

The other man rolled his eyes and gave me a gentle shove back into the room before he closed the door. The fact it was a disaster area in here probably drove him nuts, but he didn't say a word. "I want her back here safe and sound, but I don't want to throw you into the pool without a life jacket either."

"Gotta learn to swim sooner or later." I shrugged. "I don't care about me. I care about getting Boo-Boo back."

"That's my problem," Jasper growled the words and paced across my room. When he encountered a stack of clothes, he just gave them a shove with his foot. "This is not just casing a joint or lifting some beers."

"I know."

"Do you?" Jasper pivoted to stare at me. "You couldn't stand Garnet Bay. You tried to break out fifteen minutes after we dropped you off."

I shrugged.

"Two days in, you were picking fights and threatened to stab one of the nurses if they didn't let you out." Jasper wasn't quite glaring, but he wasn't calm either.

"What do you want me to say? I wanted a hit. I was strung out. I hated that place. I hated that you had to dump my ass there because I couldn't stay clean on my own." That had been bad enough. "This isn't *that*."

"No, it's going to be worse. At least then, I was right there."

Yeah, he'd slept in his car for a week. Some days, I didn't know why he put up with me.

"Then, I needed to get clean. I'm clean now. I'm not going to this place for actual treatment. I'm going to get Boo-Boo."

"But you're gonna have to play along." He raked a hand through his hair as he scowled. "You're gonna have to see what's happening to her."

"Yeah," I said. "I know. But once I'm in, I can also work on getting her out."

"You're also going to be on your own." His expression tightened. "I don't like you being out there without a lifeline."

"Aww," I said slowly, grinning. "You're worried about me."

"No shit, genius. Of course, I'm worried about you." Yeah, only his glare didn't scare me.

"You're a big ol' teddy bear, you know that, right?" The teasing helped and Jasper's dark look just turned positively foreboding. "I betcha Boo-Boo thinks the same thing, even after all the growling and snarling you did."

Yeah, it was hard not to laugh when Jasper glared at me like that. Seriously. I wasn't scared of him.

Mostly.

Clamping his hands on my shoulders, he stared at me so intensely that it was starting to make me uncomfortable.

"Man, if you're gonna kiss me, can we skip that part?"

A sharp laugh broke out of him as he shook his head. "Someday, Freddie, that mouth of yours…"

"Yeah, it's already gotten me into shitloads of trouble. What can I say? It's part of my charm."

"Don't get dead," he said after a beat. "Don't get lost."

The last part might be the hardest. "I'll do my best, *Dad*."

He glared again and I shrugged. When he gave me that rough hug though, I returned it.

"I'll be okay," I said. "You watch." Pulling back, I pasted on a smirk. "I'm gonna be the fucking hero and bring Boo-Boo back."

Chuckling, he clapped me on the shoulder again. "Just don't make me come in there to get you. One piece, you got it?"

"Oh man, you're gonna make it hard on me?" That did it, he rolled his eyes.

"You're such a little asshole."

"Yes," I said proudly as another knock sounded on my door. "Yes, I am."

Jasper yanked it open. Liam and Rome were on the other side of the door. But instead of a fight—which still wasn't out of the realm of possibility—all Jasper did was point a finger at Liam. "Bring him back. One piece."

"I'll bring them both back." Hey, no one said Liam wasn't cocky. "You watch their backs here."

"Like I'd do anything else."

"Hey," Liam said with a faint smirk. "I thought we were just stating the obvious."

I rolled my eyes and caught Rome almost doing the same damn thing. Yeah, time to go. I shoved past Jasper and thumped Liam on the shoulder. "Let's go, big bro. Time to commit me."

Yeah, that sounded way better in my head. Still, no complaints here. I just wanted to get to Boo-Boo.

Yesterday.

The Soul of Chess

LIAM

The first underground fight of the senior year kicked off in an hour. I'd made the card. That didn't surprise me. If anything, it would have been more shocking if I hadn't received the invitation to opening night. I'd lost only two fights in junior year. My stats ranked me the highest, even amongst the upperclassmen and college students who attended.

After putting my bag in the closet to deal with later, I scanned the new room I'd been assigned. No roommates. En suite bathroom. Upgraded furniture. Brand new computer waiting for me to set up on the desk. The last had to be from Mom and Dad. I'd send them a thanks when I got back.

They were—I checked my watch—still on the road after dropping me off. I sent them a text about catching up with some friends and I'd talk to them the next day. If not, Mom would probably call as soon as they got back to the city. She fussed. I didn't mind it most of the time, but phones weren't allowed at the matches.

After firing a message off to Rome, I powered the phone off and tucked it into the portable safe I'd begun bringing to school for the last two years. Inside was a gun, cash, and bullets. Securing all of it, especially this particular phone, was just a good idea. Done, I headed out. It took me less than twenty minutes to get to the venue. I didn't pull in immediately. Instead, I did a sweep of the neighborhood.

Old retail complex. The parking lot pavement sported cracks everywhere, with grass and weeds fighting to take it back. The abandoned strip mall seemed to reflect the loneliness and desolation of the area around it. The grass was too high in the fields, well what grass the weeds hadn't choked out, and rippled in the breeze.

While there weren't any cars in the front lot, there were some in the back. Including a familiar Mercedes. After one more circuit, I pulled in and parked away from the others. I also had the car angled to pull straight out onto the road. No backing up or needing to navigate around other cars would be required. The fact I was at the exact edge of the lot where no one could block me in didn't hurt either.

Adam stepped out of the Mercedes as soon as I exited the car. He paused in mid-swing to close the door and said, "Don't. I'm not in the mood. Stay in the car, Lainey. I mean it." The words carried in the silent lot, but I ignored whatever girl he'd brought with. His message had said he wouldn't be at the fights tonight.

So why was he here?

He met me halfway between our cars, in the shadows beyond the weak pool of light cast by one working street lamp. Withdrawing an envelope from the inside of his pocket, he passed it over. The weight was right, so I just stuffed it into my back pocket without opening it.

"Not counting it?" Adam challenged.

"Is it all there?" At his nod, I shrugged. "Then I don't need to count it. If you're not supposed to be here. Why are you here?"

"The cash," he said, then glanced back to his car. It was even farther from the light and the tinted windows made it impossible to see inside. "The guy is supposed to be here by the third match. He'll have on a black baseball cap."

Right, cause no one else ever wore those kinds of hats. My skepticism must have been showing, because Adam pulled out his phone and flipped it to a new screen. The man in the image was pretty nondescript, sandy blond hair, square jawed, and a nose that had to have been broken more than once.

"Warning?"

Adam nodded. "Last warning. Make it hurt. If we have to do it again, he won't be coming back from that." With that, he gestured to his car. "I'm out." It wasn't until he was back at the driver's side door that he called, "O'Connell?"

I raised my brows.

"I've got five grand on you."

"Good for you."

"For a knockout in the first round. Don't play with them. You have other things to do tonight."

Rolling my eyes, I just flipped him off and headed for the door. The cash in my pocket would get some attention but it wasn't like the crowd that frequented these couldn't afford it. Cash just happened to be the currency for the in-person betting window. Everyone else could place it electronically.

It was also a good place to wash the cash. So, I swung by the betting window, looked at the list of names on the night's fight card, and placed a bet on every single fight that I wasn't in.

Knockout in the first round?

I'd think about it. I'd been itching for a fight for the last two months and he just wanted me to one and done?

The thought no sooner crossed my mind than I smirked. No, he hadn't bet on a knockout in the first. He had to know I wouldn't go for it. So he was winding me up. That bet was for the third round.

What a dick.

Then again, we were all just pieces on the board. By the time my name was called, I'd put Adam, his job, his bet, and everything else out of my head. The guy waiting for me in the ring had about fifty pounds on me.

Oh fuck yes, this was going to be an actual fight.

Chapter Seventeen

EMERSYN

ool air brushed over my cheek. Then nipped at my nose. On some level, the vague notion of opening my eyes wandered through me without pausing. The next time I roused, hands were on me. They lifted and settled me onto a bed. The sheet was scratchy against my arms. Something cold pushed through my veins, freezing the complaints.

The hours floated. Or maybe it was days. One blink it was dark. Another was light. My bladder hurt and there was something cold beneath my bare ass. "Come on," the nurse said.

Come on and what? The words fell through my mind one letter at a time and my lips were too numb to give them shape.

"If you don't," the woman warned. It was a woman, right? She was blurry, could be a guy. The tenor of her voice suggested female. Oh, who cared? It was too hard to focus on that. "I'll have to put a catheter in if you don't pee."

Oh.

Pee.

I could do that.

The stitch in my side, a notion of discomfort vanished under a wave of relief. Oh, it felt *good* to just pee. I think I pee'd forever.

And ever.

I didn't think I wanted to stop. The elation of such a simple act buoyed me and this time when the cold rushed through me, I floated away. Maybe not happily away, happily implied caring. I just didn't anymore.

The rush of chilled air against my face was one thing. Cotton candy scented the air and I wrinkled my nose. It itched but when I tried to raise my hand to scratch it, I couldn't. Something held my arms in place. Frustration inched up from beneath the surface of the ice coating me.

"Hold still." The all-business male voice snapped through the cracks in the ice, chipping them away. Something pulled against my wrist and pinched. Tape? A ripping sound and then the sting traveled up my arm. The sensation shoved the fog away like a harsh breeze. I unglued my eyes and opened them. "Just changing the bandages, Miss Sharpe. We'll get you comfortable here in a bit."

Bandages? What? I tried to form the words but my throat burned and my lips cracked.

"Be gentler," the nurse said. "We don't want to tear out the stitches."

Why did I have stitches?

Where the hell was I?

Each flush of awareness seemed to scrape away more of *me*. What it left behind was just hurt.

"We don't want them infected," the man said, his tone nowhere near as friendly as the woman. It took some serious effort to focus on the man. Tall with thick shoulders and arms, he also had dirty blond hair and a really unpleasant expression. His hands were huge. For a moment, a flash of Vaughn went through my mind. But where his hands were gentle and kind, this guy's hands were tense and harsh. He didn't seem to care that the tape ripped at my skin or pulled at the stitches.

Every sliver of pain inflicted by his actions drained the bubble around me of the effervescent air. Air that remained too light and still smelled too sweet. I managed to lift my right hand. A nasal cannula was tucked into my nostrils. I tugged it down and the sugary flavor of the oxygen vanished.

Sucking in a hungry gulp of air, I pulled my left arm to myself as soon as he finished re-wrapping it. The skin burned and ached. More, the muscles beneath it did. It hurt to even hook my fingers closed.

"What happened?" The fact I pushed the words out exhausted me, pure and simple. My throat hurt, the sound trembling with each syllable like it added to the bruises.

"It's all right," the female nurse said, filling my vision with her plump cheeks, kind brown eyes, and easy smile. "You're in a safe place."

"Not an answer," I protested as she pushed the cannula back into place. When I would have yanked it out, the bruiser of a guy caught my hand and pinned it back to the bed. A rip of velcro tore through the quiet and then it fastened around my bicep and again over the bandage. The action pinned my arm and panic scraped its way through me.

"Shh," the nurse repeated. "You're in a safe place. We need you to keep resting. Getting upset is not going to do anything." The taste of sweetness grew almost cloying. Cotton candy and bubblegum.

Gas.

It was nitrous.

"Why?" I asked. "What happened?"

My thoughts kept scattering like bowling pins being flung apart. The crack of a ball striking them louder than any grip I could exert. It knocked them away before I could grasp them.

"You tried to kill yourself," the male nurse informed me bluntly.

"Really?" The female seemed almost scandalized. "The doctor wants her to rest and you're trying to scare her."

"Spoiled, rich bitches who try to kill themselves for attention don't deserve to be coddled. She's only here because her family can afford to put her away."

"Get out," the woman snarled with the kind of authority that actually had the bruiser paling.

That was nice of her. I didn't like him, but my vision was already blurring. The sweet smell proved inescapable. My body grew lighter and lighter, until I was floating free of it. Better. Nothing hurt here.

A hum of sound, the woman was still there or maybe she came back. "Don't worry about him, sweetheart. We're going to fix everything. Your uncle told us about those bad men who took you and the abuse you took."

What bad men?

"We'll make sure you're safe here and you won't have to worry about them again. I promise."

I tried to cling to the debris, but it slipped through my numb grasp and the darkness swallowed me whole. Nothing waited there to hurt me. Alone.

Always alone.

But alone at least meant safe.

What bad men?

That thought followed me and a pair of burning blue eyes stared into me as I drifted. I washed up onto a sandy beach where a starling flew overhead. I stared out at the ocean and then down at the sand. I was alone here too. The blue eyes had become blue skies.

Maybe if I walked, I could find… him. Yes, I needed to find… someone again.

A hand on my face woke me. The cold in my veins had tapered off. The nurse was back, she fed me by hand. The first bite was bland and tasted of nothing. Worse, I just ate it. Then she offered me water. The drink slaked what thirst there was. My eyes were too heavy and I didn't finish much before I slept again.

The cold metal was back and I got to pee again. I should have asked about a shower or using the bathroom, but I was so tired.

The shock jolted my system and catapulted me from sleep. I clamped my teeth into the rubber mouth guard. The male nurse stared down at me. No, not me. He looked at something else. The doctor entered my line of sight. Were they talking? Everything buzzed under my skin, like I was the hive and the bees swarmed.

Ice poured into my veins and the shock hit again.

A woman helped me sit up, then guided me from the bed and into a chair. I didn't protest as she wheeled me into a bathroom. There was an ugly mark on the back of my hand. It hurt when I tried to close my fingers. When she tugged away the gown and helped me stand, I had to lean on her. Then I was on a cold stool and warm water cascaded over me.

I was so cold.

"Eat," she instructed and I opened my mouth obediently. At least I thought I did, I couldn't focus for long. The first bite was mushy and warm. I just ate it. The act of swallowing took effort. "Finish all of it," she said. "You're doing a good job."

Great.

I liked doing a good job.

"Rise and shine," the woman said in a relentlessly cheerful voice. "You've got a treatment today, but we're going to get you some sunshine."

Sure.

Whatever.

"How are we feeling today?" the doctor glanced at me as they settled me on the bed. "We've been able to remove the stitches."

"Okay."

That was an answer, right?

I was pretty sure he asked me something else, but I drifted. Anchorless, I floated back out to sea. The beach was growing further and further away.

"Again," the doctor ordered.

I didn't have time to ask what when the buzzing flooded me and the static wiped out the beach, the water, everything.

* * *

The sun spilled through the criss-cross grating on the window. It made a hive pattern on the floor. On my hands. On my legs. Oh, were those my legs? I moved my toes and the slipper in my line of sight shifted.

Cool.

Music played somewhere. The buzzing wasn't just under my skin. There were other sounds. A scraping sound. Paper crinkled. I lifted my head, it weighed a thousand pounds and took forever. I wasn't in a bed, I was in a chair.

The room—the room was different. A man sat in another chair a few feet away, he stared off into space. I didn't know him.

He wasn't the only person there. A girl was on the floor, coloring in a coloring book. That looked like fun. A bell jangled and I couldn't find it.

Oh. There it was.

The television.

I didn't know the show, but they were trying to spell something.

A shock ripped through me and I jerked with each convulsion. It didn't "hurt" but it was unsettling. The static had grown persistent. No more water.

No more beach.

No more… birds?

Why weren't there birds?

"Good morning, Emersyn," the woman greeted me as she opened the door. "Time to shower. I thought we might braid your hair today."

I was still in the bed, staring at the window. It was raining, like the sky shed tears for the day. At first, I'd stared at the rain because the light hadn't come in through the windows and I didn't know what time it was. Then, I just stared because I couldn't get up. The velcro straps kept me in the bed until they came for me.

The nurse didn't waste any time. She hummed as she pulled the strips free. Then she took my temperature and looked in my eyes. I guess I'd been sick for a while if we had to do this every day. My wrists ached, but the bandages were gone.

I studied the row of stitches. They'd oozed at one point, or maybe I'd imagined that.

"Don't worry, those are coming out today," the nurse told me as she helped me sit up and then swung my legs off the bed. I really didn't have to do anything. She did it all. Easier than trying to focus, I supposed.

On my feet, I shuffle stepped into the bathroom. I could do most of this without her. Still, she stayed right there just chattering away about—something. I stopped listening. The routine of washing my hair was almost mechanical. The shower seemed weird though. It was—wrong for some reason.

Maybe it was the fact it was just a skinny stall, or the white and pale green patterned tile didn't match the curtain. Maybe I was in a different room? I debated asking the nurse, but when I asked her about birds before—it had gotten cold and I had to go back to the white static.

I didn't like the static.

So, I didn't ask. Not even if the birds were on my stomach. I liked the pattern. I didn't touch it either. That got me more ice in my veins.

After I finished showering, she wrapped my hair in a towel, then ran a towel over me briskly. I could do this, but she didn't give me the option. The towels weren't soft. They were rough and a little coarse. It sent a sensation dancing over the top of my skin, along with under it. She tugged me back into another gown, it was painfully thin considering I had nothing else on.

In my room, the doctor waited for us.

Oh, I didn't like him.

I'd never liked this doctor.

"Good morning," he said as he gave me a once over. "Let's have a look at those arms."

I didn't take any steps to him.

My skin crawled.

"Come along, sweetheart," the nurse said as she wrapped an arm around me. Even locking my legs wouldn't save me from the forward momentum. She could, and had, lift me on her own. The doctor didn't wait for me to hold out my arms, he just took each wrist and examined them.

"All right, we're going to go ahead and remove these. Janice, can you…"

"Right away."

Then I was alone with the doctor. He turned the light on my eyes and then tilted my head this way and that. I swore it felt like he was going to open my mouth and check my teeth in a minute. "Janice" wasn't long. I sat on the edge of the bed as he donned gloves then began to snip through the stitches at speed. I swore each one stung a little and it was like pins and needles interrupted under each clip of the scissors.

Still didn't know what I'd done to hurt my arms like that. How deep were they? Could I still fly?

Profound sadness suffocated me.

"You will need to take it easy still and therapy sessions will begin in earnest." He kept talking but the white noise hum buzzed back into my ears, and I forgot I was supposed to be listening. I just wanted him to stop touching me.

They both stared at me. I guess they were waiting for an answer, so I nodded.

"Good girl," the doctor said. He brushed his knuckles down my cheek. "Such a good girl for us." Then he glanced at the nurse. "Morning room, we'll do her first therapy session after lunch and then see if she needs a treatment after that."

"Of course, Doctor."

They didn't need me for this part. I ate the food she gave me, though at least I got to hold my own spoon this time. My hand shook a lot, but I managed to get most of the food in my mouth. When she wheeled me out to the morning room, I hoped for sunshine or birds.

The only thing waiting for me was more rain. Janice parked me near the windows then wandered off. I zoned out. There were other people here. There were always other people. Instead, I just traced the water sliding down the windows.

It made me think of the ocean. Water sliding up onto a beach and…

A shadow cut off my view and I frowned. It was hard to focus. I wasn't even sure why it was hard to focus, but…

"Hey," the shadow said as it—wait, not it—he, sat down. Where had the chair come from? I didn't remember there being a chair there. "Fuck, how much juice are you on?"

Juice. "No juice," I said, but it was really hard to make the words work and my voice rasped. "Water. I peed so not a lot."

"Okay." Quiet invaded after that or maybe I stopped listening. It was so hard to focus. "C'mon, Boo-Boo, I know you're in there."

Boo-Boo? I fought to lift my gaze and stared into blue eyes. They were blue. Not the ones I kept seeing, but they were…

"What happened to your arms?" Heat licked those words. So hot it threatened to melt the ice in my veins.

"Mr. Cleary," a voice intruded and then my shadow was gone. Wait…where had he gone? Or had he been there? Janice hustled me down a hallway, she was talking. Had I imagined someone had been there?

Probably better not to ask.

They really didn't like it when I asked things.

Chapter Eighteen

FREDDIE

"Mr. Cleary," the doctor said as he came into the room where I'd been waiting for my *intake*. Liam had to leave me at the front. All I had to do was play sullen and disinterested. Not a problem. I'd been dressed in pajama bottoms, a t-shirt and socks with some expensive fucking slippers on. If not for the fact we were going to the fancy pants loony bin, I might have given Liam shit about them.

As it was, Liam wasn't alone in delivering me. While Rome stayed in the car, his gaze fixed on the gothic looking building, Liam had two men escort me inside *with* him. I couldn't say I was a fan of the hired muscle. Still, we'd all had a part to play and theirs was to make sure I got in and stayed in.

What. Ever.

I barely glanced at the doc. Expert counselors, nurses, and orderlies comprised the majority of the staff of Pinetree Psychiatric. It had only one full time doctor. Convenient. Told me exactly who I needed to stab.

The fact he was within arm's reach made him a tempting target.

Really tempting. Not until I found Boo-Boo. That was the point of this exercise. Since the goal was for me to be hostile and morose, I didn't have to do shit.

"I'm Doctor Schuitevoerder," he began as he circled the room to take a seat on the opposite side of the table. Dude was pretty fucking brave coming in here by himself. Course, the guys probably hadn't added *violence* to my record.

I'd make sure to add that for them. Then because I couldn't resist, I said, "Gesundheit."

The doctor gave me a bland look. "Mr. Cleary, or do you prefer Frederick?"

Right, nope. I went back to staring at the wall. My lack of answer didn't seem to be much of a deterrent for the scumbag doc.

"It says here you answer to Freddie, but I'm going to insist on Mr. Cleary until we've developed a rapport. To that end, I will also request you to call me Doctor Schuitevoerder."

Rolling my head from side to side, I savored the crack of my vertebrae. "Gesundheit."

"And," Doctor Sneeze continued as if I hadn't spoken, "I will require your attendants to also address you as Mr. Cleary. Let's make it clear from the beginning, Mr. Cleary, you are here as a patient. Your records indicate a troubled history of drug abuse, pandering, excessive partying, and self-destructive behaviors. None of those will be tolerated here at Pinetree."

Sounded pretty fucking boring. Then again, torture probably wasn't something they wanted to advertise.

"We're going to concentrate on your routine. You will have a private room. Breakfast will be held in the common area. There's a community room for recreation. We'll have your morning sessions with group, then afternoon sessions with your individual therapists. Patients are restricted to the controlled areas for the first ten days or so, but adherence to the rules will earn you a pass sooner, rather than later."

Man, he could drone on and on and on.

"Lunches can be taken in the community room, but dinners will be in the dining hall. Again, we encourage socialization…"

Now we were talking. I definitely wanted to socialize while I was here. Specifically, with Boo-Boo.

"…to that end, however, we also require that patients maintain a healthy social distance from each other, emotionally as well as physically. Friendships can be beneficial, but not everyone here is ready for a relationship, positive or otherwise."

Man, he was a dick.

"For example, you might strike up a conversation with someone because of group, but you need to understand that their physical and mental wellbeing are as important to us as your own. That means we'll ask you to respect their space and to keep your hands to yourself."

Were we done yet?

"Do you understand?"

I could write him a fucking essay if he needed it, but I wouldn't. Right now, I just wanted out to their common area. I needed to see Boo-Boo. I needed to put my hands on her and just *feel* that she was okay.

"Mr. Cleary?"

I glanced at him.

When I continued to say nothing, he favored me with a dark look. "You should say, yes, Doctor Schuitevoerder."

"Gesundheit."

His eyes narrowed and his nostrils flared. Yep. The man did not want to be teased about his name. Thank you for playing, and showing me a weakness.

"Are we done now?" I asked. "I'm tired."

The doctor didn't quite glare at me. But he also wasn't *not* glaring. Yeah, he had buttons. I had a partial combination. Give me time and I'd drive him mad. That would be the start of the payback I wanted to deliver.

"Let's go over the rules then, shall we?"

I'd rather poke sticks in my eyes, but sure, why not? It took him a half hour to go over the rules. They were basically the same thing, just rephrased slightly differently. Boring as fuck, didn't begin to cover it. A nurse interrupting saved my sanity, this particular trip.

"Doctor Schuitevoerder?" she said as she opened the door.

"Gesundheit," I told her. The doctor slammed the file down on the table.

Temper temper.

"Yes?" It was like he had to grind the word out between his teeth. Must suck to be him. And if it didn't now, I fully intended for it to suck later.

"You have an appointment in ten minutes, you asked me to remind you?"

"Ah, thank you, Ms. Hassmen," he said.

Wow. That was just too easy.

"Mr. Cleary, this is Ms. Hassmen."

"Assmen?" I repeated cause, c'mon.

The doctor glared this time. Oh, he felt that one. Good good. "*Hass*men," Doctor Sneeze repeated.

"Oh." Bummer. I preferred Assmen. Lots more possibilities there. Still. "Ms. Assmen," I greeted her.

The doctor's teeth came together with a click. "Get Broderick, have him take Mr. Cleary to his room and get him settled. He'll need to surrender everything and change his clothes. He can check out books or other materials from the library. At the moment, he has decided to be belligerent. When his attitude adjusts, we'll discuss letting him have his things again."

"Do I have to go to bed without supper?" I called as the doctor headed for the door.

"Don't tempt me, Mr. Cleary," the doctor responded when he stood in the doorway. He swept a cool look over me. "Don't press your luck."

Doctor, I haven't even begun pressing my luck. While Ms. *Ass*men wasn't bad to look at, she had ass for miles, she also wasn't the person who took me to my room. No, that was Broderick. Big. Broad. And stupid looking. Like an ox.

Sweat trickled down my spine as he "escorted" me by the arm down the hall. Instinct told me to jerk away from the grip he had on my arm. I ignored it. Just like I ignored the sour way my sweat smelled. It was fine, I was supposed to look strung out.

The hallway was bad enough, but the room with its narrow walls and tiny cot was a lot worse. Broderick didn't leave a lot of room for oxygen to fill the place. "Strip," the man ordered after we were in there.

Yeah. I'd pass.

He didn't even look at me as he went back out into the hall. The door was wide open, the cold, white and sterile environment didn't offer any kind of encouragement. The ox didn't go far. He used keys to open a cabinet in the hallway and came back with a pair of pale gray pajamas. Dropping them on the bed, he folded his arms.

"Get changed."

The sweat trickling down my spine increased. "Tell you what, big guy," I said with a hell of a lot more confidence than I was feeling without my knife. I could hurt him. I knew how. But I'd prefer my blade, cause he had to have a good fifty pounds on me. "Get the fuck out and give me some privacy and I'll think about it."

Unimpressed would be a great word for his expression. He met me stare for stare. So, I mirrored his posture and folded my arms. No way in hell was I getting naked in front of some fucking stranger. They could knock my ass out if they wanted that. But Liam's name carried a lot of weight, so did his family wealth.

I was the cocky rich bastard's prick younger brother.

"Or we can just call Doctor Sneeze."

The ox blinked at me. "Doctor—oh Schuitevoerder."

"Gesundheit."

"Look, punk, I don't care what you call him or what he calls you. Doctor said you needed to change and get settled. So strip, put on the clothes and stop wasting my time."

"Or what?"

The man glared. A riot of fury in his eyes as he raked his gaze over me. "Or you're about to have a really bad first day."

Don't.

I swore Jasper's voice was like it was right there, as if he stood just over my shoulder.

Don't get dead.

Fighting this guy was a way to get dead. Sure. But I wasn't going to roll over and submit myself to his scrutiny either. Fuck. That.

The sweat had begun to soak through my shirt.

"Broderick," the nurse from earlier was back. "We need you to help move Mr. Delaney." She glanced past him to me. "I can stay with Mr. Cleary."

The woman had to be in her mid to late thirties, maybe. I wouldn't put her much into her forties. She seemed nice enough. Not Ms. Stephanie nice, but *way* better than Broderick nice.

"Fine, I'll deal with Delaney, but if the little shit hasn't changed his clothes by the time I'm back, I'll do it for him." Yeah, that last was definitely a threat.

Broderick's name was on the list.

As soon as he left, the nurse frowned at me. "He's a bit of a bully, but don't push him. He has no respect whatsoever for your name or your family. To him you're just another patient. Now, I'm going to close this door and count to one hundred then open it again. Please be changed so we don't have to endure what he would do next."

The moment she closed the door, I stripped out of the clothes and put on the new ones. I didn't care about keeping the pajamas we'd bought on the way here, nor did I give a damn if I ever saw them again. Resisting the temptation to hide weapons or anything else on me had taken some effort. There was no guarantee they wouldn't search me or my shit.

Or that they would do exactly what they just had, taken my clothes and left me with nothing. Raking a hand through my hair, I retreated to sit on the bed and waited. The nurse opened the door right on the count of one hundred and she smiled at me.

"Thank you," she said. "Mr. Cleary." The name seemed to be an afterthought.

"You're welcome, Ms. Assmen."

The corners of her mouth twitched. "Hassmen," she corrected.

"Looks more like a really nice ass to me, and I don't need to know if you *has* men or not."

Surprise rippled across her expression, followed by her cheeks turning pink as she retrieved my clothes. Oh? Wait for it. Yeah, she opened her mouth twice then closed it without saying anything. Finally, she retreated to the door.

After clearing her throat, she said, "This door remains unlocked during the day—for now. Behavior can dictate a change in your condition. This room opens onto the main hall and if you follow me, I can show you where the community room is. You're allowed to go there or stay in here."

Well, wasn't that just fucking special. I summoned a smile. "Lead the way, Ms. Assmen. I can't wait to follow you."

Her blush deepened and she pivoted away to hurry ahead of me. Yeah, I was being a bit of a douche, but I didn't want her paying attention to me. If anything, I wanted her to be uncomfortable and *away* from me.

The community room was just that, a big ass room with some chairs, tables, a television, and a couple of lounge like chairs. There were games, puzzles, and other shit to do. I didn't recognize the show on the television, but I parked myself in one of the chairs and waited.

Everyone came to the community room.

Right?

Three days of wash, rinse, repeat and pissing off Doctor Sneeze to the point that on the fourth day he passed me to one of the staff therapists. Fine by me. I didn't like him in the first place. Ox boy Broderick stayed away, but the blushing Assmen came to see me all the time. She even snuck me chocolate when I skipped eating the slop they served for dinner.

I bet if I worked for it, I'd get a blowjob out of her next. But that wasn't why I was here and it wasn't what I wanted.

At all.

What I wanted was…

The door opened and a nurse I didn't know walked in pushing a wheelchair, and all the oxygen in the room sucked out into the vacuum of nothingness. Boo-Boo sat in that chair, dressed in the same pale gray as me, only hers was more a gown, rather than pajamas. Her eyes were vacant, glazed over and gone.

I forgot I even needed to breathe as the nurse parked her by the window. When the nurse walked away, Boo-Boo just sat there. Nothing. No reaction. Did she even know she was in the room? My head ached and my chest squeezed. Right. I sucked in a breath of air and stood up.

"Hey," I said as I reached where they'd parked her. Fortunately, there was a table right there with some—magazine on it—so I pulled up a chair. She barely even noticed me, or if she did, there was no reaction. Her pupils were the size of saucers. I'd been there before. Fucking flying on something. "Fuck, how much juice are you on?"

"No juice," she replied in a sandpaper dry voice that made my throat hurt. "Water. I peed, so not a lot."

"Okay." Yeah, she was higher than a fucking kite. I wanted to kill every fucking person here. She'd been so clean and crisp at the clubhouse, even when she'd been hurting. The day she got stoned with the guys notwithstanding, and this was so not that. It fucking killed me. "C'mon, Boo-Boo, I know you're in there."

For the first time since she got here, she turned those sightless eyes on me and I shuddered. They were so fucking empty. What had they done to her? Just like that, I was trying to mentally inventory everything about her. Her movement shifted the sleeves on her gown. There were— "What happened to your arms?" Scars marked them—

ugly, red scars.

They were all going to die the most painful fucking deaths possible.

"Mr. Cleary," the fucking Ox Broderick was back. Dead man walking number two. "You have group."

"That was this morning," I told him.

"Things change. Let's go."

Everything in me wanted to go to Boo-Boo, but she hadn't even looked my way when I started speaking.

Fuck.

Mental fingers crossed, I followed the other guy to group. Sixty hellish minutes later, I was back in the community room, but she was gone.

The next day, she arrived at the same time and they decided to haul me out again. Okay. Fine.

I punched the therapist in the group session. That got me locked in my room for twenty-four hours, a sedative—not bad—a new therapist, and a new time.

When they brought her in on the fourth day, no one called me out.

Chapter Nineteen

EMERSYN

The coolness of a cloth over my face barely penetrated the layers of fog and cotton. I kind of liked it here. It was quiet. The air was soft. No expectations. Barely anyone to talk to or who would intrude. I could float.

The floating wasn't flying. That thought brought a twinge with it. I missed flying. Then again, if I wasn't flying—I couldn't fall. I was so tired of falling. Whether I hit a ledge or an outcropping, the battering hurt. It hurt even more when the pain lit me up inside and out. I was so tired of hurting.

"Dove, you don't have to hurt anymore," Vaughn said in that beautiful voice of his. That voice followed me everywhere. I swore it lulled me to sleep. It drifted through the air with me as I floated. "Head up, yeah? Head up and wings out."

"I don't know if I can anymore," I admitted. "I think my wings are gone."

"Clipped, maybe," he conceded. "But if you want them to unfurl, Dove, they'll be there. How did you learn to fly to begin with?"

"I was running away. It was the only way to be free. When I was

there—when I flew—I wasn't me." I didn't much like me.

"You're more than flight, though."

All too soon though, he wandered away and I drifted some more. The cold came and went. Sometimes it brought the white noise, other times there were glimmers of sun. The doctor wanted me to talk, but I didn't have much to say. It was almost too much effort anyway. No one really cared what I had to say.

"Of course, I fucking care," Jasper said with a snarl and the chair scraped against the floor as he sat down. The scent of tobacco fluttered through the air. Why was he sitting when we could float? "Because the fire is here," he pointed out and then the cool gray resolved to the roof of the clubhouse.

The wind was icy here and it made my teeth ache. Why were we up here? Then he passed me the joint and I stared at it for a moment. Oh. Maybe getting high wasn't flying but I wanted to escape. This was a good way to do it, right?

"Talk to me, Swan," he encouraged me after we sat there a while just passing the joint back and forth. The soft cotton layers separating me from the world thickened. Except Jasper was right here with me. I could reach out and touch him if I wanted. In fact, I did, and our fingers brushed every time we passed the blunt back and forth.

"About what?" Did he know he needed a haircut? Not that I minded. I liked that his hair curled under his collar sometimes. I liked his beard even more.

"Yeah?" He rubbed a hand against it. The colorful tattoos on his arm pulled my attention. "You like it?"

"I like a lot of things about you."

"Even when I make you mad?"

I grinned. The expression was almost foreign on my face. "Maybe especially when you make me mad."

"Why especially?" He waved the blunt back and forth, the haze of smoke seemed to soften him, or maybe it was the lights in his room. The soft fairy lights. Oh, I'd liked them. It was like starlight captured in one place. Kind of like being here in the gray, just us, the chairs, and the fire.

"Because you don't want anything from me enough to lie and pretend we're something we're not." It kind of made sense in my head. "Even when you didn't tell me why you knew me before, you told me why you took me. I didn't understand then."

I did now.

All too soon he drifted away, and I sighed as I seemed to be sinking. It never seemed to last. Hands grabbed at me. Locking me down. Then the ice and the static came again.

He didn't even seem to notice me as he painted and I didn't mind. If anything, I huddled into the coat and just watched him. I could watch him for hours. Instead of a beach, though, he painted a cell, the bars forming from the disintegrating pieces of my life. Always in a cage, even when I thought I'd flown away, I was still in the cage. The only thing that changed were what they used for bars.

"Miss Sharpe," the voice said. "This will go easier if you participate."

Sure, it would. I didn't want to talk to him though, I wanted to go back to the painting. Even if it was a cage. It was nice there.

"You know, Boo-Boo, this is getting awfully boring."

"Why is it boring?" The air was warmer, but maybe it was because of the way we drifted together. I was lying on my back and he was right next to me. It would be kind of funny to do the backstroke in the air, I'd done something like that before when I first learned the silks.

"This whole place is boring. Don't you think?" Freddie nudged me and a little laugh escaped.

"It's not so bad. Not really. I like it—it's peaceful."

"Peace is a lie, Boo-Boo."

I made a face. "Don't say that."

"Why not?"

"Cause I want it to be peaceful." Maybe I wanted the lie.

"Do you?"

I didn't know. "I don't want to talk about it."

"Okay." Wow, that was easy. "How about we read instead?"

I groaned. "I'm tired."

"It's okay. I'll read to you, okay?" The last "okay" sounded uncertain.

I wanted to drift, but… "Do you need to read to me?"

"Maybe," he said. "Do you remember when you sat outside my door and read?"

"You never opened the door." Sadness crawled through me. "I just wanted to help."

"You did, Boo-Boo. You did."

Then why didn't you open the door? Only the words didn't come out and Freddie drifted away just like… Oh, I was too tired to think of them right now. The cold was coming. And the doctor.

I didn't have wings anymore. If I had wings, I'd fly away.

* * *

"You still floating here feeling sorry for yourself?"

Oh, of all the people. "Don't," I said.

"Why not, Hellspawn? You don't want to be a princess, why the hell are you letting them lock you up in a damn tower?"

"Stop." I couldn't do this with him. I just couldn't.

"Not happening." Then he was there, looming over me. "Get off your ass, Hellspawn."

"No."

"Get up."

"No."

"I said…" Only when he reached for me this time, I flung my hand out and knocked his away. "No."

"It's about time, Hellspawn," he whispered. "Now fucking fight."

But I did fight. It didn't stop anything and even when the pain bit into my arms, I struck back.

"Sedate her."

"It's been a couple of days," Freddie said, sitting down with me again. There was light dappling the gray, but it was hard to care. I couldn't even float now. Chains kept me in place. Chains and ice. It would just be so much easier if they'd let me float away.

"Sorry," I whispered. "I think I got lost."

"Well, I'm here with you," he told me and covered my hand with his. "Maybe we can be lost together."

Surprise rippled through me. His hand was warm. Warmer than the dappled room with its glittering light that made my eyes hurt. My throat was dry too.

"You're touching me."

"Do you want me to stop?"

I had to think about that. Did I? "You don't like touching people." I wasn't even sure why I knew that. It felt right, though.

"You're not people, Boo-Boo."

Oh, that was fair. "Can I tell you something?"

"Sure. I'd like you to tell me all the things."

I laughed. It wasn't funny and at the same time, it was. "You guys keep coming to talk to me and it's getting quieter. Like...I can't hear you as much anymore."

"Well, we gotta be quiet right now."

"You do?" Why? Only that last word wouldn't come out.

"Yeah, for a little while."

"Okay, I'll be quiet with you."

He sighed. "Boo-Boo..."

"Miss Sharpe," the doctor said and this time he sat right in my line of sight. "I wanted to talk to you about how you are feeling today."

"Okay."

I let him talk. He didn't care what I had to say anyway.

"Hey," Freddie said and surprise dislodged some of the static.

"Freddie?"

"Yeah, it's me, Boo-Boo." He clasped my hand again.

"You came back."

"I'm here. I'll be here tomorrow, too. I promise."

No one could promise that. No one. I wish they could. "My arm hurts."

"What happened?"

What had happened? "I don't know. I don't even know why it hurts."

Freddie blurred as I blinked, trying to bring him into focus. Head tilted, he seemed really focused on me. "There she is..."

"Yep, here I am." It seemed silly to say it, but the corners of his mouth twitched and I swore my heart did a fist bump with my ribs. "I miss you so much." The words escaped. "I miss all of you."

"I've missed you, too." He squeezed my hand. "I told you not to go. Remember?"

"I had to." Another sigh. "I can't talk about this here."

"No?" He cut his gaze away from me. I would turn to look but it took a lot of effort to look at him here. "You can tell me anything."

"No," I said. "I can't. It's not safe."

"Boo-Boo." This time when he squeezed my hand, he pulled my gaze to his. "I'm here to get you out of this place."

"That's really sweet, Freddie." So incredibly sweet and it made me so sad.

"Hey, why are you crying?" His eyes changed and so did his hair. Nothing was real here. Not even floating. "Boo-Boo... godfucking

dammit if that asshole comes over here now…" The last few words came out on gritted teeth.

I went still though, maybe Freddie needed to hide. I got that. I wanted to hide, too.

"Is it okay now?" It had been a few minutes and Freddie hadn't moved. My lips were dry and so was my mouth.

"Yeah," he said slowly, then cut his gaze back to me. "C'mon, Boo-Boo, you all here with me now?"

"Maybe." I shrugged. "I don't want to be."

"With me? Or here?"

"I like you," I said then winced.

"I like you too, what are you afraid of?"

I shook my head. "This isn't a good place and it's not safe. You shouldn't be here."

"That's both of us," he told me firmly. Freddie being serious was weird. It made my heart hurt a little. The pain crept in under the number and the static, like pins and needles stabbing me as I woke up. "And I'm getting us out of here. I just need you focused, Boo-Boo. Can you do that?"

"It's really sweet," I told him. Had we had this conversation? "So sweet. No one's ever tried to before. But it won't work."

He frowned. "Come on, don't fade on me. How much shit are they juicing you on?"

"I don't know," I admitted. "The feeling comes and goes. It's coming back now. It shouldn't be. I don't even know why…"

"Well, it might be cause I've been pocketing your pills," Freddie admitted.

Pills? I had pills? I frowned. "Why would you do that?"

"Cause I need you to wake up. I need you to hear me."

"I could hear you before." I sighed. "Freddie, don't do this. It won't work. My uncle always wins. It doesn't matter how much I hate him. He's trying to take it all away again and it's fading…I don't want you here because I don't want you to fade too."

"How does your uncle always win?"

A giggle escaped. He was so serious, so intense, so—unFreddie it was almost scary. At the same time, he was Freddie. I put a finger to my lips.

"Boo-Boo, tell me about your uncle."

"Can't," I whispered around my finger. "Not supposed to talk about that. Can't ever talk about it. Bad things happen when I tell."

His whole face changed, his smile vanished and his eyes went cold. It was the gray, it was coming to fade him and I shook my head.

"Shh, no more—we don't talk about him. Not here." The more I woke up the more it all hurt. "It's time to go Freddie…you can't stay here with me."

The frown he wore worried me. Then Janice came and she glanced down at me. "It's time to go, Miss Sharpe, are you ready hon?"

"Yes," I answered. Freddie cut his gaze from me to Janice and back, but I tugged my hand away from him and pretended he wasn't there. If he wasn't there, they couldn't take him away from me.

"It's time for a treatment. The doctor is worried about your progress," she said as she wheeled me out of the room. I could barely walk anymore. That was fine. Soon, I'd be floating again. They would all be safe and hidden away. The cold room was waiting for me and the ice was in my veins. Hands gripped me and lifted me.

Fighting served no purpose, no matter what Liam said.

"Did you make a new friend today?" Janice asked as she pulled the blanket over me. Not that it helped with the cold. The shivering had already started and the gray edged my vision.

"What?"

With a gentle smile, Janice leaned closed. "The young man you were talking to? Did you make a friend? Don't worry—I won't tell. I think we could all use a friend."

The young man.

Freddie was really here?

"Shh," she said and the ice in my veins increased. "It's okay. Go to sleep."

But—Freddie was here? He'd really come to get me?

Then the white static came.

Chapter Twenty

FREDDIE

Mornings at Pinetree started the same way. A nurse opened the door, flicked back the curtains, then handed me two pills. I had to swallow them with a sip of water while she observed, then I had to stick out my tongue so she could see they were gone.

With a nod, she pivoted and left the room, letting the door half-close behind her. They weren't allowed to be completely closed unless it was bedtime or movements had been restricted. I'd already done twenty-four hours in this box under the influence. I gave it a minute for her to go into the next room before I slid out of the bed.

The bathroom didn't have a door on it. I guess I was lucky it was a bathroom. As high-end as this place was—and it was high-end, it didn't even stink—it was still a facility for whackjobs and troublemakers. I could make the argument it was a place I belonged, but definitely not Boo-Boo.

Soon as I had my dick out and pissing, I coughed into my free hand. Cupping it like a fist, I caught both pills in my palm. Everyone had skills. That just happened to be one of mine. Head back, I stared at the ceiling while I emptied my bladder. The pill regimen was to "quiet" my nerves.

Yeah, I got it. They wanted me *calm*. Punching a therapist would do that. Whatever. I needed to stay as *clean* as fucking possible. Especially while Emersyn was so completely fucking wasted. I couldn't figure out the wheelchair when they first brought her in.

I got it now.

There was no way she could walk completely plastered on whatever fucking cocktail they were feeding her. I'd done an eight ball and not been that wasted. Then again, if they were pumping her full of sedatives to keep her *calm*, it wouldn't surprise me.

I dropped the pills into the toilet as I flushed and then turned to take a seat. One thing that worked in my favor. If I was taking a crap, they weren't coming to look in the toilet bowl.

If it wasn't broke, don't fix it. They still hadn't let me have any of my things, not that I cared. I didn't want to hole up in the room. Unlike a lot of the patients, they didn't leave Emersyn alone for long when they brought her to the community room.

I needed every minute I could get with her. Especially when she couldn't even focus on the fact I was right fucking there. She was on more than pills. No one got that checked out on just a couple of tablets—unless they were risking overdosing her.

The fog in her eyes, the distance—the fact she stared right through me—yeah, I wasn't gonna take it personal. I mean, I would. But I was gonna take it out personally on every single fucker in this place. Even the nurse who made nicey nice with her. The woman looked like a grandmother.

Grandmothers could be sacks of shit. It was sexist to think it was only dirty old men.

"Breakfast," a new nurse said as she pushed my door inward. No one would mistake this chick for a grandmother. I'd be shocked if she was older than me. "Let's go, I don't have all day."

Oh, now I was just gonna go slower. I stretched. The bed here sucked. If they spent any of their exorbitant fees on the furniture, they were getting ripped. Then again, they had *plastic* chairs in the community room and the television in there wouldn't know HD if it walked up to it and bit it in the ass.

The nurse stuck her head back in. "Are you coming? Or do I need to call Broderick?"

"Who pissed in your Wheaties, Powder Puff?" Cause she looked like one of those anime characters with her stringy red hair all pulled up and done in a wild array of braids. The heavy eyeliner would look better on a raccoon. Then again… "Did you get a little tickle and poke that didn't quite hit the spot this morning? Sounds like a 'you' problem."

Her gaze went positively glacial. Man, it was too fucking easy. Poke. Poke. Poke.

"If you want, I can give your guy a few pointers. Or your girl. I mean, free world and all that."

Nostrils flaring, she took a step toward me and her hand clenched, but Broderick stuck his big ugly ass ox head in.

"Problem?"

"Nah," I said. "Nurse Mindy here is hitting on me and I get that I'm a catch, you know, who wouldn't want a piece of this? Am I right? But it's all kinds of inappropriate."

"You son of a—"

"Amber," a woman said sharply behind her and I met *Amber's* heated gaze with a smile.

"Oops, sorry, didn't realize it was a secret."

Broderick just scowled. "Stop playing around and let's go. Or you can just go hungry, Mr. Cleary."

"Well, we haven't tried that yet," I said. "First time for everything." But I shuffled along like the cooperative, stoned patient I was supposed to be. Communal meals were held in a little dining room, not all the patients were here.

Boo-Boo never had meals with us.

She wasn't the only one I saw in the community room and not at meals. There was an older guy named Chester. He had arthritic hands and rheumy eyes. I was pretty sure he wasn't even in the same year as we were, but he wasn't so bad. His favorite topics of conversation involved the Donny and Marie Show. No idea who they were, but he really liked them.

Breakfast turned out to be oatmeal. Looked more like slop, but whatever. I ate it. I just ate it all slow and shit cause, you know, stoned.

The other person who came into the community room that was never at meals was a woman who had to be like Ms. Stephanie's age. Maybe a little younger. She didn't talk to anyone. She just wandered in circles. Sometimes, she put herself in the corner and talked to the wall.

Been there, sister. Totally.

After food, it was time for group.

Let me tell you how much I enjoyed the fuck out of group. Eight people were present in my group. Two of them were considered semi-violent. They were my favorites. Julius had a habit of lashing out, so he had to attend in a straight jacket. An orderly was always with him, too. His buddy, Bodhi. First, Bodhi had a cool damn name. Second, Bodhi was certifiable.

When it was his turn to talk, he liked to tell everyone how he was going to kill them. Sometimes going into explicit details. Our therapist—Marc what a putz—tried to keep him focused, but that just made Bodhi start over at the beginning. I'd been in this group three days and I figured it out day one, just let the man get his rocks off and move the fuck on.

"You," Bodhi said, focusing on me.

"Me," I agreed. "Tell me how you're gonna do it. Give me something cool, not something cheap like drowning me in a toilet or sticking a wire through my eye and into my brain. No, wait, it was up the nose and then swirling it around like that thing they used to do to mummies. Saw it in a movie once." I tapped the side of my head. "But I want something original."

Bodhi stared at me for a long moment. "Not gonna kill you." Then he sat back in his chair.

Well, damn, and here I'd been hoping for the good shit. What a fucking bummer.

"Mr. Cleary," the therapist said. "Since Mr. Bodhi has decided against engaging you, maybe you'd like to take your turn."

"I'm good."

Marc gave me a small smile as he sat forward. Dressed in a polo shirt the color of something that got into a fight with a winter green mint and lost, Marc was way too damn cheerful. He had prep school vibrations, big money, heavy spender, and not one fucking clue about the real world, written all over him. "Mr. Cleary, that's not how this works. Everyone who comes to group has to share. It doesn't have to be deep."

Right.

"How about I share, that I don't want to share with a bunch of fucking strangers in an overpriced hotel for crackpots and madmen?"

"Crackpots and madmen," Julius repeated with the best cackle.

He could give the damn Joker a run for his money. "Crackpots and madmen."

The therapist sighed. "I understand this can be difficult…"

That was the point I tuned him out and just stared stupidly past him at the wall. He asked me a few questions, most of which I ignored.

When he said, "Is self-harm something you've struggled with for a while now, Mr. Cleary?" I checked back in.

"What?"

"Self-harm," Marc repeated. "You were very interested in what Mr. Bodhi offered."

I snorted. "If I was interested in self-harm, I wouldn't be asking him how he'd do it. Besides, he's got a lot of creative ways to kill folks. Didn't you hear the one about the ropes and the hangman's noose? I like to admire art. Too many artists aren't even acknowledged until they're dead."

"Thank you," Mr. Bodhi said and I nodded.

"You're welcome."

The fact Marc, the cheerful therapist, ground his teeth hard enough it made the muscle in his jaw twitch was just a point in my corner. Yay me.

Thankfully, he moved the fuck on and I could daydream through the rest of the session. I'd gotten to spend some time with Boo-Boo twice now, but she didn't seem to grasp that I was here.

That stung.

Not as much as it would when I figured out what they were doing to her. The marks on her arms were the ones that worried me the most. I had two long silvery scars from my wrists to my elbows. You could barely see them. One was hidden under a tattoo, but not the other. I found myself tracing that one as I waited for her to show up.

The midday pills were harder to get rid of. I ended up swallowing one. That sucked, but at least it took the edge off some of my anger. Not all of it. Nope. But some. They brought Boo-Boo in late, I almost didn't think she'd make it.

Instead of talking though, she just stared. They hadn't angled her toward the windows like they normally did. Course, the grandmother wasn't with her. It was the cunt from earlier that morning. Amber or something. Whatever. She didn't even engage the lock before she walked away with her phone in her hand.

What. A. Bitch.

Yeah, I'd work a little harder at fucking up her days. The older woman was over in her corner talking to the wall. Chester was at a table with a puzzle, but he was just staring at the windows. Right. Okay. I wandered over to Boo-Boo. Her empty stare went right through me.

Yep, really gonna make these fuckers hurt. I wanted to get Boo-Boo out of here, but I had to get her off whatever they had her on. I pushed her right up to the table with Chester, then dragged a chair over to sit with them.

"We doing the puzzle then, man?" I asked him, but Chester just twitched in his chair. Kind of like how Boo-Boo twitched in hers. And the Nutter Lady twitched and talked to the wall. The other patients in the room were either zoned out or just staring at the television. Some were doing both.

The orderlies and the nurses were behind their desk or just not around. Nurses like Amber just played on their phones. One of the other orderlies came in with another newcomer—no wait, that was Bodhi. Huh. Breakthrough in group, I guess.

"Boo-Boo," I said as I reached for a puzzle piece. "Gonna need you to shake this shit off. That pretty pussy of yours isn't doing us any good stuck in this hell hole." While I didn't focus on him, I kept track of Bodhi as he settled at a table not far from mine.

We locked eyes for a brief moment and he pointed a finger at me. Yeah, I nodded. Still me.

"Not gonna kill ya," the guy mouthed and I shrugged. Good for him. He didn't look at Boo-Boo either.

Meant he got to keep his eyes. I liked crazy. Just not near her.

"I wish you were here," Boo-Boo said, softly. "I mean, I don't. I know you're not, Vaughn. But I miss you guys."

"They miss you too," I said. "Wake up and help me and we can get out of here."

For a moment, awareness seemed to flicker in her soft doe eyes. The darkness sliding into them didn't offer any kind of comfort. Sick as it might be, I preferred it to the emptiness. The darkness we could fight. The emptiness would swallow us.

"Freddie," she said on a soft exhale. "I had a dream about you."

"Was I naked?"

For a moment, the corners of her mouth twitched, and I swore my heart slammed into my ribs in desperation to get one real laugh, one small smile, something that told me Boo-Boo was there. As it was, I wanted to kill every single person in here. They should be really happy I didn't have my knife.

I was going to have to put something together.

"No," she said, then hesitated. "I don't think so anyway."

"Did I do anything fun in your dream?" I managed to put a couple of the puzzle pieces together. I didn't even know what picture I was building, I just looked for the pieces that matched.

"You talked to me."

"Cool," I said. "I like talking to you."

A faint smile curved her lips and I had to drag my gaze off her, because even if I was supposed to be vacant and stupid, staring would get noticed. Not that anyone seemed to care that I was just sitting here talking to her.

"I like talking to you, too." A long sigh. "I wish I was there with you."

A part of me wanted to scream that she was with me. But… "What are they doing here, Boo-Boo? Why don't you want to be here?"

"Because they want me to forget. I don't want to forget."

Lainey said something about that. The Ball-Cracker had definitely been on to something. "What do they want you to forget?"

"Freedom." The weight of the world hung on those two syllables. "Birds. The clubhouse. M—" She stopped abruptly and put a finger to her lips. "No, can't say his name."

Whose— "Raptor?"

All at once her pupils seemed to shrink a little and she looked at me. Really looked at me. "Don't say it," she said in a rush whisper. "Please. They said I've been traumatized. But if he finds out about him—he'll kill him."

Who?

Her uncle.

The threats.

"We saw the pictures, Boo-Boo." It was a risk.

"Please," she whispered, fucking begging me. "He thinks I'm his. If he thinks anyone can take me away or will help me—he will hurt them. He'll hurt you."

I'd really love to see him fucking try.

"Shh," I said, covering her hand when she reached out to me and I slid a puzzle piece into her fingers. "We're going to put all the pieces together, see?"

She stared down at the piece, then at me. That's it Boo-Boo. See me.

"Freddie." Her fingers tightened under mine but I didn't let her go. I cut a glance to the orderlies and watchers. No one looked this way yet. "You're here."

"Yep," I said almost out of the corner of my mouth. "Nowhere else I'd rather be, Boo-Boo."

Tears shimmered in her eyes.

She was killing me.

"Puzzle pieces, Boo-Boo. I need you to work on the puzzle. Can you do that for me?"

It took her a moment, she turned the puzzle piece over in her hand and another chair yanked out from the table and I jerked at the sudden arrival of Bodhi.

"I like puzzles," he said as he took a seat then he looked at Chester and finally Boo-Boo. Looking at me, he grinned. "Wanna hear how I'm gonna kill the staff?"

You know… I kind of did.

"Later," I said, then nodded to Boo-Boo. Her hand still trembled under mine. "Puzzle first."

Bodhi didn't say anything, but Boo-Boo licked her lips and then she moved the piece she had to the one next to me. The one I knew matched. She put them together.

Another smile graced her lips. "This is a bad idea."

"Maybe." I told her. "But we'll have it together and you won't be alone."

"Cool," Bodhi said as he began to snap pieces together. "I like this group better."

Me too, man. Me too.

Chapter Twenty One

JASPER

"You're an asshole!" floated up the hallway from the direction of Milo's suite. Leaning back on the sofa in the sitting room of the clubhouse, I shook my head and snuffed out the cigarette.

"Maybe what you need more of in your life is an asshole," Milo retaliated, the growl in his voice punching it up a notch. If I didn't know better, I'd swear the man was enjoying it. Then again, I didn't really give a damn if he was enjoying it or not. I did have a problem with the fact that she was Emersyn's friend. A friend he seemed well acquainted with, or at least seemed to know exactly who she was before she got here. But…

But Emersyn wasn't here. Her friend was. Milo was taking it personally.

Weren't we all?

"Do you know how many assholes I already had in my life? I don't need you or yours!" The sound of a slamming door punctuated the end of that sentence. I was hard-pressed not to laugh my ass off at both of them. God, she could get under Milo's skin. It was almost as much fun as watching Emersyn make him dance.

Kellan walked out from the kitchen with a beer in hand and stared at me. I lifted my shoulders. We were stuck and there wasn't a fucking thing we could do until we either got word on the next shipment, or word on Freddie. And I was doing my absolute damnedest to not focus on the fact that Freddie was in that place with Emersyn. It was bad enough she was there. Now Freddie.

Fucking Freddie.

Making my life hell even when he was miles away.

He'd like that. Another half-laugh escaped me.

He'd really fucking like it.

Neither Kellan or I said anything, as Milo descended the steps and stalked across the room towards the kitchen, where he vanished. I was pretty sure he hadn't even noticed us. The rattle of bottles clinking as the fridge door opened suggested that like Kellan and me, Milo needed a beer. Kellan tracked the motion and then looked back at me. I shrugged again. For once, I didn't have any answers. Or even a guess really.

Milo was in his own goddamn world. I hated every fucking minute he spent in prison.

Hated it.

Hated the why behind it and the necessity of it.

I'd wanted my brother back. I'd wanted him back from the moment he left.

But the Raptor who came back? He looked like Milo. He talked like Milo—sometimes. Every once in a while, I saw Milo in his eyes. But this Raptor wasn't our Milo anymore. I had no fucking clue what to do with that. The last few *discussions* we'd had over fists hadn't gotten us anywhere. Except we'd graduated more to icy silences and dark looks.

Without a doubt, he'd take a bullet for me and I'd happily intercept one for him. But the distance dug out between us when he went to prison, just seemed to grow deeper and wider with every passing day. Try as he might, it didn't all start and end with Emersyn. Honestly, that left me with even less to work with, especially with her gone.

Gone.

Stupid fucking word.

"What's the report?" Milo asked as he emerged from the kitchen with a bottle of beer in his hand and a handful of aspirin in his palm. Aspirin he downed with the beer. When I raised my eyebrows, he just shook his head. "I want to hear the latest. I don't want to hear about Lainey. I don't want to hear about what she is doing here. What I want is something specifically to do with the hijackings, Juan Ricardo, or Ivy."

Shit, that was right. I forgot we weren't allowed to have opinions. Before I could respond, however, Kellan locked his gaze on Milo, while squaring his shoulders and lifting his chin.

"Last time I checked this wasn't a dictatorship. We work together," Kellan said, carefully enunciating every single word. "What you're doing right now…this crap? That's not you being a part of the team or working *with* us. That's you dictating what you will and won't *hear*. It doesn't work like that here and it never fucking has."

Holy shit. Kellan really had had enough. He was just done with this whole scenario.

Milo studied Kellan, running the beer bottle gently against the top of his lip before he took another drink. "I can't do much of anything right now," Milo admitted and saying it aloud cost him, I swear the taxes from it came off my soul as well as his. "Ivy's trapped in some fucking hellhole for rich people. Apparently, a place they've made reservations for her before, and whatever the hell they do screws with her memory."

A muscle twitched in his jaw.

"If I think about that too long, I am going to lose my mind, or I'm actually gonna go murder someone and commit more crimes than they tried to pin on me when they stuck my ass in jail."

Kellan raked a hand through his hair then shook his head. "Would you like me to get you a Stradivarius or just a standard violin?"

My intention might have been to dig into the conversation, but Kellan's response stopped me dead. That level of biting sarcasm usually came from me. Or Liam. I could admit that. Kellan? Not so much.

What the fuck?

"This pity party you're throwing for yourself," Kellan pressed on, not taking his gaze off Milo. "That's a table for one, right? Because no one else here actually gives a damn what happens to Emersyn? To my sparrow? Vaughn's Dove? Liam's Hellspawn?" At which point, Kellan just shook his head. Not that I blamed him. What the hell kind of nickname was Hellspawn? Then again…I couldn't fault the name choice, either. I adored Emersyn, but the label fit.

"Oh, that's right," Kellan continued as if he hadn't even interrupted himself. "It's all about you. It's been about *you* since this began *your* plan. *Your* goals. *Your* choice to sacrifice yourself, which for the record, I would like to remind you that you just fucking did. You didn't talk to any of us beforehand, you just took that deal like fait accompli and fuck the rest of us."

Yep. I took a really long drink from the beer and kept going until I'd drained all of it and then stood. With the belch, I walked past both of them and into the kitchen. The air between them swelled with tension. I was going to need another beer, and a cigarette, since I had a damn good idea of where this conversation was going. If we kept going down this path, shit was gonna get real.

Neither man had moved while I was in the kitchen, in fact they were both standing there in a little hallway between the kitchen and living room, glaring at each other. Well, Milo was glaring. Kellan wore an expression that was far closer to unimpressed resignation than anger.

"The hell do you want me to do, Kellan?" Milo demanded he spread his arms. "I don't know what I don't know. And clearly, I don't know a lot right now."

No way Kellan missed what Milo had just said. I replayed it in my head twice. I'd had one beer, it wasn't like I was even tipsy. While I wouldn't make assumptions, I was half-ready to throw myself into their conversation. Still, I held back. Milo and I had only just reached a detente where we weren't throwing fists every time we looked at each other.

If he kept going down this path though, I was not gonna be responsible for the fist that I plowed into his face.

"Well, let's try this for starters: *talk to us.*" Kellan pointed his beer at him. "You're still pissed at us because we took her. Fine. Whatever. We took her for a reason. While I might not have agreed with Jasper in the beginning, I do now. In fact, I think we should have taken her a whole lot sooner." He stepped into the growing chasm between him and Milo. "I've heard her nightmares. Heard her screams. If they were that bad after she'd been here and safe for months… I can't imagine what they will be after this."

Milo flinched. So did I. I hadn't heard her nightmares. Kellan had mentioned them in passing that she needed to not be alone and then…

Well, then Milo came home and exiled her to Liam's. I tightened my grip on the bottle and then took another long drink. Like I said, if I thought about this too much, Milo and I were going to throw down again. I didn't think he would be the one getting up this time. And there was no way in hell I was gonna take out my frustration and my anger on my brother.

Not yet, anyway.

Milo slumped back against the wall but despite his posture, it wasn't defeat. He might be exhausted from the battle he'd been waging — all on his own by his own damn choice, thank you Kellan — but he wasn't ready to give up. Surrender wasn't in Milo's DNA. Having gotten to know Emersyn, I was dead certain it was impossible for either of them. That genetic quirk definitely won out over nurture.

That knowledge just circled me right back around to why the hell she chose to leave, to go back to a place she didn't want to be. Why would she surrender when we would have fucking fought for her? Would have? We'd still damn well do it. We already were. Liam mentioned the photographs, but the prick wouldn't show me. I guess they thought I would lose my shit.

I was on the fucking edge of it right now.

Freddie knew in his soul that she did not want to go, but she went anyway. Freddie, who spent so long trying to destroy himself and not understanding that anyone would care, suddenly had a reason to care. If I hadn't already loved her — I'd love her for that alone. Yet, here we all were, fucking sitting around with our thumbs up our ass while he got himself locked up into that rich lockup.

Prison was a prison.

I've been in a cage my whole life. I'm not going back into it again.

The whisper of her voice in no way robbed it of her ferocity or her determination. Guilt raked through me. At one point, all I'd seen was a spoiled brat. A spoiled brat in danger, and being hurt. That was utterly unacceptable on every level. But nothing about Emersyn was spoiled.

No, the more I'd gotten to know my swan, the more I'd seen her grow stronger and watched her with the guys here—the idea of her being a "spoiled anything" couldn't be further from the truth. Emersyn

Sharpe belonged here. Maybe it wasn't her world, or maybe I hadn't wanted it to be, but she fit. Here. She fit *us*.

That didn't mean she couldn't be bratty. Nothing wrong with being a bit of a brat, look at Freddie.

"Milo, let us in," Kellan said. "Let us help. We're doing it anyway, make no mistake about that. And hijackers or no hijackers, the moment we get word on her and Freddie, we're going."

Couldn't agree more. In fact, I didn't say a goddamn word. Kellan pretty much had it sewed up. Maybe we should promote him to being in charge. He had his shit together.

Milo scowled. "I don't know how to fix this."

And therein lay the problem. I could have kissed Kellan for that. Because Kellan saw it just as clearly as I did. Milo's desire to control everything had to do with smoothing the way and making sure things went right for everyone. Especially Ivy.

Ivy had been the gravity binding his world together. The higher she flew, the stronger his hold was. And now, finding out that she'd gone through traumas we knew *nothing* about just left him floundering. This wasn't just her asshole dance partner raping and abusing her. We took care of that. That—that had been preferable to the alternative. So, what the actual fuck was her family doing to her?

The desire to talk to Lainey, to get answers, flooded me.

Milo looked at me. "Where you going?"

"I'm going to talk to the one source we have sitting right here, who can give us some answers." Someone who had already given us some answers.

"No," Milo snapped. I fisted my temper as tight as I could.

"Explain why, and make it reasonable," Kellan interrupted. "Or understand that you're facing a two against one on this vote right now."

For a brief moment, I locked eyes with Kellan. My brother had my back. In this—there were no words for this. We both focused on Milo. He couldn't keep controlling everything if he didn't know what the hell to do with it. Well, in this case, her.

"I'll ask the questions," Milo said. "I'll talk to her. I should be the one who hears about it."

"New plan," Kellan said, "*we'll* talk to her. Together."

Worked for me. I put my empty bottle down and headed for the stairs. Milo called after me, but he didn't follow. I don't know if it was because Kellan blocked him or because he'd given in. Part of me really hoped that Kellan had blocked him, because as hard as it was to see Milo like this, the idea that Milo surrendered — well, that shit was a thousand percent worse.

I paused outside of Kellan's door on my way to Milo's room. I wanted so desperately to walk into Emersyn's room. Spend a little time where she had been. I hadn't allowed myself once in the days since Milo sent her away.

The longing hit like a sledgehammer but I fought against the urge. I needed *her* back more than I needed to feel sorry for myself. In fact, what I needed to do was keep going down to the end of the hall, let myself in Milo's room, get Lainey whatever the hell her last name was and take her downstairs. Then *we* needed to find out everything she knew about those sharks.

That was what I needed to do.

Swan, you better hold on. You better keep fighting. I know you've got a hellspawn inside of you… I rolled my eyes at the internal dialogue. Like she could hear me. And seriously, when was the last fucking time I bothered with prayer?

Dammit.

Swan, just make it. Don't give up. Prove how much like Raptor you really are, and don't forget that while birds have wings, they also have talons. You're a fighter. Keep fighting.

Chapter Twenty Two

EMERSYN

The hardest part about being in this place was I didn't always know what was real and what wasn't. Some days, I didn't even realize I was *here*. Other days, I couldn't figure out where the hell *here* was. Or if I cared where and what here was. Those days should terrify me.

The people who worked here weren't much better. In fact, knowing *them* was worse than not knowing where I was. Of all the people I dealt with, and spotty memory or not, there were a few, only two were consistent. Janice, my nurse, bubbled over with kindness. Everything about her said trust me. I didn't dare. Then there was Doctor Frankenfurter. That wasn't his name, but I didn't care.

In and around the white static, I kept seeing the loathsome man with my uncle. Anyone who was with my uncle, or on his side, *couldn't* be trusted. No matter what the doctor said, no matter what he did, no matter how many times he told me he was there to *help* me — it was all lies.

Every. Single. Word.

Beyond dealing with the doctor and *Janice,* there were the

waking dreams. Dreams where Liam scolded me for giving up and Vaughn told me I could do anything. Other dreams, where Rome painted. Sometimes, I thought those were my favorites. He didn't say anything to me, scold me or make me feel bad. He was just there with me, like he wouldn't let me be alone—here or anywhere else. Those dreams were moments glimpsed through pinholes in a sooty window.

I wanted more. I missed the sound of their voices. I missed how lyrical and crooning Vaughn's voice was, the bite of humor in Liam's, the patience in Kellan's, the playful growl in Jasper's—even when the growl wasn't playful. I missed Rome and how he looked at the world. The simple acceptance he had for the world around him. The beauty he brought to my life.

Then there were the other waking dreams, these were worse. The dreams where Doc stared at me with such utter disappointment. I didn't want to talk to Doc. Or think about him. The half-formed ache inside came not just from the disappointment, but also the way he pushed me away. Maybe that was good. Maybe it was better. Especially since I was gone.

As much as I… No, I couldn't let myself go there. There were so few minutes during the day when it was just me and my brain. Before they brought me the pills. Before the fog descended. At least they were pills now.

They were done doing the shots or whatever it was they were putting in my IV. The white static was always there. Even worse, I couldn't always stop the direction my thoughts went in. How many times had I conjured Freddie? I swore, he was so fucking real.

More real than anything else. I could touch him, like he was literally there. For just a few minutes, I thought he really was. And then that went away too, vanished into the white static. It was all like some horrible little taunts from the past slipping through my fingers.

When the door opened to let Janice in, I didn't respond. I didn't turn my head or focus on her. Maybe she would think I was still out of it. Maybe she wouldn't force me to take more pills.

I should've known better. She hustled right over to me chattering happily. "Good morning, Miss Sharpe. Good morning, good morning, good morning. And how are we today? I hope you slept well. I know you've been having bad dreams, but I didn't see anything on the board for last night. How great is that?"

Fucking fabulous, not that I said that. I didn't think I'd had any nightmares. Then again, I'd fought going to sleep all night long. My head had been too full and it had been too hard to focus. I kept seeing puzzle pieces snapping together. Eventually, I realized it was night. The windows had been dark and the hallway too.

The rip of the Velcro restraints being released seemed to echo loudly in the room. Janice didn't even seem to mind that I hadn't answered her. After she got my arms and legs released, she wrapped an arm around me to sit me up. Like I couldn't sit up on my own or something. Arguing wouldn't have helped, not with the strange malaise seemingly lacing my whole body.

"You know," she continued almost conversationally. "I think we're getting there. It's almost time to graduate you to the next part of the program."

Yay, I guessed. I got to graduate? Did one actually graduate from a place like this? Was it like, the Third Circle of Hell… Wait, which one was the Third Circle again? Shit. I'd even done a show of Dante's Inferno. Why couldn't I think of it? Or had I just forgotten all of it? Fourth was greed, right? Maybe.

Fuck, I couldn't remember.

Janice didn't wait for me to get my shit together; she just hustled me right off the bed and into the bathroom. On the upside, she let me pee by myself. I savored the refreshing change. Normally, one of them stood there like they had to verify I was the one peeing. Of course, they'd also set me up with a bed pan more than once, the less I thought about that, the better.

Probably better to not look too closely at anything I couldn't remember. Sessions with the doctor. Sessions with the white static. The floaty place.

All at once, the desire for coffee struck. I'd kill for a fresh hot caffeine infusion.

"Breakfast today is going to be oatmeal, raspberries, and nuts." Janice was still talking in the other room as she moved about. She probably stripped and remade the bed, then tidied things up. Not that it got messy when I was literally strapped to the bed. That, or she wanted to make sure I hadn't hidden anything. I was talented after all.

Wait a minute.

I *was* talented. I glanced down at my arms. They were still achy and sore. The scars were still fresh, their pinkish color angry. If I flexed my fingers and wrists, the muscles in my forearm shifted. The pull against the scars seemed minimal.

I could get out of those straps.

"… Also, I wanted to let you know," Janice said as she stuck her head in the door while I was still sitting on the toilet. "You get to actually go to a group session today. Doesn't that sound great?"

Couldn't wait. "Okay," was about all the excitement I could muster. Especially since the only group meeting I wanted was one with—

"Also, while I'm thinking about it," Janice said. "We've been discussing your regimen. You spend an awful lot of time alone."

No kidding? Surprising, considering they strapped me to a bed every night. Apparently, Janice wasn't going away, so I finished, flushed, then moved to the sink to wash my hands. The cold water felt good over my hands. They'd even given me a brand new toothbrush. Who knew it was the little things that would matter?

"Currently, you've been enjoying an hour a day in the community room, but a change might be more beneficial. Help you integrate more. Isolation isn't healthy for you," Janice continued, all the while studying my expression via the mirror. I tried to summon up a smile. I was a performer. This was a performance. Oh, but the ache in my soul dug deeper and more painful the longer I was not in the place with the white static. I shoved it all to the side. Janice must've liked what she saw because she nodded. "We're in agreement to let you spend more time in the community room."

She looked at me all expectant, like I was going to throw my arms around her and thank her for the best present ever.

I spat the toothpaste out and then said, "okay," before I resumed brushing my teeth. Once I was done, I cast a glance at the shower. "Do you mind if I wash up?"

For a brief moment, it looked like she would balk, but then she tapped a finger to her chin and said, "Very well. I think you've earned a shower. We have to leave the door open. I'll be just out here, so I can help immediately. You know to pull the string if anything happens?" At my nod, she motioned to the shower. "Go ahead and warm up the water, I'll get your morning pills then you can shower."

Without hesitation, I turned the knob and got the water flowing. I didn't care if it was hot or cold, I just wanted to wash the ick off my skin. A cold shower might even be preferable. As much as I wanted to just strip off and get in the shower, I waited. The last thing I wanted was for her to drag an orderly in here and haul me out because I broke the rules.

She hustled back in with a little paper cup of pills. A blue one, a pink one, a yellow one, and two little white ones. Just what I always wanted. I accepted them obediently and tossed all of them into my mouth, then washed them down with the small glass of water she brought. After, I opened my mouth so she could check and just huffed a breath of minty fresh air at her. She blinked and rather than checking any further, she nodded and left me alone.

As soon as I was under the water, I shoved two fingers down my throat and gagged. The pills came right up, I hadn't swallowed them so much as held them at the roof of my mouth, then dry swallowed. They got stuck and all of them came right back up.

"All good?" she called after I coughed.

"Yes," I called back. Not even a lie. I was better without the pills. Who knew that the few bouts I'd had with forcing myself to purge could payoff? Well, payoff in an unintended fashion. The damage I'd begun to do with the constant vomiting could have gotten me kicked from performance, so I stopped.

Starving was another option. Cutting all the calories. But now I had the pills in my hand and nowhere to dispose of them. The drain had a tight grate over it, the pills wouldn't fit. The door was open. She would see if I went to the toilet. It took some time, but I ground the pills up as much as I could with the hot water and the soap. The capsules split open, spilling the contents down to wash away.

There were just a few little bits left and I wiped them on a towel. Hopefully the soap would hide them. As much as I wanted to linger in the shower forever, I couldn't. Once my skin was all pink from the heat, I stepped out to dry off. A new set of pajamas waited for me on my freshly made bed. Gray ones, just like everything else in this place.

Two hours after my shower, I questioned why I hadn't just taken the damn pills. I couldn't stand being here the more awareness swarmed through. My skin crawled. I had memories of this place. Disjointed fragments where I was terrified and others where I was just in pain. There were hands. Faces. So many blurred and shadows.

How many times had he sent me here?

All at once, a singular memory crystallized of the doctor talking to my uncle. Sending me away for treatment.

And it was not the first time.

Three weeks. He wanted me here for at least three weeks—while he had *surgery*. A smile escaped me and I couldn't help it. Sitting in the middle of this room full of strangers talking about their lives and their issues and I wanted to *laugh*. My uncle had to have surgery because I *hurt* him. I'd damaged his knee.

Oh, I hoped I got to tell Liam all about it someday. For all his scolding over the last few days—or was it weeks? Months? God, I hope it hadn't been months. I needed to tell him that I'd done what he'd taught me to do. I'd fought like hell and I hurt the person who hurt me.

I just wished it had hurt him more, or that I'd gotten away.

When it was my turn to talk in the group, I just shook my head, saying nothing.

The therapist, a woman with the most gentle voice, said, "I know this is scary. We're all strangers. But at the same time, no one is a stranger here. We're all here for you. Aren't we?"

"Yes," nearly every person in that room said in almost the same monotone. If it were possible, my skin would have shivered right off my body. That was the creepiest shit ever.

"I'm happy for you that you're not all strangers. Unfortunately, everyone in my life is and I was taught to never talk to strangers." My throat was scratchy by the end of that. It was more words than I intended to say.

The therapist nodded slowly. She acted like I just said something super profound. Whatever. Then she said, "Well, if that's the case, strangers become friends because you talk to them. How do you make friends if you never talk to a stranger?"

Well, she looked pleased with herself.

Too bad.

"I don't have any friends."

Shock rippled across her face and then she frowned. "Sweetheart, I'm sure that's not true. You have friends and you have family. "

"You know what they say about assuming."

The girl sitting next to me, who couldn't have been more than a year or two younger than I was, started snickering. Like me, she'd been silent through the whole session. From her dyed black hair to her too pale skin, she had the look of someone escaping her own private hell. The therapist glared at her, but my neighbor was unrepentant.

"Honey," she said, the peculiar inflection on the endearment echoing the therapist's empty sweetness. "If your family is anything like mine, we'd rather they were strangers. That would be better, right?"

She wasn't wrong. The only member of my family I really wanted to get to know, really was a stranger.

Milo. I had a brother.

The sense of wonder and confusion collided inside of me as I tried to reconcile those two concepts. I'd forgotten about him for a moment there. But I had a brother. A brother I'd never known, but who had known all about me.

Adopted.

I was adopted.

I wasn't even a real Sharpe.

Laughter bubbled up inside of me. I caught my neighbor's eye and grinned. She smiled right back at me.

"Fuck strangers," I said. "Fuck them all."

She high-fived me and the therapist groaned. At least I didn't have the talking group anymore. Lunch time was still in my room. I hadn't earned the privilege of eating in the communal lunchroom.

Whatever.

At least in my room for a few minutes, I was allowed to be by myself without someone staring at me... Well, presumably without someone staring at me, they had cameras, so I could be under observation and not know it.

Still, they couldn't see inside my head. The whole time I ate, I turned over the concept of my brother in silence. The brother my uncle threatened if I didn't come home. The brother who had grown up with a group of friends so tight they were willing to kidnap me to protect me. They'd kill people for each other.

What would it be like to be the recipient of all that loyalty...

They *had* killed for me.

They had shown me that loyalty. I'd had a taste of it and it was intoxicating. At the same time, I'd battled and pushed back the whole time. Why?

My brain scrambled to hold onto the thoughts, but no sooner could I catch one than another fluttered away. It was like trying to herd a flock of birds.

Birds.

Vaughn called me Dove. But he was also Falcon.

Was that why I kept seeing birds… Rome called me Starling.

Why choose birds? Because they could spread their wings and fly. They could escape. Those were the words he used, right?

By the end of lunch, I still couldn't think of what the words were. It was making me crazy.

Janice came in. I had to take another pill, and unfortunately this time I had no way to get away from it, so I just swallowed it. This whole time that they were handing me pills, I never once asked what they were. I'd just taken everything they'd given me.

Whatever this one was, hopefully it wouldn't drown the world out again. Or maybe it should. The drugs offered an escape to the floating place. All I ever wanted to do was escape. Get away from my life, my uncle—disappear.

If I could really disappear then they would all be safe. There would be no reason for my uncle to go after them.

The hum of conversation, the television, shuffling steps, and other ambient noises seemed so loud as I stepped into the community room. They scraped against my skin and made my head ache. At the same time, awareness slithered over me.

It was the first time I'd *walked* into the room. But it was hardly my first time there. The room was familiar. My gaze went to the window with a little crisscross pattern on the glass, which muted the blue skies beyond. We really were in a cage.

Janice gave me a little nudge, all friendly and encouraging. "Off you go. Have fun."

Right.

With a sigh, I scanned the room and froze.

Seated at a table next to the window I'd just been staring at, was Freddie.

It couldn't be…

That was dreamtime Freddie, right?

That was the Freddie I'd seen.

Not this one…

Freddie.

Dressed in the same kind of gray pajamas I wore. His hair had the raked off his face look, like he'd been forcing his fingers through it over and over again. There was an alertness in those blue eyes. A sharpness that was all too familiar.

On slow faltering steps, I made my way over to the table where he was sitting and stared down at him.

Oh my God, let this be real.

Let him be *real*.

"Is this seat taken?"

Chapter Twenty Three

FREDDIE

"Is this seat taken?" Four of the best words to come out of her mouth since she called me to tell me she was leaving. Even better, she said them to me directly after walking—albeit really slowly—to the table. No more wheelchair.

"Pretty sure he saved it for you," Bodhi said when I didn't answer right away. I jerked my gaze off of her to glare at him. He smirked. "What? You don't want her to sit there?"

Psychopath. And really unimportant right now. I switched my attention back where it belonged. Unease flickered in her eyes. Dammit. Guilt was a living, breathing monster slithering through my veins. "Yes," I told her. "Of course, the seat isn't taken."

Hesitation marked her as she glanced between me and Bodhi. Our buddy Chester wasn't here yet, so Bodhi had torn apart the puzzle and started putting it back together. Didn't matter how far we got, he deconstructed it every day and started over.

At this rate, we'd never finish it.

"Please," I added when she still hesitated. "Sit down?"

We could move if she didn't want to sit with Bodhi, but she only cast Bodhi another apprehensive look before she finally sat down. Awareness of the nurses and orderlies keeping an eye on us—or not as the case may be—I slid a stack of pieces over to her.

"Freddie?" She stopped my hand, covering mine with hers.

"Yeah," I said, locking eyes with her. "I'm really here."

"Prove it?"

"Boo-Boo, I can recite poetry about your pretty pussy if you want, but as fun as that would be…" Truthfully, it would be fun as fuck. "We're in mixed company. And I don't know that it would prove anything to you."

I'd been trying for days to get through to her. She searched my face, her dark eyes so intent, and there was a spark there. A spark that had been missing.

"I don't mind talking about her pretty pussy," Bodhi offered up. "We could talk about skinning people too. So, it really is up to you."

Surprise rippled over her face and she pressed two fingers to her mouth. "He's an artist," I explained. "Really, just focus on me, okay?"

Please don't slip away where I can't follow you.

"That piece," Bodhi said, dragging our attention to him. He pointed to a piece that Boo-Boo played with. She paused to look down at it then over to where he was working. Rising, she leaned over the table carefully and slotted the piece into place. Bodhi didn't take his gaze off of her the whole time. The slow, deliberate nature of her movements worried me.

Was she in pain? I skipped asking the stupid questions. She was stuck *here* and she had *scars* from slitting her wrists open on her arms. A dozen different questions hammered their way through me, but I strangled all of them. Soaking in the sight of her, I waited while she turned over the pieces in front of her—the side without the picture— and matched three or four pieces right off.

"I can't believe you're really here," she said in this sad, almost disbelieving little voice that sucker punched me.

"Well, I get that," I admitted, maintaining a visual on where the nurses and staff were. They were pretty lazy about their observation here, but it only took one slip. "I mean, I am awesome and you know, I keep a fully booked schedule. I had to squeeze you in."

A snicker escaped her. The sound was so genuine and *her* that I sagged in the chair. "You're right," she said, before reaching across the table to snake a puzzle piece from in front of me.

"Can I get that in writing?" The quip brought her smile back. For the first time in what? Ten days? Two weeks? However long this hellish empty eternity had been, I could breathe again.

"If I had a pen," she offered. The smile faded all too fast as she gave a little shrug.

"Fine," I said, magnanimously with a royal wave of my hand. "I'll allow it. You can just tell me what I was right about."

Another flash of her smile, only this one vanished nearly as soon as it appeared. "You're awesome," she whispered. "You shouldn't be here."

Not once did she look at me.

"I thought you were a dream, but you're really here. Were all of our conversations real?"

"Maybe." As much as I wished I could offer her a different answer, maybe that was all I had. "You've been pretty out of it. But you're not today…" Did I ask why and push it? Or did I just accept the gift for what it was?

She peeked at me from beneath her lashes. Her dark hair tumbled over one shoulder as she finger combed it. "I didn't take my pills this morning." Her throat convulsed a little. "I cheated. But—I couldn't not take the one at lunch."

Yeah. I got that. I'd managed to avoid most of them but it wasn't always easy. "Thank you."

"For what?"

"For listening to me." Maybe she didn't remember that part. But I did. "I need your help to get you out of here, Boo-Boo."

Her mouth formed a perfect little 'O' and I was in such a good mood, I didn't even mention blowjob face. Oh, so fucking tempting. Really… tempting. I wanted to throw myself at the crack in the glass separating her from us and blow it open. Boo-Boo was right there, within touching distance, and goddammit I wanted Boo-Boo back.

"You look shocked," I said. "I mean, I get this is like some kind of wealthy booby hatch and you got boobs—I mean they've kind of shrunk but so have you—not that they aren't nice boobs. They are. So maybe it's rude to say booby hatch. Can you hear the guys right now?"

Another giggle fell out of her and she cast a look around, then hesitated when she stared at Bodhi. He stared right back at her and I narrowed my eyes. If he told her how he would kill her…

"Who do you want to kill?" Oh, that was a way better question.

Her eyes shuttered for a minute, but she glanced toward the nurses. Grandma and Big Ox Broderick were over there. Got it.

"Anyway," she said, focusing on putting the puzzle pieces together with intensity. "Should we be talking with…"

"Bodhi," the guy said. "I'm pretty much nuts. They wouldn't believe me even if I recited back your whole conversation."

Yeah, not helping, but Boo-Boo surprised me when she stared at him for a moment. "You're Jock Cavendish's son."

"Damn," Bodhi said slowly, elongating the word as he sat back. "Pretty and smart. You want to dump him and run away with me? I'll kill anyone you want."

"Don't make me stab you," I threatened him and Bodhi grinned as he leaned back in the chair.

"That could be fun, too."

Yeah. Certifiable.

"I don't want to run away with you," Emersyn told him, and Bodhi nodded his head.

"But that's not a no to killing people. I like you."

When Emersyn shot me a mystified look, I laughed. "He grows on you."

Laughing felt so *weird*.

At the same time, I'd found her. I'd found Boo-Boo.

I shifted my gaze from her to where Grandma was. She'd looked up from the desk and stared at Emersyn. What I wouldn't give for a knife right now. We needed to get her the hell out of here.

Boo-Boo got to spend a whole three hours in the community room, but then the bitchy Grandma with the "sugar will kill you she was so sweet" attitude, brought her pills when she noticed her having a good time.

The stricken look in Emersyn's eyes gutted me, but I nodded. If we made a stink right now, she could get dragged out of here and I could end up hurting a lot of people. I was pretty sure Bodhi and I could take the ones in here. But it was the ones outside of the community room that I worried about most.

And I wasn't risking her in here. Getting her into the community room was a good start. The next was to get a message to Liam. I hadn't spoken to my "brother" the whole time I'd been here. I hadn't even tried.

When I asked after dinner, I was told "not today." Right, not waiting around to see if they changed their mind. Lockdown began a little after seven. There was no television in my room, but I had managed to score a couple of books from the library. Soon as they locked the door and left, I went to take a piss and coughed out the evening pills.

Now, I just had to wait. I sprawled on the bed and read one of the books, not that I saw much of the words. I just had to wait. The last few nights had given me a really good idea of the schedule. Even without a clock, I had the timing down. After the lights visible through the textured glass went dark, I gave it another fifteen minutes.

Stretching a hand up, I shut off the light. Then I went to work freeing the clip from the inside of the book. Dumb luck had been on my side in the library. A bobby pin had been on the floor, tucked right up against the edge of the shelves. The paperclip I'd pocketed when I'd gone to "check" out my books.

I'd been tempted to take a regular pen but there was nowhere to hide that easily. The bobby pin, flattened, tucked right into the pages. The same with the paper clip. No one searched the books. It was all win-win. Before dinner, I had to leave them in my room. That meant risking someone finding them. Luckily, no one had touched them in my absence.

With care, I kept an eye on the door while I chewed off the plastic ends on the bobby pin. I spit them out into my hand and then shoved them under the bed before I crept out of it. The whole week, I'd looked for some kind of camera in here and unless they had it super hidden, there wasn't one.

I'd deal with the one in the hall when I got there. The doors locked from the outside—comforting, right? Then again, this wasn't the first place I'd ever stayed where they tried to lock me in. The less I thought about that, the better. Forcing myself to be patient, I waited at the door for what felt like an eternity.

In my head, I hummed *Crazy Little Thing Called Love*. The song was just under three minutes. When I finished it, I went to work with the bobby pin and the paper clip. The locks weren't super fancy, it took a minute to work the angle, but it popped neatly and the tumblers gave. Twisting the knob, I swung the door inward. No lights came on at the motion and I kept my makeshift picks hidden in my hand.

So far, so good.

The nurse's station was at the end of the hall. Boo-Boo wasn't on this hall. There were two others—thank you Bodhi for noticing—he thought she'd be in the VIP wing. I did not want to know what they considered a VIP here.

When no one jumped out at me and no alarms went off, I made my way down the hall. I walked steadily, no hesitations as I followed the path I'd mapped to avoid most of the security cameras. Some were inevitable, but I had to hope if I didn't try to be stealthy, they wouldn't catch the movement. If they did, it would look like I was supposed to be out here.

It took me a hot minute to locate the doors that led to the VIP wing. They were locked and fuck my life, a card reader. Okay. I back tracked to the community room. No one was in there. I popped the lock on the door to where the orderlies and nurses retreated when we were in here.

Third drawer of the desk proved to be the jackpot. A spare white badge. I took it and checked for more, then headed back to the door.

The reader went from red to green as I scanned it, and then I was through.

Yes.

On the heels of that triumph, however, came the very real question of where to now? No nurse's station seemed in evidence. Maybe VIPs didn't need a full station? Whatever. I checked the location of the cameras and started down the hall. One perk of being on this side of the doors, all I had to do was open them.

They weren't locked on the outside. One by one, I checked the rooms. C'mon Boo-Boo. No whammies. No whammies.

Movement in the hall had me ducking into one of the rooms and I pushed the door almost all the way closed and waited. But the sound of the nurse talking on the phone passed right by without slowing down. When her voice faded away, I let myself back out. The person on the bed snored like a motorboat.

Definitely not Boo-Boo.

Six doors down, I found her.

Elation quickly turned to fury when I got a good look at her. She was sound asleep, but she was also strapped to her bed. Even in the half-light of the room, I could make out the velcro restraints.

Restraints.

We were burning this place down.

With care, I crept over to her bed, but I didn't touch her as I crouched down. "Boo-Boo?"

The sleepy eyes she opened didn't focus right away and my heart sank. Had they medicated her again?

"Freddie?" She went to sit up but the restraints kept her down. "Is this a dream?"

"Am I naked?"

She blinked, but the fact I was this close hid her eyes in the shadows. "Why would you be naked?"

"I'm always naked in my dreams," I told her. "I better be naked in yours."

Her mouth opened, then closed with a little pop before a snicker escaped her. I grinned. Making Boo-Boo laugh was the best fucking thing.

"Why are you in my room—oh shit, Freddie if they catch you."

"Key word there, *if*. They won't." If they did, what were they gonna do? For now, I just ignored that and focused on her. "I'm here because I wanted to see you and talk to you without an audience."

"I thought you liked your new friend." She shifted again and yeah, I'd had enough of these restraints. I stripped away the Velcro. The ripping sound seemed to echo loudly in the room. I'd no sooner gotten her free then she wrapped her arms around me.

Shock held me still and then I hugged her back.

"Hey, Boo-Boo," I whispered as her arms tightened.

"Hey, Freddie."

We just sat like that for a long time. I'd have to go soon, but I could stay a little longer.

"Do we have a plan?" she asked, face buried against my throat. She was so damn skinny. Even in the pajamas that seemed to dwarf her, they really did hide how much weight she'd lost. Another black mark in the book against these guys.

"Yep," I told her. "Can you hang on for another day or two?"

She swallowed. "Yes." That didn't sound so certain. Leaning back, I stared at her.

"Boo-Boo?"

"Don't ask me," she whispered.

"Is someone *here* hurting you?"

She scraped her teeth over her lower lip. "Not—exactly."

"Tell me?"

"I—" She rubbed her arms like she was cold and I wrapped around her again. Sometimes it was easier to tell secrets when you couldn't see the other person's face.

"Trust me," I whispered. "Tell me who is hurting you."

They could die first.

Chapter Twenty Four

EMERSYN

The night after Freddie crept into my room, he snuck in again. I tried to stay awake, but I had no idea when he would get there. Or if he would. He'd asked me to trust him and to tell him who was hurting me. But the words got stuck in my throat. Then he had to go.

When he showed up the second night, I wanted to cry. I was having trouble focusing. After he freed me from the restraints, I wrapped my arms around him again. Freddie wasn't a hugger. Sure, he would sit next to me or hang out, but he wasn't the cuddling type. Yet, here I was climbing all over him.

Thankfully, he didn't shove me away. I clung to him even when he squeezed all the air out of me. "We gotta feed you more, Boo-Boo, don't they got like the expensive stuff over here?"

A watery laugh escaped me. "Controlled diet," I told him and he pulled back to peer at me.

"What the fuck is that?"

"Just—controlled. No carbs. Lots of proteins. Some veggies. Though I was getting really nasty oatmeal for a while." I tried not to slur, but it was hard to make my lips form with the words when they were numb.

Searching my face, even in the half-dark since there was a nightlight in the bathroom, Freddie frowned. "More pills?"

I shook my head. Not tonight. "I had a relapse, I think." I frowned. "It's kind of foggy."

"You were fine in the community room earlier." Something weird was going on in his voice. Freddie all sober and stern wasn't Freddie. It was so weird.

"Did I go to the community room?"

Had I? I didn't remember that.

I sighed. "I'm sorry, Freddie. I don't know how much help I'm going to be."

Even if we were alone and the door was closed, I kept whispering. I didn't want him to get into trouble. "It'll be fine. The plan is all on me, anyway."

No. "You said you needed my help."

His teeth flashed when he grinned. "I'd love your help, but I'm the one who came here to rescue you." The brightness of his smile vanished. "You were the one who got stuck here."

Guilt raked through me and I shifted to let him go. He was right.

"I'm sorry," I whispered to him. "You shouldn't have had to come here."

"No, I absolutely *should* have come here," he argued. "You're here. Besides, don't tell me what I shouldn't do. I'm terrible at the reverse psychology thing, it just makes me want to do all the things and none of them."

A reluctant smile skated over my lips, but I couldn't hold onto it. None of them should be in this place. "You're only here because I left."

"No, I'm only here because they put you here. Or someone did. I can't decide if it was your parents or not."

This, I didn't want to talk about.

"How did you get in here, anyway?"

He hadn't told me that part. Freddie sighed and slung himself back against the bed. "This bed sucks. For as *exclusive* as this place is."

I shrugged. "They don't care. It's not about our comfort." It really wasn't.

"What is it about?"

"Compliance. Cooperation. Silence."

"Three things I suck at," Freddie mused. "Well, maybe not the cooperation part, I can be very cooperative—sometimes."

I stole a look at him.

"Boo-Boo, why won't you trust me?"

"It's not about trusting you," I promised him. "It's about…"

"The threats?"

My stomach bottomed out.

"Rome found them," he told me.

I swallowed hard. The images were kind of fuzzy. A lot of stuff had gotten fuzzier. The white static—it was getting louder. The inexplicable sadness seemed to grow deeper. "I shouldn't have left them…"

"No, *you* shouldn't have left." The scolding tone was so different from how Freddie normally spoke to me, I blinked at him. "But I forgive you."

"You do?"

"Yep. Cause I've done dumb stuff, too."

"It wasn't *dumb.*" Anger burned away some of the fog. "He's hurt people before. He's dangerous."

"So are we."

"Freddie," I sighed. "That's not the point."

"It is the point, Boo-Boo.' He sat up and moved to sit right next to me on the bed. "We would have protected you. We want to protect you. *I* want to."

"So why can't I want to protect you, too?"

Instead of arguing, Freddie bounced his knee. When I stole a look at him, he had his chin down and his expression hidden in the shadows created by his hair. "A lot of people have protected me." The soft confession held me riveted. "Sometimes, too many times. Jasper—"

My heart twisted at his name. He was probably furious with me.

"He's never given up on me," Freddie confessed. "Even when he should."

"I don't think he wants to give up on you."

A faint snort escaped him. "Prolly not, our boy has issues, you know."

"We all have issues." The moment those four words passed my

lips, I could taste the absolute truth there. "I'm adopted."

Two simple words. Best news I'd had in my lifetime and…

"When Milo—" Dammit. Milo was probably mad I left. Or maybe not. "Was Milo happy that I went home?"

Freddie cut a look at me. "When he thought it was your choice, he accepted it."

That wasn't an answer.

"He wasn't happy, Boo-Boo."

Relief swamped me all over again. "I don't have the right to want him to miss me."

"Boo-Boo, Raptor's missed you since the day you were adopted. I didn't even know him then and I knew that. That's the thing, you know—you've always been a part of our lives. My life. For as long as I've known them… Wait, scratch that. For as long as they trusted me, I knew you were one of us."

That part still left me mystified. "You didn't know me."

"Eh," he said with a shrug. "Ivy is a part of Milo. You're Ivy. Ergo—you're a part of Milo. Milo is also one of us. Used to be the best of us. Not so sure about that anymore." He paused, almost thoughtful. "Maybe he's more human now. Kind of like the shine has been knocked off. Whatever—the point is—you're a part of Milo. Milo is one of us. You're one of us."

"Just like that?" Was it really that simple?

"Pretty much." Twisting, he sat sideways so he could face me. "Look, I'm a fuckup."

"Freddie…"

"Nope, I'm a total fuckup. I know it. They know it. Just—I'm also a Vandal, and they don't let me go, even when they should. They will haul my sad ass right up out of the gutter, get me clean, and sit on me until I get my shit together."

Tears burned in my eyes. "That's kind of beautiful."

"Agree to disagree," he said with a snort. "It's—it is what it is." Then he sighed. "Boo-Boo, I know you're scared to tell me things. Maybe you think I can't handle it. Or maybe you don't think I mean what I say…"

It wasn't that. I swallowed, all the moisture in my mouth drying up. "It's—it's not that I don't believe you."

"I think it's part of it."

"I don't even know how to tell you."

Standing up, he held out a hand to me. I slid my palm over his and he tugged me to my feet. The world swayed a little and I tightened my grip to keep from falling down.

"You okay?" he checked and I nodded.

"Dizzy."

"Okay. Plan B."

He snagged the pillow and dropped it on the floor, then had me sit on it. Instead of sitting with me, he moved behind me and sat down. Then his back was against mine.

"What are we doing?"

"Confession."

"Confession?" I tried to twist around, but the pressure of him leaning into my back kept me from moving too far.

"Yeah," he said. "Just—go with it. When you go to church and you confess to the priest, you're in the little box and they can't really see you and you can't see them. It gives you the freedom to admit what's going on with you without having to see judgment in his eyes. Mostly, cause you know in church, you're not there for the priest's judgment."

A shudder went through me. "I'm not real big on church." I literally couldn't think of the last time we'd been to one. If ever.

Freddie snorted softly. "It's not about going to church, Boo-Boo. It's about whatever you tell me, I'm not going to judge." Then before I could respond to that offer, he said "And whatever I tell you, I'm trusting you to not judge me too."

I would never. "Freddie, I think you're awesome."

"Well, I'm glad you noticed, but then we know you're the smart one."

A wet laugh escaped me, and I pressed a hand against my mouth. I wasn't in the floaty place or the white static, but I was—still a little disconnected.

"If you like, I can go first," he offered. "I know it's ladies first and all that, but I figure if I do it, you can see it's not so bad."

Apprehension struck with every thud of my heart. The dryness in my mouth was back. "You don't have to."

"I should tell someone," he said quietly. "The guys know, well, I think they know. They know parts of it, but I've never talked about it."

All at once, I wanted to run away and take him with me. He didn't have to…

"My earliest memory was being in bed with a man," he said, his voice so soft I had to strain to hear it. "It's literally like the first thing I can remember from when I was little. There were lights and a camera, and they were hurting me."

I closed my eyes. Then I forced them open again. If Freddie could tell me this, then I could damn well listen. The disjointed sensation eased.

"I mean, there's a word for it—child pornography—two words." A self-deprecating laugh. "Didn't know what it was called. Just knew it hurt. I wasn't the only one there. And I didn't have to do it every day, probably good, 'cause they tore me up."

Bile burned the back of my throat.

"I was—four, I think. Maybe I was younger. But I think I was four. That was my life until I was eight or so."

His life?

He went quiet, and I swallowed against the burn in my throat and in my eyes. "I don't remember a time when my uncle didn't touch me." It was so hard to push those words out and I stared at the darkness of the room, terrified someone would hear it. Hear me.

Worse, they would hear me telling Freddie.

His back stiffened against me.

"He used to dress me up, or he would have his staff do it…" I licked my lips but there was no spit. "He liked to take my clothes off and to pet me and to dress me up again."

The bile from earlier just seemed to sit there and one of the tears slid free.

"He calls me his princess."

I hated that name so much.

"And it was always just touching…until I turned ten." Then it was so much worse. "I—had to touch him sometimes too. Every person I've ever told…they've died."

Silence greeted my confession. Then again, I hadn't really known how to respond to his.

"When I was six," Freddie said. "They sold me to a man for his collection. They said I'd gotten too old, and they needed me to do other things. I was supposed to call this new man Daddy." The snort he released said exactly what he thought of that. "That was the first time I ran away. I didn't make it very far, but he locked me up in a little room after. Eventually, he got tired of me and gave me back to the movie people."

Horror crawled through me. "I thought I could get away when they first sent me to school. It was a boarding school. But my uncle—he didn't like having me so far away. He really didn't like that I had a roommate. So, he took her away. Well, he took away the room and I had to be by myself. Looking back—he always wanted me alone. The dancing…he knew I liked it, so if I wanted to dance, I had to ask him nicely. Then eventually, I got to go on tour. I was still alone but—I was farther away."

"I ran away from the movie people," Freddie said. "I did it a lot. I don't even remember their names. I don't want to remember them. I just know that I bled a lot and I hated people touching me."

I shuddered. Understanding that just ripped through my soul.

"One day, I got picked up by the cops for vagrancy or some shit. But it wasn't long before they came and got me, like they were real parents or something." His laughter didn't hold an ounce of humor. "I have no idea how they did it. I remember getting punished. I couldn't walk after. It was why I was there when the cops raided the place."

"That's why I'm here," I whispered. "I tried to get away after we were home. I punched him in the balls and wrenched his knee. I got away. I ran—but the fence—" I looked down at my hands. "He's never going to let me go again. No more dancing. No more tours. Just me with him."

"Fuck. That."

I swiped at the tears on my cheek. "I'm broken, Freddie."

"Me, too, Boo-Boo. Me too."

When I leaned back into him, my head rested against his. "You think we can really get out of here?"

"I know we can," he told me. "Liam and Rome aren't that far away. If they don't hear from me soon, Liam's gonna raise hell. Boo-Boo, we're going to get out of here. You. Me. We're going home."

If I ran, he would come after me. He would hurt them. Fear sank its icy claws into my spine. At the same time…

"Do you believe me?" Freddie whispered.

"Yes."

Bad idea or not—I wanted to go back. I wanted…

"Then hang on, Boo-Boo." He squeezed my fingers. "Just hang on. We're going home soon."

Chapter Twenty Five

LIAM

It was a little after four in the morning when I rolled out of bed and gave up on sleep. Rome sat in the corner of the hotel room we'd grabbed while we waited on Freddie. The point was for him to get in, find her, then contact us. So far, he'd been there several days without a word. It had bugged me enough that I had *called* them.

The staff had been *less* than forthcoming. "Limited to no contact is better for patients during their first seven to ten days," the woman on the phone explained to me in the most unctuous tone. "Your brother is well, he has begun his therapy, and he is adjusting. We don't want to disturb this delicate balance."

Right.

"Tell the doctor I expect a return call within the hour or I'll be making an appearance there and you can all explain it to me in person." They wanted to placate me. I had zero interest in being placated. The cool, deadly tone and threat did what all the politeness in the world hadn't managed to achieve. The doctor called me back.

He'd been singing an entirely different tune, however. "Mr. O'Connell, I understand your concern. The point of bringing your brother to Pinetree was to let *us* take care of him. Part of that is the isolation procedures. We need him to adapt and to be comfortable. It will encourage him to participate in group and we've already had one incident."

Oh, really.

"And that was?"

"He had a bit of a disagreement with one of the therapists during a group session and attacked him."

Real altercation or manufactured one? With Freddie, it was fifty-fifty. But he'd been damn focused when he went in there.

"I'm afraid we had to sedate him for a day and put him on lockdown, but he responded quite well. He's also in a new therapy group and we're seeing active engagement." If the man's attitude were any more oily, it would leak through the phone.

"Lockdown?" Fuck. "What exactly does that entail?"

"We're hardly a prison, Mr. O'Connell." Patronizing fuck was gonna get his teeth handed to him. "But we are a facility equipped to handle these kinds of slips. Lockdown essentially kept him in his room for twenty-four hours. His privileges were restored the next day."

Right. "And the sedatives? I thought the medical paperwork made it clear he has a substance abuse issue…"

"Yes, as you also stated clearly upon committing him to our treatment. We have taken his past issues into account. The use of therapeutic pharmaceuticals is a common practice. His level of agitation was counterproductive. Attacking one of my staff is also not acceptable. Sedating him gave him a measure of calm."

Goddammit. The doctor wouldn't budge on that. He indicated they were still cycling through their treatment options, but Freddie was doing well. They could arrange a visit in four days, but the doctor wouldn't bend on sooner. Seven days. Freddie had been in Pinetree for seven days.

The doctor wanted him there for another four. Having him admitted as a patient allowed him to look for Emersyn within their isolated walls. We needed to find her. Freddie was supposed to contact us as soon as he had made contact with her. Then we'd get her out.

Agitation vibrated under my skin. It was entirely possible that it was taking so long because Freddie and Emersyn weren't even in the same ward or wing. Maybe he had to actually find her. That could be what punching the therapist was all about.

Or maybe he punched the guy because he was an asshole.

My thoughts raced in circles following the call. It made sleep damn near impossible and barring breaking into the joint ourselves, we were stuck in this holding pattern.

This was the *plan*.

The guys back in Braxton Harbor would be less than pleased. Especially Jasper. Every day since we'd left, he texted. Every. Single. Day. I'd talked to Jasper more in the last week than I had in the last year. It was kind of nice.

"I'm going on a run," I told Rome. No way I could sit still here, not for another fucking minute. I needed *movement*.

My other half glanced up from his sketchbook. The weight of his stare followed me as I yanked clothes out of the bag. We'd basically kept everything ready to leave, even our toiletries were repacked after every shower. Speed, right now, was far preferable to comfort.

"Okay," Rome said. He didn't follow it up, but he nudged me to the side to grab his own clothes out. It was my turn to track his movements while he got dressed. From the moment I found him at my place, Rome had been… *withdrawn* was the only word for it. Where Freddie had been laser focused, Rome had been almost non-communicative. I still couldn't believe him and Freddie had gone after, and then brought Lainey back.

Then again…

"We going?" Rome's question knocked me out of my musings.

"Yeah," I said, then dragged on my shoes. "You don't usually go running with me."

"You never ask."

He had a point except… "I didn't ask this time."

"I know."

Right. Let it go. Rome wanted to run with me, I wasn't going to complain. Not when I needed to burn off some of this aggression. The window during which I could continue to stay here dwindled rapidly. The king hadn't made mention of my absence from Braxton Harbor, nor had he made any more requests. However, that wouldn't last.

I'd been absent from the fights for over a week. If nothing else, word of *that* would get back to him. Better to keep him from looking any closer at me right now than he already had been. I could explain seven to ten days. Anything more?

No, that wasn't going to fly.

After my shoes were on, I clipped my gun into place at the small of my back. It was a lighter caliber, but it would do, and it didn't bulge. It was also easier to access. I covered it with the shirt and then we were out the door.

Our hotel wasn't fancy. If anything, we'd taken a downgrade. No sense in running into anyone who traveled in my circles, or the ones that Emersyn used to inhabit. Pinetree was hardly located in a dense area of population, so the number of five star resorts remained small.

The place we had was off the interstate, clean, serviceable, and absolutely anonymous. Probably better if Rome and I didn't go out together, twins tended to be noticeable. That said, it was still dark and I needed to run.

One thing about my brother, we didn't need to talk. He let me pick the direction and then fell into step with me, matching me stride for stride. Just because he didn't *run* for exercise, didn't mean he couldn't run.

Hell, I was aware of how fast he could go when he pushed it. Thankfully, today wasn't about racing. The route I chose didn't have any particular destination. There was a small little tourist town about two miles down the road. It had New England quaint written all over it. We'd only passed through without stopping.

Supply runs meant we went a lot further afield. No sense in leaving tracks. A town that small? We'd definitely get noticed. The slap of my shoes against the damp pavement offered a lulling cadence that soothed some of the rougher edges. The plan—we were sticking to the plan.

I hated the fucking plan.

Four more days, I reminded myself.

Four more days, then I could see Freddie. Hopefully, he would have news on Emersyn. A flash of Hellspawn's defiant chin lift when we trained, or the way her lips twitched when she gave me hell—the images burned against my mind's eye.

The first thing I planned to do when I got my hands on her was hug her until she couldn't breathe. Then make sure she was okay. After that? Well, I figured after that, the spanking she got would keep her off her ass for a while.

"Company."

The one word warning from Rome forced my attention back to

where we were. Shit, I knew better than to let my mind wander. A car swung around us and then yanked over to stop ahead. The expensive make of the car was my first warning.

The man slamming the door as he stepped out of it was all I needed for the second. I moved in front of Rome and met Ezra head-on as he came at me. No idea how the fuck he found us, but I'd known for a long time he wasn't an idiot. No matter how much he liked to play that he didn't give two shits about anything that didn't involve his own pleasure.

I caught him in the mid-section with my foot and shoved him backwards before his fist could land. Air whooshed out of him and he rushed me again. This time when I caught him in the solar plexus, he gagged at the force and staggered back.

"Stop, Ezra," I warned him. "I don't want to hurt you."

"Yeah?" Ezra wheezed. "Well, I plan to hurt you."

Dammit, his hand dipped to his belt. Like me, he was probably armed. I didn't want to have to shoot him. I liked Ezra—for the most part. He was a dick, but most of the guys I knew were also dicks. He'd also tried to warn me, when he didn't have to.

I made one flat palmed motion to Rome to keep him out of the fight. If Ezra didn't want to be reasonable, we would have to do this a different way. I closed the distance before he could pull the gun and this time slammed my foot into his sternum. It knocked the air out of him and doubled him over. The uppercut sent him staggering, the second cross strike took him down. It was fast, it was dirty, and he was gonna have one hell of a fucking headache.

One of my knuckles cracked with the blow and pain shot through my hand. Good, I needed the lash of it. I managed to catch him before he hit the ground. With care, I located his gun and his phone. After handing them both to Rome, I hauled Ezra up and over my shoulder.

"Fuck, he's gained weight," I grunted. Lean as he was, it was still all muscle. Rome got the passenger side door of Ezra's low slung sports car opened and I dumped the other man in it. His head lolled and blood trickled from the corner of his mouth.

Shaking my hand, I buckled him in while Rome circled to the driver's side. Ezra hadn't even turned the engine off. The backseat was a joke, but Rome climbed in there. I slid into the driver's seat and we headed back to the hotel.

It was still dark when we pulled up. While I got Ezra inside and secured, Rome took care of his car. We didn't need to get rid of it entirely, but it sure as shit didn't need to be parked right in front of the hotel we were staying at.

One of the best parts of doing this with my brother, we didn't have to talk. Dropping to sit on the end of the bed, I stared at Ezra. I'd secured him to the desk chair. It wasn't really gonna hold him if he fought, but it might slow him down long enough to listen.

The shortness of the run *and* the fight hadn't done much for me. Fuck. I scrubbed a hand over my face. I liked this son of a bitch. I really didn't want to have to bury him.

I downed a bottle of water before I filled up a glass, and then splashed it on his face. Better to get this over with while Rome wasn't here. They knew I had a twin. They'd never been formally introduced to him and I'd prefer to keep it that way.

Ezra let out a grunt and jerked his eyes open as I sat back on the edge of the bed. I had his gun right next to me, so if I had to calm him down I had another option too. It took all of ten seconds for recognition to flash into his eyes and he glared at me.

"You son of a bitch," he began.

"Well, probably, not that we've ever bothered to check. Though, I'd recommend you not talk about my mother that way."

He curled his lip, then winced, before he glared all over again. "I've been looking for you for a fucking week."

"Well, you found me." Clearly. "Want to try this again while using your words?"

"You asshole."

"Okay." If he wanted to call me names, I'd let him get it off his chest. "This isn't productive, Ezra. What pissed you off?"

"Like you don't know!" The scoff might aggravate me coming from someone else but there was just enough *real* disappointment amongst the outrage and the fury to give me pause.

"Let's pretend I've been off the grid for a week and we haven't spoken since you called to warn me about a certain someone's impatience."

He snorted, then spit. Blood flecked spittle hit the carpet at my feet. Yeah, I'd seen worse.

"Then let's pretend that you just rolled up on me in the dark armed and ready to attack."

"Don't have to pretend that part," Ezra snarled, then grimaced.

"How fucking hard did you hit me?"

"Hard enough," I commented. If we were gonna keep this up… My phone buzzed and I pulled it out to look at it.

Rome

Getting food. Coffee. Need a shovel?

I didn't laugh. It was tempting, but I didn't. I did answer though.

Me

Food and coffee are great. Thanks.

That didn't mean he wouldn't still bring a shovel, but I hoped we wouldn't need it. Ezra continued to glower at me, I just opened up another bottle of water and took a drink. Hoped Rome hadn't had to go far for the coffee.

"Well?" Ezra demanded and I spared him a look.

"Are you ready to talk and stop hurling insults and generally acting like a jackass?"

The other man's expression darkened. That would be a no.

Right. My phone rang and I frowned at the unknown number. This wasn't my Royals phone. I rose, pointed Ezra's gun at him and hit answer.

"Yes?" I kept it short and to the point. Ezra's eyes widened.

"Fuck me," Freddie said. The tension banding me snapped like so many rubber bands breaking. "Trying to find a phone to make a fucking call is a joke."

It was just before six in the morning. Didn't matter. It was damn good to hear from him. "Heard there was trouble." I had to watch what I said because we had an audience. No way I was betraying Emersyn to Ezra. Like I said, I liked the guy but she wasn't negotiable.

"Hey," Freddie countered. "It's me! What trouble could it be?"

"Do you want that in order of occurrence or alphabetically?"

"Fuck you too, big bro," he said in a half-cheerful tone. "The assholes wouldn't let me use a phone. I've been trying, then I've been trying to find one I could use here. They've got them all coded. It's stupid. Finally lifted a cell phone."

Great. Someone was going to be missing it. "And you called me first?"

"Don't worry, I'll make sure they can't—"

I growled a sound, cause I couldn't just snap his name. "Get to the point. I have company."

Silence. "Good company or bad company?"

"To be decided."

"I found her."

Thank fuck.

"She's messed up and I'm working on a plan. We need to get her out of here sooner rather than later."

"What do you need?"

"Shit," Freddie swore, then the call ended.

Discipline was the only thing that kept me from throwing the phone. I had the number that called me. I knew where they were. We'd wanted to avoid guns blazing, didn't mean I wasn't willing to do it.

"Problems?" Ezra taunted.

I just stared at him. "What the fuck do you want?" Because I didn't have time for this game.

"Just tell me if you're having problems or not." The demand seemed almost ludicrous considering he was the one tied up.

"Yes," I told him. "Happy?"

"No." Exhaling, Ezra said, "Adam's missing."

Fuck.

"And then they took—" He edited himself. "You know fuck it, then someone took Lainey."

Me.

Took Lainey.

That was why I'd known the damn name.

"So, we both have problems."

Chapter Twenty Six

FREDDIE

"**S**he's messed up and I'm working on a plan. We need to get her out of here sooner rather than later." Understatement of the year. I hadn't brought up her confession once since she'd offered it. Nor had she brought up mine. But as bad as my story was, at least I hadn't been related to any of those assholes, no matter what they wanted me to call them.

"What do you need?" The all-business attitude really helped. I was running late to get back to my room, but the fact they weren't letting me call anyone and I hadn't heard from the guys since I got here made this critical.

The door to the community room opened. It was dumb luck I'd found the damn cell in their office. I'd checked every single time after seeing Emersyn, but tonight, I'd found one. Taking it back to my room was an option, but not the best one.

"Shit," I swore, ending the call and hiding the phone. There was no way to move, so I just stood where I was when Amber the bitchy nurse walked in. She gave a start when she saw me and her eyes narrowed.

"What are you doing here?" She immediately looked at the clock on the wall and I shrugged. Not saying anything bought me some time and just zoning out like I was stoned—lots of practice with that—might give me a bit more. I had to get rid of the phone or the nurse.

I had better chances with the phone, but this bitch's eyes narrowed. She took another step toward me. Sweat dotted the back of my neck. Some people just had that vicious air about them, a coldness that didn't allow for any kind of compassion. Amber the nurse definitely fell into that category. Unlike the overly warm grandma that hovered around Emersyn, Amber was an ice queen.

Whatever brought her into the field of nursing, it had nothing to do with taking care of people. Then again, very little about this place seemed geared to making people better. Docile. Compliant. What had Emersyn said? Compliance. Cooperation. Silence.

Yeah. They didn't want to hear from the people here. They wanted them quiet.

"You're not supposed to be in here," Amber said, narrowing the gap between us. "In fact, you shouldn't even be out of your room. The door behind her opened to let another guy in. I didn't know this one, but he was dressed in the same white clothes the other orderlies wore.

He missed a step. "What the fuck?"

"I don't know what he's doing here," Amber whispered, teeth grinding. "He shouldn't be here."

I didn't respond to either of them, just kept sort of swaying in place. The new guy approached and he glanced from me to her then back. "How did you get in here?"

Yeah, didn't answer her. Not gonna answer you.

"Shit," the guy said as he began to back up. "This is not good."

"Shut up," Amber barked in a sharp tone. "He's checked out. Look." When she snapped her fingers in my face, I didn't flinch or look at them. The sweat dripping down my back wouldn't fool anyone, but I kept my attention off-focus. Maybe they'd hustle me back to my room and that would be that.

Might take a day or two and cool it, except I had no intentions of leaving Boo-Boo trapped on her own. Especially since these fuckers were *strapping* her to her bed. Sick bastards.

"We can take care of this."

"Yeah, I came here to do the pill swap, not to deal with one of their overpriced paper dolls."

Paper dolls?

"Yeah well, he's a classic fuckup. Big on the drug abuse. Broderick told me all about him. We can deal with him and probably pick up a bonus while we're at it."

Who the fuck were these clowns?

"Are you insane?"

"No, Paul," Amber informed him. If she'd been an ice-cold bitch before, she was positively frigid now. "You're going to do what I said. We have…" She checked her watch. "Less than twenty minutes before they start rounding on the rooms. The minute they realize he's not in his, they're going to trigger the alarms."

"Then send him back to his fucking room."

"Oh, you coward." Not to be dissuaded, Amber grabbed my arm. "Do the swap and meet me at the south doors."

She didn't wait for Paul to say anything, just tugged me along. I stumbled, and she dug her fingers into my biceps. The sharpness of her nails stung, but I moved woodenly, hopefully neither of them would see the phone.

Once we were in the hallway, she guided me past the doors to the VIP wing and into another area. She used her card to open it.

"Move it," she ordered in a shrill tone. "We don't have all day. I can't believe you're just wandering around here."

Every stumbling step I took slowed her down and incensed her more. I wasn't even sure where she was going. I hadn't made it down here, but it was definitely less friendly than my hall or Boo-Boo's.

All of a sudden, she paused at another door and yanked it open. "Here. In you go." She tried to shove me, but I just glanced off the wall and staggered away. It gave me a glimpse inside the room. I wasn't sure who was more surprised. Me or Bodhi. Fortunately, Amber didn't seem to catch on.

"Dammit," she snarled, yanking my arm and this time the phone slipped. It hit the floor and skittered all the way into Bodhi's *cell*. Because his room wasn't a treatment room, it was definitely some kind of cell. "What the hell was that?"

Bodhi now stood in the doorway to his "cell" and he looked from her to me. I focused on him briefly. Bodhi in the community room was kind of funny, standoffish, but funny. Bodhi in group therapy was certifiable, but I liked him. This Bodhi?

The sweat slicking my back made my shirt stick to me. Bodhi wasn't focusing on me anymore, he was looking at the nurse as she tried to drag me forward. I wasn't moving. In fact, when she hauled particularly hard, I yanked my hand away and she stumbled backward. The next words out of her mouth were going to be shrill.

Not that I needed to worry. Bodhi just grabbed her by her head and twisted hard. The crack of her neck echoed loudly in the hall. The nurse dropped, lifeless eyes staring and her mouth open in a silent scream.

Huh.

Bodhi looked down at her then at me. "I'm keeping the phone."

Nodding slowly, I gave him a thumbs up. "What are you going to do with her?"

The other man looked thoughtful, then dragged her body over his shoulder. "They have drain cleaner here." He wandered off with her. Even closed his door behind him.

Yeah.

Skip.

I made it two steps before I paused and glanced back. "Bodhi?"

The other man turned to walk backwards, but kept moving. "Yeah?"

"Thanks."

He grinned and gave me a little salute. "Not my best work."

Right. Don't laugh.

I abandoned this particularly gloomy region of Pinetree and hurried back to my room. I barely made it. Literally collapsing on my bed as the door to the room opened. I jerked up, a sweaty, stinking mess as another of the orderlies—a guy name Gary? Yeah, didn't know, didn't care—came in.

Fuck.

I almost welcomed the pills, cause it came with water. Still didn't swallow them, even if my heart was racing.

Course, now I also needed to find another damn phone.

Bodhi wasn't in the community room that day. Neither was Paul. A couple of the nurses talked about Amber missing her shift, but no one seemed to think anything was wrong. The weird thing was all the surveillance.

The section she'd dragged me down where Bodhi's cell was, it had cameras everywhere. How did their security not notice? I'd been damn sneaky, but there was no way I should have been able to make it back to my room this morning unseen.

When Boo-Boo showed up, she moved slowly, her eyes were out of focus and I wanted to kill all over again. She didn't even see me as she wandered through. I waited for her to pick a place to sit—instead of one of the tables, she went to the sofa in front of the television.

Ignoring the puzzle, I walked over to sit with her. She didn't even look at me and I kept trying to study her without staring. This was bullshit. I'd left her only a few hours before, what happened?

Halfway through some house renovation show, she gave a little shudder then glanced at me. "Freddie?"

"I'm here, Boo-Boo," I told her quietly, careful to talk out of the side of my mouth. "You okay?"

"No," she admitted and that made my whole heart just drop. "I thought you were a dream again."

"Yeah?"

"But you're not naked."

I grinned. "I could fix that."

Not here. Preferably. But if it would make her smile.

"No, it's okay," she said softly. "At least I know you're real." That little hint of disbelief in her tone made me sick. "They took me to the floating place and the white static."

The floating place?

I didn't know what those were. Goddammit. I needed another phone or to talk to Liam. We needed out of here. But I didn't think we could afford to wait for Liam or Rome to "visit."

"Are we still getting out of here?" There it was again, that hint of fear lacing the question, like she wanted to believe but it wasn't true.

"Yes," I promised.

"How?"

"I've gotten into and out of more places I didn't belong than I can count, Boo-Boo. Keep fighting for me. We're getting out of here."

Maybe tonight.

I knew some of the layout of the place from my nocturnal

wanderings. But the grounds were extensive. Depending on when we got out of here, we'd have to hike a bit—unless I could steal a car. Modern cars were not easy to hot wire. In fact, some were downright impossible. You needed code keys and shit.

Wait—what if Amber had a car?

Shit, what if she did. When would they notice it in the lot? Yeah, definitely needed to get out of here tonight. The next day at the latest.

"Freddie?"

I glanced back at Boo-Boo, her eyes were huge. Well, her pupils were, huge and completely blown. The darkness swallowed up the brown. How she wasn't squinting, I had no idea.

"I'm here, Boo-Boo."

"You won't leave me, right?"

"Never. I promise."

Relief slid across her face and she sank into the sofa. I was going to seriously fucking kill them all.

In fact, we'd already started that.

That night on the way to her room, I was careful to not stop anywhere. I wanted a phone or something, but not this time. Probably not the best idea, after everything, to sneak back in there. But no way in Hell was I leaving her alone. She'd been so damn *sad* this afternoon when she wasn't just drifting away.

Floating place.

What the hell was the *floating place?* The static?

At her room, I got inside and found her sound asleep. She didn't even stir when I got over to the bed. Asleep or not, I undid the restraints. We always had to put them back on and while she didn't seem to mind, I hated them.

I still didn't get it. What had she done that required she be restrained? The more I thought about it, the more I had to wonder about the records. Maybe I should stop into the doctor's office or get into one of the computers.

Right. Because hacking was something I could do. I'd had dumb luck with the phone. It had a four-digit pin number passcode one. 1-2-3-4 worked. Not everyone was that dumb.

My eyes were gritty, but I didn't let myself go to sleep. I needed to plan. I needed to sit here with her so that if she did wake up, she'd find me here.

I drifted off a couple of times, but snapped myself awake. Soon, Boo-Boo, I promised. Soon.

Bodhi was back in group therapy the next day and in the community room. He was in a good mood too. I didn't ask him about Amber and he didn't offer anything. At the same time, we were both working on the puzzle and I kept waiting for Boo-Boo to show up.

When the time she usually arrived came and went, I tried not to fidget. Bodhi had started putting our puzzle together face down. We were matching shapes, not the picture. Well, Boo-Boo had actually started that. We just kept going.

One hour late.

Two hours late.

At the three hour mark, I slumped back in the chair. She wasn't coming. Was she in the floating place? Or the static one?

Broderick the Ox was in today or I might have gone wandering during daytime. They weren't really paying attention to us.

"Bodhi?"

"Yeah?"

"I'm going to break out of here and take Boo-Boo with me."

The other man nodded, didn't even slow down putting the pieces together on the puzzle. "Okay."

"I need to borrow that phone back."

Bodhi slid me a look. "I like you."

"I know."

"But I want the phone."

"You can keep it. I just need to call someone."

He scratched his chin. "I'll think about it."

"Thanks."

"Yep."

The rest of the afternoon passed with agonizing slowness. It was almost time for us to leave the room for dinner. She never showed up.

"You think I'll get to kill someone on the way out?" Bodhi asked.

"Oh yeah," I told him. "There are a lot of people here who can die."

He nodded again. "Sounds like fun."

I hoped so. "Just have to find Boo-Boo first."

"When?"

I wanted to say tonight. "Tomorrow night." If she was too out of it, I didn't want to risk her if we had to carry her. I liked Bodhi, I really did. He wasn't gonna be touching Boo-Boo.

Yeah, that was a hard nope.

"Sounds like a party."

Chapter Twenty Seven

DOC

"**A**ny news?" The fact Milo was at the clubhouse without any of the others suggested otherwise. I'd sent Liam one text to check on their status. *Still waiting.* His two word answer hadn't exactly been enlightening. Then again, maybe he hadn't known much more. The only read I had on Pinetree involved its exclusivity and the fact it catered to a very particular class for its clientele.

Beyond the brutal suppositions Lainey Benedict offered, and what detail I'd been able to turn up, I didn't know enough other than a shady medical operation was a shady medical operation. Little Bit was right in the middle of that.

Milo shook his head. He was flat on his back on the sofa, an arm over his eyes and an open beer on the table.

"Problem?" I asked when he offered up nothing else.

"What could possibly be wrong?" The dry as the desert tone didn't help, despite the nature of his rhetorical question. "Everything's just fucking fine."

"Good. I thought we were having a pity party in here and I was about to worry."

The words did what little else had managed, Milo went from his prone position to sitting up. A red mark decorated the corner of his eye, a fresh bruise. The glare on his face, though, that was all him. "What?"

So was that snarl.

Right. Folding my arms, I studied him. "Spill."

"Fuck you, Mickey." He picked up his beer and took a long pull.

"You're not my type," I reminded him.

"No, but I bet my sister is." The dark accusation scored deep.

Thankfully, he wasn't looking at me when he said it and I had a second to get a grip. Locking my expression was an old habit and when Milo finally met my gaze, I just raised my brows.

"What? You have to have noticed. Every damn one of them is after her. Every damn one of them and…" He didn't finish the sentence, just stood as he drained the beer. "Look, if all you came for was an update, then I've got nothing for you. Liam's being circumspect. Rome isn't answering. Freddie's actually inside that place."

"That explains why you're in a shit mood."

"I'm not in a shit mood," Milo practically growled. "I'm fucking tired."

"Then take a nap," I said. "Take a shower. Shoot some caffeine instead of some beer. Whatever the fuck you need to do to get your head out of your ass and stop this moping, do it."

Disbelief morphed over his expression. "Jesus, Mickey. What the hell?"

"My question exactly," I told him. Arms folded, I studied him. "Kid, I've given you a lot of leeway since you got out. It's an adjustment. You shouldn't have been in that place—"

I held up a hand the moment he opened his mouth to argue. A quiet kind of rage burned in his eyes. The kind that consumed a person from the inside, hollowed them out, and left a shell behind. I'd seen it overseas. I'd felt it in the burn ward.

Sometimes, I saw it in the mirror.

There was a reason I focused on healing others. Because destroying them would be so much easier.

"As you've stated," I continued when he listened and didn't interrupt. "You had your reasons. You haven't chosen to *share* those reasons. That's your call. You were always the kid with a dozen irons in the fire and this time—one of them burned you. I'm not the guys. You're not going to intimidate me into backing down. Lash out all you want, I'm not going anywhere."

Milo drained the last of the beer, then he stared at the glass bottle for a long moment. It was like he questioned why it was even in his hand. In the next moment, he turned and threw it at the wall. The glass shattered, raining down the broken bits and what few drops of beer remained.

I said nothing as he sucked in one breath after the other. He flexed his hands as if he was torn between lashing out and sucking it all in.

"Does it stop?" he asked finally.

"The buzzing beneath your skin? The agitation in your blood? The desire to destroy it or fuck it and you can't tell which would be more provocative?"

Head down, Milo went dangerously silent. "I guess that answers my question."

"Well, you know what they say about assuming," I said. "When you're ready for the answer, I'll be in the kitchen."

I left him to stew, more to get my own shit together. The darkness writhing inside of him mirrored the shadows housed in my own skin. War changed people. So did prison.

Milo had been at war his entire life. First, he battled for his mother, then his sister. Then he gave up his sister to protect her. Along the way, he found brothers to protect. Battle after battle, he'd waged in the war life had given him. It could have cost him his soul, but by some miracle, he'd held onto it.

After the last few weeks, particularly his reaction to Emersyn— fuck she was Ivy, that was never not going to mess with my head— after his reaction to her and how hard he wanted to push her away? I worried he'd lost more than time to the prison, that he'd come out with his soul in tatters.

The kitchen boasted a sink full of dirty dishes and a garbage can overflowing with trash comprised of empty take out cartons. A glance in the fridge didn't say much for the supplies on hand. Yeah, this was hitting all of them.

It's hitting you too, asshole. The snide little voice in the back of my head could fuck right off. I sacked up the trash and changed out the liner. Then I started on the dishes. I wanted to make coffee, but it would have to wait until I could actually clean out the pot.

It took a half hour, but I scrubbed down the dishes and the kitchen, even the damn coffee pot. After I got fresh coffee brewing, I took the garbage out. That helped improve the smell. I'd just poured a cup when Milo walked into the kitchen. He hadn't changed his clothes, but his hair was wet and his eyes seemed more alert.

The stink of beer wasn't on him.

It was an improvement.

Saying nothing, I sipped the coffee and cleared the way so he could get his own.

"How did you know?" Milo asked with his back to me, as he got one of the cups I'd cleaned out and filled it with coffee.

"Hard to miss when all the signs are there, Kid."

"Right." Not that he sounded like he believed me.

More silence filled the room around us, but it wasn't a harsh or uncomfortable silence this time. It was easier, allowing us to take a breath. Allowing *him* to take a breath.

"Mickey?"

"Yeah?" I pulled out a chair and sat down.

"What was the answer?"

I shoved out a chair from the table with my foot in invitation then waited. He huffed a breath, but carried his coffee over. Once he'd taken the offered seat, I studied him.

"It doesn't," I said, bringing us back to the conversation about the agitation and the buzzing. "It gets quieter. Sometimes you can soften it, but it's there because you've been put in a place between survival and dying. It's a cold place, the fight is the same, the only difference is you get up after one and you don't after the other."

Rubbing a hand over his face, Milo shook his head. "That's not the answer I want to hear."

"That's the only answer I have."

"Didn't you do something when you got out?" The question, however serious, amused me.

"I did lots of things—I went to a burn unit and fought to make it through each day. I learned to walk again. I finished the last of my degree. Got my medical license."

"While you were recovering?"

"Yep, because if I didn't do something, then the pain won. I wasn't going to let it win."

"You're better now?"

"Depends on who you ask." I took another drink from the coffee and stared into the cup. "I try to focus on the good I can do. The healing. Helping others. I have more good days than bad."

The quiet ballooned again. The dreams didn't change though. No matter how many good days I had. Course, a good day was a day where I didn't have to think about what I'd done or explosions that killed the guy standing next to me or the smell of flesh burning where chemicals splashed on my skin.

Yeah, those were the good days.

There was a sound, faint, but of a woman yelling. At the shout, I glanced at Milo who just sighed.

"Lainey's pissed I locked her in my room."

Eyebrows raised. Did I want to know? There'd been issues with her when she first came, but… Yeah. Fuck it. "Why is she locked in your room?"

He shrugged. "She threatened to go after Ivy herself. She had some pretty headstrong ideas. Figured she'd be better off—safer—here, where I can keep an eye on her."

Right.

"Milo," I said. "This habit you boys are developing regarding kidnapping girls for their own good? Not a good plan."

The other man paused, then straightened as he stared at me. Eyes narrowed as a frown took over his forehead, he glared at me. "It's not a *habit*."

"Well, your boys did it and now you have. Seeing a trend here."

"We didn't *kidnap* her. She came of her own volition." Then Milo took a swallow of his coffee. "Just not letting her leave right away."

"Cause that makes all the difference in the world."

His grunt said he couldn't argue the point. I sighed and leaned back in the chair. "Fine, but don't leave her locked up in there by herself for too long. That's cruel."

"She's fine," he argued and this time I did roll my eyes. "Trust me, she's got teeth and claws. She's *fine*."

I snorted. "Little Bit has teeth and claws too, you wouldn't want her caged up that way."

His expression tightened all over again.

"And you're going to have to stop hating on the boys for wanting her."

"Shut up." There was absolutely no heat in the statement. "This wasn't—"

"No, she should have grown up in that apartment with you and your mom," I reminded him. "Not the foster system and not with strangers. And I hadn't..."

"Mom would have gotten the drugs from someone," Milo told me. "It didn't matter that it was you. It was just a job to you."

"That doesn't make it better, Kid," I told him.

"It doesn't make it worse. Like I said, Mom would have gotten the drugs. She could barely function on them, but she didn't function at all without them. What matters is what you did after."

When she died. Fuck my life. Leaning back in the chair, I stared at the ceiling. The woman's shout carried, it was faint but definitely there. "You might want to make sure she doesn't hurt her throat."

"She can go for hours, it'll be fine."

Nope, not touching that with a ten foot pole.

"You might also want to remember she's your sister's best friend." At least that was who I thought she was. I hadn't really focused on *her* details too much.

"Yep, that's why I'm making damn sure she's all right."

Okay, Milo, whatever you need to tell yourself.

"Mickey?"

His question stopped me from standing to refill my coffee cup. "What's up?"

"Do you think I screwed this up?"

I frowned.

"That she's been in trouble all this time and I didn't know it?"

"Kid, I don't have an answer for that." Rubbing a hand against my neck, I used the rough and raised ridges from the burns like some kind of self-soothing exercise. "I think—I think she's got a lot of secrets and reasons to keep them."

It was a fine line to walk, to keep from betraying what few confidences she'd given me, while also giving Milo the comfort he needed.

"But if her home life was good..."

"Even good homes have secrets." At his skeptical look, I shrugged. "Steph and I do. She knows I did shit I shouldn't have, she never asked. She's never cut me off either. We don't tell each other everything—sometimes I just don't want to see the disappointment in her eyes."

Kind of like I didn't want to see it in Emersyn's. The hurt had been a thousand times worse.

"Liam and his parents have secrets. You know they aren't aware of half the shit he does. I'd be shocked if they knew even a small percentage."

The twins might have been separated by their own choices, but Liam had never left his brother or the Vandals behind. The only thing that changed was his address. They were still tight—or they had been until Liam took off to that expensive prep school. Then again, some of it was all about planning and I wasn't too stupid to think there wasn't a plan.

"So good or bad, she could still hate her family?" Even as he asked the question, he answered it with the shake of his head. "No, that's not it. Because I'm her family too and she—doesn't know what to do with me. To be fair, I don't know what the hell to do with her either. None of this went the way I planned."

"Life is what happens when we're in the planning stages," I told him as I stood. "You know Steph likes her proverbs."

Milo groaned. "We plan. God laughs."

"Yep." I refilled my coffee cup.

"You going to talk to me about her?"

"Who," I said, glancing back at him to find he'd turned to stare at me. "Steph?"

"No," Milo answered, his tone and expression even. "About Ivy. You've been really circumspect about her, but I didn't miss the way you looked at her that first day I was home."

Fuck.

"I'm fond of her, she's a good kid." And that was all she could be to me.

"Right," Milo said. "Well, when you're ready to actually answer. I'll be right here."

Chapter Twenty Eight

EMERSYN

I missed Freddie. I didn't even know if he'd visited. Would he leave me something so I'd know? We hadn't actually discussed that. Then, I forgot to look the first morning. I didn't even think about it until I was halfway through group. When I made it back to my room, it had been cleaned. No evidence of a note anywhere.

Disappointment curdled in my gut. I hated that I hadn't seen him in the community room or after lights out. How long since I'd last seen him? I thought it had been a couple of nights. Maybe longer. I'd gotten into an argument with the doctor about—something. I couldn't remember. They made me do more medication.

Freddie did wake me. I didn't get to go to the community room. Maybe I'd imagined Freddie. Imagined him, just like I'd imagined them. That's what they kept telling me.

"This is a natural response to trauma."

What trauma?

"The mind will act to protect itself."

From what?

"This is another sign of your post-traumatic stress, the

sleeplessness. The nightmares. The violent acting out."

Violent acting out?

"I understand how difficult this must be for you, but that's why we have the group therapy sessions and why you need to also talk to me."

No thanks.

Doctor Skate-Boarder always put his hand on mine.

"Talk therapy is an important part of the process."

Right.

"All right, I think another session, then we'll come back. All right?"

Did I really have a choice?

The answer to that was clearly no.

We didn't come back, I didn't think. I got lost in the floating place. The next day, after group, it was right back to Doctor Skater-Boarder. I really didn't like him. At all.

There was a reason for that.

Oh, right. He was friends with my uncle.

In his office, he put his hand on my knee. Instead of sitting apart, he'd moved the chairs so that I had nowhere to look but at him. Gross.

"Let's start again," he said. "A few months ago, you were kidnapped."

"No." I hadn't been. Even when I thought they had, they hadn't.

They saved me.

"Miss Sharpe—Emersyn, I know this is difficult."

"Yeah," I told him, lifting my chin. "Because you're an asshole."

As hard as it was to form words, I fought against the numbness in my tongue and my lips. When he put a hand to my cheek, I slapped it away. It lacked the force—my mind stuttered, searching—Liam. The force *Liam* taught me to use. But the move still worked and he stopped touching me.

The doctor sighed. "Acting out is just another symptom." Was he cautioning me?

"You don't need to touch me to talk to me." There. That was what made sense.

Only that just started us over again. A few months ago, I'd been kidnapped, or so he claimed, and I argued the point. After all, it happened to me. Right? Not him?

There was no community room or group today. They took me

straight to the white static and the floating place.

The hum beneath my skin followed me everywhere, blotting out sound. When I went to the community room, Janice had to guide me with a hand on my arm. The table she sat me at was empty. The room was mostly empty too. I tried to focus on the television, but the buzz kept everything muted.

"Pretty Pussy Girl," a voice greeted me and I blinked slowly. It took a moment to bring the man into focus. "Knock, knock."

"What?"

"Nope, wrong answer." The guy knocked the table twice with his knuckles as he sat down, then he emptied a box onto the table. Little cardboard pieces scattered everywhere. A couple of locked ones slid toward me. "Let's do that again. Knock knock."

"Who's there?" I blinked slowly as I picked up one of the pairs and pulled them apart then put them back together again.

"I am." The answer came so fast it took me a moment to turn it over in my head.

"I am, who?"

"You tell me," he responded, then slid a piece over and matched it to my pair. I studied him for a moment.

"I'm—" Who was I again? I wanted to lick my lips, but there was no spit in my mouth. I was… "Emersyn," I exhaled slowly, then I shuddered. "I'm Emersyn."

"Pretty Pussy Girl sounds better," the man told me as he slid another pile of pieces to me. "But I'm Bodhi."

The name was familiar. "I know you."

"Yep. I know you, too."

"Then why did you ask me…" Wait, what had he asked me? I rubbed a hand over my face. The buzzing noise just seemed too loud all of a sudden.

"See that nurse?" Bodhi asked, but when I looked up, he was focused on the puzzle pieces. "I'd probably just gut her, you know, slam the knife in and twist it—maybe wiggle it around a bit so I made sure I nicked a major organ or four. Then I'd let her die slowly, gut wounds take a while. It's painful."

Oh.

"That guy? Yeah, he'd need some correcting. Maybe break a few bones." He matched a couple of pieces and when I reached over toward them, he let me take them, cause they matched the pair I was putting together. "Yeah, broken bones. Sounds good, right?"

There was only one "guy" over there. He was the big guy. The mean one. "He's mean."

"How mean?"

"I don't like him." I went back to the puzzle.

"So, definitely breaking bones. Work from the inside out or the outside in?"

Something tickled in the back of my mind. "I know how to break someone's fingers."

"Cool," Bodhi grunted. "Useful."

Especially if people kept touching me when I didn't want them to. I turned the idea over in my head along with the puzzle pieces. "Hands first."

"Oh, I can work with that. Knuckles, like at each joint of his fingers, then down to his wrists. Think tools would be better or just keep it really 'hands' on?"

His chuckle made me smile. "Could do both. Is that an option?"

Bodhi stared at me for a moment. "Give me that piece there," he told me and when I slid it over to him, he grinned. "You want both. I can do both."

Some of the buzzing quieted and the giggle that escaped didn't seem appropriate and at the same time, it was funny.

"Now that chick," Bodhi said with a scoff. "She needs something special."

It took me a second to realize Janice was "that chick."

"She's my nurse."

"Got any good ideas?"

No. Except… "You have to be really happy when you hurt her," I said. "She's always cheerful when they take me to the white static."

"I can be very cheerful."

That was good.

We had almost half the puzzle together when Freddie got there. His arrival heralded an almost audible pop in the muted bubble around me. Relief flooded through. I hadn't imagined him. He really was here. What if…

"Boo-Boo," he said as he slid into the chair next to mine. Dark smudges under his eyes worried me and I wanted to reach over and brush the hair away from his face. He looked terrible. "You're here."

"So are you." Did he think I was a dream too? Were we both

dreams? Wait… "I'm not naked."

He blinked for a moment and even Bodhi looked at me, then he leaned sideways as though to look under the table. "Nope. Do you want to be?"

Freddie snorted. "That's my line."

I grinned. "I mean, if I were in your dream, I'd be naked. So, I'm not and you're not. That means we're real."

For his part, Bodhi just looked thoughtful then nodded before he went back to the puzzle.

"Definitely not in a dream here. You haven't been here the last few days."

"Days?" How long?

"Three," Freddie continued as if I'd ask the question aloud. He kept his voice pitched low. "And you've been out of it when I came to your room."

"You didn't forget me," I whispered, soothed that he'd still come, even if I hadn't known he was there.

"Never," he promised.

"I probably will," Bodhi said. "But you didn't ask me. Probably a good thing to forget. If I don't know you, can't testify against you."

That actually made sense.

"What about her?" The woman who came in seemed familiar, but I couldn't place her. She wore white like the other orderlies and her resting bitch face just didn't quit.

Freddie frowned. "What about her?"

"Depends on if you want it to hurt or not," Bodhi offered.

Yeah, I didn't know that answer yet. I didn't even know her.

The next two days were better. Freddie's agitation had taken on a life of its own. Fortunately, I remembered when he came to see me. I worried too. How many more times could he sneak into my room and not get caught? What happened if they did catch him?

They sent me to the white static because I slapped the doctor's hand. But Freddie told me it would be fine. "Course, we're not waiting anymore."

"We're not?" It was almost time for him to go back to his room.

He'd brought a book with him and we'd been taking turns reading it. I had no idea what it was about, but listening to him soothed me.

"No," he said. "I think Bodhi will help us and I have a couple of ideas. So tonight, when I get here—we're going to go."

I wanted to believe him so badly.

"I know, Boo-Boo. Should have done it two days ago, but you were still—"

Out of it. I was better now. I nodded.

"Today," he said as he scooted off the bed so I could lay down. He reached for the first strap and his expression darkened. "Today, do everything you can to not have them drug you. Pills only."

Yeah, the pills I could gag up sometimes. The shots—I couldn't do anything about those. I swallowed as he secured my ankles first, before he came up to wrap the strap around my arms.

"The last time was cause I hit the doctor."

Freddie scowled. "Do you have to see him today?"

I lifted my shoulders. No one told me my schedule. I didn't even know how long I'd been here. Time had kind of lost all meaning.

"Why did you hit him?"

"It doesn't matter," I said. "I won't hit him today."

The fierceness of his frown intensified. "Boo-Boo, I don't care if you hit him. If he deserves it, you lay his ass out."

"But you can't get out of here if I'm drugged." Because clearly, he wouldn't leave me.

"We'll make it," he promised, then pressed a kiss to my forehead. "We'll make it. Tonight."

I nodded and then he was just gone and I was strapped back to the bed.

I hated this place.

When Janice took me to the doctor's office instead of group, my heart sank. The doctor waited for me, dismissing Janice and waving me in to sit down.

"How are we feeling today?"

I just had to play along. Then Freddie and I could leave. "I'm fine."

"Good," he said as he waved me into a chair. Instead of sitting down across from me, he circled behind me. That was enough to make my stomach plummet, but when he put his hands on my shoulders I went cold. "Glad to hear it. You know we've been worried about you."

With hard fingers he began to squeeze and massage the muscles. My spine went rigid and I had to fight to keep from yanking away. "So you said." When he rubbed toward my neck, I flinched.

"Sore?"

What would I be sore from? It seemed like forever since I danced. My arms were achy. The scars on them ugly as hell. A reminder of what happened at—no, just focus on here. I told myself that over and over. Focus on here and on getting out of here. "Not sore. This is uncomfortable."

"What is? Your neck?"

"You touching me."

He stilled, but he didn't take his hands away. "Withdrawing from contact, alienating family and friends, even resorting to physical violence—these are all symptoms."

That sounded familiar.

"I know you've been struggling, that's why you're here." He started his massage again. The ice under my skin began to spread like a wild frost. "The kidnapping has left you traumatized and we need to reacclimatize you to—"

I had no idea what the rest of that sentence was because he slid his hand toward my chest from my shoulder. I gripped two of his fingers, and twisted until they popped. Grabbing the first thing in reach with my free hand, I struck back at him with the stapler. He swore, stumbling back, but his grip on me pulled me with him and the chair went over. I twisted and struck him with the stapler again. It flipped open and the end snapped against his face.

Blood sprayed from his nostril.

His fingers dug into my arm, but I just grabbed the stapler with my free hand and bashed it down on his head. Once.

Twice.

Three times.

Four.

I lost count. But he let me go.

His fingers unlocked and his hand fell away.

I was half sitting on his chest and my hand was soaking wet.

The world was a blurring, whirring mess. Then I looked down at the doctor. There were little metal staples in his face. What parts of his face I could make out.

His mouth was open, but his chest didn't move. Scrabbling backward, I bounced against the wall and stared down at him.

Doctor Skate-Boarder didn't move.

The blood on his face matched the blood on my hands and on my shirt.

And the wall.

I'd killed him.

Stapler.

I'd killed him with a stapler.

Had Bodhi ever used one before?

What the hell did I do?

The doorknob rattled and began to turn.

Too late.

Chapter Twenty Nine

EMERSYN

The stapler still dangled from my hand when the door pushed inward. Nowhere to hide. Nowhere to run. I tightened my fingers on it, ready to strike the next person if I had to. No more. Just no damn more.

Bodhi stuck his head inside and glanced around. First at the doctor, more curious than anything, then he looked at me. What—what was he doing here?

"Hey, Pretty Pussy Girl," he said, slipping all the way in and closing the door behind him. "Didn't know you'd be here."

"I didn't know I'd be here," I said slowly. "Why are you—wait, how are you here?" Wasn't he a patient too?

He held up a white electronic badge. "Have key, will travel." Crossing the room, he paused to stare at the doctor. "Messy."

"He's dead." Pretty sure he could see that.

"Yeah?"

"I think so." I mean, he hadn't been breathing. Bodhi crouched down for a sec, then gripped the man's head. He twisted it viciously. The sickening crack echoed through the room and I would have covered my mouth with my hand, except they were both red and speckled.

"Definitely dead now," Bodhi offered. "You should go use his bathroom and clean up."

I had blood on my shirt and on the stapler. I went to put it down, then hesitated. It was slick with blood. My stomach rolled. The blood wasn't just on my hands or the stapler. It was on my top and my pajamas.

"It's that way," Bodhi offered as he walked around the doctor's desk. He motioned toward the other corner where a door stood open. I hadn't even noticed it. Then again, I didn't like being in this room.

Hands trembling, I headed for the bathroom and I took the stapler with me. Once inside, I couldn't believe my state. The blood speckled my face, soaked my shirt and coated my hands. I didn't know whether to sob or scream. The trembling in my hands spread everywhere.

"Use soap," Bodhi called. "Cold water would be good too."

The words jarred me and I stared down at the bloodied mess on the stapler then the sink. "I can't touch anything."

A minute later he popped in and I jerked as he twisted on the water. It was also when I realized he had on gloves. I lifted my gaze from his hands to the mirror, where I found him staring at me. "Stapler?"

I nodded slowly.

"Cool."

Then he left me to "wash." Even if I could get all the blood off the stapler and my hands. There was still my shirt. And my face. A shudder went through me and the tremors grew more violent even with the cold water. The blood smeared on my cheeks and wouldn't come off until I grabbed the high thread count cloth towel.

"I can't clean this all off."

Bodhi came back and stared at me. "Okay."

That was it before he turned and left.

Just—okay?

What...

I looked back at the body on the floor and the air in my lungs backed up. There was a phone on the desk. I was alone. Alone for real and not strapped down somewhere for the first time since I'd gotten on my uncle's plane.

My uncle.

A vise squeezed all of the air out of my lungs. I couldn't get a breath. Then the door opened again and I probably would have screamed if I could have sucked in even a drop of oxygen. Bodhi was back and he had Freddie with him.

Knees buckling, I tried to brace myself up with a shoulder against the door jamb. "Holy shit, Boo-Boo," Freddie said in a hushed whisper as he hurried over to me. He didn't even look at the doctor. "Fuck me. What happened?"

A dozen explanations collided in my head, but when I opened my mouth, the only words that came out were, "He touched me."

Both of them paused. Bodhi, from where he stood back at the desk, and Freddie, from where he stood in front of me, and they *glared* down at him.

"He's dead?" Freddie checked.

"Definitely dead," Bodhi confirmed. "We can do it again, though. Maybe cut the head off. I did that once. It's messy. But not as messy since he's already dead. Shouldn't gush too bad."

I grimaced at that description. Yeah, I didn't want to see that. But I couldn't find an ounce of remorse inside of me for it. "I killed him."

"Well," Bodhi said before Freddie could respond. "Maybe. You weren't sure. I definitely killed him."

Oh.

But…

"It doesn't matter right now, Boo-Boo. Are you hurt?" Freddie studied me. "Is any of that blood yours?"

I shook my head.

"Good." He stripped his shirt off and I blinked. There were two of them. Why did he have two shirts on? "Bodhi, give me your pants."

"No," Bodhi said, then pointed at the second chair the doctor usually sat in. "I brought another pair."

"Smart."

"I thought so."

Rolling his eyes, Freddie grinned at me. "Okay, Boo-Boo, don't take this the wrong way, but you need to strip so we can clean you up and put you in fresh clothes."

"Okay."

Mouth open, Freddie hesitated then glanced behind him at Bodhi then back at me. "You know what, Boo-Boo. Back into the bathroom a little more and let's get that off all careful like. I can help, or not. What do you want?"

I wanted his blood off of me.

"I want to go home."

Head tilted, he studied. "Home—home or…"

"The clubhouse. Liam's. Home."

The corners of his mouth curved. "Good. That's where you belong. Okay. Let's get you changed."

Once I got out of the top, I spotted all the blood on my chest. It had soaked through. I didn't have on a bra, but I didn't care about that as much. Freddie didn't even so much as playfully leer at me or comment while he bagged up the clothes in the plastic liner he'd taken out of the trash can. Once I changed pants, we realized the shoes had to go too. They were slippers.

"It's time," Bodhi said. The floor was cold under my feet, but I didn't care. Freddie frowned, then looked back.

"Yeah, we need to go. We'll get you shoes out there."

Out where?

Bodhi was already out the door and going when Freddie clasped my hand. "Stay with me, okay, Boo-Boo? No running off. Trust me."

I did, but the earlier shaking was back. Before he could pull me out of the bathroom, I grabbed the stapler. I didn't want to leave it there. "I promise."

Shooting me another small smile, Freddie headed for the door. We were in the doctor's office. The doctor was dead—how were we—an alarm started ringing out in the hall. Its shrill scream punched through my skull at an unrelenting cadence and painful decibel.

As soon as it went off, Freddie moved faster, pulling me with him. I had to take two steps for every single one of his. There were flashing lights along the corridors. I had no idea where we were going, but I didn't ask. Instead of going out, we went down a flight of stairs and then along a hallway. Where were the people?

The alarm changed, growing more intense. Then Freddie opened a set of doors I didn't recognize. This part of Pinetree wasn't nice at all. It looked like a prison. Even the doors looked like cells. They were open too. All of them.

"Freddie—"

"Hang on, Boo-Boo, almost there."

Where were all the people?

At the end of the corridor, he hit the crash bar on the door and another set of alarms went off. I could barely hear anything beyond the cacophony. The fresh air slapped me in the face as soon as we were outside. There was a driveway there, circling a couple of dumpsters tucked into a bricked cubby. The light actually hurt my eyes. It was so bright.

The sun blinded me and I squinted and tried to stay close to Freddie. We didn't head up the driveway, instead, he headed for the grass and the woods. It was soft against my feet, but I didn't care if it was rough or cold. I just wanted to go.

I glanced back to see the bellows of huge black smoke escaping one side of the building. There were people everywhere—out front. But it was pure chaos. Orderlies. Nurses. Patients. More smoke, and I tripped.

Freddie kept me from falling and I twisted to face front, but a movement behind us made me jerk back.

"What—" Freddie started to ask, but I pulled the stapler up like I could throw it at the huge orderly charging us. "Stay behind me," was all Freddie said before he went for the big man. The guy was huge, he could hurt Freddie. The plastic bag was at my feet, where Freddie dropped it and there was silver in Freddie's hand. The sun glinted off it.

The big man barely said anything as Freddie cut him. He never stopped moving and the guy never touched him. Little rips of blood began to soak through his white shirt, and pants. One minute he was on his feet and the next he staggered to his knees. Then he had both hands on his throat, but blood rushed through his clenched fingers.

Freddie retreated from him and then he shot the guy the finger. "Fuck you very much, Ox. Good riddance and good night."

The man crumpled and then Freddie faced me. His grin demanded I smile, and I couldn't help it. Even the gleam in his eyes was happier. The buzz under my skin and the static in my head couldn't compete with it, especially after the deafening cacophony. Despite the shakes still gripping me, I took Freddie's offered hand as he snagged the bag with my bloodied clothes.

Then we were off again.

Behind, there was the sound of an explosion, shattering glass, and screams. The smell of smoke clung to the air, but Freddie kept us moving. I fought to stay on my feet, despite stumbling over what amounted to air. It was like my limbs were too heavy to be graceful.

Freddie only slowed when we got to the huge brick wall. It was at least eight feet high. Not a problem. I could climb that normally. The sound of leaves crunching behind us, had us both turning. Bodhi was there, with another guy who wore—was that a straight jacket? Only it was all loosened up.

Grinning, he passed Freddie a bag. "This was fun," he said. "Definitely invite me to the next party."

"Thanks man," Freddie told him.

The other two didn't even slow down as they climbed over the wall. We waited a minute, then Freddie hoisted himself up and I had to pass him my stapler before I scrambled up after him. At the top of the wall, I looked back one more time.

Pinetree was burning. The smell carried. More glass shattered in the distance and there was another boom.

"Come on, Boo-Boo," Freddie said and I looked down. He was already on the ground and when I pushed off, he caught me. Hand in hand, we ran. There were more woods. I was panting when he finally slowed down. We were right at the edge of the woods and there was a road below us when he urged me to stop.

I leaned against a tree while he rooted through the bag Bodhi gave him. The sound of sirens carried on the wind. When he pulled out a phone, I nearly sagged with relief.

"Come on," Freddie murmured as he powered it up. When the company logo appeared on the screen, I sagged. "Told you we had this." Then he pressed a button and put it to his ear.

Whoever he called must have answered on the first ring. "I got her and we're out." After hitting the speaker button, he held the phone out toward me. "Say hi, Boo-Boo."

"Hi," I said and it came out really shaky.

"Goddammit, Hellspawn, if it wasn't so good to hear your voice I might threaten to beat your ass when I see you. Where the fuck are you two?"

I hit my knees at the sound of Liam's voice. A crazy little laugh bubbled up out of me. I was so happy to hear him, I just might let him.

"We're—at—mile marker twelve," Freddie said. "On that winding fucking road we took."

"We'll be there in ten minutes."

"Five," Rome said and tears burned in my eyes.

"Right, Rome's driving," Liam said. "We'll be there soon,

Hellspawn. And Freddie?"

"Yeah, Big Bro?" Freddie just grinned.

"You did good."

"I know, I'm awesome." He was still grinning when he hung up.

Sitting back against the tree, I stared up at the blue sky. Puffs of black smoke streaked across it. There were still sirens in the distance. The sun was shining, the air was warm but the breeze was cool. Freddie sank down to sit in the grass right next to me.

"We're going home, Boo-Boo."

Home.

Chapter Thirty

EMERSYN

An eternity passed between the phone call and when the sound of a motor approaching had Freddie waving me back behind the tree. Granted, we were *near* the road, but not on it. The heavily wooded area afforded us shelter from sight. Freddie didn't duck back with me, though, he stood up.

Exhaustion swarmed me the longer we sat still. The trembling came back to my hands and despite the sunshine peeking through the trees, it seemed to get colder. The stapler still firmly in my grip, I stared at it for a moment before putting it down next to me. Knees to my chest, I wrapped my arms around my legs.

A car door slammed, but only one. The motor continued to idle. It all seemed so loud. Freddie whistled, two short, sharp notes.

"She's back here," Freddie said, but even before the words were out of his mouth, Rome crouched in front of me. The blue of his eyes was so intense. That was the color I'd been seeing everywhere, the color I'd wanted to see. It wasn't the sky or the sea, it was his eyes.

Movement pulled my gaze up and Liam stood a couple of feet behind his brother, wearing a near matching expression. Only the hum of the engine broke up the silence. So many words died unspoken as I locked eyes with Liam.

He'd been there—at the airport. He'd tried to stop me and I couldn't let him. Now…

The lightest brush of fingers against my jaw. A whisper of contact. "Your blood?" Two words. The only sounds Rome had made since he got there.

"No," Freddie said as I tried to get my erratic pulse and breathing under control.

"It's the doctor's," I said slowly. My voice cracked, it sounded horrible.

"The doctor's?" Liam did a sweep and when he turned, I caught sight of the gun holstered at the back of his jeans.

"He's dead," I said in case he was looking for them. A shiver stole over me and I rubbed at my arms. "I killed him."

That got me Liam's attention and he jerked his gaze from me to Freddie then back. "It's handled," Freddie said. "I'm starving and she's exhausted. Can we go and tell you all about it in the car?"

Rome held out his hands. No judgment lived in his expression at all, but he waited for me to decide. Guilt hardened like a rock in the center of my chest, forcing the air out of my lungs. "I'm sorry," I said as I grasped one of his hands but grabbed for the stapler with my other. I didn't want to just leave it there.

"For what?" Rising to his feet, Rome tugged me to mine. When he scooped me up though, I nearly dropped the stapler.

"I left," I said. "I—"

"Protected us." Rome nodded. "We know. Now we'll protect you."

"What he said," Liam told me as he plucked the stapler out of my hands. Freddie had the bags and we were heading down the hill to the car.

"You don't know…"

"I also don't care," Liam retorted then he opened the back door to the car they were driving. "Just—get in the car."

Rome shoulder checked him as we passed, but Liam just grunted. I half-expected Rome to put me down, but he climbed into the backseat still holding me. With a shake of his head, Liam closed the door and Freddie climbed into the passenger seat.

"I want the biggest fucking burger we can find, a chocolate

milkshake, a beer, and chili fries," Freddie announced as he slouched into the seat. "Real food. What do you want, Boo-Boo?"

Sleep was the first word that came to mind. Rome had buckled the two of us into place, but I was still in his lap. This close, there was no way to miss how he studied me. I still couldn't believe they came for me.

The vehicle gave a little jolt as Liam put it in gear and I flattened a hand against Rome's chest to keep from bouncing off of him. He was so warm. Rome flicked a look ahead then at me before he covered my hand with his.

Liam and Freddie were talking in low murmurs, but I barely registered it. When I tipped my forehead toward Rome and pressed against the side of his head, he slid a hand up to my hair.

"I smell," I warned him.

"I don't care," he echoed his brother's earlier statement. "You're here."

I was.

Right here.

Another shudder went through me, then another.

I was out of there.

No more white static.

No more floating place.

My uncle…

Rome tightened his arms, locking me against him as I shivered. It didn't seem all that long before we were stopping again. Lifting my head, I tried to figure out where we were. The outside was so strange. Even when Rome opened the door and shoved it back before he slid out of the car, still carrying me.

"I can walk," I offered.

"No."

That was all he said and honestly, I didn't want to let go of him, so I held on. Over his shoulder, I met Liam's gaze and the shivers intensified. I swore he could see right through me and I didn't want him to look. Freddie was a half-step behind them. Exhaustion seemed to hover in the air around him.

Rome paused only to let Liam open the door. Then all four of us were in a—hotel room. It wasn't anything exclusive or upscale. Just a standard hotel room, like so many others I'd stayed in over the years.

"Starling is going to shower," Rome said as he carried me all the way to the bathroom. "Order food."

"Yes, sir," Liam called, the corners of his mouth quirking into a half-smile. "I'll get right on that."

Rome set me on my feet carefully, then flashed his middle finger at Liam. The tile was cold against my feet and all at once they ached. When I glanced down, I stared at the mess of mud and grass sticking to them. There were cuts too. I had no recollection of hurting my feet.

While my skin didn't hum and the white static had quieted, I didn't feel all the way connected to me. Even the shivers seemed to be happening at a distance and I only noticed when my hands kept jumping or twitching. So weird.

"Yeah, I want three large pizzas," Liam said into a phone and Freddie all but fell onto one of the beds and just lay there. I should say something to him. Anything. He'd risked so much to come for me, when he begged me not to go. Now, everything I'd tried to protect them from could happen anyway.

I didn't even make it a half-step though before Rome caught my hand, then lifted it. His gaze wasn't on me or the shirt, or even my feet. Instead, his gaze fixed on my arm. I tugged my hand away and turned, but Rome followed.

"Show me." The quiet words washed over me. Rome's gaze locked on mine in the mirror. He seemed so much bigger than me, but no trace of fear swam in my system. The sense of him wrapped around me rather than towered over. With his chest at my back, he was so close and he could see over my shoulders clearly. At the slide of his fingers down my forearm, I lifted my hands so he could see the scars now decorating me from my wrists halfway to my elbows. The jagged cut had healed to a line of thickened, angry pink.

As impossible as it seemed, the little holes made by the stitches were still present. In some ways, it felt like it had happened months and months ago. Had it only been a few days? Weeks?

Three weeks.

That was how long my uncle would be gone. Getting his knee fixed.

So—only weeks? Maybe?

The calluses on his fingers traced a light, if rough, path along the jagged cut all the way to the reddened and still scabbed line on my palm. I'd scrubbed off the scab—oh, when I'd washed my hands earlier. I'd barely even noticed it. The skin beneath the scab was also fresh and flushed. A flash of Mr. Cole digging the glass shard into my forearm and raking it toward my wrists flooded my mind.

I pulled my hands away and folded my arms. These were the kind of scars that lasted a long time.

Scars I couldn't hide inside.

"Who?" It was the only thing Rome asked. When I would have answered in the negative, he wrapped a hand around my nape. The gentle pressure had me tilting my head back to meet his gaze. "Who, Starling? Who hurt you?"

The voices from the other room stopped abruptly. It was as though the sudden lack of noise reminded me Liam and Freddie were still here.

Looking down at my arms, I flexed my fingers. It still hurt to touch my fingertips to my thumbs. The flexion reminding me there was scar tissue inside as well as out. Not that I'd even been able to dance in the last—however long it had been. No dancing. No music.

No…

"She had them when I found her." Freddie's quiet voice carried. "I know why I have mine. But maybe leave her alone for now and just let her shower? It's been a shitty, shitty day."

Maybe. "But we're out."

Rome hadn't moved, his presence warm and solid at my back. The worry darkening his eyes tore at me. Worry. Hurt. Sadness.

I'd done that.

Twisting away from the mirror, I faced Rome. My heart thudded against my ribs in a painful cadence. "I'm sorry."

"You didn't do that," Rome said patiently.

"No." I hadn't tried to kill myself. A wave of pure fatigue struck and I leaned back against the counter. The cold seeped through the pajamas. "I left."

"I know." Rome shrugged.

"I had to, he threatened all of you."

"No, you were wrong. We'll protect you."

"It's not that simple."

"Actually," Liam said as he joined us, but he didn't push into the bathroom, which was good cause it wasn't that big. Arms folded, he stared at me. "It is that simple, Hellspawn. We *will* protect you."

The earlier fear resurfaced from beneath the layers of cotton and static. "You don't understand what my uncle…"

Reaching past Rome, Liam caught my wrist lightly. The warmth of his hand on my skin just seemed to emphasize how icy I was. A fresh wave of shudders washed over me. Just like his brother before him, Liam studied the fresh scars.

"Your uncle did this?"

It was a yes or no question and the twins stared at me with equal intensity. All the moisture in my mouth fled. "No." I managed to croak out the word. "One of the men who works for him."

"Name?" Rome asked, even as Liam stroked his thumb over the pulse in my wrist.

"He was new…"

"Name?"

I owed the guard nothing. Absolutely nothing. But I didn't want Liam or Rome getting hurt. The weight of their patience closed in around me. It could have been suffocating, but it wasn't. Neither was going to give up. "Mr. Cole."

"Did he hurt you anywhere else?" Liam flicked a look over me.

"A threat, only," I admitted. "One of the other guards stopped him."

"How many guards, Hellspawn?"

"Six. That I remember." I frowned. "I tried to get away when I first got there. I thought—if I ran once we were back—he'd focus on me and not all of you." I licked my lips. "I hurt my uncle."

"Good," Rome said.

"But they electrocuted the fence and I didn't realize it before I grabbed it."

At that, Liam ran his thumb from my wrist to the mark across my palm. It had been a burn. I could see all of that almost clearly, but I was so divorced from the emotions around all of it.

"Hellspawn?" His soft voice coaxed me to look at him. "Do you want to stay here? Or do you want to go back? To Braxton Harbor?"

"He'll know I'm there."

"I don't care."

But I did. And at the same time—"I want to go back." I closed my eyes. Closed out all the torment and intensity the two of them seemed to carry. "I wanted to keep you safe, but you followed me. You guys—came to get me." It was so hard to wrap my mind around.

"Did you think we wouldn't?" Disappointment edged Liam's voice. "I was right there at the airport."

Another wave of guilt hit.

"She's learning," Rome said. "Leave her alone."

"Shower, Hellspawn." Liam seemed to be relenting. "Food is coming. I want a doctor to look—"

"No." I straightened. "No more doctors. No more drugs. No floating places with white static." The cold on my skin seemed to have made it all the way to my bones.

I didn't care what they said. No more fucking doctors. None.

Rome nodded. "Doc can look at her. You want us to stay or be alone to shower?"

Doc? No, I did not want *Doc* to look at me either. I shook my head and then folded my arms. A part of me wanted to ask them to stay but the rest of me…

"Can we leave the door open a little?"

There was something in the way Liam watched me that left me with no doubts that he wanted to know what was going on inside of me. What secrets was I hiding? What hadn't I told them? If he kept looking—he just might find them.

They came to get me. The shock of finding Freddie at Pinetree renewed all over again.

"We can do whatever you need," Liam promised.

"I'll be right outside," Rome offered.

"Thank you."

Then they were out of the door and it was three-quarters closed, leaving the smallest gap. If I looked at it through the mirror, I could see Rome's arm where he leaned against the wall. He was doing exactly what he said.

He was waiting.

Freddie came into Pinetree.

Liam and Rome were waiting for us as soon as we were out. We were *nowhere* near Braxton Harbor. They didn't just *happen* to be here.

Bracing my hands against the counter, I stared at myself in the mirror. All I wanted to do was close my eyes, curl up and go to sleep without being doped, tied down, or monitored.

Or touched by people I didn't know.

If no one ever touched me again, it would be nice.

My wrist tingled where Liam had gripped me. For all the strength he and Rome possessed, they hadn't squeezed or made me feel anything other than safe.

"Starling?" Rome's voice was so soft I almost didn't hear it.

"I'm here."

"I'm glad you're here."

"Me too," I admitted. "I'm sorry I left."

"Don't do it again."

No, I wouldn't. This was going to be so messy.

"Take a shower," he said. "No one will bother you."

He didn't have to add the words "I promise." I heard them loud and clear. Finally, I stripped off Pinetree's pajamas. The doctor's blood was still on my skin. But the tattoo on my abdomen was right there—thankfully. They'd discussed removing it, but they hadn't.

Head up, wings out.

I could do that.

I could do this.

"I'm here, Starling," Rome reminded me and I smiled again.

"I'm glad you're here," I echoed back his earlier words, then made myself move. I was shivering all over again and I needed to shower.

Chapter Thirty One

ROME

Freddie was asleep before the food arrived. Liam stripped off his shoes, moved him more onto the bed, and covered him up while I waited for Emersyn to finish her shower. It had taken her a while to even turn on the water. The crack in the door let me check on her if I needed to, but I didn't look inside.

The scent of the pizza reminded me I hadn't eaten, but I didn't care. Liam just stacked the boxes on the desk and moved to lean against the wall, arms folded. Neither of us would touch anything until they had eaten.

"She's lost weight." The comment from my brother only echoed my own thoughts.

"Mr. Cole."

"I'll find him."

I didn't even have to ask, Liam understood. In fact, he dragged out his phone and began typing things into it. He had connections. Ties. Resources. I didn't usually think about them. He'd been using them while we were here. The life he led away from us opened doors sometimes. It also brought its own problems.

One problem still waited for us.

I couldn't care about that guy right now. Ezra Graham attacked Liam. People who attacked didn't deserve second chances. "She's hurting."

"I know." His sigh said more than his words. He glanced up from the phone. "We knew it wouldn't be pretty."

Had we? I turned that over in my head as the water finally turned on. The fist in my gut eased back a bit. But only a bit. Since the moment I discovered she'd left, breathing had become an act of will. So had putting one foot in front of the other. Going to Lainey, bringing her back, getting Freddie in place, they had all been things to do.

The waiting though, I didn't like it.

For the first time in days, my fingers itched for a can of spray paint. All of my supplies were in a bag that I hadn't opened once. Now I wanted to paint. More though—I wanted to inflict harm on those who had hurt *her*. She'd been wounded before, black and blue with bruises, tender-headed, and troubled.

The one we blamed for that had suffered as she had suffered. It was enough.

Now?

"Got him." The quiet mutter carried despite the water. The steam rolling out of the bathroom promised it was a hot shower, the scent of the shampoo and soap wasn't familiar. We needed to get her the right things. There were clothes for her in our bags. Clothes I'd packed from Liam's apartment. Things he promised she picked out herself.

When he turned his phone and showed me the picture of the man, I studied him. Big. Thick-muscled. Unsmiling, his eyes promised violence. I accepted the promise. "He works for her uncle?"

"Freelancer, it looks like," Liam murmured. "I don't know the company. Never heard of them before."

I didn't care about the company, unless they were part of hurting her. If they had, we would deal with them too.

The water cut off and I pushed up from the floor. Liam tucked his phone away and passed me a stack of clothes, including clean panties and a bra. Then he nodded to the door. "Gonna go grab some drinks."

He was also giving her space. Freddie was still out.

After the door closed behind Liam, Emersyn said. "Rome?"

"I'm here," I promised, right next to the door where I said I would be.

The huff of a sigh carried a relief I understood. Hearing her voice in Freddie's messages had brought a kind of comfort I didn't understand until now. I needed to *hear* her almost as much as see her.

"I have clothes for you."

She pulled the door open. Wearing only a towel and with another wrapped around her hair, she looked so painfully thin and haunted. The shadows in her eyes had shadows.

"Thank you," she said, then swallowed. Her eyes shimmered as she blinked. I passed the clothes to her, but her fingers brushed over mine. Stilling, I let her hold my hand. "Why?"

Head tilted, I met her watery gaze. "Because you're you." There had only ever been her. I understood what she asked. "You're ours."

A shudder went through her. Fresh worry assaulted me, but then she pressed forward and I moved the clothes so I could close my arms around her. The heat from her skin, the dampness, the feel of her heart racing beneath my palm—it was all my starling.

"You've always been," I promised her. "Nothing that happened changes that."

Her sniffle added another tally to the list of injuries I planned to inflict on those who had hurt her. "Even though I left?"

"Did you really want to go?" Freddie had said she didn't. That she didn't want to go back to them. The photos I found said she'd only done it to protect us. Liam hadn't been wrong when he said we would protect her.

If they came for her again, they would have to go through us to get to her.

"No," she whispered in a hoarse voice so thick with tears it made my own eyes burn. I didn't cry. For Emersyn, I just might.

"You leaving doesn't make you not ours," I said. "It just means we have to come get you."

The wet laugh escaping her made me smile. "I missed you."

Closing my eyes, I cradled her closer. The world was better with her in it. It was perfect with her right here. As reluctant as I was to let her go, when she began to pull away, I opened my arms again. A long, shuddering sigh escaped her.

"I need to get dressed."

I nodded. "And eat."

This time when I gave her the clothes, she hugged them to her. When she hesitated, I turned around. I would have walked away, but she put her hand against my back.

"Thank you."

I wasn't going anywhere. The rasp of the towel let me know she dried off. Then the rustle of clothes as she pulled on the shirt—one of mine—and the sleep shorts. Those were hers. Maybe I should have gotten her pants.

"Do you have a comb?"

"Yes. Go sit on the bed." I waited for her to pass, the lightness of her fingers brushing against my back so welcome.

When she was out of the bathroom, I gathered up the clothes from the floor. The visible blood inside them reminded me of what she'd said about the doctor. I'd talk to Liam about it later. After I disposed of the clothes, I carried the pizza box over and handed her a comb. Then I sat down next to her and kept one eye on her and the other on the door.

We didn't say anything as she ate. Liam took a long time to return. I expected that. He probably had arrangements to make. She only ate two huge slices and drank water, pausing only to comb her hair.

"I want to wake Freddie up to eat and at the same time…"

"Don't," I said. "Pizza is good cold."

"Yeah."

When she finished, I put the pizza boxes back and moved the blankets so she could get into the bed. Liam returned with the sodas. They went into the little fridge, then he locked the door. Once everything was secure, he tugged off his shoes then stripped down out of his jeans. I did the same and he climbed in on one side of her and I climbed in on the other. The bed wasn't that big, but she really didn't take up any space.

Liam took the side closest to the door. He also put his gun on the table over there. There was another in the drawer if I needed it.

"Is this all right?" Liam asked.

Emersyn let out a sigh only to yawn in the middle of it. She burrowed against me and held out a hand to Liam.

That was an answer. Meeting Liam's gaze over her head, I read the concern. With a nod, I shut off the light and pressed my lips to her damp hair.

She was back where she belonged.

Tomorrow, we would take care of things so we could take her

home.

Liam woke me at dawn. Freddie was in the shower and Emersyn slept. She'd barely moved throughout the night. Even in sleep, her expression didn't relax.

His damp hair suggested he had also showered. Liam said, "I'm going for food and supplies for them. Shower when Freddie is done. I'll be back soon."

Rubbing my face, I nodded. "What time do we leave?"

"By eight."

Emersyn was still asleep when I ducked into the shower after Freddie. I left him eating cold pizza and drinking a soda. Liam was back and she sat up in bed when I came out. The smell of eggs, bacon, waffles and more filled the room. He'd gotten her a little bit of everything.

"You're leaving?" Instead of eating though, she stared at Liam with uncertainty.

"Yes," he answered. "Don't worry, Hellspawn. We'll be back within a day. That's why I brought you two supplies." The bags lined the top of the desk. "There are microwavable meals in there too. More drinks. I also bought a real coffee maker. "

Freddie leaned forward. "It's gonna be fun, Boo-Boo. You and me. I bet they have porn on the hotel tv. We can charge it all to Liam."

The comment worked, a flash of a smile dispelled some of her worry. But when her gaze tracked to me, it all came back.

"You'll be safe, Starling. We'll be fast." As possible. I didn't say the last two words aloud.

I wasn't sure if she believed me, but she nodded.

"Hellspawn," Liam said and the snap in his voice made all of us look at him. "Behave. Stay in the room. We'll be back. Listen to Freddie—except about the porn." The last he said with a hard look at Freddie, who just grinned.

"Do you have to go?" The quiet question had me ready to toss all of it and stay. I would, except… Except staying meant we didn't deal with this Mr. Cole. Mr. Cole needed to be dealt with. She needed to know he would *never* touch her again.

"Yes." I crossed to the bed and nudged her plate. "Eat. Sleep.

Shower again if you want. The bag by the closet is yours. We brought things for you from the apartment."

"Boo-Boo and I are gonna be fine," Freddie said. "Aren't we?"

She smiled, but it wasn't a real one and it didn't quite reach her eyes.

"We'll be back," I reminded her. "I promise. Promise to stay in the room?"

Another soft exhale, then she nodded slowly. "I will. Promise."

"I don't." The comment made her smile for real. "I am done with rules."

"Freddie," Liam said with the most aggrieved sigh.

"Damn, take the stick out man. I'm kidding. We made it. We rescued Boo-Boo. Well, I did, but I'll give you guys twenty percent of the credit. Go and do all the things and come back. We're gonna be fine, right?"

"Right," she said, though her voice didn't sound as solidly believing it as he did. "I'm sorry," she said again as I straightened.

"For what?" Liam asked, he'd already turned to the door.

"I'm not usually this needy."

"You're not needy," I told her, then did what I'd been wanting to do since I picked her up in the woods. Cupping her cheek, I nudged her chin up and then brushed a kiss to her lips. Just a touch. To remind myself she was real. "We'll be back."

"Okay." There was a real light in her eyes again. Not as bright as it should be, but at least one shadow seemed to have drawn back. "Hurry?"

"Yes."

Hurry. Go and deal with this. Then come back. To her.

I glanced at Freddie.

"I got her." It was a promise. Just like when he said he'd get her back. I cut a look to the drawer. Had Liam told him? He nodded. He knew.

Good.

Leaving was harder than I thought. Liam didn't seem as troubled by it. Once outside of the room, he led the way to the SUV. "They'll be fine and we'll be back before morning."

"We'll be back tonight," I told him as I climbed into the passenger seat.

"Or we can be back tonight," he agreed. Almost too easily.

"First, Ezra. We're gonna have to let him go."

I didn't like that idea. "Do we?"

He pulled out of the spot, not once looking back. I kept cutting my gaze to the side mirror. I didn't want to leave them at the hotel alone. But this one was even more anonymous than the other. Freddie would look after her.

"Yes, Rome," Liam said in a firm voice. "We do."

"He attacked you."

"Well, he had his reasons."

Whatever. "If he does it again…"

"Leave it." We didn't argue much. "Just don't bring up Lainey while we're there."

"Why would I bring her up?" I'd barely thought about her, other than she'd given us the info on where Emersyn was.

"You know, just—never mind." All at once, he sounded aggravated. I left it alone. The other hotel was a good fifteen minutes away. We'd moved after we parked Ezra at the other one. The silence lasted until we were pulling into the parking lot at the hotel. "You up for this?"

"Letting him go?" I frowned. "No, but you said you wanted to."

My brother twisted in the seat and stared at me. "I meant what we're doing after. Going after Cole. I have a line on him, it's gonna take us a couple of hours to get there, then we gotta track him down…"

"Him? Yes. Him, I'm ready for."

At least four hours in travel time and there was still Cole to deal with. We could spend a few hours and make it back before she went to sleep.

"Rome." The snap jerked my attention back to Liam. "Focus, bro. If your head is back at the hotel, I can take you back and leave you there."

Tempting.

"Cole first. He hurt her."

Liam nodded. "Then focus. You're not gonna get hurt cause you can't stop thinking about her. Got it?"

"We're wasting time." My fingers twitched. The desire to paint and to draw slid through me. "You can't stop thinking about her either. Don't pretend you can." I shoved open the door and he sighed.

Pacing me all the way to the door, Liam said, "We'll be back with her soon."

Yes. We would.

"But first, your friend."

"Yeah," Liam agreed with a sigh. "My friend."

Chapter Thirty Two

LIAM

"That's it?" Ezra demanded, glaring at me. "You're just letting me go?"

"I'd have let you go a few days ago if you hadn't been such a dick," I told him honestly. Rome was dead silent and had been since we walked back into the room. "You weren't leaving me a lot of choices."

"But whatever the fuck you were doing here, you're done now, is that it?" Anger soaked the words but it was more than just rage. For all that he acted like he didn't give a damn about anything, Ezra fell prey to the same fears as the rest of us. The fear of losing the ones we cared about.

Lainey. She had to have been the leverage that Adam kept shutting him up about. I'd had time to think about it since the near miss the other day. The king used leverage when you didn't cooperate. The threat designed to keep you in line, should you suddenly develop independent thinking. Rome was on that list.

He'd made the mistake of going for him once. I returned the message in kind. His would-be assassins had all gone back in body bags. Still, even if the message had been received, the king could still try to leverage him against me. It was why we could never relax our vigilance and why I kept my parents as far away as possible.

They didn't need to be dragged into this fight.

"For the most part," I said, finally.

"I suppose you're not even going to tell me what it is." He dragged a hand through his disheveled hair. The abrasions on his wrists said more about how much he'd tried to get out of the zip ties than anything else. I'd set him free as soon as we got back and he moved around the room with slow, halting steps.

In hindsight, restraining him to the chair and limiting his movements probably hadn't done him any favors. But I didn't have time for his volatile temper or unpredictable actions. The only person I'd ever seen come close to tempering him was Adam, and even then— that was fifty-fifty.

"No." Arms folded, I kept an eye on him. "We picked up your car, it's outside. It's got gas. Go home."

"Man, you're not even going to fucking help me?"

"I can't," I said. Unfortunately for him, it was the honest truth. "Right now, I have my own problems that I need to deal with."

Ezra cut his gaze past me, then back. Rome stood by the door, a silent sentinel. "Then answer this for me…"

"If I can."

"Have you seen Adam?"

It was a direct question and deserved a direct answer. I didn't think he'd like mine, but I couldn't offer him much more. "The last time I saw him was almost three weeks ago. We were both summoned to a meeting."

"Fuck," Ezra swore. Yeah, I didn't have to explain who summoned us. Technically, Rome wasn't supposed to know anything about this life or those choices. So Ezra would risk a hell of a lot *if* he brought it up. "You haven't seen or spoken to him since?"

"Nope." Then, before he could bring up Emersyn's best friend— which I didn't want to focus on how strangely intertwined this knot of connections was—I added, "I can't help you, right now. Once I get this shit sorted out, I'll see what I can do."

It was the best I had to offer.

The glower he wore didn't offer much in the way of understanding or acceptance. "Remind me not to do any more favors."

I snorted. "I've never asked you for any. And you're not asking me now." Because he absolutely wasn't. He wanted information. He wanted me to come to his aid. Like I said, we weren't friends. The Royals didn't show their loyalty that way.

They never had.

At the moment, he'd just have to take what I could give him.

Pivoting, he stuck his hand out. "Give me my gun."

"No," I said with a shake of my head. "Your wallet and your phone are in your car. The phone's got no juice and there's no charger in there. It'll take you a minute to work on that."

Not leaving him at my back armed. I might like the guy, but I wasn't an idiot. Pivoting, I headed for the door.

"Where are the keys?" Ezra asked as Rome opened the door. I held up the set in my hand as I walked outside. I lifted my chin to Rome to head for the car. We'd ripped the phone out of the hotel room. If Ezra cooled the fuck off, he could go ask to use the phone in the office.

I wasn't waiting around for that.

Three steps from the SUV, I pitched the keys to his Porsche 911 toward the green belt that bordered along the side of the hotel. It wasn't exactly a heavily wooded area, but it'd take him a minute to find them in the grass.

"You're an asshole, O'Connell," Ezra said from the doorway, glaring at me.

"Yep," I agreed. I was definitely an asshole. "Go home. I'll call you when I'm free."

"Don't do me any favors," the other man yelled, and I touched two fingers to my temple and saluted him before I slid into the driver's seat. Rome waited until I had the SUV started before he joined me.

"This is a bad idea," he said as I accelerated out of the lot.

"Maybe, but he can't help us with this and he's already caused us enough delays."

"You going to help him?" Rome drummed the fingers of his right hand against his knee. The eerie stillness gripping him since Emersyn vanished on us seemed to have been cured by her return.

Thank fuck.

"That's what I told him." I shrugged. The GPS told me we were roughly 98 minutes from our destination.

"You lied to him."

I frowned. "What?"

"You lied to him about his friend."

"I haven't seen Adam in almost three weeks."

"That part was true."

I sighed.

"But you have spoken to him."

"Actually…" I resisted the urge to punch the dashboard. I needed a fight, badly. We couldn't get to our destination soon enough. "I haven't spoken to him. So no, I didn't lie to him."

"If I asked you?"

Cutting my gaze to the right, I met my twin's stare. "Don't." Then I added, "Please."

Rome nodded. "I don't really care."

Yeah, I knew that.

"But you're hiding something."

"We're all hiding something."

"I'm not."

I laughed. "No, bro, you don't hide anything. You just don't talk about something if you don't want to talk about it."

He nodded, but when I glanced at him, his attention was on the window. Impatience seemed to writhe in the air around him. The only thing keeping him in the seat was that we needed to deal with this guy.

Fact was, I *wanted* to deal with him. The last time I'd seen her before I went to meet her so-called uncle, she'd been whole and there'd been a light in her eyes. Now, she was marked up and the shadows in her eyes were thicker than ever. Her curves were gone, the subtle form of them she'd been gaining all seemed to have been worn away in the last three weeks or so.

Three weeks shouldn't be a damn eternity.

"We'll get this done and then get back to her."

And after that, I was going to make sure no one ever laid a finger on her again.

* * *

We parked down the street from the firm—Legionnaire Preservation Service—weird name for a place that specialized in asset protection and threat mitigation. Of course, they also offered other services, like private investigations, process servicing, and transportation. The company wasn't listed, all of their contracts came through private references, and you couldn't walk in off the street and hire them.

It had taken me three months to uncover the damn name when I first began looking into Bradley Sharpe and the rest of the Sharpe family. This firm handled all of the uncle's security concerns. Greasing the wheels with some former classmates had scored me a reference. But I hadn't actually used it beyond tracking where they were "based."

I'd been too busy, especially after Milo sent Emersyn to live with me. That reminded me, we hadn't called the guys yet. We should probably do that. Except…

"How do you know he's going to be here?"

"I don't," I answered. "I just know this is who he works for and they're required to appear at the offices once a week if they aren't on an assignment."

"And if he's on assignment?"

"Then I'm pretty sure they'll call him in for the box I had couriered over here this morning." A box I'd sent with a return address of Bradley Sharpe and the promise of a bonus. Greed got to everyone.

Rome shifted in the seat. "You hope."

"I have a plan b."

"Good."

I sighed, then cut a look toward him because the weight of his stare bored into me. "What?"

"You like her."

Pulling my gaze from Rome, I focused on the doors to the building. It wasn't a huge one. They weren't located in some downtown metropolis, but instead they were in a suburb. I supposed it made sense.

The pressure of his gaze didn't shift. I watched the building and he watched me. "Yes," I said, finally. "I like her. She's a pain in the ass, but she's also a fighter. What does it matter?" She was his girl. I wasn't going to get in the way. Even if he'd wanted me sleeping on the other side of her, I got it.

It was the same when she'd been at the apartment. Keep the bad dreams away. Make her feel safe.

"It's okay to like her."

I frowned, then twisted to look at him again. He wasn't looking at me but at the building.

"You were right. He's here."

Jerking my attention back to the target, I flexed my fist then pulled up the photograph of Mr. Cole. My contact hadn't been able to get me much more than a picture and the confirmation he worked here. Anything beyond that would cross a line they didn't want to cross. Fine, whatever. I just wanted to get my hands on the son of a bitch.

I paid good money for the information.

Worth every penny.

"Mr. Cole" wasn't inside long. I didn't touch the ignition while he made his way down the street toward a public lot. As soon as he turned the corner, I started the car and rolled forward. He got into a silver car.

"Get the plate," I told Rome as we passed it. The car had backed out of its spot and I pulled into the next drive like I was going to get into the drive-thru.

"Got it."

Then I "changed my mind" and went to the next exit.

"He's going south."

A left turn and I was back on the road. We were three cars behind him. There we stayed as he got on the interstate. He didn't stay on it long. Fortunately, he wasn't the only one who got off at his exit and we moved with him. I dropped back another car length. His car was lower to the ground, but the SUV gave us the height to look past the other vehicles.

When he pulled into a lot near a grocery store. I glanced at Rome. "Here or wait?"

"Here."

I let Rome off at the door, even as I tracked Cole's movement through the parking lot.

"I'll be around back."

Fifteen minutes later, Rome half-carried "Mr. Cole" as he walked right out through a service door and shoved him into the backseat. I glanced back as Rome climbed in with him. Blood trickled from the guy's forehead. Not that Rome was especially gentle with the prick.

"He resisted."

"I didn't say anything. You didn't leave a trail?"

"I did—it won't matter—" Alarms went off inside the building and I pressed the accelerator.

"I'm not going to ask."

"Okay."

"Get his phone and shut it off."

"Done."

The next twenty minutes passed in silence. Mr. Cole began to groan at one point and Rome kicked him. That shut him up.

We needed a good spot and this wasn't our territory. Hell, we were hell and gone from our territory. But I had a few ideas. While Rome went shopping, I'd done a couple of web searches locally.

The place I'd picked out should work.

We had everything we needed in the back.

It took another half hour to get to the abandoned train yard. There were rail cars sitting idle, covered in graffiti. A chain link fence was all that stood between us and getting in. They didn't even have cameras.

I clipped the padlock and replaced it with another.

Cole had begun to really resurface and he thrashed in the back, at least until Rome put a foot on his throat. Then the guy just gurgled until he passed out again.

My brother was pissed.

So was I.

After driving through the gates and securing them with my own padlock, I headed for the northwestern corner of the train yard, where it backed up toward a deserted field covered in trash and debris.

Yeah, no one came here.

Maybe some kids.

We could deal with them.

I found exactly what I was looking for, a stack of rail cars I could park in between. A couple of them stood open. Between us, it took no time to drag Mr. Cole into one of the cars and lash him up.

"Who the fuck are you?" he demanded, but neither of us answered.

Once we had him lashed in place, I went back for the kit and wrapped my hands. Rome waited, almost dispassionately, for me. Once I was back and we had the plastic spread out, the guy tried to lash out. He kicked at us—well me. But he never landed.

"I said, who the fuck are you?"

Rome raised his phone. There was a picture of Emersyn on it. The guy paled.

Yep. He knew her.

When Rome slid the photo to the next and showed the scars on her arms, sweat broke out on his forehead.

He did it. He cut her up.

Confirmation.

"We're vengeance," I informed him. "You touched someone you shouldn't have."

"You won't do it again," Rome said.

We really didn't have anything else to say to him. The first strike I landed against the guy's jaw rocked his head back. That hurt.

The next fifty or so were going to hurt a lot more.

Chapter Thirty Three

EMERSYN

After the twins left, I found myself staring at the door and waiting. I didn't touch the food or the drink. Just stared at it. The last few days—well, I'd done nothing without being directed. The nurses came in, the orderlies fetched me, we went to see the doctor, or we went to the floating place. Even when I showered, I wasn't alone.

When Rome asked me if I wanted him to close the door or not, I'd been torn. Privacy seemed almost novel, but at the same time, I didn't want them to disappear. What if I opened the door after the shower to find myself back in my room at Pinetree?

Not that the bathroom had a door. But if I imagined all of this—the escape, killing Doctor Skate-Boarder, Rome and Liam—I didn't want to wake up. No, the door had to stay open. When he'd said "I'm here," everything in me just seemed to sag. Somehow, Rome understood.

The bed had made for crowded sleeping quarters, but I didn't care. The minute they were on either side of me, all the panic and the fear subsided. Sinking into the exhaustion had been the easiest thing in the world. Made only that much better when I woke to Rome being right there with me this morning.

But now they were gone…

"Boo-Boo."

I jerked and twisted to stare at Freddie as my heart slammed against my ribs.

He had a biscuit halfway to his mouth, but he paused and frowned at me. "Did you forget I was here already, Boo-Boo?"

"No." The fact the syllable came out a bit of a squeak made a liar out of me. "I was wondering if I was going to wake up and all of this wouldn't be real."

"I get that," he said slowly. "But you're not naked."

Laughter bubbled up through me and the balloon of tension just seemed to pop. "Right. I forgot."

"You forgot you weren't naked?" Freddie clasped his hands over his heart. "Boo-Boo. We need to work on that."

It was funny, except it wasn't. I'd been having trouble remembering a lot of things. Like my damn name. It wasn't so bad here, but after the floating place and the white static… Tears escaped while I laughed and I swiped at them.

Freddie sobered almost instantly. "Come on, Boo-Boo. Don't cry. I suck at tears. You start crying and I'm going to feel like I should be crying with you and no one wants to see me blubbering."

Another soft chuckle escaped me, and I sniffed while I wiped at my eyes again. "I'm not going to cry—I just… My head feels so full." Did that even make sense? "And, they were here and now they're gone and—"

"And?" he prompted when I didn't say anything more.

I shook my head. "I don't know. I don't even get why I'm upset they left. It's better here, right? I mean, we're in a hotel room." It was kind of small, but it had clean sheets. There was food. I looked back down at the breakfast I'd stopped eating. Yeah. I didn't want any more of that.

Cleaning it up, I climbed off the bed to put the containers on the desk with the others and then I stood there, just staring at the room. What were we supposed to do? They said stay in the room. But…

"You want to talk about it?" The question tugged at me. Freddie was cleaning up his own debris from eating. His pizza box was empty though.

"Not really." I wouldn't even know where to begin. "Do you?"

"If it will help you."

I frowned. This wasn't like confessions. It was daytime for one, and we were looking at each other. He held out his hand to me after he put the empty box by the trash can.

"We don't have to talk about anything," he offered. "We could watch tv. I bet they really do have pay-per-view movies."

"I don't really want to watch porn," I admitted but let him tug me back to the bed. Only instead of mine, he patted his. When I sat against the headboard, he sat next to me then he put a pillow between our hips. "What are you doing?"

He dropped another between our legs. "This is no man's land. You're on your side and I'm on mine." Even saying that, he rested his hand palm up on the pillow between us. "That way, we only touch when we want to."

The tears burned in my eyes all over again. Clasping his hand tighter this time, I leaned my head back. "Thank you." The relief was right there and some of the chaos churning in my mind quieted. Rome and Liam touching me when I was in bed with them hadn't bothered me, but the longer I'd been awake the more the agitation was right there.

"I get it, Boo-Boo," Freddie said, not looking at me as he picked up the remote. He turned on the television but muted the sound as he began to flick through the channels. His fingers threaded with mine easily and his grip was steady. "Touch is something you allow people to do. When they do it and you don't want it, it's—bad."

That seemed like an understatement. Yet, he did get it. "I wished you didn't know."

"About you?"

I kept my gaze on the television, I think Freddie was too. But he didn't loosen his grip from my hand. "About any of it. I wish you didn't understand what it was like."

"I could say the same thing, Boo-Boo."

But he hadn't. Maybe I shouldn't have. "Sorry, I won't bring it up."

He squeezed my hand. "I don't mind if you bring it up. I told you for a reason. It was weird—I don't tell anyone, but telling you helped. I think."

"Yeah?" I frowned. "Like group?"

I stole a glance at him when the channel flipping stopped. He stared at me. "Um—I wasn't a big fan of group," he admitted.

"But Bodhi was in your group."

"That's true." Freddie grinned. "Weird guy, but I liked him."

"Me too."

Neither of us mentioned the doctor. The office. The blood—

"Where's my stapler?"

"It's over there," Freddie assured me. "It came in with us. Don't worry."

The chill skating over me was stupid. Taking that stapler with me was probably kind of dumb too. He squeezed my hand again.

"Do you need me to get it for you, Boo-Boo?"

I frowned. Did I? Closing my eyes, I tried to suck in a deeper breath of air past the panic scrabbling against the inside of my skin. "No," I whispered. "I just—I wanted to know…"

Letting go of my hand, he slid off the bed. By the time I opened my eyes, he had rescued the stapler from behind the bags of takeout and food. I still couldn't figure out why Liam brought so much. "It's right here." Freddie set it right in the middle of the desk and shoved everything around it back. "Better?"

Stupidly… "Yes."

He grinned. "Good."

When he came back to the bed, he reclaimed my hand and I sighed. Tilting my head, I let it rest against his shoulder. "Is this okay?"

"Yep," he said. "You're fine." He didn't add anything, just kept scrolling through the options. I had no idea how many times we went through the channels over and over until he stopped on a show. "This will work."

I frowned, but he turned the volume up as the credits rolled. Apparently, we'd found the show right at the beginning. Apparently, there was a whole marathon of *Murder, She Wrote* on. It was—nice.

After the third episode, Freddie put popcorn in the room's microwave and grabbed us sodas. The scent of the buttered popcorn made my stomach growl. After the sixth one, I glanced at the door.

"Want to watch something else?"

"No." I needed to pee though. "This is fine." Especially since I kept zoning out. The television helped, but the headache throbbing behind my left eye seemed to be growing in intensity. At the next commercial break, I scooted off the bed and went to the bathroom.

When I came back, Freddie had traded out the empty cans for bottles of water. "You don't look so good," he said.

"I don't feel so good."

"Then maybe we can take a nap?" He shoved a hand through his thick blond hair and twisted to sit sideways. "Maybe eat some more?"

None of that sounded good. The hot-cold sensation washing over me was uncomfortable. The headache was worse. At least the water bottles were cold and I pressed one to my face. My stomach twisted.

"Boo-Boo, what can I do?"

"Nothing," I told him. "Not even sure why I feel this way, why my skin wants to itch off my body, or my heart is racing." We were watching television.

Freddie grimaced. "Don't focus on that."

"Okay." Easier said than done. "What do you want me to focus on?"

"The show. Me. Um…Hell, I brought books." He was off the bed again and this time he went for his bag. When he came back, he had three paperbacks. "Remember when you would read to me?"

Flushed, I fanned my face with my hand and moved the water bottle to press against my neck. "I remember."

"Well, I can read to you if you want."

"We can watch the show too," I offered. "It's okay. I'm just— maybe I'm getting a cold?"

"Maybe." Freddie raised his hand toward me, then hesitated. "Can I?"

I lowered the water bottle and nodded. Freddie wouldn't hurt me. With a light touch, he pressed his much cooler palm to my forehead. His frown deepened.

"Told you I was hot."

He snorted. "Too easy."

A hint of laughter escaped around the pain throbbing in my skull with my heartbeat. "I am not."

Grinning, for real, Freddie shifted his hand to my nape and I closed my eyes. His hand was so cold. "Yeah, you're on fire, Boo-Boo. Cold shower or ice."

"I can do a cold shower." I'd done those before. He plucked the water bottle from my hand and then offered to help me up, but I waved him off. "I can do it. I showered last night."

"Yeah, you do not look good."

The temptation to flick his nose vibrated through me, for now, I just stumbled into the shower. "I'm not closing the door."

"Does that mean I get to watch?" The question was so light and so Freddie. "Fuck me, I didn't just ask that."

The laughter swelling up now was a little more freeing. "It's okay, I can pretend I didn't hear it. I'm very good at pretending."

Very good. Too good. I turned the water on. The cold was almost too icy against my skin, but I stripped down before I slid inside. Holy shit. I grimaced. I could do ice showers when I was really sore, but this was so much colder than normal, and it wasn't even that cold.

"Fuck, fuck, fuck," I cursed the litany as the shivers hit, but the flushed feeling retreated and it took some of the headache with it. Wimping out, I turned the hot water on and let out a shudder when the frigid water warmed up.

More awake and a lot less nauseated, I didn't linger under the warm water too long. Rinsing off felt good though and a quick wash also helped. I managed to only get the ends of my hair damp. The smell of coffee teased me as I got dressed.

"Did you make that for me?" I asked.

"No, I made it for the ghost next door," Freddie called. "She gets real cranky without her coffee and I figured we didn't need to be jumping at shadows."

With a snort, I shut off the bathroom light and stepped back out into the room. He'd done a little more tidying up. At least he'd gotten rid of the empty popcorn bag. He held out the full disposable mug with the lid.

"Fancy."

"For the ghosts? Absolutely."

"Are we talking ghost boobs and ghost sex too?"

I had no idea where that question even came from. Freddie did contortions with his eyebrows and the smirk on his face was adorable. "Ghost sex—gotta imagine that's a cock tease."

"Why does it have to be a cock tease?" I asked, climbing back onto the bed and walking on my knees to where I'd been sitting. I was a lot clearer and the coffee was bitter, but sweet. There was no creamer in it, but he'd dumped enough sugar in to cut the edge. "It could be a cunt tease."

"Ghost dick?" Freddie's smirk grew. "Telling me a fantasy,

Boo-Boo?"

"I wasn't the one courting the ghost next door." The bland response was almost perfect. He cracked up and sat down next to me. When he lifted his coffee cup to tap mine, I smiled. "Thank you, Freddie."

"Anytime, Boo-Boo." He grimaced after he took a swallow of the coffee. "Maybe I need to get a job as a barista next."

I didn't laugh at him, but I did study him. He had so many different jobs. At least, it sounded like he did. "What do you want to do?"

"Me?"

"No, your ghost girlfriend in apartment 'boo'."

His eyebrows danced their little dance as he fought against the laughter. "You're the best, Boo-Boo."

"No," I said slowly, my own smile fading. "I think we both know that's not true."

"You are not them," he said suddenly. "Am I those people who used me?"

His gaze locked on mine and I couldn't breathe for the pressure in my chest. "No."

"Then you're not your family or your uncle or anyone else who put their damn hands on you." The absolute sincerity in his words and tone were impossible to argue.

"It doesn't always feel that way."

He sighed. "Yeah. That part sucks."

"I keep wanting to ask you to forget what I said."

It was his turn to nod slowly. "I want to wish I hadn't told you, too."

"I'm sorry that happened to you."

"Ditto."

But what did that leave us? When he held out his hand, I took it. When he turned the show back on and after I finished my coffee, I tucked my head against his shoulder. When my eyes got heavy, I let them close.

I wasn't alone. Freddie was right there.

Chapter Thirty Four

FREDDIE

Liam and Rome were back before midnight, Boo-Boo didn't see them arrive because she'd finally gone to sleep—after throwing up everything she'd eaten. I wasn't a fan of puking. It made me want to puke. The fact I barely held on had everything to do with the fact I refused to throw up on her. The dull thud of the headache I nursed reminded me that as much as I'd avoided their drugs, I'd still taken some.

When she'd gotten all flushed and overheated once more, I ushered her in to take another cool shower. This time, I stayed close, cause she also wasn't steady on her feet. Pretty pussy or not, I was more worried about her falling than I was ogling. Besides, she really didn't need me looking at her. The "he touched me" explanation floated around in my head alongside that confession.

I sat up because until they were back, I wasn't going to sleep with her vulnerable in this room. I had my knife and there was a gun in the drawer. Didn't matter. No one was going to get at her on my watch. Whenever a little whimper escaped her, or she shifted in her sleep, I moved my leg to put pressure on the pillows between us. That put pressure on her via the pillow. It worked and I wasn't crowding her.

"What happened?" Rome asked not even a minute after they came in. They were quiet, she didn't even twitch. Sweat dotted her brow again and I tossed a washcloth at Liam.

"Can you rinse that down in cold water?"

He didn't even ask, just went to do it, while Rome came around to the far side of the bed I was sharing with Boo-Boo. His grave expression said he knew *something* was wrong.

"Waiting for Liam," I said. "I don't want to have to explain this twice." Between my own tiredness and headache, I really wanted to go to sleep. With them back, I could do that. They'd take care of her.

After his brother came back with the washcloth, Rome snagged it and began to wipe her face down slowly and gently. Yeah, he got it.

"Withdrawal," I said to Liam's questioning look. "They were loading her up pretty hard on drugs. I didn't even think about it. She got sick earlier. Couldn't keep anything down. The tremors and the shakes are there too."

"Drugs." Liam's whole expression darkened. "Fuck. Why didn't you say anything earlier?"

"One, I didn't think about it," I told him. "Two, I was fucking exhausted. And three, what the fuck did you think they were doing in there? You heard what the Ball-Cracker said about that place. I'm pretty sure they were doing some kind of other treatments too. I couldn't get into that medical ward though, to see what they did."

I hadn't even noticed they had a medical ward until after Bodhi came to get me. The doctor's *office* had been next to that ward. It would make sense, but I just—fuck, I knew they'd been doing something.

"She called it the floating place or the white static." As much as it killed me to reveal anything she told me in confidence, they needed to know this. "There were days she didn't know me at all." That had scared me more than hurt though. Because in all the time I'd known her, she hadn't once treated me like an afterthought or someone to be ignored.

The sight of her in that wheelchair, completely checked out? Yeah, that wasn't going away any time soon. Liam glanced past me to Rome then down to her. "We don't know what they were giving her?"

I shook my head. "Didn't have time to steal records. The escape turned out to be a little more spontaneous than my original idea."

Not that I was going to cry one fucking tear for that asshole.

But maybe I should have tried to get her file or something. Fuck, did I mess this up?

"Hey," Liam said and he rested a hand on my shoulder. It was light, but also brief and he let me go after one gentle squeeze. "You did good. You got her out and you didn't get dead. We can handle the rest."

I nodded, then glanced over at her again. I hoped he was right.

* * *

We weren't flying back. Liam debated it with himself, cause Rome didn't seem to have an opinion and I didn't care. Then again, taking her through an airport meant security, which meant no weapons, which meant—yeah, we were driving.

Instead of leaving first thing the next morning, they waited for her to not be nauseated anymore. If the day before had been bad—the next morning was awful. Liam had gone out to get coffee and when he came back, she just couldn't hold anything down.

When she fell into an uneasy sleep, I caught the twins looking at each other. At least I didn't have to hold her hair when she puked this time. I would have if she'd needed me, but Rome hadn't moved away from her. Not once.

Late afternoon, she managed some water and some crackers without puking. She also made the decision for all of us. "I want to go home."

Home.

Yeah.

The twins shared another of those telepathic looks. But the decision was made before Liam said a word. Emersyn wanted to go back to Braxton Harbor, then that was where we were going. Good. Doc could look at her there. Make sure she was okay.

It didn't take us long to pack the room up, wipe it down. We still had her bloodied clothes to deal with, but I'd rather they were with us until we had a safe spot to burn them. The stapler came too.

Liam and Rome swapped out the driving, I offered to help but they waved me off and that was fine. The tremors came and went. So did the vague sensation of motion sickness. Not something that had ever been my problem. Then again, they'd been giving me shit too. But I wasn't a mess.

Emersyn was. She sat in the backseat and had a bucket and a bag. Rome was back there with her at the moment, though Liam had been trading out with him. I needed to be more useful, but neither of them asked me.

Fortunately, the one time she'd puked in the car so far, we pulled over and opened all the doors. That was a smell that not even she could make attractive.

It was afternoon, the sun was way too fucking bright to be any other time the next time I roused. Rome was behind the wheel. Soft music played, but my brain was too fuzzy to identify what the song was.

"It's fine, Hellspawn," Liam said in a droll voice. "Puke anywhere in here you want. We can clean it up."

I didn't gag. It was a close thing.

"I don't want to vomit anymore," Emersyn said in a voice both exhausted and aggrieved.

"Want to try the motion sickness stuff we got you again?"

What stuff? I rubbed a hand over my face. Maybe we'd stopped somewhere while I was sleeping.

"It didn't work last time." Despite the complaint, it wasn't a no.

"Just give it a shot," Liam told in a far gentler voice than I was used to hearing from him. "We got some of the lemon-lime soda too. That helped, right?"

"Some. Okay."

My head still thumped but it wasn't anywhere near as bad. A bump of a bottle against my arm had me opening my eyes. Rome held out an unopened water bottle to me. Yeah. Hydrate. Probably a good idea.

I twisted the cap off and drained about half of it before I leaned my head back against the seat again.

The only sound in the car was the hum of the wheels on the road and the music playing. Pretty sure I drifted back off to sleep. The next time I woke up, we were pulling off into one of those rest areas. Liam was back behind the wheel and he'd barely gotten the SUV stopped before Emersyn was out. She didn't even make it to one of the trash cans before she threw up into the grass.

Fuck.

I pressed a hand to my mouth and Liam slapped some peppermints in my hand. "Suck on those."

Yeah, good plan.

We all took a break. I had to take a leak and the twins had Emersyn. When I got back, Liam was there by himself and he'd cleaned out the backseat again. I didn't ask. He didn't tell. I just sucked on another peppermint. They helped.

Maybe it was a placebo, I didn't care.

"Should we take her to a hospital?" It wasn't a question I wanted to ask and I knew how long it could take to come down. That was when I had some idea of what I'd been taking. Fuck, what I wouldn't give to be high right now. Then I wouldn't have to think about all this shit.

At the same time, if I were high I couldn't help her, so that wasn't going to work.

"No," Liam said. "She's keeping down more fluids, we just have to be careful about what she eats. We'll be back in the harbor in a few hours."

"Where the fuck are we, anyway?"

"Copper Town City is about thirty-five miles up this road. Then we'll have six, maybe seven hours before we're back in the harbor."

Holy shit. "How fucking fast have you guys been driving?"

"Do you care?"

No, except... "Boo-Boo is in the car."

"Exactly," he said, giving me a level look before he reached into the back and cracked open the cooler. There were sodas, water, and what looked like more of the lemon-lime stuff. I wanted one but I wasn't taking anything from her. So, I settled for one of the others. The first sip wasn't bad, even if I had been sucking on a peppermint. It was getting dark again.

We'd been on the road all day and all night the night before. Weren't they tired? I was fucking dead.

"I'm surprised the guys aren't blowing up the phones." I swore what few brain cells I had left seemed to be sparking. Pretty sure my phone was dead. I hadn't even looked at it since the twins showed up.

Probably dumb on my part, but both Liam and Rome had their phones.

"They don't know we're on the way back."

I blinked. "What the fuck?" Was he insane? Jasper would kill him. "They need to know we found her."

"They know we found her," Liam reminded me. "They don't know we got her out, and before you decide to blow your stack, think. She's having a lot of trouble right now and that's with the three of us hovering. She does not need to answer their questions or try to make them feel better right now."

"They wouldn't—"

"They would." He cut me off with a wave of his hand. "They would because I want to. A part of me wants to paddle her ass for taking off like that, and then I look at her." When his gaze went past me, I twisted around. Unsurprisingly, there she was, walking back to the SUV with Rome. He wasn't holding her hand or touching her, but he was right there.

"She looks like hell."

"Yeah, so, no, I haven't told them. We're not telling them until Doc has a look at her. I'm worried about dehydration at this point."

That made sense. "I didn't think she'd be this sick."

"We don't know what they gave her."

And we didn't know what to give her to stop it either. If it was just the matter of scoring her something, I could do that.

But Liam didn't ask and I didn't offer. Probably a terrible idea. She was back, we had her. That was the important part.

Liam and Rome swapped out again, with Liam climbing in back with her.

"You okay, Freddie?" she asked and I twisted in the passenger seat to grin at her. For her, I could smile.

"I'm great. Still not naked, though." When Liam snapped his gaze to me, I ignored him because Boo-Boo laughed.

"Go back to sleep," she suggested. "Though, I kind of feel like crap so I don't even think naked would be good."

"I'll let you know," I promised and she smiled again. As I started to face forward, I got Liam's dirty look and couldn't help myself. The guy was just asking for it. "I get to dream of her naked and she gets to dream of me naked. It's our thing."

Probably any other time, Liam would grouse at me, but Boo-Boo laughed again and yeah, that point was mine. Go me.

It was way too fucking early in the morning when we got to the clinic. There was a relief in being there though. Being somewhere familiar. Course, the last time I was here someone had been watching the place. The guys must have had the same thought, because we went around the block a couple of times.

Checking.

Smart.

When we pulled into the lot behind the place, Doc straightened up from where he leaned against his truck. Fuck, it was good to see him.

It'd be better when we had the rest of the guys and she was safely tucked back into the clubhouse, but Doc would do.

Doc was at the passenger door of the backseat, but Rome beat him to the punch by lifting Boo-Boo out himself.

"She's asleep," Rome said. "Keep it down. Don't scare her."

Doc's gaze fixed on her and I understood that look. The need to make sure she was real. That she was there. I'd felt the same way when I first got a look at her in the community room—especially when she'd been so checked out.

"Bring her in." Doc said, pivoting sharply and stalking toward the door. That was when I noticed the gun tucked into the back of his jeans. The holster was in no way hidden.

Yeah, Doc wasn't playing.

Good.

My back cracked as I climbed out, and Liam waited for me at the door. Fuck it was good to be home.

Chapter Thirty Five

EMERSYN

The barest touch of fingers against my cheek roused me. The hum and motion of the car was gone. Whatever I was lying on was stable. A part of me just wanted to go back to sleep, but the medicinal scent combined with heavy cleaner tickled my nostrils.

Awareness flooded through me along with panic, and I jerked my eyes open. Heart hammering, I sat up and stared around the room. It was a—clinic. The clinic. I'd been in this room before. Disjointed fragments broke apart like the puzzle pieces we'd had in the community room. Panting, I paused at a calm pair of blue-green eyes.

Rome.

He stood right next to the bed, within touching distance, but he hadn't moved until I saw him. Then he only raised a hand slowly, as if asking. The pounding force of my heart seemed to echo in my ears. The nausea was still there, but not as bad as it had been. Rome's presence helped and bit by bit, I got my breathing under control.

When I would have reached out to take his hand, I froze. There was an IV in the back of my hand.

"Fluids," Rome explained in an easy voice. He still held out a hand to me and when I set mine in his he gave my fingers a gentle squeeze.

"We're back in Braxton Harbor."

A nod.

A shudder passed through me and I leaned forward. He moved so I could press my head against his shoulder. The care he took in putting an arm behind me, hand on the bed to brace me. It all made me want to cry.

"Doc's clinic." It wasn't a question or even a guess.

"Yes," he said when I didn't look up. I sighed. "Do you feel better?"

Did I? "I don't know. Maybe?" My heart was still taking time to calm down. I hurt down to my bones. "So tired."

"Sleep." He touched his lips to my hair like he was just resting them there. Kind of like I was leaning into his shoulder. The contact, careful and light.

"I don't want to sleep in—" I started to say hospital bed or a hospital of any kind. This wasn't that. It was a clinic. Didn't matter. I wanted out of here. "Can we go back to the apartment? Or something? No. We can't go there." I answered the question myself before Rome could say anything. "He knows about Liam's. He knows I was there."

The last place I wanted to be was where my uncle could find me. He knew about the Vandals too. He'd had all those pictures of them.

"You're safe."

Two words. They carried so much weight.

"Not if he knows where I am." A tremor went through me. In my desire to get away again, to come back, should I have not? Maybe I shouldn't have let them bring me…

"Starling." A request and a command. I raised my head and glanced up at him. "You're safe."

He meant every single word.

"Trust us."

Squeezing his hand, I nodded. "I want to."

"Good." A knock on the door distracted him for a moment and he let out a sigh. "Doc wanted to see you when you were awake."

I made a face. Did I want to see him?

"You don't *have* to." It was like he read my mind. But when he met my gaze again, he shrugged. "You needed a doctor. They made you sick. Doc can help. But if you don't want him, we'll find someone else."

He meant that too.

"Don't leave me alone?"

"I promise."

That helped. I was digging my fingers into his hand, not that he'd complained. Still, I forced myself to loosen the grip a little.

"Come in," Rome called.

The door opened almost immediately and even braced for it, I wasn't ready to see him. The room shrunk as Doc entered. It shrunk even smaller when Liam followed him inside. While Rome stood right next to the bed, Liam parked at the door.

"Where is Freddie?"

"Got him hydrating, just like you, Little Bit." Though I'd directed the question at Liam, it was Doc who answered. But the answer worried me.

"Is he all right?"

"He'll be fine." Doc had stopped about halfway to the bed, but I focused on the wall to his left. The last time we'd been alone—well, it didn't matter. I was here because he was a doctor. "Right now, I want to ask how you are."

"I'm peachy." I flicked a look at him, then shifted on the bed. I didn't want to be lying down or even sitting. In fact, the longer I sat here, the more I wanted to leave. "How long before I can go?"

A frown tightened his forehead and he snagged a rolling chair and sat on it as he came closer to the bed. It put his head more on level with mine. Well, no, it was a little lower. I shifted a little and then looked past him again.

The last thing I wanted to see was pity in his light brown eyes. "Soon," he promised. "The guys told me you've had trouble keeping food and water down."

I shrugged. "I was really hot and—uncomfortable. My meal choices have been limited. The food was probably too rich."

"Well," Doc said slowly. "That's possible. Or it could be the medications they had you on."

Shock stiffened my spine. I shot a look at Liam. He gave me a small shrug. "He knows, Hellspawn. We needed his help to get Freddie in there."

"Does everyone know?" I ignored Doc.

"Yes," Rome said. "It doesn't matter."

It mattered to me. The spit in my mouth went away.

"Little Bit…"

"Don't call me that."

Doc frowned.

"It's not my name. Apparently, Emersyn isn't my name either, but it's better than the other." I didn't want his pet names. Not after… I shifted. "Look, it doesn't matter, what do I have to do to get out of here?"

I really wanted to go.

"Okay," Doc said slowly. "I'm going to stand up. I wanted to do a physical exam, but I didn't want to do it without your permission."

"I don't want you to touch me." I dug my fingers into Rome's hand and he held fast. "I just—they didn't beat me or anything."

Not that I remembered.

"It's not like before."

"Okay." Everything in those two syllables told me Doc didn't believe me. "Emersyn, you were a patient at a facility that possibly used psychotropics, antipsychotics, antidepressants, and other pharmaceuticals in your treatment. Probably sedatives. While not all of those medications are addictive, they do have mind-altering properties which can cause issues when you come off of them cold turkey."

"It goes away."

Liam sighed. "Hellspawn… Let Doc do the exam. It'll be over and done with, then we can go. You'll feel better if you know."

"Will I?" I asked, rebellion curled in my stomach. "Will I really feel better if I know? Cause I know a lot of things… I know how I got these." I held up my free arm. "That doesn't make me feel better. I know where I was and I know why—that doesn't make me feel better either. The medication—the drugs—it goes away. If you stop taking them and you let it get out of your system."

"Speaking from experience?" Doc asked, his gentler tone had hardened.

"Leave her alone." Rome shifted to step between me and Doc. He never once let go of my hand. "You asked. She said no. Move on."

With a groan, Liam ran a hand over his face. "Is there a test we can run? Something else we can do to find out if there's something she needs?"

He sounded so very aggrieved. "There were shots and pills and IV bags," I told them. That much I remembered. "Some were blue.

Some were pale white. A couple were yellow. Sometimes they made me feel really floaty, other times—other times it just took all the noise away."

I didn't look at any of them as I spoke. The chill icing through my system seemed determined to spread frost everywhere. If not for where Rome touched me, I didn't think I'd ever be warm again.

"It doesn't matter."

"It matters more than you know," Doc said, the gentleness back in his tone again. "I have some uncomfortable questions for you."

A snort escaped me. "Because everything else has just been a softball."

The corner of Liam's mouth kicked a little higher. There was no mistaking the worry in his eyes. For all that he acted put upon, he'd been nothing but kind, if a little pushy.

"Do you want some privacy for the questions?" Doc pressed on, apparently not impressed or moved by my response.

Did I want to be alone with him? Let me count how many ways I didn't. Not after what he said. Not—after that humiliating display. I'd just rather not. "Just ask, please."

"All right," Doc said on a long exhale and then sat once more on the rolling stool. "Were you sexually assaulted that you're aware of?"

The direct question just ripped that Band-Aid right off. Truth and lies danced on my tongue, but I didn't want to give voice to any of them. "It doesn't matter." Now I didn't dare look at Liam or Rome.

"It does."

"No," I said, shaking my head. "It doesn't. I have the IUD, so pregnancy isn't an issue." I didn't want to go through that again.

"That's not the only issue that comes from sexual assault." Doc mouth firmed into a line. "Little Bit—yeah, deal with me calling you that—this isn't just about pregnancy. There's tearing that can happen, there's disease—there's the psychological trauma."

I almost laughed. "Pretty sure we've established that I've got that. They put me in Pinetree, didn't they?"

When he said nothing, I closed my eyes.

"You want to do a physical exam for that." It wasn't a question.

"I want to make sure you're all right," he said. "I can't imagine how uncomfortable this is for you. But you don't have to hide anything from me. In fact, I'd prefer it if you didn't. Let me help you. I won't do anything I don't tell you about first, you have my word."

The element of soft gruffness in his tone invited me to believe him. "If—*if*—I do this. Can we go after?"

"I'm going to give you a couple of shots—antibiotics only. Just to be on the safe side. Then we'll make sure you're fully hydrated and after that—yes. You can go." The last few words seemed to cost him, but he still made no move to close the distance.

That helped more.

"You guys don't have to stay for this part," I said to Rome and Liam both, even though I was still holding Rome's hand. No matter how much I'd rather skip this part of being exposed, he was right. It probably needed to happen and the sooner it was done, the sooner I could try to forget about it all.

Pushing away from the wall, Liam walked over to us. "You don't want to be alone with anyone, we can do that."

It wasn't just anyone, I just didn't want to be alone *with* Doc. That said, Liam gave me an out and I nodded. "This probably won't be as interesting as me dancing at the club."

The corners of his mouth quirked a little higher. "I'll survive. What do you need?"

Rome stared down at me with the same intensity and I exhaled. "Probably a stupid gown."

The fact Doc was about to get up close and personal with my cunt in a purely medical way hadn't been lost on me. Yeah, I could have gone my whole life without this. With a little assistance from Rome, we got my pants down. My shoes were already off, but I got to keep my socks.

Liam focused on the floor and Doc turned his back. Once my bare ass and I were back on the bed with the sheet covering my legs, Doc got moving. He got gloves and set up a light, laying everything out. Liam moved to stand on the other side of the bed, opposite Rome, and they both stayed by my head.

As promised, Doc spoke to me all the way through the internal. I focused on the ceiling and not on the discomfort. When he finished, he helped take my feet out of the stirrups and then backed off while I sat up.

"I'm gonna do some general tests, the blood work and like I said, the antibiotic."

I kind of only half-listened. They'd gotten almost all of one bag in me, he wanted me to stay long enough for another. That was fine.

He was giving Liam a list of things to look for and he kept casting concerned glances at me. It wasn't until he prepared to step out that I roused.

"Doc…?"

"Yeah?"

"Thank you." Even if he hurt me, he wasn't trying to hurt me now. He'd been nothing but kind to me.

He studied me for a long moment. "You need anything, big or small, you need something, just tell me."

"Don't tell Milo."

That got all of their attention.

"Little Bit…"

"Just don't tell him. He knows about Eric, that's enough." I hadn't even been the one to mention that to him. But it didn't matter. My brother had given up so much for me, he didn't need to know this.

"I was going to say, doctor/patient privilege. I'll keep your secrets." Then he focused on the twins.

"No problem," Liam said, meeting my gaze. "I've got your back, Hellspawn. Now get dressed, I'm going to check on Freddie and then we'll get you guys home."

Rome had been still and quiet through it all. After the door closed, he lifted my hand where I still held his and moved to sit on the edge of the bed.

"Mr. Cole?" I knew what he was asking.

I shook my head. "No. Don't ask. Please—I just—want to forget it all."

"Starling, are they still out there?"

Could they still hurt me?

"Yes. But they've always been out there." I didn't want to tell him. I'd hated telling Freddie and at the same time… "Rome, promise me you won't go after them?"

"No."

I blinked. "What?"

"If I promise, it would be a lie. They hurt you. We'll hurt them."

The raw honesty shifted one of the stones sitting on my chest. "It's ugly."

"Tell me?" Not an order. A request.

I swallowed. Could I handle saying it aloud? After the exam, I was already raw and exposed. What was one more secret? My uncle was—a horrible man. What if when I told him it changed how he saw me? But Freddie knew and he hadn't changed. Then again, Freddie got it on a level I really hoped none of the others did. I didn't want them to know what this was like.

Meeting Rome's gaze, I searched his eyes and there was no judgment in them. Only patience and need reflected back at me. The flash of his dick, how it felt on my tongue, and the fact he'd inked me on his cock. It had to have taken a long time. That day with him and Vaughn flooded through me, it was like I could feel them both. It had been a good day. So much better than the last few weeks.

As much as I craved that loyalty and affection they'd given to Milo and showered on me, they deserved so much better. Just say it, I told myself. Just say it.

Reaching for his other hand, he rewarded me by gripping both of mine.

I could tell him.

"My uncle…"

Chapter Thirty Six

EMERSYN

Rome was curled around me when I woke. Awareness crawled through me in stages. The leaden weight of my eyelids. I didn't want to open them even if I wanted to check the time. The warmth of his arm wrapped around my middle. Maybe it should have been confining, but the comfort vastly outweighed any unease.

It was Rome.

Safe.

Some distant part of my brain just recognized him. He had one leg tucked over mine. When I shifted, however, he adjusted. The arm around me tightened and pulled me more firmly against him, my back to his chest and his knee nudged between my thighs. Even half-awake, a smile pulled at my lips.

It was *nice*.

I'd fallen asleep next to Freddie. And Rome and Liam had both tucked me between them when we were at the hotel in New York. Later, in the car, I always had one of them with me. When I managed to sleep, they were right there when I opened my eyes.

The scratchy, burning sensation in my eyes had me closing them again. I still hadn't managed to look at the clock. The room was lighter, though, I could tell that it was brighter against my closed eyelids.

Burrowing my face against the pillow, I sighed at the brush of Rome's breath against my nape. I could curl up tight and I had the feeling he'd wrap all the way around me. Bit by bit, the weight of the last few days settled. The hum under my skin. The static. The weird dreams. The floating place. Freddie.

Oh, Freddie. I still couldn't quite comprehend that he landed himself in Pinetree to get me. That he'd—the memories poured through me, like water through a filter. Some of it was hazy and distant. Others, too sharply focused and visceral.

"You're safe," Rome mumbled against my hair. It didn't even sound like he was awake, but his arms tightened. Strapped down. I'd been strapped down for days. Being caged up against him was so very different.

Safe.

Shuddering, I pressed back against him. I didn't think I could get closer, but he just tightened his arms again. As tired as I was and as bad as my eyes burned, I didn't want to go back to sleep. Nightmares could be waiting.

"Tell me." The softness in that command looped around me, sanding against the jagged edges. When I told him about my uncle the night before, Rome hadn't said a word. He'd held my hand and locked his gaze on me. The laser focus grounded me when my footing seemed to slip beneath me. The grip on my fingers promised he wouldn't let go.

I wouldn't drown.

I hadn't.

"I think I'm talked out," I admitted in a hoarse rasp. The rawness in my throat ached. My eyes were sore. Even my chest just—hurt. Bruised and battered. Yet, there wasn't a mark on me. My scars had never been on the outside… before.

Lifting my right arm, I stared at the scar that stretched from my wrist halfway up to my elbow. Ugly slashes against the skin. Not anymore…

Closing his hand around mine, Rome rolled us both over. He sat half up against the pillows tucking me against him. It was nice.

Really nice.

But he didn't let go of my arm. Resting my head against his

shoulder, I glanced up to find him looking at the marks. He lifted my other hand. The bandage across the back of it covered where the IV had been inserted. The way he cradled my wrists while he studied my arms peeled away the self-consciousness about the scars.

"I didn't try to kill myself." It seemed important that he understood that.

"I know."

He lifted my right wrist and pressed a kiss to the angriest of the pink lines. The place where the glass had probably gone in first. It was weird. Flashes of the attack popped through my mind like a slide show being played out. The fear and the pain were present, but behind a wall of thickened glass. I could see it, but it didn't quite touch me.

The soft caress of his lips along the scar trailed all the way from my wrist to where it broke off just before the crook in my elbow. Then he repeated the process with my other arm. That line didn't stretch as far, but it was far more uneven. The whisper of a touch, barely there, and yet I felt it everywhere.

"Never again."

"I won't go back again," I promised. Those five words had been impossible to articulate the night before. After the whole ugly story lay torn open between us, I'd exhausted my vocabulary. Or at least, it was how it felt.

Still holding my wrists, Rome brought them up to my chest, hugging me and holding them there as he rubbed his cheek to my hair. The rasp of his stubble filled the silence. "If you do," he said slowly, startling me out of the quiet. "You won't be alone."

No if. I couldn't go back. If I hadn't— "Rome, if I hadn't done what Liam taught me, I don't know that I'd have been in Pinetree or that I could have gotten away." Mr. Cole. The electrified fence. The other man—a flash of his indifferent expression which clashed so soundly with the way he'd put that chokehold on Mr. Cole.

Walking willingly into that trap had been my choice.

"I had to protect you guys." I swallowed. "You didn't know about my uncle. You don't know the things he's done…"

So many terrible things.

"Not alone," he repeated, then pressed a kiss to my temple. "We would have found you."

A little laugh escaped me. It was hardly funny, but he sounded so damn certain. Tilting my head back, I gazed up at him. "You mean that."

"Yes."

No posturing. No bragging. No raging declarations. Just—the conviction of inevitability.

That—helped.

I stared around the room. We were back at Liam's apartment and in Rome's room. It seemed both familiar and alien in equal measure. The room itself had been a wreck when we got here. Then I saw the folder, the photos, my IDs and the cash. It had all been heaped together on the dresser.

Without a word, Rome had just dumped it all in a drawer and went to work straightening. I would have helped but he kept shuttling me back to the bed, so I finally just sat there while he put the room back in order. Liam hadn't followed us inside and the door was closed to the rest of the apartment. Freddie and Liam were out there, but not in here.

After being in such tight quarters, it seemed weird. Weirder still that we were here. Exactly where my uncle had found me. At my shiver, Rome squeezed me again.

"What do you need?" The question surprised me, not because he asked it, but because I literally had no idea what the answer was. I was afraid of being here, but I didn't want to be afraid. Liam said it would be safe. So did Rome. But did that mean it was safe because they were here? Or did it mean it was safe because my uncle wouldn't come looking for me?

What did *safe* even mean when he'd known where I was all these months?

"I wish I could forget," I said, but those words just tasted wrong. "Then if I forgot, I wouldn't be here, would I?"

He frowned. Yeah, maybe it didn't make sense to him, but I understood it.

"I hate that you know." Even if I'd been the one to tell him.

"I don't. I needed to know. I can't protect you if I don't know."

That was sweet. "But now you know how ugly it is inside of me—how—broken I am. I can't…" With Freddie, I could still pretend because he let me. When I told him, I hadn't been looking in his eyes. Not once had I looked away while telling Rome.

"Not ugly, Starling," he said. "Broken isn't bad."

As I twisted, he loosened his grip and I turned so I could face him. Not an ounce of deception reflected in his expression.

"What?" I'd heard him but…

"Broken isn't bad," he repeated. Then he tapped his chest. "Broken. Liam? Broken. Jasper? Vaughn? We're all broken, Starling." Head tilted, he cupped my cheek and I leaned into the contact. "Broken isn't ugly, or wrong. It's not bad."

"It feels…" If bad wasn't the right word then… "Exposed? I can't just act like you don't know and I've spent so long—"

A knock sounded on the door.

"Go away," Rome said without taking his gaze off me.

"I love you too, bro. I'm making food."

"Don't care," Rome replied. "Go away."

I frowned, but more because I didn't want them to fight. Then again, Liam sounded like he was laughing as he walked away.

"You don't have to act," Rome said after a beat, like he waited to make sure Liam left too. "I know. It's better. I can protect you better."

"But…"

"You're still my Starling," he said, not blinking. "You're still you."

"Broken bits and all?" I didn't mean to sound so self-pitying, but Rome just nodded.

"You like me?" The question surprised me.

"Yes."

"Then why can't I like you?"

It was different. Before I could make an argument though, he brushed his thumb over my lower lip. The soft stroke made my breath stutter.

"This is okay?" The intensity in his eyes riveted me. "You said the doctor touched you."

I made a face, but I didn't pull away from Rome. "I didn't want him to touch me."

A nod. "It's okay for me?"

He'd been telegraphing every hand movement, except for when we'd gone to sleep. Then he'd just wrapped around me like a blanket and I hadn't wanted to be anywhere else. "Yes," I whispered. I licked my lips and dipped my gaze to his lips when he mirrored the action.

This was weird. I was still feeling off center and disconnected, as though I were in the floating place, only I could focus and Rome tethered me to the here and now.

"I want you to touch me," I said. "I like that. Even if—" I didn't get to finish that thought because his mouth claimed mine. What might have begun as a whisper of contact, turned into something far deeper. The gentle pressure from his hand tilted my head, and then his tongue swept across the seam of my lips.

The fierce contact steadied me, chipping away at my fear. The rasp of stubble against my skin sanded away at the jagged little bits. The massage of his lips on mine and the thrust of his tongue kindled something deeper. He still tasted a bit of his toothpaste, but it was like he breathed fire into me.

The scars, the broken bits, and the damage were all still there, but the rush of touching him painted over them. It was like I was one of his projects or murals. Air-brushing away the invisible injuries until the only thing present was where his skin pressed against mine. The fact I was only in a t-shirt while he was in pajama bottoms just left me skin to touch.

When I hesitated, my hands just hovering over his shoulders, he nipped at my lower lip. "You can touch me, Starling. I like it when you touch me."

Heat licked at the ice threading in my veins, melting it until I shuddered under the weight of it all. When I slid my fingers over his collarbones, Rome stilled. Then he lifted his head to watch me. I hadn't even realized my eyes had opened again, until the wonderful blue-green of his eyes filled my vision. This close, I couldn't miss a single nuance of the color.

It was perfect.

His skin was so warm. The tension in his muscles beckoned for me to explore them. He and Liam were so alike, even how they bulked. But Rome was definitely leaner. Then he flexed his arms and a laugh escaped me as the muscles rippled over his chest. When I glanced up, he watched me steadily. His lips were kiss swollen and damp.

My belly tightened at the look on his face, the openness in it. "Rome…"

"I'm here."

Two words, just like when he was outside the bathroom and they wrapped me up in an embrace of their own. He was right here. When I moved to sit more firmly on his lap, I had to straddle him. He dropped his hands to my hips and then settled me there. There was no hiding the thickness of his erection.

But… "I'm not…I don't want to just…" The words kept stuttering out. How did I tell him I didn't want to ruin anything for him? He'd been so surprised when I'd sucked him off, so— "You've never done this before, have you?"

I suspected. I thought. Had we talked about this? The buzz under my skin and in my head was back.

"Kiss?" He looked curious.

"No, I know we've kissed." The kisses I remembered.

He raised a finger back to my lips and stroked the lower one before he pressed it forward gently. The question in his eyes didn't need explanation. I sucked his finger against my tongue and his pupils dilated.

"I liked this," he said.

I kissed his finger as I let it go and nodded. "I liked that too."

"You liked it when I kissed your cunt too?"

A grin slipped through, even as another rush of heat flash fired over me. "Yes. I liked it when you licked me—even when you licked Vaughn, too."

"He was in the way."

"So you said."

"He's not in the way now."

No. He wasn't. But… After Doc insisted on the test. "Maybe we should wait?"

"For Doc." It wasn't a question.

I made a face, but then I nodded. "I don't want to hurt you." I didn't want to hurt any of them.

He ran his fingers through my hair. "We can kiss?" I nodded even as he patiently loosened a snarl. "I like kissing."

Maybe it hadn't been an invitation, but I leaned into him anyway and he went still again as I kissed the corner of his mouth gently, then the other side, and when I slid my hand to his nape, he clasped mine. Then his tongue was there to duel with and I sank against him. Yes, I liked the kissing too.

Another knock on the door and Rome ignored it. His mouth held me captive as he nipped, licked, and sucked at me until I groaned. The knock came again.

And again.

The fourth time, he lifted his head. "Fuck. Off. Liam."

He spit each word like a bullet.

Outside the door, his twin laughed and I blinked, glancing from Rome to the door then back. Rome's expression declared pure mutiny and I smoothed my fingers over his lips. "It might be important…"

He sighed, before he called, "We'll be out in five minutes."

"I'm counting!"

"Fuck. Off."

Liam was still laughing when Rome dragged my mouth back to his, but I let go of all of it. Five minutes sounded really good right now.

Chapter Thirty Seven

EMERSYN

Freddie let out a huge sigh when we finally came out of the bedroom, probably because it had been more than twenty minutes. Maybe longer. We'd taken a shower. Well, showers, Rome sat and watched me and I waited for him. Way past the five minutes Rome had declared. Then again, my lips tingled and my body hummed.

For the first time in weeks, I wasn't cold. I'd dressed in one of Rome's sweatshirts and a pair of my leggings. The fuzzy socks I'd apparently forgotten, so they worked. He'd even waited until after I'd gotten dressed to kiss me again. That had to have taken at least five minutes more.

"Thought you guys were never going to come out," Freddie said almost mournfully. "Liam is *starving* me." The melodrama and the way he clutched at his chest made me laugh.

"Yeah," Liam agreed, expressionless. "What happened to five minutes?"

Rome headed into the kitchen. "I wanted five minutes more."

His twin snorted, but he wasn't watching his brother. No, Liam focused on me and I shifted under the scrutiny. Sometimes, he saw too much, and as raw and exposed as I'd been feeling earlier, Rome had helped to paper over the cracks. I didn't want to tug on any of that.

So, I focused on Freddie instead. Despite his antics, he still looked a little pale and worn out. I felt that so much right now. "Why is Liam starving you?"

"Because I got you donuts, Hellspawn." That dragged my attention to Liam as he shifted to the side and revealed four stacked white rectangle boxes. Rome emerged from the kitchen with two huge mugs and he carried one over to me.

The smell of the coffee hit me. I hesitated. The last time I'd actually drunk any coffee, I'd thrown it back up. Then again, I'd puked up a lot the last few days and kind of lost track. My stomach didn't protest, so when Rome handed it to me, I cradled the mug.

"Okay?" The quiet question asked so much.

"I'm here," I promised and his whole expression relaxed.

"Donuts?"

"Coffee first—maybe." I stole a look at Liam. Neither his watchfulness nor his folded arms betrayed anything. "I don't want to get sick."

Instead of being disappointed, he nodded. "Freddie, get cereal."

"Oh man," Freddie grunted. "It's a good thing I like you Boo-Boo. I've been known to kill for donuts."

"Well," I said, still debating whether sipping the coffee would go well or not. Right now, I was actually enjoying how it smelled. "Would you use a weapon or your hands? I suppose a blunt object would work." How had Bodhi put it? "How creative are you feeling? Or are you just in a hangry hurry?"

There was a beat of total silence. Rome frowned and Liam straightened, dropping his folded arms. "What the fuck?"

Freddie, though, he got it and his laughter was its own reward. Color flushed his cheeks as he shoved off the sofa. He pressed a kiss to my cheek as he passed. "You're the fucking best, Boo-Boo. Never leave me again."

It was the again that robbed it of some of its humor, but I nodded anyway. "I'll do my best." The twins were still staring at me though, and I lifted my shoulders. "It's a long story."

"We have time," Liam said.

"Nope," Freddie called from the kitchen. "You held out on the donuts, so no story for you. That's *our thing*, right Boo-Boo?"

I had to bite back a smile because the cheer in Freddie's voice was worth leaving Liam in the dark. At least for a little while.

"Sorry," I said. "It's our thing."

That earned me a grunt from Liam and a shrug from Rome.

"Drink," was Rome's only response and now they were both watching me. Well, there was no time like the present, so I sipped the coffee. The first taste was like a gift. The second was near perfection. I could have cried when my stomach cooperated, but for now I settled with just sipping my coffee.

"Okay," Liam said after Freddie returned with his cereal. "We need to talk."

Dread shivered up my spine. That was one way to kill my appetite.

"Hellspawn?"

The questioning tone from Liam pulled my attention back to the warehouse. We were half a block from it, but he'd pulled over. It was a rainy, sunny day. It kind of fit my mood. The breaks in the clouds let enough sunshine in that it glared off the droplets on the windshield. The rain itself came in dribs and drabs. Like the sky couldn't make up its mind.

Rain or shine?

Why choose? We could have both.

"We can go back," Liam said. "You don't have to do this today, if you aren't up for it."

From the moment he brought up going to the clubhouse, I'd been on some wild pendulum swinging ride that alternately trapped me and sent me soaring. I *wanted* to see the guys again. I'd *missed* them. Missed them more than I thought possible.

But I'd also chosen to leave, and maybe they didn't want to see me. None of them acted like it was a problem. As far as I knew, they hadn't called them yet either. My stomach bottomed out as I shifted to meet Liam's gaze. Even if he wore sunglasses like I did, I could feel the weight of his stare. Without an ounce of rancor, he put the SUV in park.

Freddie had gone quiet and Rome just held my hand. I had

managed to eat one donut, but I was all tied up in knots. Jasper and Vaughn—they'd need more than an I was sorry. They *deserved* more. Kellan and Milo too.

Hell, Liam deserved more right now, and I was having trouble finding it.

"It's okay, Boo-Boo," Freddie said into the quiet. "Even if they're mad, they aren't gonna be mad at you. They're gonna be mad for you. They're gonna want to fix it. Jasper's gonna stomp around and growl. Vaughn will just want to hug you. Kellan's gonna be salty, but he's also gonna want to figure out how to fix it. They all will. Trust me."

The last two words pulled my attention from Liam to where Freddie sat in the passenger seat, staring straight ahead.

"I'm the fuckup, I've fucked up more than everyone put together. They always forgive me, they always fight for me, and they always try to fix it."

Tears burned in my eyes.

"That is all true, but they can also wait another day or two if you need the time. I can make sure they know you're okay and we'll keep you buttoned up until *you* are ready," Liam added gently, and it was that gentleness that snuck in past the nerves. Normally, he'd push me, scold me, tease me, and *had* irritated me until I fought back, stood up for myself. He'd *never* treated me like I was fragile.

Broken wasn't bad.

Not bad.

I glanced at Rome. "I'm here," he reminded me. "So is Liam."

"Yeah, Hellspawn, right here."

"Me too," Freddie said. "But I'm not going in there to tell them we got you back and you're not ready to see them yet. Liam can do that. He volunteers for that job."

A laugh escaped. "That's mean, Freddie."

"Eh," Liam said. "Wouldn't be the first time I pissed them all off."

Reaching forward, I put my hand on Liam's shoulder. "You don't have to do that for me." When he covered my hand with his, I didn't pull away. "I'm just being a big chicken. I left—I left all of you."

"You thought it was the right thing to do, Hellspawn." Man, that sounded like it hurt for him to say. "You should *never, ever* do something like that again, but you did it to protect us. We do a lot of things to protect each other and it wouldn't be the first time a choice we made pissed someone off."

"No?"

"Nope." He squeezed my hand. "Guess you really are one of us."

The painful thud of my heart echoed in my ears, but they waited me out. Without a doubt, I could say no and we would go right back. I could do it. A safety net. I could run and hide. They wouldn't blame me.

But the guys deserved so much better than that.

"Let's go see them," I said before I lost what little courage I could cobble together. "I need to see them."

I needed to see them like I'd needed to see Freddie in Pinetree. Then Rome and Liam when we made it out. This was the last step to going home. To seeing the guys—and my brother. I tried to suck in a deep breath, but it was hard.

"Okay, Hellspawn. You got this." Liam squeezed my hand again, then he put the SUV in drive and we were moving again.

My mouth was dry by the time the door rolled upward. It was surreal. If going back to Liam's apartment had been strange, this was—bizarre. At the same time, I found myself leaning forward. Inside, Liam turned the SUV around and parked it facing outward. They all did that, out of habit. The darkness inside left me blinded after the glare, even with the sunglasses on. There were two big rigs parked inside.

"Here we go," Liam said, shutting off the engine and getting out of the SUV.

He wasn't alone, Freddie glanced back at me first though. "Catch your breath. I'm gonna go brag about how awesome I am." Then he was out of the SUV before my first giggle could escape. I dragged the sunglasses off. The windows on the vehicle were tinted. I could see movement out there.

"I should get out of the car," I said.

"When you're ready." Rome seemed perfectly content to just wait. "We can kiss if that will help."

Another wave of laughter bubbled up through the fear choking me. The faint tilt to his lips made me smile for real. "Thank you." Then before I could change my mind again, I brushed my mouth to his. "I'm ready."

Getting out of the car was probably one of the hardest things I'd ever done. But Rome followed me. I wasn't alone. My eyes had adjusted and I stared at the little cluster of guys around Liam and Freddie.

They were all there. I didn't see past them.

Jasper.

Vaughn.

Kellan.

Milo.

"Son of a bitch," Jasper swore and he strode straight toward me. It erased the last little flutters of fear. I met him halfway, crashing into him and letting out some soul deep breath as he hugged me to him. "Don't you ever do that again," he muttered against my neck, his arms half-crushing me but I didn't care. "Shh, Swan, it's okay."

I held on and it took me a moment to even register that I kept saying I was sorry. "I'm sorry," I repeated even as the hot tears I hadn't wanted to shed slid down my cheeks. "I'm—" Jasper pulled back, clasped my face, and kissed me. The searing touch burned past everything else. It was like he breathed life back into me and I clung to him.

When he lifted his head, I met his wondering stare. The relief in his eyes stunned me. He brushed away the tears on my cheeks with his thumbs. I didn't have any words except the litany of "I'm sorry," but Vaughn was suddenly there.

Jasper blinked hard as he let me go and I swore there was dampness on his face, but Vaughn lifted me and cradled me to him. "Dove," he exhaled the single word and it held a wealth of emotion I couldn't even begin to define and I didn't try. I just sank into it and wrapped my arms around his neck.

That voice. The soft croon of it. How it held so much comfort and kindness, that even when I didn't know who he was, it helped. It made me feel better then and now. My feet weren't even on the ground and I didn't care. When Vaughn kissed me, I pressed my lips to his and just drank in the contact.

His strength was right there, a steadying force, a gift and foundation that wouldn't give way. Broken wasn't bad.

That refrain echoed within me as Vaughn pulled back to study me. A dozen questions lived in his eyes, but he gave voice to none of them. "Welcome home, Dove."

The fist around my heart redoubled, but it wasn't pain, no matter how much pressure it applied. Movement behind him pulled my attention and I found myself staring into Kellan's eyes.

"Go see him," Vaughn whispered against my ear. "He needs to see you too."

Needed.

Yes, I needed to see them. When Vaughn set me down, Kellan just opened his arms and I walked right into them. Why I'd been so damn scared I didn't know, but the lingering shadows of fear died as I clung to them, one after another. Kellan didn't say a word, just held me close and I pressed my head to his chest.

Cars. Oil. Coffee. Tobacco. Ink. A citrusy-like smell that was in their shampoo. All these familiar scents just confirmed it for me. I really was home. It was my turn to pull back, but Kellan didn't let me go far before he dipped his head.

"Waited too damn long for this," he whispered. Then his mouth claimed mine and my heart forgot to beat. Or maybe the world hesitated. It was a sweet kiss, but it burned. It was a giving caress, but it demanded. Nothing about this was friendly and everything about it was open and possessive. Nothing hidden. I sighed against his lips.

I could live here, forever. As fanciful as the thought was, it didn't seem so impossible. They would find me. They would bring me back. They would protect me.

They would keep me safe.

It was in every touch, every kiss, and every embrace. I just hadn't understood it. If Jasper's kiss had given me breath and Vaughn's granted me strength, then Kellan's filled me with understanding.

I didn't have to be alone.

The feel of Kellan pulsed against me, even as he lifted his head. I had no idea what he was looking for when he gazed down at me, but I hoped he found it. Words just failed me. He wiped the tears from my cheeks, just like Jasper had.

Milo stepped into my line of sight and I braced for it. He didn't want me around the guys. He'd been so adamant about sending me back. But I didn't want to go then, and I didn't now. More, I'd fight him if he made me.

The hesitation in his stance scored deep inside of me. I rubbed a circle against Kellan's chest, but when I took a step, he let me go as

I faced Milo.

"I'm back," I said, finally finding my words again. "Don't make me go. Please."

Pain flickered over his tense, fierce expression. "Come here, Ivy." I don't know which of us moved first, but I was in his arms and hugging him tight. "You don't have to go anywhere. I promise."

Home.

My home.

Finally.

Chapter Thirty Eight

EMERSYN

"I take congratulations and thank yous in the form of gift cards to my favorite dining spots and also the occasional beer," Freddie said as he led us toward the clubhouse doors. Milo had an arm around my shoulders and didn't seem in any hurry to let me go.

I was okay with this. Strangely enough. After all the weeks of not believing him and then hoping desperately it wasn't true because of what it meant—I wanted to be a little selfish. I wanted my brother.

I wanted *Milo* as my brother.

"You did good, Freddie," Jasper said.

"I did *great*," Freddie corrected, thumping his chest. "Great."

"We know," Kellan said, almost patiently, and he glanced at me. There were so many questions in their eyes. Liam hung back, but he didn't leave and for that I was grateful. Rome stuck to his brother and that made me happy too.

"You only think you know," Freddie said with a near flourish and it wasn't until he winked at me that I got it.

He was distracting them—for me. "Maybe, but I do know," I

said, meaning every single word. "You were my hero."

When he skidded to a halt and blinked, I grinned a little wider. He'd saved me. Just fucking *being* there had helped save me. He could play and tease and distract them for me and I would adore him for it. But he really was my hero.

He should know that.

Coughing, Freddie actually glanced away from me, but Jasper gripped his shoulder. "Okay, hero, first coffee is on me. Let's go."

When I would have followed them, Milo tugged me back. "Go on guys, we'll be there."

I wasn't the only one who hesitated. Kellan actually pivoted and moved back to us and so did Liam. Before I could ask though, Milo let out an aggrieved sigh.

"Guys, I'll bring her in, just go. Give us a minute."

Kellan glanced from Milo to me. "You good with that, Sparrow?"

The question surprised me. No, surprised was far too mild a word. It stunned me.

"Really, Kel?" Milo asked and the aggravation in his tone dialed down some.

"Yes, Milo," Kellan answered him without looking away from me. "Really. We had this conversation. I thought I made myself plain. Let me know if you need a refresher."

The faint smirk on Liam's face had me curious, but he just shook his head when I looked at him. Fine, I'd ask him later. The quiet reminded me they were still waiting for an answer.

"It's fine," I said, finally. "Sorry, I'm still a little—tired." Tired sounded better than out of it. But this time when the question flared in Liam's eyes, it was my turn to shake my head. I was okay. I'd meant what I'd said at the clinic. There were some things I wasn't going to tell Milo.

There would be questions. About Pinetree. About why I was there. Probably about the scars on my arms. Thankfully, the sweatshirt covered them.

I reached a hand over to Kellan, it was an impulsive act but he caught my fingers. "I want to talk to him, but I'm not running away. I promise."

Maybe even that morning I couldn't have said that, cause I was very much considering running, but not now. Not after seeing them. Not again. Not if I could help it.

"Don't take long," he murmured. "We have a lot of catching up to do."

We did.

With one last squeeze, he left us but Liam lingered and Milo let out another sigh. "Do you need to get her permission too?"

"Hey." I jabbed my elbow into his gut. Not that it did much to move him. His abs were rock hard. "That's rude and Liam doesn't deserve that."

I swore I could feel the tension shiver through him and I glanced up to find Milo glaring at Liam, then he seemed to work on softening his expression. It looked more pained than kind. "Fine, you're right. Rude is wrong."

"Take it easy, Raptor, that looked particularly painful for you to say. Besides, I can handle you being a jackass. Just keep it in check with Hellspawn or you and I are going to have a far more unpleasant conversation. Clear?" Not even an ounce of threat shifted Liam's pleasant tone, but the pure menace made the hairs on my arms stand up and a chill go up my spine.

"I'm not planning on being a jackass. Keep it up, though, we can solve this in a different way."

The glare between them was getting us nowhere and I shook off Milo's arm. The moment I moved, they both shifted their attention to me. "I don't want a fight," I said, folding my arms. I wasn't altogether sure I could handle it if they fought.

It hit me. We were standing in the great huge warehouse outside of the clubhouse, and it was just the three of us. I didn't see any of the ones they called rats and while I recognized some of the cars, I didn't recognize all of them.

The air seemed almost colder in here and I was really glad I'd brought the sweatshirt.

"We're not gonna fight, Hellspawn," Liam said almost too easily. So easily, in fact, I swore I heard the unspoken *yet* at the end of his sentence. "Going inside now, going to be right on the other side of that door if you need me—"

"For fuck's sake, what the hell do you think I'm going to do to my own sister?" Milo demanded.

"Nothing," Liam told him with a smile. "Because you know I'm not the only one who is going to kick your ass if you upset her again. We're not doing this your way anymore. Remember?"

The annoyance on Milo's face and in his posture made me feel bad for him. But it would be a lie if I didn't acknowledge that Liam's casual defense and statement left me warm. "Thank you, Liam."

"Yup," he murmured. "Right on the other side of the door." I wasn't sure if that was a reminder for me or a warning for Milo. Then Liam pressed a kiss to my head before he turned and walked away. The squeak of the door signaled the fact Milo and I were finally alone.

Shifting my foot, I focused on him again. He stared at me.

"Is this as weird for you as it is for me?" I asked.

A faint, but genuine smile appeared, and it softened his face. "Maybe," he admitted. "Probably should be awkward and maybe this is gonna sound weirder still, Ivy—fuck Emersyn."

No. "You can call me Ivy," I reassured him. "That's the name you think of me as. I'm your Ivy. I'm okay with that. I know I was a bitch to you—"

"You weren't a bitch to me and if you were," Milo said, shaking his head. "I started it by being a raging asshole when you didn't deserve that."

"Well, yeah." I could agree with that.

The corners of his mouth curved a little higher and he chuckled. "Tell me how you really feel."

"I think we did that once and you were pretty insistent that you weren't a virgin." It was a weird thing to remember, but he'd been almost apoplectic. My own lips twitched and then Milo laughed for real.

"Yeah, we're not going there again."

"Probably a good plan." I scuffed one of my shoes against the ground. The weirdness hadn't diminished, even if I was okay with the discomfort at the moment. "So, what did you want to talk to me about?"

"Nothing specific. I have questions, but you look tired and I don't want to push you away by demanding a lot of answers."

"I'd appreciate that."

"But—"

Why was there always a but?

"—you've been through hell."

How did he…

"None of them said anything." That fact pissed him off. "At least not the specifics of what happened this time."

This time?

I frowned.

"But my point is, you need to see someone, to talk to them. I want to be that person for you, but I don't think I am."

An inescapable sadness lived within that statement. "Milo…"

"Nope, you don't have to make me feel better. This is one of the things that I should be doing as your big brother, but we're not there yet."

The big fierce guy with his tattoos and dark, furious eyes had shifted my whole worldview. Challenged everything I knew about myself. Proved that someone could care and want the best without wanting anything from me. I hated seeing him upset. Not that I could fix this either.

At least, I didn't think I could.

"That said, I want to take you to meet someone."

"I don't want to be sent anywhere…" All at once I wanted to retreat. "You said you wouldn't send me away."

"I'm not going to," he promised, hands raised with his palms outward. "She lives here—in Braxton Harbor. She's a good person. Fuck that, she's a great person. The point is, she's been there for me. Hell, she's been there for all of us. I don't know a better person to confide in. She knows you—well, she knew you when you were little."

"Okay," I said slowly, not entirely certain of what to do with that. "Can I think about it? I'm not really big on strangers right now."

Strangers. Doctors. So-called mental health professionals. Pretty much not anyone.

"That's fair," he said, then raked a hand over his head. "Are you—planning on staying here at the clubhouse?"

"Do you not want me to?" It was hard to tell.

Dropping his hands to his hips, he dipped his chin down as if he needed to gather himself. "It's not a call you want me to make."

"Wow. That really did look painful for you to say."

His snort made me smile and when he lifted his head, he was chuckling again. "It is painful for me to say. Do I need to point out that you literally just kissed Jasper, Vaughn, *and* Kellan?"

"Nope. Pretty sure I was there for that part." He rolled his eyes and I lifted my shoulders. "I'm not going to apologize for that."

"I didn't ask for an apology."

"Good." Okay, maybe I was being snippy.

"Apparently." Him too.

Sighing, I tried to relax and dropped the defensive posture. "This is hard."

"Fuck yes, it is." He clasped the back of his neck. "Any chance you can just—go back to being someone who doesn't know anything about boys?"

I hadn't been that person in a long, long time. "Sorry."

"Right. I'm kidding—well, half-kidding." The pause elongated. I swore it was like he really wanted to tell me something but didn't want to at the same time. Or maybe that was just me. "Look, if I have a preference, I'd rather you stayed at Liam's place or we get you a different place if you need to. We can come to you…"

"But you don't want me here."

"Don't want is a strong set of words."

That was something.

"I just don't know if it's safe enough for you here." A fact which clearly bothered him. "That said, I'm not going to order you to go back to Liam's or—anywhere else."

"You're getting better at saying those words."

"Bite me." It came out so damn grouchy it took everything I had to not just laugh at him. As it was, he glared up at the ceiling. "I'm trying."

"Yes," I said softly, swallowing the laughter. "You are, and I appreciate it. I don't mean to tease."

"No, teasing is fine." He rubbed his jaw. "It's actually kind of nice."

"Yeah? I've never had a sibling before."

"You can't tell," he assured me, and I wasn't entirely certain if that was a compliment or not. While the awkwardness was still there, the weird factor had dialed down. "Just—can you think about it for me? Like I said, if you want somewhere else, we can do that too. Not going to make you go anywhere."

"I can think about it." It wasn't asking a lot.

"Thank you." He exhaled. It was like maneuvering around landmines, but neither of us wanted to set off the other. "Can I ask about the Sharpes?"

I flinched. I didn't mean to, but it escaped before I could suppress it at the sudden left in the conversation. Maybe it wasn't a sudden left…

Milo's frown tightened. "You really didn't want to go back to them."

It wasn't a question. This wasn't something I wanted him to know. Me, having some magical blessed life was important to him. "We should probably go see the guys now."

We'd been out here for a while.

"Yeah, about that—" He grimaced. "Before we go inside…"

"You just said you weren't going to ask me to go."

"I'm not. Just—there's something you need to know and it would probably be easier to show you."

"What?"

"Just—we had a little help in figuring out where you were."

He already knew I'd been at Pinetree. "How?"

"C'mon," he said, gesturing to the door. He didn't wait for me and I folded my arms as I followed him. My stomach kept doing the drop thing and I couldn't quite seem to stay on solid emotional ground. There were a lot of questions waiting for me inside, but it might be easier with everyone there.

Maybe.

As promised, Liam stood right inside the door and Milo just rolled his eyes as he waited for me to go in. Liam wasn't alone. Jasper straightened, as did Kellan, then Rome stepped forward. Were they all waiting right here?

"Really guys?" Milo said. "Subtle."

"Not trying to be subtle." Vaughn nodded to me. "Actually, we were just talking about food, Dove."

"Save it for a minute," Milo asked, holding up his hand.

They all gave him a variety of suspicious looks, but Rome shifted his weight. Then nodded and when he held his hand out to me, I took it. Milo headed up the stairs and I followed, with Rome, and apparently everyone else. It was weird. The guys didn't follow us down the hall as we passed most of the rooms I knew to the room at the very end.

At the last door, Milo pulled out a set of keys and unlocked it. Why the hell was it locked from the outside?

"Oh, you're back. Be still my heart…" The voice from within the room was as familiar to me as my own. Oh my god.

"Lainey?"

Chapter Thirty Nine

EMERSYN

"Lainey?" It was like a grenade had been dropped. She was here? What was she…? Before the thought could even complete, she was just there. Dressed in shorts, a t-shirt with a hole in the sleeve, sans makeup and even with her hair pulled back into a messy ponytail, Lainey looked like a million bucks.

"Oh my god," was all she said before she wrapped me up in a hug and I was holding onto her. I hadn't seen her in almost a year. It seemed so much longer. Devastatingly longer. All the tears I'd been trying to hold back just poured out of me.

"Come on," Milo said from behind me. "Let's—give them a minute."

Some part of my mind didn't want them to go, but I needed to hold onto Lainey. The one bright, truly good spot in a world I kept trying to escape. Running away from that world didn't mean leaving her behind. Not when she refused to let me go and followed me.

Followed me.

I pulled back to meet her wet gaze. At least I wasn't the only one sobbing. But she cried so pretty, and I always looked like someone scrubbed my face raw. That, and I had to keep sniffling or I'd be a snotty mess.

"What the hell are you doing here?" I almost choked on the words trying to push them out.

"Looking for you," she retorted, then fisted my hands in hers and hauled me back into—where were we? I glanced around at the room with its bed set up on a platform, desk, oversized sofa and bookshelves *everywhere*. "Are you okay?"

"But—how did you know to come *here*?" I hadn't told her about the boys. Not really, or exactly where I was, because I didn't want my uncle to have any reason to look in her direction.

"Well, it started with a message from your phone. Ended up with me meeting Freddie—where did you find him? He's nuts. Cute, but nuts." She dragged me back toward the sofa and sank down on it. I perched next to her, twisting to face her and our knees touched, just adding to the connection. "His friend, tall, blond, very literal, and gorgeous? He was there too."

Very literal. "Rome?"

Lainey nodded. She gave me a quick sketch of her meeting them and how she insisted they bring her back because she wanted to help find me.

"Wait…" I swiped at the tears on my face. My eyes hurt and so did my throat. "How did *you* know about Pinetree?" Horror crept through me.

"Oh, sweetie," Lainey said, squeezing my hand as she propped her elbow against the back of the sofa and braced her head against her fist. Sympathy flickered in her eyes. "I've known for a long time. I made Adam help me figure it out, but it's been a while since he sent you there and you never seemed to really remember it—"

No, I'd remembered. A little. But I kept blocking it out. The white static hummed in the back of my mind and I shook my head. Or maybe I hadn't remembered because that was what they'd been trying to do.

"Sometimes, you didn't recognize Adam," she said, almost gently. "Once it took you a real minute to even remember me."

That crushed some of the air out of my lungs.

"Sometimes, he can be a real prick, but I was almost sure he was looking for you this time because it's been months. But when they sent me that message and said you'd gone back…" She shook her head.

"Would you leave *me* somewhere like that?"

"Never." It wasn't even a question. "Lainey, I never wanted you to know any of this."

"It's your uncle." It wasn't even a question and I flinched. "Yeah, you don't have to answer that. If the fact Adam hates him with the fury of a thousand suns wasn't a big enough clue, the way he watched you was another. Uncle Fuckbucket is a disgusting toad."

"I was adopted." The three words just broke free. "He's not even my real uncle." It did not make it better. Not even close. "I'm not actually *related* to him."

But that last part?

"Good." Lainey didn't need me to explain it. She sniffed, then let go of me for a moment to wipe away her own tears. I glanced around for tissues or something.

As if she read my mind, she stood and crossed to a bathroom I hadn't even seen hidden in the corner. How long had she been here? She seemed to be right at home. When she came back, she'd already removed the evidence of her tears and held a tissue in her hand, but she passed me the box.

"Lainey... you shouldn't be here."

"Not happy to see me?"

"Oh shut up, you know I am. I just..."

"Keep trying to push me away to protect me?" The droll observation stabbed me with guilt. She dropped to sit next to me again. "I get it. But have I ever not come when you called?"

No. Not once. "You never asked me, either."

"I only ever said if you needed to talk, I was there. I'm still here."

I sighed and shifted so I could lean back against the sofa. Staring up, the lights across the ceiling reminded me of Jasper's room. Stars, everywhere, even if the actual lamps turned on in the room gave it this cozy atmosphere.

Whose room was this?

"So much has happened," I whispered. "I don't even know where to begin." Or if I wanted to try. "A part of me just wants to forget." I'd been trying to forget *forever*. For a little while, here, I'd actually begun to let that ugly part of my life go and then...

"Then tell me something good," she suggested. "Tell me about that pretty boy brother of yours."

Pretty boy? I blinked and glanced at her. A flush touched her cheeks and I raised my eyebrows. Was this *Milo's* room?

"Do I want to know?" was what I asked. Lainey didn't talk about guys that much. Well, she talked about Adam and Ezra—oh hell, I needed to tell her about Adam. That seemed like a million years ago and at the same time, he made her crazy. He also hurt her and when he did that, it made me want to kick him in the nuts.

Considering Liam's training, I could probably do it now.

"He's stubborn, annoying, bossy as hell, and he adores you. So, he has at least one admirable quality." The last was offered almost grudgingly. "To be fair, he only locked me up when I said I would go after you at Pinetree myself when they told me I wasn't invited on their little rescue plan."

Wait— "They *locked* you up?"

"It's fine," she said and I stared at her. "Okay, it's not fine. But let it go, for right now? Okay?"

"Kidnapping you is not okay." It really wasn't.

"Is it kidnapping when I insisted on coming back with them?" The question gave me a moment of pause. "I mean, I kind of insisted, then I refused to tell them anything unless they brought me back here."

"So, Freddie and Rome just brought you back here?"

"Yes."

"But Milo locked you up?"

"Technically."

Technically. When she glanced away and the flush left her cheeks pink, I frowned. "Are you okay? Really? Cause if you're not, I'll go kick his ass. Liam's been showing me how." The disconnect and distance seemed to all be collapsing at once.

Lainey was the one person who had *always* been there. From everything they said, Milo and the guys had been too, but I hadn't known about them. She'd been my family, better than family, for as long as I could remember.

"I will hurt him," I promised her. I didn't want to. "I mean, I kind of like him and he's pushy and overbearing and absolutely annoying when it comes to growling at everyone around me. But he cares…" That meant something.

"He adores you," was her response. "Like I said, one redeeming quality. Well… okay maybe he has two."

"Uh huh."

"Don't look at me like that, we're talking about you."

Yeah, we were and that reality was so much more unpleasant. "I'd rather tease you, though—if you're having sex with him, I don't know if I want you to tell me that." While I wasn't looking directly at her, I didn't miss the way she shifted her gaze away or the vulnerability that flashed through her eyes. "But if he isn't good to you, I will hurt him."

"He hasn't hurt me," she assured me. "Besides, I'm more than capable of dealing with emotionally constipated men. At least he appears to have more emotional depth than a teaspoon."

I grimaced at that. "Look, I don't know exactly what happened with Adam…"

"Nothing," Lainey said firmly. "Absolutely nothing has or will. That's been made abundantly clear. He can barely stand the sight of me." Then she cut a hand through the air. "You know, let's not worry about him right now. The less said the better. I haven't seen or heard from either him or Ezra in weeks. I kind of like it that way."

That wasn't true, but I didn't call her on it. Not yet. Exhaustion settled on me like a lead weight. "You know I'm on your side."

"I do." She settled so we were side by side and like me, she looked up at the ceiling. "You know, for a gang living in a warehouse, this place is not a dump."

That should not be funny.

It really shouldn't.

But I laughed until I wanted to cry again. Thankfully, Lainey didn't let me cry alone.

"I'm on your side too," she reminded me.

"I've always been so damn grateful for that."

Eventually though, we needed to leave this room. But that required me washing my face. I wanted to tell her everything and at the same time, I didn't want to burden her anymore than I had.

"Are you really okay?" she asked me when I came out of the bathroom. I still couldn't get over that this was Milo's room. A part of me was curious and I kind of wanted to look around, but the rest of me didn't want to intrude.

"No," I said. "I'm not."

Surprise and worry vied for dominance in her expression.

"But I will be." I had no idea how long that would take, or even what it would look like. Telling someone—Freddie, then Rome—that seemed a good start. At the same time, everyone else who learned the truth had died.

One step at a time. I closed my eyes. I couldn't handle it if something happened to them because of me.

"I had to, he threatened all of you."

"No, you were wrong. We'll protect you." Absolute certainty in Rome.

"It's not that simple."

"Actually, it is that simple, Hellspawn. We will protect you." Echoed by Liam.

That loyalty, it was everything. Clasping Lainey's hand, I smiled at her. "Have I said how damn good it is to see you?"

"No, but I rather thought that was implied. After all, I'm me and you're you."

A laugh escaped and she grinned. "Yes, we are. And Lainey?"

"Yeah?"

"Later, we need to talk about Adam." As angry with him as she always had been, his rejection had also hurt her. But after the last few months, especially after his visit on the road, I had to wonder if that was more tangled lies, like the Vandals trying to protect me had been.

She made a face. "If you insist, but I'm good if I never talk about him again."

It wasn't true. She knew it. I knew it. But sometimes, we needed our little lies.

"We could talk about all these boys who seem very invested in you," she suggested, and I made a face.

"Not sure I'm ready for that. Not even sure I totally understand it." Even if I craved it. Craved them.

"We'll figure it out." That seemed like a plan, when we got to the door and I opened it, she let out a little grunt. "Well, I guess I'm off house arrest."

Milo was in the hall when we came out and Lainey made a face. He zeroed in on her and I swore the air went electric before he looked at me.

"Then again, the pretty boy is right here, so maybe I'm not." The droll comment was so Lainey. Was there a bull she wouldn't wave a red flag at?

That said, "Milo, have you really kept her locked up?" Because that wasn't going to fly.

"She needed to sit down," he grumbled without an ounce of apology. "She takes off with two strangers and just shows up here like she's in charge, then thought it was okay to go after you to a place she insisted was terrible for you."

My heart fisted. He'd protected her.

"Actually, it is that simple, Hellspawn. We will protect you."

"You must really think I'm an idiot."

"No," Milo retorted. "I think you're hotheaded and foolish."

"Oh, Pretty Boy, you have no idea what I'm capable of."

The words flew back and forth between them, but Milo didn't look impressed, even if he couldn't quite keep his gaze off her. As for Lainey, she was enjoying herself, so I just bit back my next comment and settled on. "Thank you for looking after her." That seemed to surprise him and when Lainey opened her mouth to object, I focused on her. "Thank you for coming to help me, even if you had no idea what you were getting into."

Maybe it was foolish, but it was also brave. It meant a lot to me.

"But don't lock her up again," I finished, swinging my gaze back to my brother. "Or we're going to have a real problem."

"She's stubborn," Lainey advised.

"I've noticed," Milo grunted.

Yes, I was.

"I'm also kind of hungry," I admitted. Hungry for food and for the guys. Hungry to try and put the pieces all back together.

My stapler was still at Liam's, but if I moved back in here, then I needed to bring that with me.

"C'mon," Milo said, jerking his head toward the hall. "What do you want to eat? I can send one of the boys to get it."

Maybe whatever we had on hand, cause I didn't want anyone to leave. The guys were staged out around the couches, coffee in hand, talking though the conversation stuttered when we came in. Doc had arrived and he locked his gaze on me as soon as I walked in.

My stomach dropped at the concern in his eyes. While I hadn't been expecting him, maybe I should have. Hopefully, whatever test results he had were good news.

Yes, we all needed more good news.

Lainey squeezed my hand, a reminder she was right there and I grinned at her.

Yes. She was.

We weren't alone.

They were all there.

"Boo-Boo," Freddie exclaimed. "Ball-Cracker! Together again!"

Ball-Cracker?

The bubble of tension exploded from around me and I laughed.

When I glanced at Lainey, she grinned and shrugged. Yeah. Ball-Cracker fit.

"Come, sit down, tell them how wonderful I am."

I could do that.

Chapter Forty

LIAM

Everyone danced around where Emersyn had been. We'd discussed it, some, while she was visiting her friend. Her friend. Her friend was Ezra and Adam's Lainey. The leverage the fucking King had over them and the girl Ezra worried about being missing.

How it all became so tangled in this Gordian fucking knot I had no idea, but it was gonna get messy.

Really fucking messy.

Emersyn encouraged Freddie, but in his tales regaling us with how he'd gotten in and out of his room, maneuvered around the facility, and gotten to her, were kernels of the shit that happened to her there.

We needed a list of names. One glance at Jasper told me he was thinking the same thing. Look at that. We were absolutely in agreement on this one. Then again, I rather doubted a single one of us wouldn't walk right into Hell for her. She tugged at her sweatshirt at one point, pulling the cuffs down.

The scars on her arms pissed me off on a visceral level. Beating Cole until he was half dead, then cutting him up like he'd done her. It helped. But he wasn't the sole cause of what happened to her.

No, that we could lay at her uncle's feet. That son of a bitch had a lot to answer for.

A lot.

Then there were her parents. Where the fuck were they in all of this?

We'd both been adopted, but I'd won the fucking lottery compared to her freak show of a family, with their proper breeding and wealthy bank accounts. Doc had shown up, but he kept his distance, even if he was very focused on every breath she took.

Yeah, that was all of us. Dragging my gaze off her, I caught Rome's glance. I understood the message. He was just waiting for me to admit it.

Right. Fuck that. At the moment, she had enough guys wanting her, she didn't need me on top of the rest. What she needed was for me to deal with the threats. Including the one pointed at Lainey, one that could spill over onto her, that meant I needed to deal with it too.

After putting my empty coffee cup in the kitchen, I headed out. She was safe here. They both were and I needed to take care of things.

"You're leaving?" Her question silenced the hum of conversation.

I just smirked. "Don't worry, Hellspawn. I'll be back. But there's shit I need to do. Entertain the boys. I've had you for the last three days, they deserve a chance."

Oh, that worked even better than I thought. Jasper's expression darkened and even Kellan gave me a distinctly unfriendly look. Doc actually sighed, but Rome shook his head. Yeah, bro, I get it. But focus on your girl. If I started, well, Jasper and I had enough things to fight about.

Not that Hellspawn wouldn't be worth it.

Milo caught my eye as I passed him, but I just bumped his shoulder with my fist. He had his hands full with Lainey, and there was another problem I didn't want to think about. Whatever shit had gone down in the last few weeks—it had shifted things between them.

Fuck. My. Life.

The interior of the SUV wasn't entirely pleasant, but I could deal with that later. No one followed me. Leaving the warehouse behind, I headed back out of the city. My destination was an hour away. As it was, I'd already been cutting it close with how off the map I'd been, but there had only been one message from the king and no missed calls.

The message involved a fight that was a month away. It didn't require a response. When the O'Connells first adopted me, they had a manor estate in Bay Ridge. The affluent area had gradually become something of a bedroom community in the last decade, but prior to that, it had been an escape for the wealthy in summer.

In some ways, it was like the Hamptons, only instead of being on an island in New York, it was spread out around a lake. Fishing, water sports, and hiking were all easily accessible. In winter, they were an hour away from semi-decent slopes.

A lot of families had places out here. Huge estates on isolated bits of land, where the closest neighbor was several acres away. Private property where just about anything could happen. Back in our school days, there had been any number of parties at the various estates, reopened even if they had been closed for winter.

Parties no one reported and where anything could happen.

Parties where the Royals could gather to plot or celebrate. Gang territory, only in a different zip code and income bracket. It was also where the Royals got their name. Particularly because it wasn't the only Bay Ridge area.

I'd repurchased the old O'Connell property a couple of years earlier. It had gone back on the market, so I set up a shell to snag it. Always have a fall back plan. Currently, the only staff was a caretaker who maintained the property and a cleaning crew that came through once a month to freshen the house up.

No one else lived there. Made for privacy when I needed it. If we had to hide Emersyn—this would be where I would suggest. Though she wouldn't care for the isolation.

The gates swung open as I pulled up and then I was through. They closed silently behind me. The whole drive, I'd been turning this conversation over in my head. Once in the garage, I checked the security cameras. I had a company monitor them to let me know if anyone tried to get on the property, but it never hurt to review them myself.

Yeah, I was only delaying the inevitable, but it helped to assure myself nothing had changed in the last three weeks. The last person in and out had been me.

Inside, I followed the sound of the television toward the living room. Adam Reed shoved up from the chair he'd been seated in and glared at me.

"It's about fucking time," he said.

"I told you it would take time," I reminded him as I crossed to the bar. I didn't care what time it was. The next part of this conversation was going to need a drink.

"You didn't mention weeks, prick." Despite his anger, he hadn't left. Then again, the king thought he was dead. More, he thought I'd killed him. He couldn't really afford to leave, could he?

"No," I said, agreeing with him as I added three fingers of whiskey to the tumbler and glanced at him to see if he wanted any. "But things changed and I was needed somewhere else. Now I'm not."

"It's not even lunchtime," he argued as if that was a reason not to drink.

"So, one finger?"

His dead-eyed, unimpressed look almost amused me.

Almost.

"Suit yourself," I told him as I tossed the drink back and refilled my glass before facing him. "We need to talk." Probably better to just dive right in. "About Ezra. Lainey. The king." His eyes narrowed and his lips flattened. "And a girl named Emersyn Sharpe."

Emersyn and the Vandals will return in *Brutal Fighter*
To keep up with Heather and all her series as well as enjoy bonus scenes and other content join her reader's group on Facebook:

https://www.facebook.com/groups/HeathersPack/

Brutal Fighter

Broken dreams.

Broken lives.

Broken bird.

Our feelings for her were like wild animals finally freed from their cage. But my Sparrow, she was the most brutal fighter of us all. She'd had to be.

The battles she'd survived, she'd done in silence and alone.

Not anymore.

Never again.

Milo let her go. Jasper took her. Vaughn sheltered her. Liam taught her. Rome connected with her. Doc rejected her. Freddie went after her. All because we wanted what was best for her.

Me?

I was in this fight. Our promises might lie shattered in the debris of the life we'd thought she had, but we weren't abandoning them or her.

Oh no, I would never leave her again.

My name is Kellan Traschel, I will be whatever she needs me to be. And if war is what must be waged, then hell was what we would rain down.

Breathe.

I can wait.

Seriously.

Breathe.

That was not *cliffhanger* per se. Oh, you're still yelling? Right, okay. I'll wait.

Done?

No?

Right, feelings. I know there are a lot of feelings. Yep, I'm hushing. Get yourself a drink, a cup of coffee, a glass of wine, maybe a soda—whatever you need. I'll be here when you're done.

You're ready now? Wonderful.

From the beginning, I said this was a dark journey, a dark romance, a dark past, present, and quite possibly future for these characters. That said, this ending is way more a WTFhanger than it is a CLIFFhanger.

I get it, you have a lot of questions. Trust me, so do Liam, Jasper, Kellan, Vaughn, Doc, and Milo. Freddie and Rome know her story and she knows Freddie's. So they have far fewer questions—right now.

The characters in this series have always been on a collision course. We're seeing some of those impacts right now between Lainey being with the Vandals and eventually reuniting with Emersyn. We're seeing it with how Ezra went after Liam because he has no idea where Adam or Lainey are. We're seeing it in how Kellan, Vaughn, and Jasper, specifically, but the rest of the Vandals aren't following Milo's lead in this anymore.

So, what happens next?

For me? I'm working on the next book already, I'm also working on finishing up the Untouchable series. I probably need to take a couple of days off but I'm kind of a workaholic. So, if you need to curse my name or rail or debate theories be sure to head over to my group and spoiler groups on Facebook.

You will not only find your people there, you'll find me

xoxo

Heather

Reader group: facebook.com/groups/heatherspack

Spoiler group: facebook.com/groups/teammadatheather

About Heather Long

USA Today bestselling author, Heather Long, likes long walks in the park, science fiction, superheroes, Marines, and men who aren't douche bags. Her books are filled with heroes and heroines tangled in romance as hot as Texas summertime. From paranormal historical westerns to contemporary military romance, Heather might switch genres, but one thing is true in all of her stories—her characters drive the books. When she's not wrangling her menagerie of animals, she devotes her time to family and friends she considers family. She believes if you like your heroes so real you could lick the grit off their chest, and your heroines so likable, you're sure you've been friends with women just like them, you'll enjoy her worlds as much as she does.

Follow Heather & Sign up for her newsletter:
www.heatherlong.net
TikTok

Bravo Team Wolf
When Danger Bites
Bitten Under Fire

Cardinal Sins
Kill Song
First Chorus

Chance Monroe
Earth Witches Aren't Easy
Plan Witch from Out of Town
Bad Witch Rising

Her Elite Assets
Featuring:
Pure Copper
Target: Tungsten
Asset: Arsenic

Fevered Hearts
Marshal of Hel Dorado
Brave are the Lonely
Micah & Mrs. Miller
A Fistful of Dreams
Raising Kane
Wanted: Fevered or Alive
Wild and Fevered
The Quick & The Fevered
A Man Called Wyatt

Going Royal
Some Like It Royal
Some Like It Scandalous
Some Like It Deadly
Some Like it Secret
Some Like it Easy
Her Marine Prince
Blocked

Heart of the Nebula
Queenmaker
Deal Breaker
Throne Taker

Lone Star Leathernecks
Semper Fi Cowboy
As You Were, Cowboy

Magic & Mayhem
The Witch Singer
Bridget's Witch's Diary
The Witched Away Bride
Mongrels
Mongrels, Mischief & Mayhem

Shackled Souls
Succubus Chained
Succubus Unchained
Succubus Blessed
Shackled Souls (Omnibus)

Space Cowboy
Space Cowboy Survival Guide

Untouchable
Rules and Roses
Changes and Chocolates
Keys and Kisses
Whispers and Wishes
Hangovers and Holidays
Brazen and Breathless
Trials and Tiaras
Graduation and Gifts
Defiance and Dedication
Songs and Sweethearts
Legacy and Lovers

Wolves of Willow Bend
Wolf at Law
Wolf Bite
Caged Wolf
Wolf Claim
Wolf Next Door
Rogue Wolf
Bayou Wolf
Untamed Wolf
Wolf with Benefits
River Wolf
Single Wicked Wolf
Desert Wolf
Snow Wolf
Wolf on Board
Holly Jolly Wolf
Shadow Wolf
His Moonstruck Wolf
Thunder Wolf
Ghost Wolf
Outlaw Wolves
Wolf Unleashed